Altered Creatures Epic Fantasy Adventures
Book 1 of the Thorik Dain Series

Fate of Thorik

Historical Date 4.0649.0913
(4th Age, 649th Year, 9th Month, 13th Day)

Artwork by Frederick L. Wedgeworth

ISBN: 978-0-9859159-2-6

Library of Congress Control Number: 2008902777

**Altered Creatures Epic Fantasy Adventures
Historical Date 4.0649.0913
Thorik Dain Series
Book 1, Revision 1.2
Fate of Thorik**
www.AlteredCreatures.com

Printed in the United States of America

No thrashers or Chuttlebeast were harmed in the making of this book.

Dedication:

For all the years you worked with me as I struggled with severe dyslexia and feelings of inadequacy, your constant encouragement to overcome all the obstacles in my life, and the endless hours you spent editing my manuscript. I love you, mom.

Acknowledgments:

My lovely wife, Tami, for putting up with the years of working on this book, telling me what does and doesn't flow,
and believing in me.

My brother, Rick, for pacifying my wild ideas of creating a new land by rendering it in 3D. Thanks for your support.

Everyone who took the time to read my manuscript to help me work out the details and issues. These include Kristina Walker, JoAnn Cegon, Robert Cegon, Michelle Richards, Josh Crawford, Rick Wedgeworth, Alexander Wedgeworth, Tami Wedgeworth, Bob Cegon, Zak Larter, Jonathan O'Brien, Barefoot Editing and my business mentor Dennis Shurson.

**Altered Creatures Epic Adventures
continues with the following books:**

**Nums of Shoreview Series
(Pre-teen, Ages 7 to 12)**
Stolen Orb
Unfair Trade
Slave Trade
Baka's Curse
Haunted Secrets
Rodent Buttes

**Thorik Dain Series
(Young Adult and Adult)**
Fate of Thorik
Sacrifice of Ericc
Essence of Gluic
Rise of Rummon
Prey of Ambrosius
Plea of Avanda

Fate of Thorik

by

Anthony G. Wedgeworth

Chapter 1
Messenger of Doom

Grasping the weather beaten boulder with his blood covered hands; Ambrosius dragged his torso out of the freezing river water. Fluids oozed out from ruptured burn blisters across his face, neck, and one arm. Leaning against the flat side of the cold rock, he paused to rest and reflect upon his situation. *Now that the council members are dead, no one else knows of the upcoming attack.*

Pressure squeezed his head from all directions, blood tasted coppery upon his lips, and stabbing spikes of pain ran up his legs. Survival was not guaranteed. His first order of business was to get to a safe location, and then to determine the extent of his injuries. Fighting the river's current, he swung his lower limbs out and onto the rocks that lined the rushing waters.

Pulling his body past the top of the boulder, he quickly found himself rolling over the other side onto yet another set of rocks. His spine cracked as he landed flat on his back. Losing whatever breath he had regained since leaving the river, he lay on the newly found surface for a few minutes and stared up at the stars. They were difficult to see as a haze clouded them and prevented any clarity.

Ambrosius' tall lean body appeared frail among the resilient stones. Wet shoulder-length mahogany colored hair matted to his face, which was outlined by a properly trimmed beard and mustache. Made of the finest cloths, his clothes were burnt, ripped, torn and soiled with mud. He was out of his element, but he was a survivor.

Once rested, he dragged himself off the rocky banks and into a grassy area to assess his health within the night's dim light. Starting at his hips, he used his hands to inspect his lower limbs for injuries. Thick wet clothes made it difficult. Nevertheless, rips in his pants legs allowed him to make contact with his skin and he quickly recognized the problem. His right leg had a long gash with a stone shard wedged deep into one end.

The other leg was obviously broken as he felt one of the bones pushing the skin out an inch from where it should be. Instinctively reaching for his side bag, he realized it wasn't there, nor was his metal quarterstaff. He would have to get along without them.

He had healed his own wounds in the past and he doubted that this would be his last.

A sudden overwhelming feeling of sickness washed over him. He felt flushed, nauseous, and lightheaded. Fighting the sensation only increased its intensity. Immediate action was required before he passed out. The injuries could be worse than he had assumed.

Ambrosius sat quietly for a moment to regain his composure and thoughts before focusing on the stone embedded deep into his thigh. Reaching out with the unique powers of his mind, he began to pull the granite shard out of his flesh. The stone began to vibrate. Making a slight lurch forward, it became blocked from its escape by his own skin. Pulling harder with his powers, the shard finally ripped out of his leg, tearing the flesh which held it in place. Catching the rock in his left hand, he screamed as blood gushed from the wound.

Still tormented from this newly self-inflicted pain, he tore a piece of his tunic off and wrapped it around his leg to stop the excessive bleeding from the now larger cut. *One down, one to go.*

Reaching out again with his powers, he then focused on repairing his broken limb. Normally his abilities were second nature, such as walking is for most. Instead, he struggled to use them to do nothing more than lift his lower leg off the ground and begin pushing the bone toward its original position. He was getting weaker with every passing moment.

Excruciating pain shot up his leg causing him to yell in agony. It was becoming too great to handle. One last quick burst of power from his thoughts gave it the needed shove, popping the bone back into place.

Snap!

"Awwww!" Ambrosius screamed, dropping his leg to the ground and collapsing from the pain. His entire body hurt. How much of what he thought to be water was actually blood? How much had he lost?

His self-concern stopped once he heard the sound of an animal from behind him, away from the shore. Silence followed. Looking through the haze was difficult and resulted in no answers. Rushing waters raced by on one side of him, while the trees blowing in the wind could be heard on the other. He turned to face the trees, gathering his bearings and options.

Sitting ever so still, he waited to see or hear something. Anything. It finally came in the form of a deep growl from within the trees. Perhaps up in them. It was not the call of a wolf or any large cat species that he knew of. Patiently, he waited for it again. A few moments later he heard another noise. This time the sound was from his right as he faced the woods. The growl was slightly higher pitched and had various clicks within it.

Thrashers

Ambrosius had seen these carnivorous apes in captivity but never in the wild. Tribal in nature, thrashers attack all creatures entering their range in a crazed frenzy like a swarm of bees or ants. They were aggressive to anything, regardless of its size.

Changing his location, he pulled himself the short distance back to the rock formations near the river. The pain was intense with every move he made. He was again feeling faint. Leaning back on a boulder, he faced the trees and looked up at the ever-darkening starlight. He could taste blood dripping down from his face and his breathing was no longer a subconscious effort as he struggled to keep it under control. He tried to sit still and relax.

A series of barks came from the left, followed by a single howl straight in front of him. If it wasn't the sound of the river drowning out the movement noise of the thrashers, then it was the ringing in his ears that had been nonstop since he woke up on the rocky shore. *Where are you?* Squinting, he tried to see any activity to focus his powers on. *Perhaps a friendly shove will scare you off and send you on your way.*

He listened to a few more clicks and howls from the trees at various elevations. By this point he couldn't see anything. The haze had totally removed all visibility. He focused his thoughts and energy on the blackness directly in front of him and waited for a noise to come from it.

Eventually, one of the barks and clicks came from the area of his focus and Ambrosius pushed with his mind in hopes to scare the creature off. Tree limbs snapped and crashed to the ground, followed by a moment of silence. It was short lived as it was shattered by a screaming howl filled with clicks. The trees came alive with noise. Sounds of tree branches slapping against each other and howling filled the air from every direction along the shoreline woods.

One of them had jumped out of a tree and landed with a thud. A second one hit the ground and then another. Ambrosius' heart sank as it sounded like an apple tree that had lost its fruit all at once.

A screaming roar came from directly in front of Ambrosius and was followed with growls by a multitude of others. The first beast charged toward him and was cut short as Ambrosius lifted his hands and used his powers to shove the creature back. Quickly realizing that it did not stop the rest, he spread his arms out to his sides to push them all away. A force emanated from him in a hundred and eighty-degree arc bowling over anything in its path. The sounds of surprised creatures resounded from every direction except one, behind him.

It was too late. A slash across his outstretched arm ripped open his forearm. A second assault from the other side caught his neck. There were several thrashers on the boulder behind him, mauling his upper torso.

The fallen creatures in front of Ambrosius quickly regained their footing and joined the attack. It was only moments before the hairy beasts had grabbed onto his arms and legs in an attempt to rip them off. Ambrosius was now off the ground in a tug-of-war for body parts.

This is it, he thought. *This was how the great Ambrosius was going to die, devoured by wild animals. No longer will I be remembered for the Dovenar Civil War. Instead, the death of the Grand Council will ring in the ears of those who would speak my name.*

In one last-ditch effort, Ambrosius pushed away the pain for a brief moment. Pulling all of his energy into focus in that fraction of a second, he shoved as hard as he could in every direction.

He was airborne and there was silence. Calm encapsulated his body and mind as he floated and began to recall the memories of his life. He wondered if he had died.

A wave of wind interrupted his bliss followed by a thunderous crack of tree limbs. It was the last sounds he heard as he crashed back to earth, knocking him unconscious.

Chapter 2
Farbank and Polenums

Thorik Dain still had his thin and agile sixteen-year-old youthful body, as he walked with a slight bounce in his step. His clothes were clean and neat but without question old and weathered. Like most Polenums, Thorik had soft facial features and hair salted with various colors from nature's palette. His happened to be colored with shades of tree bark browns as it feathered back from his face naturally.

Polenums, or "Nums" as they were referred too, had the gift of looking young and spry well into their fifties, making it difficult to tell their real age. That being said, the youthfulness of their exterior did not prove true for other attributes. Like most species, the eyes and dexterity of the body would start to fade and their hair would lose its luster and thickness as it began turning gray. In addition, the mind of Nums tended to regress with age, regaining a sense of childlike playfulness in their elder years.

Thorik walked along a path near the river as he breathed in the crisp and cool fall morning air. He loved this time of year. The changing colors of the leaves made the entire valley look like a gallery of art. The local villagers enjoyed the wondrous seasonal sight.

Mountain foothills on both sides of the river were rich with plant life, providing every color imaginable. Several areas of exposed rock added their own peculiar scheme of browns, reds, and tans as veins of mineral and crystal deposits were uncovered by the rains.

Small streams ran down the mountain walls and merged at the bottom with the mighty King's River. Thick vegetation and narrow valleys could be seen upstream, while downstream it unfurled into softer hills and scattered open ranges.

Living upstream of the village of Farbank, the young man had taken this windy path as his own. Not because he owned it, but because the only home it led to was his. Seeing that few people came to visit, he had adopted the dirt trail as his responsibility to keep well trimmed. A similar path downstream of Farbank traveled to the

Frellican house and not beyond. Farbank's outside trading transpired only a few times a year with their cousins in Longfield.

Working his way from the steep hillside to the boulder-lined King's River, Thorik made his way downstream to the village. Orange and red leaves, moist with morning dew, clung to his leather boots as he strolled down the path.

Thorik pushed his single wheeled barrow filled with skins and meat from recent hunting & trapping trips. The skins were cleaned and dried and ready for use while the meat had been smoked and spiced with the Dain's secret family recipe.

Along his way he noticed Gluic at the shore on her hands and knees, reaching into the bitterly cold water. She was in her sixties and showed signs of aging for several years now, giving her a more mature and wise look. This was in direct contrast to her actions as she played in the river like a small child.

Swirls of dark skin blossomed from the crest of her nose, up across her forehead and beyond her dull silver hairline. The same style swirls were on her palms and were known to Nums as soul-markings. These natural skin paintings were unique for each Polenum.

Resting the barrow on its two legs, Thorik stepped over to her. "Gluic? Have you lost something?"

"Found, my dear boy." Gluic reached deep into the chilled water, soaking her entire sleeve before pulling it back out. "See?" Opening her hand, she showed him a handful of mud and a single black weathered river rock.

Keeping his distance so as not to get mud on his clean clothes, he eyed the river stone. "Very nice. But the water is cold and the current is moving fast. I don't want my only grandmother to be swept downstream just to be caught by some fishing net in Longfield."

She smiled with a delight that warmed her entire face. Various weeds, grass, and flowers had been used to decorate her hair, clothes, wrists, ankles, and around her neck. Stepping forward she extended her hand out in front of him. "Touch it."

Thorik had been through this enough times to know he wouldn't get out of it, so he smiled half-heartedly and touched the muddy rock with the tip of one finger in hopes not to get dirty. "It's a good smooth rock."

With her other hand she grabbed his wrist and flipped his hand around to be palm up before she slapped the rock and mud into it.

Gluic's eyes widened as she waited for Thorik to get excited about it as well. "Can you feel its energy? Very old and many stories to tell. Even helps you remember what you forgot. It is a good one, isn't it?" She nodded her head to answer her own question.

"It's a fine addition to your collection. You have few that are this -" Thorik stumbled as he tried to come up with the right wording. "- perfectly round and smooth."

She agreed with him. "And as wise. It'll be useful for our trip."

"What trip?"

She slapped the back of his hand, shooting the rock and mud up in the air. Catching the stone in mid flight, she eyed it like a treasure. Mud had splattered everywhere, coating Thorik's face and shirt with small brown droplets.

Her expression of joy outweighed his feeling of frustration over being dirty and Thorik grabbed a cloth rag to wipe his face clean. Watching her return to the river to wash the new collectable, he could hear her talking to the stone as she properly cleaned it with no regard to the chilling of her own fingers in the water.

Thorik patted himself down with the rag to soak up any remaining mud on his clothes before putting it away and grabbing the arms of the barrow. "See you later, Gluic," he said to her back. She stopped scrubbing long enough to raise an arm into the air to signal goodbye. With that, he lifted the barrow's legs off the ground and wheeled it downstream.

It was only a few minutes down the path before he reached the outskirts of the village. The subtle smell of burning logs lofted from the chimneys and mixed with the occasional aroma of meals being cooked.

Out beyond the cattails that lined this part of the river, several children sat on the docks with their fishing poles and lines waiting for some action. Rolled up pant legs exposed their bare feet, which periodically kicked water at one another.

"You won't catch any fish making all that commotion," Thorik yelled over to them.

They laughed and continued to play as they soaked up the last few days of warm fall weather.

The path turned away from the wide river and into the village, consisting predominately of wooden houses placed on short rock walls that often connected to each other. Roofs of thatch were the most common but moss and grass were used as well. It was difficult to see one from another this time of year as a blanket of fall colored leaves covered everything.

Each house had a fireplace and smokestack that was often shared with another. Sometimes even three or four would utilize one large chimney in the corner where they all met. Even though the houses shared up to three walls, they were each expressive of the family that lived within them. The Nums took pride in their homes and would decorate them with items gathered from nature that best expressed their families.

Various sidings were used which included the blackened oaks to the white birch barks and everything in between. It was amazing the range of wood types that existed in the valley and how the treating of them brought out unusual characteristics.

Erratic placement of houses and paths often became dead end streets without warning. As chaotic as the homes and patted down dirt paths were, they were kept quite tidy and clean. Among the odd shaped alleys were open areas that served as places for entertainment and relaxation. Children would run and swing from tree branches, while adults gathered to talk and play various tile games.

Trees grew in most open areas, then again they grew everywhere, including in the streets and in the houses. Many houses used them as part of one wall while others used the trunk in the center of the home to hang coats and clothes. It was stylish to have a tree as their front door frame. Besides its status symbol it also provided shade from the summer sun.

Thorik wheeled his cart around various sharp corners as he made his way toward the market place in the center of Farbank. Greeted often as he walked down the angled paths, he always returned the sentiment with a smile and a nod.

Thorik stopped to say hello to Trumette, as the old man squinted to see his tiles during a game of Runeage. Trumette's soul-markings circled his mouth and chin and continued straight down to his chest like a mustache and long goatee. Thorik stood behind him for a moment and quickly pointed out a play to make. Trumette then placed the tile on the table causing the man across from him to grumble and complain as Trumette laughed and Thorik continued on his way toward the market.

Several times along the way small groups of children ran up to him, asking questions about the Harvest Festival awards. But Thorik was not willing to give up any of his secrets as he teased them with hints and sent them on their way.

Upon reaching the market place, Thorik stopped and looked across the wide opening for a specific face. This was the only place inside Farbank that was not sheltered by trees. Therefore, several large tents were erected to protect the Num's fair skin from the sun's rays.

He quickly found his person and headed straight toward her. Emilen had a smile that melted Thorik's heart. Petite in frame, she was far from frail as she bartered with storekeepers for goods. The bright autumn leaf colors of her red and gold long curly hair reflected the sunlight as she stepped out from under one of the tents.

Thorik couldn't hear or see anything else when he gazed at her face and into her large greenish blue eyes. Thin lines of darker skin traced her eyes and extended to her ears. He felt queasy and soft every time he looked at her beauty.

Her demeanor was cheerful as she flirted and sweet-talked several men into giving her what she wanted. She knew how she affected them and used it to her advantage.

Thorik wheeled his cart into the market and greeted her with excitement. "Good Morning, Emilen. How have you been?"

She smiled. "Fine, thank you. But I haven't changed a lot since yesterday when we talked."

"Oh, right." Pausing, he thought about how to continue. "Speaking of that, remember when I was telling you about the maps I was making of the upstream valley? Well, I brought them to show you."

Taxing her memories from the night before, she didn't recall the conversation. "We talked about maps?"

"Yes, I told you how I was mapping out the valley to help with my hunting and trapping patterns." He removed a rolled up map from his pouch and unraveled it for her to see. "So, if this is Farbank and this is the White Summit, then this is what I have mapped out so far."

Glancing over the sketches on the paper, Emilen pacified his interest. "Well done."

"Every peak and valley is titled. I created names for those that hadn't been given one yet."

"That's very brave of you, Thorik. Taking it upon yourself to name an area which belongs to the Mountain King," she mocked with a giggle. But his excitement was contagious. "This is by far the best made map I've ever seen." A wink of approval gave him comfort in her words.

Thorik blushed slightly as he rolled up his map to put it away. "Are you going to the festival with anyone yet?"

"Yes she is," Wess Frellican announced as he stepped up behind Thorik and put his wide arm across Thorik's back and onto his far shoulder. "She's going with me, once I ask her." Wess was a few years older than Thorik and more developed. His broad chest and back rested on a lean muscular torso and waist. Sharp soul-markings on his neck and exposed arms resembled long deep claw marks.

Wess was the youngest of the four Frellican of Farbank brothers who hunted on the downstream open fields. They had always been a successful family with plenty of soft rolling hills to hunt on. The easy hunting grounds provided them with more luxuries than most of the villagers, including nice new clothes and a large hillside house that boasted three trees. Two of them ran the sides of the front double doors while the third tree trunk was used as a support for the center of the house, much like a tent pole.

Thorik never particularly liked the Frellican family. They had always mocked the Dain family for only having their little cottage, small hunting rewards, and even smaller name. Nums were proud of many things. At the top of the list were their family names and soul-markings. Thorik had the shortest last name of any in the village. The villagers with longer names carried more status in the community and often were looked at as the upper class. Last names like Mullenfrather added credit to your character and respect at gatherings. Trumette Mullenfrather of Farbank was definitely a respected old man.

It was customary for Nums to give their full name at the first meeting with others. This included their first and last name as well as the place they were born. Some had the slight benefit of having a prefix for spiritual rank that included 'Fir' for the community's spiritual leader and 'Sec' for the Fir's assistants.

"Ah, Dain." Wess always reminded Thorik of his short family name. "Will my date be watching you lose the race in the festival? Or are you going to save your effort and concede to me now?" He paused with a grin. "I've noticed lately how your skin has thinned over the past year." Picking up one of Thorik's mink skins, he held it up to the sunlight. "Your trapped skins, of course."

Thorik felt the back of neck heat up while listening to Wess' comments, but knew that Wess would easily be victorious if Thorik were to challenge him.

Wess looked back down at Thorik and then at his clothing. "What's the matter, Dain? Couldn't you find anything clean to wear this morning?" He tried to dust off the mud droplets on Thorik's shirt with his free hand.

Before Thorik opened his mouth Emilen stepped in. "I think I will just meet you both there." She smiled, turned and then walked away to continue her shopping.

"She looks good from any angle, doesn't she?" Wess commented as he watched her stroll away.

"Get your arm off me." Thorik pushed out from under Wess' heavy arm and turned to face him head on. "I'm tired of your games, Wess. Just back off!"

Wess looked surprised at the feedback. "Slow down Fir-pet, what's your problem? Can't you take a little harmless fun?"

Thorik straightened his shirt. "You don't know what its like to be me. I have duties to perform for the Fir and at the school. I perform all the hunting north of Farbank without any brothers to help," he said to justify his attitude. "It must be nice to still live at home with your family without any real responsibilities."

Wess smiled at how ruffled Thorik's feathers were. "Yes it is, no-soul." A sharp nod of his head added extra arrogance to his words before he walked away.

No-soul. The lowest thing that he could be called, especially under the circumstances. Thorik was the only Polenum ever to not have any soul-markings. Embarrassment he could live with, but the thought of disappointing his family with such a deformity was torturing.

Arms straight and fist clinched, Thorik stood there motionless as he tried to regain his composure. Ever since he was a child, Wess had always been able to make Thorik feel uncomfortable. His words ate at him, taking bites from his emotional flesh.

After several minutes of stewing about Wess, Thorik started noticing the good things about Farbank again. The sound of flutes in the air while people came together and traded and socialized; it was enough to start him on his way again.

He stopped periodically at shops with an armful of skins and meat on his way in and a load of various harvested goods on his way out. Life was grand and he hoped it always would be.

After a swift day of trading he returned home to his cottage at the end of the path, close to the woods, upstream of the village. In his mind it was the best place in the world to live. Not a grand house nor colorful, but well built and maintained. Strong and sturdy, it would hold up for many more generations. It was sound and warm, making Thorik thankful for what he had.

He opened the door and wheeled his barrow right through the doorway. This was much more efficient to put things away, and he did so in a quick and orderly way. Then with a spin of the cart he pushed it out of his home, around to the side of the cottage and up toward the hillside. He stopped at an outcropping of rocks and placed it in a location designed just for his sturdy barrow. A single long rock arched over his tool shed, providing his items with perfect protection from the elements. "Harmony in the home brings harmony to the heart."

Pleasantly, he walked back to his comfortable single room home. Once inside, he sat down for a bite to eat. The fresh fruits and vegetables were better than he had remembered. He loved harvest time. After eating he cleaned up and began to boil a pot of water to which he added various herbs and pinches of items from many little jars on his open cupboard shelves. Each jar was well organized and labeled as they faced forward for easy reading.

He let the broth boil for nearly an hour before letting it cool to a simmer. During this time he spent endless moments looking over maps and drawings at the only table in his home. Every place he had ever been was recorded on various maps with details of unique canyons, bluffs and rock formations. Animals had been cataloged with sketches and notes from his limited travels. He removed each valuable sheet from a decorative two-hinged wooded coffer, which he used to store them.

Daydreaming of what was beyond the next set of foothills, he drew his own conclusions. It was his only escape away from the small village and hunting grounds to the north. If it were up to his uncle, Thorik wouldn't even go past the first ridge.

Two crisp knocks at the door interrupted Thorik's peaceful pondering of distant valleys. Fir Brimmelle Riddlewood the Seventh of Farbank opened the door and walked in as Thorik stood from his chair after hiding the papers he had been looking over.

Brimmelle was twice the age of Thorik, about the same height, but more robust in his size and clothing. His dark chestnut and coal colored hair added width to his already round face that centered attention on his thick bushy eyebrows. Broad strokes of dark skin traveled from his left hand up to his neck, stopping abruptly at his jaw line.

Fine threads were used in Brimmelle's suit, adding color to an otherwise colorless man. He was clean and sharp in his mannerisms, stale and shallow in his charisma. As the spiritual leader of Farbank he had respect from the villagers without having to earn it.

"Has he spoken again?" Brimmelle asked.

Thorik finished cleaning his items off the table while answering. "Yes, this morning I was able to get his name."

"I told you my daily readings would do him good. He said nothing else?"

"Bits and pieces. He's still saying the date of December 13th, but the rest I can't understand," Thorik answered.

"Have you soaked the wounds yet?"

"I was just about to." Thorik collected several small thick cloths and dunked one into the simmering herbal water. Fully saturated, it was removed and folded tightly to remove most of the water before being placed on the neck of a human lying in Thorik's only bed. Humans tended to be a head taller than Nums, with stronger facial features and darker tan skins. This thin human met all those attributes.

Brimmelle looked upon the sleeping man. Covered with a clean blanket, the badly burnt side of the man's face and neck were still visible. "And what is it?"

While patting the cloth on the man's burns, Thorik looked up at Brimmelle confused by the question. "Is what?"

"His name. What are we calling this outsider?"

"Ambrosius."

Fir Brimmelle helped himself to one of Thorik's pears and took a bite. "Well, don't get to attached to him. No good ever comes from dealing with outsiders. The sooner he heals, the sooner he can leave."

Discouraged by the comment, Thorik asked, "Why do you dislike anyone that doesn't live among us?"

"It has nothing to do with disliking them. I don't trust them." Brimmelle's conversations were short and to the point. He didn't allow pondering other options. Issues were easier to resolve when they were black and white. "I have had poor luck with the few that have come to our village, including Su'I Sorat. I still blame him for your parent's death. You would have been gone as well if I hadn't saved you." Pear juice sprayed from his mouth as he pointed a stern finger at Thorik. "Remember, outsiders don't do things for others unless there is something in it for themselves. It's that hidden something that costs us in the end."

Thorik lowered his head at the thought of his parent's death and at what he owed Brimmelle for saving his life.

Brimmelle pulled a chair up next to the bed and opened his finely crafted wooden chest filled with scrolls. He began reading the spiritual limericks from within them. Each scroll had its own topic that related to a specific rune symbol.

He read the colorful words of inspiration in a dry tone that paled their complexion, much like listening to a beautiful song, sung by a tone-deaf singer. It was pointless for Brimmelle to unroll each one and read them, for he had a perfect memory and had been able to recite them easily after his first reading. But it was tradition and he followed the teachings without questioning them.

Monotone scroll reading went on for an hour before he suddenly stopped and stood to leave. Setting the dry pear core on Thorik's table, he walked to the doorway without a word. He paused for a moment at the open door looking into the night air and taking in a deep breath of cool fall air. "I noticed that you have missed my teachings several times in the past month. It will not happen again. Is this understood?"

Thorik didn't have to speak. He bowed his head and it was understood. A parishioner missing Brimmelle's reading was unacceptable, but Thorik was Brimmelle's nephew as well as one of his spiritual assistants. Missing his readings was serious and Thorik had missed more than one while out on hunts.

Without turning away from the night sky, Brimmelle made one last comment before stepping out the doorway. "You are too old to be playing with maps and fantasies of distant valleys. I want all of those papers you hid, when I arrived, to be set aside so you can focus on memorizing the Rune Scrolls. It's time you grow up."

And with that, he left Thorik standing in his one room cottage with a mysterious man recovering from severe injuries. Struggling between his mentor's words and investigating this man's adventures would keep Thorik from having a good night sleep far more than the inconvenience of having to sleep on the floor.

Chapter 3
Painful Extraction

Jolted from his sleep in the middle of the night, Thorik woke to the sound of Ambrosius screaming in pain.

Throwing off his blanket, Thorik quickly stood up to see what Ambrosius was yelling about. To his surprise, Gluic was kneeling at Ambrosius' side as she tried to calm him down. Her hooded cloak was still on and the front door had not yet been shut. She had just arrived and had left a trail in through doorway of flowers from a broke necklace.

She looked over at Thorik. "Close the door and grab your Runestones," she called out over Ambrosius' screams.

This was not the first time Thorik had witnessed Gluic arrive at just the right moment. In some ways the locals came to expect it.

Shutting the front door and grabbing his sack of Runestones, he met Gluic back at the side of the bed. By this point, her cloak was off as she finished strapping down Ambrosius' arms and legs in an effort to keep him from flailing around and hurting someone.

Ambrosius' entire body exploded with sensations that nearly made him pass out. Instead he arched his neck, opened his mouth, and let out a murderous cry for help. He grabbed onto the side of the bed in an involuntary response to his dilemma. His back arched and he gasped for breath as though he had just surfaced from the water after a long dive.

"Shhhh, it will be all right." Gluic spoke in a warm voice as Ambrosius was trying to deal with the pain. "You need to slow down and relax before you pass out again. We thought we had lost you last time."

"Last time?" Ambrosius questioned as he gritted his teeth together. With a great deal of focus to get out each word he continued. "How many times have I gone through this torture?"

"Its okay, son. Just let the pain flow out of your system. Focus with me." Gluic placed several stones into key positions on his head and body. In addition, she set Thorik's Health Runestone on his forehead. She then placed her hands around the top of his head with her thumbs touching each other between his eyebrows. "Listen to me, we haven't much time. I want you to focus on my hands. We are going to pull the pain spirits out of your body." Her hands began to move down his head past his eyes and nose. "Help me pull it out! I can't do this alone. You have to be here with me." The warmth in her voice was still there but now much sterner.

The flat hexagon Runestone on his forehead gave off an energy that Ambrosius could feel as heat and a slow wave-like humming sound.

Listening to her words he fought the enormous pain and did as she instructed. Impatiently, he waited for the next instruction. Focusing on her voice had reduced his pounding headache and allowed him to hear more clearly. But the pain was so strong. It was everywhere. He hurt with such overcoming agony and his fingers burned from an internal flame. "What happened to my hands?" Attempting to pull his hand to his face to see the problem he found that he was restricted from doing so.

"Reach with your mind and push the pain out as I pull it out." Her hands worked their way down his neck and then separated as they each grabbed a separate shoulder. She had noticed that he was slipping again into his own battle. "*Focus!* On my hands. Nothing else. There is only one thing important to you right now and that is *my* hands."

Her hands stayed firm on his shoulders for a period until she felt he was focused again before she continued. "My hands and your mind are going to focus on your right arm and then down past your hands. We will not stop at your hand to make sure it is well otherwise the rancid energy will stop and fester in it." With both hands on his right shoulder she pulled the energy down toward his hand. "Focus on pushing it out of your wrist, your palm, through your fingertips and then out past them."

He did as he was told, but then paused for a moment to move his fingers to make sure they were still functional.

"No!" She screamed, tightly squeezing her hands around his wrist she began moving her grip toward his fingers which were now starting to turn dark red and becoming increasingly painful to Ambrosius. "Ignore what you feel, and focus on me." It wasn't working, the pain was drawing his attention to it and his fingers were thinning and turning black. Multiple heat blisters were expanding and bursting on his palms and fingers. Dark blood oozed out of them.

If Ambrosius could imagine what it felt like to have taken all of his pain and condensed it to one spot, it still wouldn't have been this bad. He screamed as though his hand was dipped in lava. His heart began to pound out of control and his breathing was again erratic. Tossing back and forth, he knocked the stones off his body.

"I can't stop it," she shouted over his screams of pain. "I'm going to have to cut off his arm to prevent the dark energies from going back into his body. I need to get his metal armband out of the way so I can start to cut. Give me a saw, I don't care what kind it is," she yelled at Thorik as Ambrosius felt her grab his armband on his forearm. Pulling it down for the amputation, she quickly removed the arm restraint to pull the band off.

Instinctively, Ambrosius attempted to use his weakened powers to keep the armband up, to prevent this butchering from happening. He focused on the band with all his might as it continued to slide down. Regardless of his attempts to pull it back up with his mind, she pulled it past his wrist and fingers.

The metal band flew off the end of his arm and across the room. Several loud noises instantly erupted with a combination of shattering glass and items falling off shelves. The negative energy had followed the armband and had shot out of Ambrosius' hand crushing the shelving on the far wall and tipping over a lantern. A fire had started and Thorik ran over to stifle the flames.

"Good job son, now let's get the rest of it out of your body," she stated very matter a factly. His hand was now fine, except for a few remaining blisters. Her deception to get him to focus on her actions, instead of his pain, had worked successfully. She winked at Thorik for helping with the ruse, although he had no idea it was one at the time.

Once completed with his other arm, Gluic started in the center of his chest and went down to his stomach before separating at his legs, all along talking him through every step. She finished with the feet in the same manner as the hands but this time without any issues.

In a warm motherly way she said, "Now then, you lie there and get some rest." It was over. His pain was washed away and he could relax. She collected her stones & cloak and handed Thorik his Runestone of Health.

Thorik thanked Gluic for her help and walked her to the door before coming back into the room to clean up the mess created from the extraction. He had already put out the fire caused by the lantern that was knocked off the shelf and was still in the process of cleaning up the glass and various and powders from the jars of herbs that had previously resided on the destroyed shelf.

Ambrosius' throat was raspy even though the pain had subsided. He still didn't understand what had happened or where he was. Regardless, he was relieved not to be in pain anymore. "Thank you."

"You're welcome. I am Sec Thorik Dain of Farbank."

"I am Ambrosius." Finally having a chance to look at Thorik's face, it triggered fragments of memories, but nothing solid. Perhaps they had met in the Dovenar Kingdom or at Kingsfoot. "You look familiar to me, though I don't recognize your name. Have we met before?"

"I think I would have recalled meeting you." Thorik laughed at the thought. "Very few humans have visited Farbank."

Thorik continued, "I found you lying unconscious in the woods during my last hunt, so I brought you here. You've woken several times and have seen my face before passing out again. It's most likely that which you recall." He had finished picking up the large pieces of debris in the kitchen and now grabbed a broom to sweep up.

Ambrosius twisted his wrists and ankles to stretch them out. "I don't want to sound ungrateful but why is my eye covered?"

Thorik glanced over at the cloth wrapped around his patent's head to hold a paste of root and herbs against his right eye. "It still needs to heal."

Heal from what? Ambrosius thought. "I thought I was healed."

"Oh no, you aren't healed. Gluic just removed the pain for a while. She'll be back when it starts to get out of control again."

"I'll let you know when I get to that point."

"No need. Gluic will know before you do." Thorik chuckled. "As far as I can tell, you were in some sort of fire before you ended up in the river and then nearly torn apart by animals," he said in a very observational voice while finishing his cleaning.

"Fire? River?" Ambrosius rolled over to his side before slowly sitting up on the bed. "We were in a council meeting having an argument." He thought for a moment and asked himself, "Then what?" Impatient, he didn't like the lapse in memories. "The room began to shake. Everyone was running. The mountain came down on us. The Grand Council was crushed," he recalled.

"You're part of the Grand Council?" Thorik asked, staging his wood working tools neatly on his table from longest to shortest.

"Member?" snorted Ambrosius. "Dear lad, I created the confounded council," Ambrosius replied, taking a deep breath of pride. Releasing the air out his mouth he quickly relished, "Not long ago I was one of the most notable men in Australis. I had orchestrated the unthinkable, to hold a Grand Council meeting in the sacred Mountain King Temple to unite ancient enemies against a common scourge. To cease the hostilities amongst the free people and act as one, before it was too late." He paused and then continued in a more humble tone, "It was to be what I would be remembered for, my crowning achievement. Now with the attack, the death of the council, and the destruction of the temple this much will surely become true."

Thorik looked on with interest but did not grasp the depth of Ambrosius' words. "I'm sorry to hear about your loss. I've never been that far upstream, but it's my understanding that the city and statue of the King are more inspiring and grand than anything else in the world," he said, closing his eyes to envision it. "Seems a shame to mar such a magnificent place."

Gathering his wits about himself, Ambrosius straightened up and commanded, "Thorik, this is more than *my* loss or the devastation to a temple. The tide of Australis will change for the worse without its governing body. I need to return to the Mountain King Temple and find out if there are any survivors. There still might be a chance."

Sitting down at the table, Thorik began carving the head of a long thick wooden staff. "You aren't going anywhere."

"I'm sorry Thorik, but you cannot stop me," he said in a friendly and still authoritative way.

"Nor would I have to try. Your leg will take care of it for me."

Ambrosius recalled the broken leg and lifted his body slightly to see if it could take the pressure of standing. *Not yet. Perhaps with a good walking stick.* Disappointed, he sat back down on the bed. "How long before I can use my right eye?"

Thorik walked over and placed his nose near the bandages around his head and sniffed. "Not long. The root paste is just starting to smell of rot; it will be a few more days before it's finished reducing your swelling. You'll have time to collect your vision before the Harvest Festival but your leg will take much longer."

Thorik went back to work on the long staff as Ambrosius' realization of his injuries sent him into a depressed state. He was dependent on the charity of others, a feeling that he'd come to loathe over the years. On top of that, he had a date with destiny for which he could not be late.

Every morning and evening Fir Brimmelle came in to read from his Scrolls of Wisdom for an hour, but Ambrosius almost didn't realize he was there. His mind was miles upstream. In fact he didn't even recall being introduced to Brimmelle. He came, read, and then left with no conversation.

Another daily ritual became the cleansing of his pain by Gluic. This odd healing technique seemed to hold off the pain for nearly a day and each time the effects would last a little longer. She would come in and take control, perform her cleansing, complain about Ambrosius not helping enough, and then leave. This also became a blur to him.

Ambrosius was beside himself with a lack of answers and not willing to face the facts. His life was in the hands of others and he was helpless to do anything about it. It was a devastating position to be in for such a man.

Chapter 4

Harvest Festivities

The sounds of music and cheering of crowds could be heard by Thorik and Ambrosius as they approached the normally open grass field along the river, downstream from the village. The Farbank Commons had been transformed into a carnival of celebration and contests. It had been a great year for the villagers with bumper crops and an abundance of fish and hunted meats.

Small groups had formed near the tents as the adult men boasted to each other of their successes throughout the seasons and compared their fortune to past years when the Mountain King had blessed them with even greater bounties. Each year the older stories continued to grow and become more extravagant. Just ten years prior, the melons were told to be twice that of today, but now the stories tell of melons three times that size. The same was true for the tomatoes, deer, and fish.

Wess was the youngest of the elder group of men as he stretched out his arms while describing the deer that he recently hunted. His large muscular arms rose on each side of him and he spread his fingers apart toward the sky as he conjured up visions of the size of the deer's antlers. The men around him cheered and congratulated him before the next man stepped in to tell his story of triumph.

At the tents near the river, groups of women had gathered to set up tables and fill them with pies, gourds, melons, and many fragrant dishes. The melons couldn't compare to how the men had described them, but they were of good size none the less.

As they worked together, the women chatted and gossiped about who would win this year's contests and whose husband was going to get hurt in the games. They also compared how well behaved and mature their children were to how childish their husbands acted.

Using the wooden staff Thorik had made for him, Ambrosius limped his way past the tents. Groups of men and women would quiet down and stare at the intense burns along the right side of his face and neck; the pain currently relieved, however the skin would never recover. Although seen as an oddity to the villagers and a topic of conversation, everyone was respectful and pleasant.

Thorik helped Ambrosius past the tents and sat him in a chair facing the temporary stage and the open grass field where the children played. Ambrosius could overhear parts of the women's conversations but he couldn't keep up with them. They all talked at once about unrelated topics and yet kept up with each other. Ambrosius resigned his attempts to eavesdrop and relaxed in the cool air and warm sun as Thorik excused himself.

Ambrosius watched the children play in the field before him as they jumped and tumbled in the grass. He smiled for the first time in many a week as he envied the freedom and easy life this village offered.

A short distance away, a group of children sat in a circle and chanted a rhyme while a young girl walked around the outside of the ring. Older than most she played with, she had a spark in her eye of cleverness and curiosity which stood out from the rest. Glancing over at Ambrosius, she grinned before returning to her game. Her long straight hair was woven with various shades of spring flowers, swinging from side to side while bobbing her head back and forth to the other children's voices.

When all the jewels are in his crown,
The mighty King will drop it down.
All but one of the gems will break
As it plummets into a nearby lake

At this point in the poem, the young girl tapped a darker hair boy on the shoulder and ran as the boy sprang up and chased her around the circle while the youthful group continued.

This treasure will again appear
Striking disbelievers with great fear.
But if the one is cleansed, you see
Rebirth to the kingdom is foreseen

Once the poem stopped, the young girl raced the remainder of the lap around her seated peers to the location her chaser had once sat. He had just caught up with her and tagged her sleeve after she sat down. Safe, it was his turn to walk around them.

This went on for a few more rounds until the young girl got up and approached Ambrosius. Three thick soul lines twisted into a simple, yet beautiful, pattern around her neck and her wrists. The other children had stopped the game and turned to watch her.

Tilting her head in question, she looked him up and down for answers while he smiled at her. "What are you?"

Stunned at first by the brashness of the question, Ambrosius' face softened and warmed up. "Dear child, I am just a man like your father."

"My father isn't nearly as tall or thin as you, and you have no soul-markings on your skin." Placing her hand on the back of his, she felt its texture. "Your rough skin feels more like an old dried beaver skin Uncle Wess gave us."

Ambrosius chuckled at the comment. "Sometimes I feel like an old dried beaver skin."

"He says that you're bad luck and the reason for the dead fish in the river recently," she commented very openly without agreeing or disagreeing with him.

Just then, Thorik returned with drinks and food that he had acquired from the women's tables. "That's enough Avanda, go play with your friends," Thorik directed as she removed her hand and quickly smiled before heading back to her group.

"My apologies, Ambrosius." After handing the older man a mug and plate, Thorik sat down to enjoy his meal. "She doesn't always think about what she says before she opens her mouth. It doesn't help that she's living with Wess while her parents are in Longfield."

Taking a sip of the sweet juice, Ambrosius was pleasantly surprised by the drink. "She was just curious."

"The last thing she was curious about ended up at the bottom of the river this morning." Thorik noticed Ambrosius' confused look. "Her aunt's nine-time award-winning pie is so fluffy and light it can float on water. Avanda wanted to test that theory by seeing if it could stay afloat between our two main fishing docks." He paused and smiled. "And that pie almost survived the voyage to the second dock before it was pulled sideways in the current, took on water and then sank. Needless to say her aunt didn't have a second one to enter into today's contest. So there are tongues flapping about who will take her place this year."

They both grinned at the thought of the youthful entertainment for a few moments before Ambrosius finally chimed in. "Perhaps if she added a rudder to the bottom she could avoid the side current next year."

They both went quiet and then laughed out loud at the thought.

The day continued with contests for the children first and then the judging of the pies, fruits, vegetables and more. Fir Brimmelle was the head judge for the contests and by the end of the day his stomach stretched over his trousers as he began to wobble as he walked. Avanda's aunt cried as the winning pie was selected, knowing that it would have been hers if it were not for Avanda's failed experiment.

Full of food and ale, it was now the men's turn to compete in the games as the women and children cheered them on. Contests of strength, speed, and accuracy were usually made to impress the unmarried women of the village. Sometimes, a few married men would enter to show their spouse how young and vigorous they still were.

This was the case of old man Trumette who every year entered the running contest from the grassy common into the woods, through the ancient cliff dwellings, up to the top of Dula Peak and back again. Red flags were made up by Trumette's wife, Sorla, and the children placed them in the spiritual hut at the top of the peak earlier in the day. The runners would grab them for proof that they made it up to the top.

Many years ago, when Trumette was in his sixties, he took one of the red flags from his wife's bag the night before the Festival and hid it deep in the woods. During the race he fell behind and grabbed his hidden flag halfway up and raced back down to barely win the race. Each year after that, he hid the flag closer to the bottom of the hill and each year his wife made one extra flag for him to steal from her. It became a tradition to see him come in first place as the crowd cheered him on. Sorla always made a big fuss about the event for his benefit, as he would tell her how he was getting younger and faster every year. It was a joy to see him happy and everyone supported the ruse.

The participants of the contests changed for each sporting event including the Dula Peak Race. This was the only event that Trumette entered as he stood at the starting line with all of the young bucks.

Ambrosius looked at the old man before peering up over the cliff dwellings, which once held their ancestors, and to the rocky peak that needed to be hiked. He looked forward to seeing Trumette make his way up.

Wess stood next to Thorik in line, waiting for the race to begin. He attempted to talk to Thorik in an effort to distract him from the race. Thorik did not listen. Wess then pointed at Emilen. Her smile and charm filled Thorik's chest with warmth and he couldn't help but smile when he saw her. Shaking off his gaze at her, he looked back at the track to get his mind focused at the task at hand. Wess blew her a kiss and nudged Thorik to look at her blowing one back at him. Thorik glanced over to see her standing with her arms crossed, just as the signal was given to start the race. Thorik had fallen for Wess' trick and was now several lengths behind him.

The thirty-four racers ran along the grass field toward the trees with Thorik at the back as he followed Trumette who tripped and fell only a few paces out. Thorik stopped and helped the old man up before quickly returning his attention to the race.

The group left the grassy field and ran into the woods with Wess in the lead and Trumette far behind. One at a time, they slowly disappeared into the timber going up the hillside. All except for Trumette, who only made it a few yards into the woods before he slowed down to find the flag he had hidden the night before.

Ambrosius looked around at the crowd as they cheered Trumette on while they watched him through the trees. Wandering from bush to bush, he searched for where he had placed the hidden flag. He obviously had forgotten and had picked up a stick to beat at the shrubs to see if anything would fall out.

Meanwhile, the group of racers had worked their way above the trees and into the ancient ruins of a Polenum civilization long gone. Walls were mere stumps and easily climbable. Each runner was respectful of this spiritual land and moved quickly between the short borders instead of stepping over them. The time lost was the same for all racers.

They then raced up the rock face toward the peak. Wess was still in the lead but Thorik was right on his tail and gaining on him.

Wess lost his footing when the small rocks that he stepped on gave way, causing him to roll down the steep hill. Grabbing onto a small bush that grew on the hillside with one hand, Thorik snatched Wess with the other as he slid past. With Thorik's help, Wess stopped and regained his balance. The added weight, however, pulled the small plant out of the ground and Thorik let go to prepare for his fall. As he began to slide down he reached back out for Wess who retracted his hand allowing Thorik to tumble down the cliff.

By this point the crowd was dismayed that Trumette had sat down and given up on his quest. Seeing her husband's frail body exhausted and tired against a tree, Sorla walked over to Avanda and whispered in her ear while removing an extra red flag from her apron and handing it to her. Avanda ran off to the side into the woods and then turned sharply toward the old man. She quickly moved in behind him and quietly placed the new flag on the bush just to his right, before sneaking back out the way she came.

Wess arrived at the top of Dula Peak, ran into the hut to grab his flag, and began his race down the hill before passing Thorik. As he glanced back and smirked at Thorik with a smile, Wess tripped and rolled his way down into the cliff dwellings.

Thorik reached the top and grabbed his flag. He stopped only a second, to help a friend up the last rock, before he began his chase for Wess. Quick and nimble, Thorik made the loose rock face look very easy to descend.

Collecting his dazed head and his battered body from the fall, Wess sprinted over the short walls to ensure his lead over Thorik. Tradition and respect would slow the smaller Num for he would weave his way through the ancient site.

The crowd chanted Trumette's name in an attempt to get him started again. Trumette was still catching his breath and his poor vision didn't allow him to see the obvious red flag near him. Finally he stood and turned to his left and began to walk. Everyone screamed, trying to tell him that he was going the wrong way. Looking for a few seconds more, he then followed the crowd's orders by turning around. The villagers went wild with delight. The suspense was killing them as he took a few steps toward the flag while moving the thick fall leaves around with his stick. Just as he started walking past the flag, his stick hit the bush and it fell onto the ground before him.

Trumette stood there staring at the red flag for a moment in disbelief. He picked it up and started his walk out of the woods into the green grass as everyone yelled his name. Raising the flag over his head he walked slowly toward the finish line. His eyes were beaming and his cheeks were red while he passed the young children on his way to his thirtieth consecutive victory. "Never give up," he told the children as he passed them. "You can make anything happen if you want it bad enough." Trumette huffed as he continued the last stretch of grass.

But it wasn't over. Wess launched out of the woods and toward the crowd with Thorik in his wake. Dirt and cuts covered their bodies as they rushed in for the finish while Trumette stood in their way. Still several paces from the ribbon, Trumette made a move for it but it was too late as Wess passed him by in a blur and crossed the finish line. Thorik saw Trumette moving the best he could and slowed down to allow the elder man second place.

Thorik followed in third before he walked to the side and bent over to catch his breath. He looked up to see Wess with his hands over his head holding the finish-line ribbon as his three brothers ran over to reward him with hugs and pats on the back.

Sorla walked over to Trumette and gave him a big hug while she explained that she was still very proud of him. But it was an end of an era for him. His body language spoke volumes as though he suddenly felt as old as his ninety-two year old body looked.

The crowd was full of mixed emotions, for many had never seen anyone but Trumette win the race. Some cheered while others stood silent, but most of them still came over to Trumette to congratulate him. Being polite they also congratulated Wess in a more solemn manner, although Wess ignored them and continued to revel in his victory with his brothers.

Fir Brimmelle stepped in toward Wess with the award and raised his hand in victory. He handed Wess the Runestone of Success while he read a few chapters from memory of the scroll about the meaning of the rune. Wess stood tall as the words spoke to him while grinning at Thorik, making Thorik's neck hairs stand up on end. Once Brimmelle was finished, the Fir asked Wess for the Red Flag to which Wess looked down at his hands and realized he didn't have it. Panicking he looked about the ground near his feet and then his pockets while questioning his brothers if they had taken it. But it was nowhere to be found, for he had dropped it during his tumble down the cliff face.

Clinching his fist, he appeared to be ready for a fight. "You all saw me reach the top." Walking over to several spectators, he used his height and broad shoulders to intimidate them. "I still made it there and back first, and you know it."

But they didn't back down and screamed for his elimination from the race.

Brimmelle tried to settle them down by explaining that Wess had made it to the top, but he was finally pressured to give into the rules that the contestant must have a flag on their return.

He reached to receive the Runestone from Wess who clinched his fist around it. "This is your own fault," Brimmelle told him. "I know you've won, but the rules are the rules."

Looking at the group of friends and neighbors getting upset with him, Wess finally opened his hand and allowed Brimmelle to take the awarded stone. Wess and his brothers stomped off to get some ale as Brimmelle awarded Trumette with the Runestone and then read the same passage again for him. Everyone cheered and Thorik beamed back to life for Trumette's victory as he looked over at Emilen and winked at her. She was caught up in the crowd's enthusiasm as well and smiled back at him.

After the group dispersed, Thorik dusted himself off and made his way back to Ambrosius. He let himself fall into the chair while he wiped sweat from his face. "That Trumette sure is fast." A smile grew across his face. "He's like a gust of wind. I didn't even see him pass me."

Ambrosius grinned. "Do you think you'll ever beat him?"

Still smiling, Thorik answered in a thoughtful tone. "I hope not."

"You are very lucky, Thorik. You live in this isolated lush valley, protected from the rest of the world and surrounded by wonderful friends and family." Ambrosius looked upon the bright smiles of the young and old. "Yes, you are one fortunate man."

Thorik eyed Wess who had walked over to Emilen and started a conversation. "Perhaps."

Leaning back in his chair, Ambrosius contemplated his own life. "I don't know if I would say that I have had as much luck over my years."

Thorik continued to watch Wess as he escorted Emilen to the next contest where he would compete for strength. Wess would win this contest just like he had for the past several years. He was obviously the strongest member of the community. "You're lucky I found you." He then returned his attention back to his patient.

"Yes, my friend. I was lucky that you found me."

"My mother used to always tell me that things happen for a reason. So, we just need to find out the reason why I found you."

Ambrosius found the comments amusing as he looked about the crowd. "Where is your mother?"

Thorik's eyes tightened as he answered. "My parents aren't with us anymore."

Ambrosius realized that he hit a sensitive nerve. "I'm sorry to hear that." He let Thorik get some blood back in his face before he continued. "Do you still believe things happen for a reason?"

Thorik nodded his head in a soft motion. "I have to. It's the only thing that keeps me going."

"In that case, I will tell you why you found me."

Thorik's face came back to life with a look of intrigue. "Go on." His brow rose with curiosity as he looked Ambrosius square in the eyes. "Let me hear it."

"I cannot travel up the river valley to Kingsfoot by myself. You will help me determine who destroyed the Mountain King Temple and the Grand Council which held forum within it, so we can prevent the next such attack upon the innocent. Why else would you just happen to find me in the middle of the forest?" Ambrosius placed his hand on Thorik's shoulder while finishing his thought. "I've seen you looking over your maps and notes. You want an adventure out of this valley. Finding me, gives you that opportunity. It is fate."

Thorik's eyes widened, he had never been that far upstream. "I think not. Even if Brimmelle would allow me to travel such a distance from Farbank, you have not recovered enough to make such a trip. It will take Gluic another few weeks to get you healthy enough."

"I would like you to ask Gluic if she will come with us. She can continue healing me during our travels. While at Kingsfoot, you can see a true testament of your faith and once we are complete you can ride the river to bring Gluic home."

"Do you realize how far downstream we are from Kingsfoot?"

"It couldn't be that far. Or how would I have floated down without drowning?"

"You couldn't have without a boat. By walking, I would assume it will take us several weeks," Thorik estimated, not knowing how far Ambrosius could travel in a day.

"All the reason to leave sooner than later." Ambrosius twirled the hair of his beard between two fingers, feeling confident that he convinced the young Num to help him.

"You don't understand the dangers in such a trip. You will need to be stronger. The passes will be snow covered soon and the river cuts will be overflowing from the after-harvest rains. We should wait until spring."

"Thorik, I cannot wait until spring. Someone has killed the governing body of our world and destroyed a sacred temple of your faith. I need to find out who and how they did this, before they strike again." Ambrosius' passion came out stronger than he had intended. "As you said, the after-harvest weather will be moving in soon. We need to leave before it arrives."

"Do you need to be there by December 13th?" Thorik's scrutinizing look waited for an answer.

Fighting to not display his sudden shock by this question, Ambrosius tamed his voice be replying. "What do you know of this date?"

"I know you repeated it several times in your sleep. Is it important?"

"Extremely, my young friend." Ambrosius made sure they were out of hearing distance before leaning forward and continuing. "Keep this date to yourself. If we don't stop the murderer of the council by that date, he will unleash a devastating attack on the land which could wipe us all out."

Ambrosius paused until Thorik made eye contact with him again. "So you see, I will go on my own if I must, but I believe the reason you found me was to help me prevent the deaths of thousands of innocent people. Children at play, loving wives and husbands, and the elderly all are at risk from this killer. Just because you don't see it here around you doesn't mean it's not coming. But it is, and you can help me stop it."

"Why me?"

"You have a strong foundation which a significant future can be built on. Stronger than most I have met. Plus, there is something about you that I still cannot place. Something that tells me you have greatness."

Thorik thought about it for only a few moments before shaking his head as he looked back at Ambrosius. "I'm sorry about what happened to you and about your challenges outside this valley, but I'm happy here and-"

Brimmelle interrupted Thorik as he walked up to them, "It is time for the Rune Awards." Towering over them as they sat, he made his presence clear and official, like always. "Come along then. We shall not be late for it." Brimmelle stood firm as an oak tree waiting for Thorik to jump up and get his items ready for the speech.

After a slight hesitation and a deep breath, Thorik slowly stood and did as he was told by walking over to one of the tents and grabbed various scrolls and bags. By the time he made his way to the stage he had the usual spring in his step again. Quickly organizing his items onto a table, several children came up to look at what was on display.

Showing the children various stones that hung on leather necklaces Thorik asked them questions as though they were back in school. As they raised their hands, he called on them to give the answers about the rune symbols for each of the stones. Each of these Runestones was similar in size, shape and symbol to the ones used on Ambrosius, without the radiance or gems embedded within them. Thorik's personal Runestones had been handed down from his father and were unparalleled to any seen in the village.

Thorik beamed as the answers came from the children. His weekly teachings of the Runestones and the Rules of Order to the children obviously paid off. They knew every answer and went on to explain at great length the rune name, its external meaning on the white painted side, and its internal meaning on the stone finished side.

Brimmelle stepped onto the stage and walked to the center before turning toward the crowd. He spied his mother, Gluic, playing with the children as though she was one of them. He was very uncomfortable about the changes in her during her elder years. Regressing to a childlike mind was common among the older Nums, but she had also started talking to stones and plants, as well as people that didn't exist. In addition, she would change from a playful child to a serious scolding mother in an instant. He never knew who he was going to be approaching. Because of the discomfort he felt with the situation, he never spoke of it, nor did he allow anyone else to. The villagers had learned to ignore her odd behavior.

Thorik quickly waved away the children and grabbed the first of many scrolls on the table before he walked out next to Brimmelle. A crowd formed in front of the stage as Brimmelle reached his hand out to his side, waiting for the placement of the scroll. Thorik removed the string from the scroll before placing it in Brimmelle's hand.

Thorik quieted the crowd down prior to making an announcement. "It is time now for Fir Brimmelle Riddlewood the Seventh to present the Harvest Festival Awards. Can I please have the children come to the front?" Avanda moved to the front with the rest of her young friends and waved at Thorik as he waited for the few stragglers before continuing. "Over the past year there have been some special accomplishments by our youth. One of which is the saving of Marla Moondy's grazers from a bushdog last spring by Norby Grenwicker."

Everyone cheered as Thorik motioned for Norby to come up on stage. Once there, Thorik placed a leather necklace over the boy's head with a Runestone hanging from it. Thorik made sure that the white face of the stone faced out as he adjusted it to the center of Norby's chubby body. Thorik then placed his hands on Norby's shoulders and turned him toward the audience as they applauded. Standing directly behind Norby, Thorik asked him to read the rune and describe what it meant to him.

Looking down at the stone now resting in his palm, Norby looked at the symbol in the center of it. "It's the Rune of Symbiosis." He looked out at his hefty mother and father smile from the back of the crowd. "It means that I have to help keep Mrs. Moondy's grazers from being eaten, so my mom will have wool to make me clothes and to trade for food." He scrunched up his lips as he worked his brain for more. "So, we all need to help each other to have food?"

"That's pretty close." Thorik smiled as he reached around and flipped the stone over to show the polished stone side. "Go on."

"Well, um." Norby's lips pushed to one side as he thought about it. "It means that each part of my body needs to help the other parts and what I do to one part can affect the others?" He looked up at Thorik in hopes that he had it right.

"Keep going. Give an example that you have experienced."

He thought for a second and then realized he had it. "Last week I ate a whole basket of blueberries that upset my stomach and I ended up getting sick all over Margi's new dress," he giggled as his belly bounced at the thought. "My mouth loved them but my stomach didn't. I guess they weren't working together."

Disgusted, Fir Brimmelle glared at Thorik. A Sec is responsible for educating the children on the Rune Scrolls. Apparently he had not done his job.

Sec Thorik let it slide. "That's not exactly where I was going. So why don't you listen to Fir Brimmelle as he reads from the Symbiotic Rune Scroll."

With that Brimmelle uncoiled the scroll and began reading the meaning of the rune, while Norby stood proudly on stage displaying his award to his friends. Brimmelle continued for several minutes in a monotone voice while his parishioners stood quietly and listened.

Once Brimmelle had completed his readings he coiled up the scroll and handed it back to Thorik who tied a string around it and set it back with the others. He then handed Brimmelle the next scroll after removing the string from it.

Thorik began to talk again and the crowd slowly came back to life with smiles and light chatter. "This past winter someone had stolen a large wall carving from the school. It had been made by last years graduate Benly Harcaloff in the shape of a huge Runestone of Trust. After several days of questioning we gave up our search. Not long after, it was returned with an apology. It had been taken by a child to be used as a snow sled. And after several successful runs down Turtleback Mound she lent it to another to ride. But on their way, they crashed into a tree and broke the wood sled in half. The person who returned it blamed herself and took the full punishment without making excuses or blaming others."

Thorik looked down at the children in front. "Avanda, please come up here," he said to his student of only a few years shy his own age. "This Runestone is for the lesson you learned the hard way and I hope you are wiser for it." She stepped up on stage and he placed the necklace over her head. "Now, it's your turn," he whispered into her ear.

Avanda looked down in her open palm at the white side of the Runestone. "It's the Rune of Responsibility, and it means that you have to take responsibility for your actions to others and to nature. Even if you didn't mean to hurt them." She stopped as she turned the stone over. "And I have to be responsible to myself by knowing that I did something wrong and I did the right thing in the end."

Thorik prodded. "You're getting there, keep going."

Avanda looked behind her and asked Thorik, "Would I have still received this Runestone if I had told you that Uncle Wess broke the sled?"

The crowd overheard and erupted in laughter as Wess' face turned red and his brothers began to laugh and push him around. Humiliated, he left the group.

After everyone settled down, Brimmelle uncoiled the scroll and read the official meaning of the rune.

Several more awards were handed out to the children before a few adults received some. The routine was the same for each with Brimmelle reading after each award was given. When they had finished, the crowd dispersed and went back to eating and drinking as the sun set on Farbank's Common.

Lanterns were lit and music began to play as Ambrosius sat in his chair and watched couples begin to dance. Partners changed frequently allowing everyone a chance to socialize with each other. The night was still young but his body was not. Gluic's healing from that morning was wearing off and he was again starting to feel great discomfort.

As Thorik finally received a chance to dance with Emilen he glanced over at Ambrosius who was hunched over in his chair. Regretfully, he excused himself and left the dance area to see what was wrong with his patient. "Ambrosius, can you walk?"

"Yes, but the pain is starting to return with a vengeance," Ambrosius squeezed out.

Thorik helped him from his chair. He then acted as a crutch for Ambrosius as they made their way through the village and to Thorik's cottage, where he laid his tall friend gently onto the bed. Gluic had been waiting there long enough to make herself a pot of tea and sip half a cup down. Her Healing Stones were laid out and ready to be used as she moved them onto key points of his body.

Chapter 5
Leaving Farbank

Ambrosius opened his eyes the next morning just as the sun began to warm the frigid air. He slowly sat up and noticed something different from the other days. Although the room was very tidy like always, there was a pack sitting on the center of the table, along side it was a Runestone. He also noticed his wooden staff leaning against the chair. Thorik had fashioned a thumb grip at the top of the staff out of antler, ideal for negotiating inclines.

Standing up and moving over to the table, he pulled out a chair and sat down to investigate. He opened the pack to find various hiking gear and rations. *He's packed my bags for my trip.*

Disappointed that he was not able to sway Thorik, he took in a deep thoughtful breath and considered his options; wait until he was fully recovered or take his chances now on his own. His frustration in not knowing what exactly happened at the Mountain King's Temple was fueled by the idle time that he had had in the small village. He felt unproductive in helping others that could have survived the Temple's destruction, uncomfortable in not knowing how the council was located and destroyed, and furious in knowing the assassin was victorious and roaming free. *Where would your next attack be? And if not me, who would be there to stop it?*

Utilizing the wooden staff to lift him from his seat, he threw the pack over his shoulder and grabbed the Runestone to begin his walk to Kingsfoot. Looking around the little cottage, he commented to Thorik who wasn't there. "Thank you for your help, my friend. I understand why you wouldn't want to leave this peaceful place."

He tossed the stone in the air before him and caught it as he turned for the door. Stopping just before opening it, he looked into his palm at the rune in the center of the hexagonal stone. It was the Runestone of Symbiosis. Looking puzzled for a moment he suddenly realized what it meant. "I knew you would come through for me." Although Thorik couldn't possibly hear him, ironically the Num approached the door from outside sharply after the words were spoken.

The door swung open and Thorik walked in with a handful of blankets neatly folded after being freshly removed from the clothesline. "Good morning. Do you feel strong enough for a hike upstream today?"

"I've climbed the east face of the Shi'Pel crest, I think I can handle a little tour in the woods," he said with a smile. "I'm glad that I could change your mind about helping me."

Thorik set down the thick blankets and walked to the kitchen area. "You didn't. Looking into my student's faces did." Grabbing several pieces of fruit for them to enjoy on their trip, he tucked them into a sack before tossing one to Ambrosius. "How can I teach the words of the Mountain King if I don't follow them myself?"

"Either way, I appreciate what you're doing for me."

"You're welcome." Thorik went back to his task of collecting items for the excursion. After lining up silverware, plates, oils and spices onto the table, he placed them into his own pack in specific locations around his coffer to keep them protected. Instinctively, he kept the coffer hidden so Brimmelle wouldn't see it and berate him for wasting his time.

Ambrosius stepped out the door into the sun's morning rays peeking between the colored leaves in the trees. Closing the door behind him, he walked out onto the path to test his leg strength as well as Thorik's recent modifications to the staff's handgrip. It felt much better. Not as good as his old metal staff, but an improvement from the prior day. Walking up toward the hillside behind the cottage to test his leg capabilities, the outcroppings of rocks acted as an ideal site for stepping up and down. His legs were holding, weak and wobbly, but holding.

Putting the last few items into their designated locations, Thorik was interrupted by a knock on the door to which he went to answer. He was surprised to find a small party outside his small cottage packed for the trip. He had expected Gluic, seeing that she had agreed to help Ambrosius while Thorik would lead them to Kingsfoot. But he was disappointed to find two others had joined her.

"Brimmelle? What are your plans on this day?" He had hoped that Brimmelle strictly showed up to see his mother off on her journey.

Brimmelle raised his head and chest slightly. "You need a leader. I'm the obvious choice. And I brought Wess with us to ensure our safety from wild beasts."

This was a direct insult to Thorik by his mentor, the Fir of Farbank. He was just reminded that Brimmelle felt he didn't have what it takes to be a leader nor a protector.

Bringing Wess made it even worse. Wess had been malicious and condescending to Thorik over the years, and yet he was a loyal follower of Fir Brimmelle. The contradiction annoyed Thorik.

Regardless of any feelings Thorik had, he welcomed them both in.

Wess politely thanked him as though they were close friends. "You have done well for yourself, Dain." Picking a few jars off the cupboard shelves, he read the detailed labels before setting them back with the labels facing the wall. "Your mother would have been very proud of how clean you kept her shack." Looking at his fingertips for dust after glazing them across the back of the chair he found them clean.

For no apparent reason, Wess pulled a chair out as he rambled on before moving over toward the shelves of books and knickknacks. He observed several items by holding them to the light from the window and then setting them back down in new locations.

Brimmelle, meanwhile, had made himself at home by pulling up his normal reading chair and was entrenched in reviewing the Scrolls of Wisdom as though the journey was completed and it was time to relax.

By this time Thorik was slowly following Wess around the room trying not to look obvious as he turned the jars back so the labels faced out, pushed the chair back in and reorganized the various objects Wess had moved.

Threading a new feather into her hair, Gluic looked at the group and shook her head in disbelief. "Are we going to Kingsfoot or rearranging your home? Take the lead," she ordered Thorik, before looking at Brimmelle and Wess. "And I didn't ask either of you two to come so you walk behind me. I'm not going to spend the next week downwind from you."

Thorik tried not to smile. She knew just what to say to ruffle Brimmelle's feathers and make Thorik feel better.

Stepping out of the cottage, Gluic turned upstream to head through the woods. Ambrosius was already waiting for the group. Approaching him, she adjusted a shoulder strap. "I see you've found your legs this morning."

Placing a hand on his leg, he nodded at her statement. "Thank you for your help."

Reaching for a small sack hanging from her belt, she pulled out a yellowish clear stone and placed it in his right hand. "Moonstone," she explained. "Releases all the tension and emotions you're hiding inside you." She reached up and pointed at his head. "And *you* have plenty of that up there."

"I'll be fine. Thank you anyway." Ambrosius politely rejected her help by trying to return the item as she walked past him and into the woods.

"Well, of course you will be, as long as you do as I tell you." Her soft but stern words stopped his returning of the gift. "Now hold onto that stone today and I'll need to cleanse it tonight so you can use it again tomorrow."

Ambrosius chuckled to himself at her odd leadership role and placed the moonstone into one of his pockets before following her through the trees.

Without looking back, Gluic notified Ambrosius, "I'll strap that to your palm if you don't take it back out and hold it on your own."

Stopping in his tracks he had to give her motherly instincts a nod of praise as he took the stone back out and grasped it in his fist.

Thorik, Brimmelle, and Wess grabbed their items and followed as well. Brimmelle was out the door and in pursuit of his mother while Thorik made a turn and headed up the hill to grab a few last items out of the shed next to his well positioned barrow. He hummed a few rhymes and phrases as he put items in his pack. "Lack of plans, provides fallow lands." He was just glad to get going. Stuffing his pack to its limit, he tested the stitching that held it together. Satisfied that he had what he needed, he headed back to catch up with the group to find Wess just leaving his home.

Wess headed into the woods to meet the group and didn't notice Thorik was a short distance to his right, walking down the hill toward him.

Thorik thought it odd that Wess would stay in his home after everyone left, unless, "Oh no." He ran to the front door. Heart racing, his imagination went crazy with the potential damage that Wess could have done. *Why would he? How did I do him wrong?* Upon opening the door he stepped in to see what had been done.

He ran to the cupboard and looked the items over. Finding everything in order, he worked his way over to the bookshelf to find the same thing. Nothing. It was just as he had left it. Taking a deep breath to get a hold of himself, he started to laugh at his own paranoia. Shrugging it off, he walked outside where he nearly bumped into Wess.

Wess smiled at Thorik before glancing over his shoulder into his home. "Did you forget something? I noticed you were missing." Wess had one of those smiles that made Thorik's skin crawl. "Is there anything I can help with?"

"No, I'm fine," Thorik replied before mustering up the courage to continue. "I did notice you leaving my cottage a little later than everyone else. Did you forget something?" It was difficult for Thorik to be confrontational.

Wess' smile never wavered. "Why yes I did. But luckily I remembered it before we got too far."

This was going to be a long trip and now was not the time to create friction. Besides, what was he going to do? Complain about Wess' annoying smile? No, Thorik needed to get going and just ignore him.

So off they went to catch up to the three in front who had no idea where they were going.

It wasn't long before they were all together again. Ambrosius was the hold up, but then again he was the reason they were going. His thoughts were again on other issues and only reserved enough focus to walk the slightly rocky woods. He paid no attention to conversations around him unless he was literally poked to get his attention in an effort to give him water or food.

Ambrosius was vacillating between denial of the destruction and the grief of accepting it. His own internal struggles seemed to control his walking pace. Not mindful of the path, he wandered from side to side and requiring periodic assistance from Thorik. It was a more difficult hike than Ambrosius had suspected.

Over time the group slowly spread out, walking at different speeds. Shortly into the walk, Wess and Brimmelle fell a few lengths behind the others to talk privately. Wess watched Ambrosius limp and stumble through the forest, like some drunk after a long night of festivities. "So, this is the one that has put a plague on us? This weak pathetic man," Wess quietly said to Brimmelle. "Wouldn't it have been easier to just sacrifice him to the Mountain King?"

Typically Brimmelle was reserved about saying anything unless it was read out of his spiritual scrolls. "We will not taint our village with his blood. He is either the one that will save us or the one who will destroy us and I will not be the one who orders our savior's death."

Wess slowed their pace a bit to increase their distance from the rest as they rounded a bend in the old path. "How much more proof do you need that he is evil? The river has been filled with dead fish ever since he arrived. Even with the great harvest we had, we will run out of food if he is not sacrificed and the fish return. Several of us talked about this and I know that most of the others agree with me that-"

"Others?" Brimmelle interrupted. "Who else knows that we suspect him of carrying out the words of Portent Scrolls?" Brimmelle stopped Wess in his tracks and looked him in his eyes. "Listen here, Wesstiford Solen Frellican." He pulled Wess close to him with a handful of his shirt. "I am the Fir, not you. I make this ruling and I decide who knows what. Is that understood?"

Wess was leaner than Brimmelle, several inches taller, and about half a life younger. Regardless of his physical abilities, Wess was not going to be disrespectful to a Fir. Disagree with him perhaps, but never disrespect him. Knowing how far he could push the issue, he nodded to Brimmelle signifying that he would obey.

Keeping his grip tight onto Wess' shirt, Brimmelle relaxed his arms to give some distance between them. "Who else knows about this?"

Before he could respond, they both heard a voice in the woods from which they had come. It was a woman's voice shouting Wess' name. It was Emilen running through the woods trying to catch up to them. Her long curly hair bounced with each stride as it was loosely held together with several colorful hair ribbons in a single ponytail. Following behind was the youth, Avanda. Brimmelle released Wess before they arrived.

Emilen joyfully approached the two while looking farther into the woods. "Where's the rest of the group?"

Brimmelle crossed his arms and pulled his shoulders back. "Young lady, what do you think you're doing?"

She listened to him as she walked past them both and started walking the direction she hoped was the correct way. "We're going with you. Which way did they go?"

The timber was very thick at this point but the river could still be heard to her left so she assumed she was going the right way.

It seemed very cut and dry to the Fir. "Nonsense. Return home at once. This is no place for the two of you. Return to Farbank and watch Avanda for Wess like you were instructed."

"My family lives in Kingsfoot and I want to see if they are safe. As far as Avanda goes, I can watch her while we travel," she replied, before sighting Thorik and Ambrosius. "There they are." Ignoring him, she rushed forward into the woods before Brimmelle could utter a rebuttal.

Brimmelle stood silently and watched her run until she rounded the path's bend. "Is she one that believes he is a savior or a demon?"

Wess finished straightening out the creases in his shirt. "Savior." He also had watched her run and skip over fallen branches and rocks, but with different thoughts in his head.

"Unfortunate."

"True, but perhaps I could persuade her to think differently." Wess smiled as he viewed her leave them.

"You won't get that chance," Brimmelle noted. "It is not safe for Avanda out here."

"She'll be fine, we will all watch her."

"Avanda is your responsibility until her parents return to Farbank in the spring. Take this seriously and order Emilen to return her at once."

Wess was captivated by Emilen's looks. It was difficult for him to stay in Brimmelle's conversation. He eventually added, "This will be good for her to learn how to travel. I'll take care of her, I promise."

"I don't like this," the Fir replied as Avanda followed Emilen toward the group in front.

It wasn't long before Emilen had reached the forward group and jumped onto Thorik's back. "Surprise!" she shouted as they both fell to the ground and rolled to a nearby log. Flinching from the stabbing pain inflicted by various objects in his backpack, Thorik tried not to move. She was on top of him laughing at his expression, not knowing why he was making the faces he did.

Hopping off once she saw Ambrosius standing near Gluic, Emilen approached the older man slowly and bowed her head. "I'm grateful to finally meet you."

Ambrosius looked down to see Emilen at his feet. "What's that child? What did you say?" he asked as he pulled out of his own frustrated daydream. She looked familiar. Then again, she wasn't the first Num he thought that of. His head had been scrambled and his memories were a mess.

She looked up at him and replied, "I am at your service to save our people."

"Save your people?" He thought about it, figuring Thorik must have caught on to more than he thought. Then Ambrosius said, "I've tried to save your people. All people in fact, but I'm afraid I have failed. Now I'm struggling just to keep my own vitality."

"But you are the one, the one written about in our Portent Scrolls." She looked into his tired eyes and waited for his reply.

"Emilen, he doesn't know what you're talking about," Thorik said after dislodging himself from his pack. "We're just here to return him to the Mountain King Temple."

Emilen looked in disbelief at Thorik. "Why didn't you tell him?"

Brimmelle responded as he and Wess caught up to them. "We don't even know if it is true about the Mountain King Statue, the council, and if he is who he claims to be. Contain your excitement until we know what's going on here."

"Why would you think his story is false?" she asked.

Brimmelle answered her loud enough for Ambrosius to over hear. "First of all, how did he end up so far downstream? If he had fallen in the river, he would have surely drowned or froze to death before reaching Farbank."

"We'll be at Kingsfoot soon enough and know what happened," Thorik added, in his attempt to dissolve the friction in the air.

By this time, Ambrosius was confused and exhausted from limping through the woods and comforted himself by sitting down on a large log. Brimmelle's words were valid, but he was unable to protest them.

The rest of the party also relaxed for a moment as Brimmelle and Wess sat on a few large rocks off by themselves to continue their conversation. Gluic and Emilen found comfortable locations sitting on adjacent logs. Avanda sat next to Emilen and proceeded to inform her of all the misadventures she had over the summer.

Thorik reviewed the items in his pack to ensure everything was all right. Noticing Avanda, Thorik questioned her. "What are you doing here?" He was obviously upset that she was subjected to the dangers of the woods.

Avanda frowned. She had hoped Thorik would have been excited to see her.

"This is too dangerous for you," Thorik told her before turning his attention to Wess. "Wess, you need to take responsibility for her and take her back to Farbank."

Wess didn't take kindly to Thorik giving him orders. "Listen Dain, I gave her to Emilen to watch, so don't be lecturing me. Tell Emilen to take her, or better yet, you can take her back and Emilen and I will lead this group upstream."

Wess looked up at Emilen's sour look and quickly changed his response. "Personally, if Emilen feels that it is safe out here for Avanda, then I will defend her decision." With a quick smile he added, "Emilen and I will work together to keep her out of trouble."

Thorik couldn't believe his ears and looked to Brimmelle for backup.

Brimmelle shook his head at Wess. "Avanda is your responsibility. You better rise to the occasion." It was quickly followed with, "Of course, if anyone asked me, I would tell them that this entire trip should not be taken."

His comments were ignored as were his normal growling and stodgy comments.

Wess winked at Avanda, telling her that she could stay.

Avanda cheered and everyone grabbed their items to continue their travels.

Chapter 6
Curious Discoveries

Once again, the party was on its way through the woods as bushes thickened and boulders became more common. Steep slopes began to appear, small hills at first and then large ravines. The trees here were taller with trunks the size of three men.

After many more hours of walking into the evening, Wess noticed that moss seemed to grow on almost everything in this area. The exceptions were several logs and a few large rocks scattered about.

Wess, like Thorik, was a proficient woodsman, so when he noticed the unnatural looking growth he grew curious and investigated it. The rest of the group continued on their way. All except Emilen and Avanda, who returned to see what had caught Wess' attention.

"Some of these logs have no moss or mushrooms on them, and they're different from the trees standing. The fallen trees also have no fungi on the broken ends." Wess chipped off a few wood fragments as he tried to determine the reason. "There must have been one terrible storm in these parts." Looking over a twenty foot section of one of the larger trees that lay before him, he glanced around to see where it came from but couldn't find any stump that would be its origination point.

Looking at a series of long scratches toward one end, he noticed the bark had been scratched off many times with continued scabbing over it. "This is a base of a tree," he mentioned to Emilen as she walked over to see what was of interest.

"How do you know?" she asked.

"See these marks?" Wess pointed to the cuts. "This tree was used as a scratching post for a ry'horn goat. But I can't find the base of the trunk." He scanned the area without any luck.

Wess continued his investigation by looking at several large rocks with earth stuck to the side of them. He assumed it was some type of mud wasp nest but found it to be nothing more than clumps of dirt, as though the rocks had been uprooted and flipped. He showed Emilen various items that were inconsistent or out of place.

As the slight breeze changed direction they all noticed a new odor. Emilen and Avanda covered their noses with their hands and looked at Wess. He was starting to get nervous. "I know that smell. It's the smell of death. Rotten flesh," he noted as he followed the stench.

Emilen was visibly uncomfortable. Looking around, she noticed that the rest of the party had left and she didn't know in which direction. "Let us be on our way." She grabbed Avanda's hand and walking the direction she hoped was correct.

Wess paid no attention to her as he was in search of the odor. He had pinpointed it to one of the fallen trees and hopped up on top of it to walk its length. Noticing a patch of black fur attached to the backside of the log, he took a stick to pry it off to find that it was an arm of some animal. "Thrashers." His eyes darted about before looked over to warn Emilen, who was now running through the forest while pulling Avanda, before Emilen fell and let out a scream.

Wess raced over to find Emilen's eyes shut tight as she tried to cover Avanda's eyes from the sight of the mutilated creature, which they had tripped over. It was a decomposing ape-like beast with both legs missing. Shards of wood pierced through the creature's body. Facial skin had been chewed off half its face and the insects where running rampant over it.

Avanda fought to free her eyes from Emilen's hands. "Let me see!"

Emilen was paralyzed from the sight as she tucked her head away with her eyes closed. If it wasn't for holding onto Avanda, she would have curled up into a ball and waited for the sight to be taken away.

Avanda finally broke free and stood up, staring at the corpse. She looked to her uncle for answers. "Uncle Wess, What is that? What happened to it?"

Wess' eyes searched the trees for movement. "I think it's a thrasher. We best be leaving quickly and quietly." As he stood, readying to leave, his eyes were now registering bits of thrasher hide in all directions as if some sort of massacre had taken place. "I've heard that thrashers kill each other for dominance, but this doesn't seem like an attack from their own kind. But I don't know what would even attempt to attack a tribe of thrashers."

Wess talked his way through the scene, "This doesn't make sense. A tribe of thrashers ripped apart. What could have done that? And those fallen trees, they don't belong here, and they weren't dragged to this spot either." Looking upwards, he noted a lot of breakage in the canopy. "It's as if they were dropped here. And these rocks, they look water worn from the river." He thought for a moment before stating nervously, "I know of no creature that could do this, but I am sure we don't want to run into whatever it is."

Wess had never actually seen a thrasher before, but he had seen hides that had come from the south side of the mountain. He had heard stories. Horrific stories of thrasher raids on villages. Every child had been warned by their parents in an effort to keep them from wandering off into the forest. "But thrashers don't live in the Kings Valley." He shook the child's horrifying fable out of his mind. "So, why are they here? And so close to Farbank."

Though still puzzled, Wess finally decided to focus on getting them out of the area and to discuss this with the others. He looked over at Emilen still frightened by the sight as she peered up from her hands to view it. Wess failed to realize the trauma she was in. "No, you can't have it for dinner, we've made other plans." His laugh was joined by Avanda's giggle. His niece was used to Wess' crude sense if humor. He would have said the same thing to his brothers or Thorik. But he failed to realize that Emilen didn't appreciate it, until it was too late.

Emilen looked up at him in anger and then back down at the creature in horror.

Wess helped her to her feet and dusted her off.

She slapped his hands away. "I don't *need* your help."

Wess backed up a step. "Calm down, it was just a joke." His cavalier tone fell flat as he looked back at the oddities of these woods. "Even so, things are not right here."

Avanda sensed the tension and stepped in between them, grabbing their hands. "Come on Emilen, Uncle Wess didn't mean anything by it. We just need to train him how to talk to us women." She gave off that innocent smile of youth that relaxed everyone. "Now, which way did Thorik go?"

The three walked briskly in the direction Wess pointed.

Avanda looked up at Wess and winked with a smirk. It was obvious that she wanted to see her uncle and Emilen together.

Though still wary of their surroundings, Wess saw the opportunity and followed Avanda's lead, but Emilen was still reeling from the sight they had witnessed and took no notice.

The pungent smell of rotting flesh grew as they caught up to the rest of the group after a few minutes. The party had stopped, standing on the edge of a rim looking across a small valley clearing.

Emilen caught up first and had a look to see why all the interest.

The bowl shaped clearing sat in front of them about half the size of Farbank. Its rim was lined with fallen trees and large boulders as they pressed up against the trees still standing along the rim.

The small round valley was free of all life and extended into the river with a dam of earth and rocks, preventing the river from flooding it. It was a strange contrast of rock and dirt surrounded by the lush forest and snow capped mountains. It was out of place and oddly unnatural.

They started down the side of the crater's valley wall and then moved toward the middle as the smell lessened and the ground became hard. As they approached the center, the solid rock was stripped clean of all dirt. The group fanned out as they looked at the deep scars in the bedrock floor of the crater. Each scar was straight with one end pointing toward the center of the valley, which is where Thorik brought Ambrosius. Brimmelle accompanied them.

"Do you recall this place?" Thorik asked Ambrosius.

Ambrosius was in great pain by this point. He had pushed too hard today and was in need of a treatment from Gluic. Regardless, he looked at his surroundings with no memory of it. "No."

"This is where I found you, right here in the center."

Ambrosius slowly looked around. "No, I have no memories of this place." Thinking a bit more, he added, "But I do recall climbing out of a river, not unlike this. I remember pain. And then being attacked. They came from everywhere. I was certain this was my end. They were clawing and biting and ripping me apart." Ambrosius thought deeply to remember. "Then I pushed them away." He paused as he fought the overpowering urge to collapse from the pain, the day's travel, and the memory of the events. With the help of Thorik he lowered himself to sit on the ground. "No, not *them*," he corrected himself. "I pushed everything away. Everything. Then blackness and peace." After a moment he continued, "I remember nothing else; in fact I'm not certain it's even a memory.

It's so unclear, like a faded dream. If I hadn't still the pain in my legs, I surely would have thought it was precisely that."

Thorik noticed Brimmelle's tense expression and face turning deep red. "Brimmelle, I know what you're going to say. However, understand he was going to die, his powers to kill the thrashers and create this crater match the powers in the Portent Scrolls about the evil that is coming, but they also match the description of the one that will save us."

"You found him out this far?" Brimmelle said to Thorik's surprise. "I had forbid you to exceed the boundaries of Fawn Hollow without others. If you had been hurt out here we would have never found you. You may play lightly with your life, but I will not."

Thorik's shoulder's lowered. "Yes, yes, you are right. But-"

Brimmelle continued over the top of Thorik's words. "Have you forgotten how your parents died? Are you trying to tempt fate?" He was furious at the youth's actions.

"No. You don't understand the whole story."

Grabbing Thorik by his hair with one hand to stifle the young man's words. "No, it's you that doesn't understand the entire ramifications. You knew that thrashers had traveled this close to Farbank and you never alerted us? You know the stories. You know what they do. And you didn't tell anyone? You endangered all of us, so you didn't have to confront me with the extent of your travels?" Angry and disappointed, the Fir looked at Thorik's now sagging shoulders and saddened eyes. "I would not have thought you, of all people, would have put yourself before the clan. When are you going to start looking at the bigger view of life instead of your little insignificant piece of it?"

Thorik attempted to get a few words into the conversation. "I was just-"

"I don't want to hear it. When we return to Farbank you will surrender your family home and your position as our Northern Valley hunter so you can focus on the Rune Scrolls. I will *not* let you make this mistake again."

Thorik's eyes widened and filled with tears as he began to protest. But he knew that look from Brimmelle. With every word Thorik spoke to argue the point, Brimmelle would make the deal even worse.

Chapter 7
Campsite

Thorik tried to work off his frustration with himself, the situation, and those he had let down. Rationalizing his decisions, he justified them with the understanding that this trip with Ambrosius was still the right thing to do. He assembled various beds of grass, leaves, and sticks for the night. This busy work took his mind off his problems and put him in a slightly better mood.

A campsite had been quickly set up toward the upstream wall to block the wind. Collapsing from the pain and fatigue, Ambrosius lay next to Avanda near the fire as Gluic covered them with blankets.

Fir Brimmelle, Wess, and Emilen began to argue about what to do with Ambrosius. The options proposed ranged from helping him reach Kingsfoot to leaving him to die where Thorik had found him.

The two men argued that anyone with the power to create this crater was surely a threat. The destruction of so much nature, along with the animals that lived among it, showed a lack of morality. Brimmelle wasted no time in reading verses from the scrolls that applied which forbid such destruction of nature.

Wess added, "We've had weeks of dead fish in the river ever since *he* showed up, and now thrashers in the valley, near Farbank no less!" Wess peered into the darkening surrounding woods, partly out of wariness of these predators, and partly to emphasize his point. He continued, "These bad signs shouldn't be ignored. We don't even know what he is. I know of no man who can do what was done here. He's probably some kind of demon." He enjoyed a heated debate. The outcome meant very little to him. It was the bantering back and forth that excited him.

Emilen held her own against the two, however, emotion played a factor for her. It was very uncommon for anyone to raise their voice to a Fir, let alone publicly disagree with them. But she did, and didn't hold back at all. She pointed out verses in several scrolls that spoke of the coming savior that fell from the Mountain King's Crown and then helped rebuild their kingdom. "The animals that were killed around the crater were thrashers, who have never come to this valley before. Another day or so and they would have attacked the village. Ambrosius prevented the attack and saved our lives. As far as the fish are concerned, I recall a scroll passage that reads 'where great good comes, great evil tries to destroy it'. It is *our* responsibility to protect Ambrosius from an evil that will try to kill him."

Brimmelle took offense to being challenged. No one had ever questioned his interpretation of the Runestone Scrolls or the Rules of Order, at least not to his face. He allowed Wess to do most of the arguing and then would interject with phrases from the scrolls when he could.

Wess was quick to return a pointed question back to the sender and he knew just what and how to say things that got under Emilen's mental armor, throwing her off balance. He never lost control of the situation and often flashed that irritating grin of his.

Emilen fought the good fight but became so frustrated with Wess that she finally had to walk away and take a break near the river. "Thanks for your support," she stabbed at Thorik as she walked past him, his shocked look irritating her even more.

Thorik had avoided the debate. His focus was on helping Ambrosius get to the point he could make it on his own, regardless of his intentions. He reached into his sack of Runestones and pulled out one at random for guidance. Mentioning the rune's name, "Respect," he looked at the hexagonal stone's white side. *Show others the same respect that you would have them show you.* Pondering over a few more phrases in his mind helped set him at ease and understand his error in judgment, as he finished preparing the camp for the night.

Brimmelle found his bed laid out for him and fell asleep shortly. Avanda was moved to another bed by Emilen to distance herself from Brimmelle. The youth never woke as she was guided to her new resting place near the Fir. Thorik and Wess took turns as lookout throughout the night while Emilen slept off her frustration.

After collecting new flora to wear, Gluic ignored everyone and focused on healing Ambrosius before her own slumber. She never got into debates or the Rules of Order for that. She just did what she felt was right when she felt it needed to be done. Life seemed so much simpler that way.

Ambrosius woke to the sound of a campfire and Brimmelle snoring up a storm. His vision was hazy at first as he looked at the firelight washing against various bodies surrounding the camp. They were all lying on thick neatly constructed beds.

One figure was leaning over the fire, and judging by the smell, was making breakfast.

Thorik looked over at him. "You gave us quite a scare again. You passed out when we first arrived and then screamed in pain several times last night." The night's sleep had washed away the arguments from the prior day as Thorik challenged himself to start each day with a fresh outlook.

The Num continued to focus on his cooking. "How are you feeling this morning?"

"I hurt, but I'll survive." Sitting up to face Thorik, Ambrosius squinted as he looked about and realized that he was still in the crater, and still not recalling the place. It meant nothing to him, but something else did. "Do you know the name Ruddlehoth of Kingsfoot?"

"Yes, there's one sleeping right over there. Why, what do you need with Emilen?"

"I'm not sure exactly. I had a dream, recalling someone with that name. What can you tell me about her?" Ambrosius inquired.

"It's hard *not* to dream about her." Smiling, Thorik glanced over at her sleeping under several blankets. "What do you need to know? She has a great gift for teaching the Runestones and helping others. She's a good leader and everyone loves her." Thorik stumbled on his words to quickly correct them. "Her personality, that is. She's enjoyable to be around. Just don't get on her bad side." Thorik smiled and then noticed that his breakfast hadn't been given attention for a bit.

"Any relationship to Fir Beltrow?"

"Yes, that would be her father. Why do you ask? Do you know him?"

"Yes." Now was not the time to inform the young lady of her father's death while he had attended the council meeting. Ambrosius wasn't even absolutely convinced of it himself. It all seamed vague and dreamlike. Instead, he changed the subject. "How is your Order structured?"

Thorik was too busy finishing up the cooking to notice the change in conversation. "Same as all of them I guess. What do you mean?"

"I understand that each community has one Fir of the Order and if I remember correctly they usually have more than one Sec that is in training who helps with the daily tasks."

"We have three. Thea, Shucan, and myself. It is a great honor to be selected. We each have our own ways of supporting Fir Brimmelle. Someday one of us will become the Fir, after Brimmelle has left us."

"So who does Fir Brimmelle receive guidance from?"

Thorik looked puzzled. "The Order."

Ambrosius also looked confused. "The Order?"

"The Scrolls of Wisdom provides the details of how to live by the Rules of Order."

"Isn't there a higher power than your village Fir to monitor their teachings?"

"No." Brimmelle words were abrupt and heavy. "The Rules of Order and the Rune Scrolls tell me what I need to know. Seeing that the Mountain King himself wrote the Scrolls of Wisdom to be self-evident to those who know how to read them, there isn't a need for others to tell me how to interpret his writings."

Thorik looked over. "Ah, Brimmelle, you're awake. Your breakfast is ready." He proceeded to scoop some onto a plate before handing it to him. Thorik continued by making a plate for Ambrosius as well as the rest of the party, as he woke them up before serving himself.

"Our beliefs are of no concern to you. They have served us well for generations and don't require outsiders poking their nose into our business." Brimmelle began shoveling food into his mouth.

Ambrosius stared at Brimmelle's image which was slightly clearer now that the sun was starting to rise. "Recently your Order has acquired representation on the Grand Council, and I haven't had the time to learn much about your beliefs. I was just curious and meant no offense."

Brimmelle continued eating while talking. "I'm not represented by anyone at your council. The Rules of Order and the Rune Scrolls were written by the King, which the Fir's teach to their faction. The Sec's provide the support for the Fir's and carry out actions to help the faction. The faction provides the needs of the Fir. In return, the King provides strong crops, abundant fish in the river and fruitful hunts. It is cut and dry, easy to understand."

Ambrosius questioned Brimmelle again. "Can I safely assume that Gluic is a Channel? I've never met one personally, but she seems to fit the description that I have heard."

Thorik's brow raised and eyes opened large at the question, for he knew how Brimmelle refused to allow anyone to talk about Gluic's odd ways.

Defensively, Brimmelle responded, "She's my mother. Don't you dare try to label her."

Ambrosius took a different angle in his questioning. "Understood. Your mother aside, may I ask how Channels fit into your Order?"

"They don't," Brimmelle cut short.

Thorik broke the awkward silence that followed. "Some people have been given the gift to channel these special powers, which we are thankful for and use from time to time. But they have nothing to do with the Order. There is nothing in our Scrolls about them and we don't understand why they are given. Many channels have been killed for having such abilities, believing they are evil powers." Glancing at the Fir, he continued. "But Brimmelle has taught us that the powers come from the Mountain King and we are not to question it, for it would be like questioning the Mountain King himself."

By this point the rest of the party was eating their breakfast. They all sat on the beddings facing the fire, some with their blankets covering their head and body. The meal was warm and helped them shake off the night's cold chill. The camp was oddly silent as they ate, unlike the night before after Ambrosius had passed out. They quietly finished their breakfast, eyes glaring at each other with obvious tension amongst them. No agreement had been made as to Ambrosius' fate.

Ambrosius noticed his party's disposition with interest, wondering what he had missed. Obviously he had struck a nerve with his questioning but the stiffness of the group seemed to be more than just that.

Thorik finally stood, gathered dishes and his cooking gear, and headed off to the river to clean them. Emilen stood up to help Thorik with the items.

It wasn't far to the water. They had camped near the edge of the crater, toward the river to reduce the cold winds that came down from the mountain top and headed down the valley. The crater's northwest edge sloped up to a wall of boulders and dirt that acted as a dam, keeping the water out and encroaching into the river by a fourth of the river's width. Wess had done some scouting earlier, before breakfast, and found no signs of thrashers in the area in the last few weeks. It seemed safe.

"I bet you wish you had brought your fishing supplies," Thorik said to Emilen as he set his items down on a flat-sided boulder, attempting to lighten the mood. He received no response, so he continued, "I mean, look at this natural dock. It's perfect for fishing wouldn't you say?"

Thorik and Emilen started washing the pots as he continued in his pursuit of reducing the uncomfortable silent tension. "I might have to stop here and do some fishing next time I'm in these parts. Yes, some very nice fishing could be done at this spot."

"Why didn't you support me?" Emilen briskly stated as her eyes looked up from what she was cleaning to look at him.

Thorik wasn't sure which was worse, the uncomfortable silence or the conversation that was just starting. He looked up from his work and replied. "Hang on a second; I thought you were mad at Wess. Why are you upset with me?"

"Yes, I'm mad that Wess' misguided understanding of the Scrolls of Wisdom could cause an innocent man to die. A man that I believe has been sent here by the Mountain King to strengthen our faith, guide us, and unite us across the land. Of course it upsets me and it should upset Brimmelle and you as well. Brimmelle is either to afraid of losing his authority or too bullheaded to see what's going on. On the other hand, you are close to Ambrosius and can surely see that he is not here to harm us. You also know the words of the scrolls and should be helping me in carrying them out. Wess may not agree with me, but I respect the fact that he stands up for what he believes in and is willing to fight for it." She finishes.

"I just don't see how yelling at each other is going to help any of us." Thorik sighed as he recalled the hours of arguing that accomplished nothing.

"So what would you have me do? Watch as they kill the savior of our people and do nothing? What kind of Sec are you? I thought you were a good person. Someone who carries out the Rules of the Order and followed the words from the scrolls. At what point do *you* stand up for what you believe in and fight for it? Or should we just do whatever Fir Brimmelle orders even though everything inside of us is saying different?"

Thorik felt this wave of questions crash upon him and he began to drown in them. He didn't know what question to answer first and he was concerned that any answer he gave would unleash another attack. But he had to reply. He wasn't a coward by any means. He just didn't see any reason to make this issue any bigger than it really was. "No, of course not," came out as he kept his eyes on his work. It was a safe answer, simple and not retaliating which would have caused more conflicts.

"No? No What? No, you don't have the valor to fight for what's right? No, you can't disobey your Fir even when you know he's wrong? Or, no, you don't care about anyone but yourself and unless it hurts you it isn't worth bothering yourself. Is that why you live outside the village, so you don't have to bother yourself with the problems of others? Ignoring the problems doesn't make them go away."

Thorik was wounded. This wave hit deeper than the prior one and there appeared to be an endless supply of them ready and waiting. He had worked extremely hard all his life to be the best person that he could and tried to follow the Rules of the Order. He thought he performed this better than most others by helping people whenever they asked without looking for anything in return. How dare she suggest otherwise. "You're wrong." He finally looked her square in the eyes. "I'm always helping others. You have no right to question my beliefs and convictions." Pausing to take a breath, he finished with, "I am a good person."

"Yes, you are," she agreed with him. "But it takes more than being a good person to make things right." Emilen picked up the items she had washed and walked down the hillside and back to camp without saying another word. In her haste, one of her hair ribbons fell to the ground near Thorik.

His natural reaction was to return it to her, but instead he picked it up and pulled it tight between his fingers. Tight, just like he felt inside after his confrontation with her. His chest and shoulders were straining and his stomach churned.

Thorik was frustrated and was deep in denial of her stabbing words as well as disappointed in himself for not defending himself better. He played back the argument in his head several more times and came up with actions which this time placed him as the victor of the verbal battle. Each time he got better at it until he realized how exactly he should have handled it, and how he would handle it the next time he was confronted with such criticism of his character. But there was no way to turn time back and the likelihood of the same confrontation happening was less than slim. This exercise in tongue-lashing defense had given him a temporary feeling of heroics that quickly died when he realized how fruitless it was.

He sat there, near the river, not understanding what he had done wrong. He continued for a bit, justifying himself to himself before realizing that this too wasn't doing any good.

Looking down at his feet dangling over the boulder he continued to pull the blue ribbon back and forth between several fingers until he lost control of it and dropped it. It floated down toward his feet near the flowing water. As it reached the water's surface he noticed a frog warming itself on a rock in the morning sunlight. Thorik smiled slowly. "How simple life must be for you. You're free to do what you want without the worry of how others will take it. You'll never know the pain of hurting someone's feelings, especially someone you care about."

The frog leaped into the water and disappeared from sight. Thorik was alone again.

He finally realized that he felt badly about what had happened and that he hadn't supported Emilen. He just wanted the conflict last night to end. But she was right; ignoring it wouldn't make it go away.

Chapter 8
Fesh'Unday

Thorik's Log: October 2nd of the 649th year.

My journal of our travels begins on a sour note. Our journey up the river has not been as I had hoped. I'm looking forward to reaching Kingsfoot and seeing the Mountain King statue with my own eyes. – Sec Thorik Dain of Farbank

Shortly after breakfast, the group had packed and prepared for the day's journey. Most of the group began walking as Thorik doused the campfire ashes and began stacking the beddings before leaving.

"What are you doing?" Wess asked Thorik.

"Just cleaning up before we leave."

"For who?" Wess asked with that laugh that made Thorik's shoulders tense.

Thorik realized it didn't make sense to be stacking the bedding, it was more of a habit than anything, but to save face he changed the focus of conversation. "As a man of the woods, you should know the importance of making sure your fire is properly extinguished."

Wess was onto Thorik's game and allowed the change of conversation. He looked around them at the crater's lifeless base. "When was the last time you saw rock and sand catch fire? There isn't a shrub to burn in over a hundred feet."

Thorik hated these conversations with him. Wess was always ready for a verbal match of wit and was always poking at his weak points. He flashed his smile that again drove Thorik crazy.

Thorik spoke up. "Perhaps you'd like to take some responsibility during this hike instead of complaining about what I do. I suggest you take over camp cleanup chores, starting right now." Thorik grabbed his items and looked Wess in the eyes while waiting for his response.

Wess smiled at Thorik and then turned his head to look at the camp. Half the beds weren't stacked yet, there were glowing cinders still visible in the fire, food that had fallen off plates continued to lie there, and various logs sat about for firewood and sitting. He bent down and picked up one of Emilen's many hair ribbons. He held it to his nose and breathed in her smell from the cloth with obvious enjoyment. "Camp cleanup is done, let's go."

Wess turned and quickly caught up to Emilen. While walking next to her he apologized for the confrontation the night before. He explained that he had thought about what she had said and he would give her ideas a chance. She obviously warmed up to what he was saying and thanked him. Presenting her with her dropped hair ribbon, he explained how beautiful she looked with it in. She was very happy to see her grandmother's gift returned and gave him a quick excited hug.

Emilen looked at Wess for a moment. He was actually very dashing, ruggedly handsome and carried himself very well. He had a charm that either had people eating out of his hands or irritated them to no end. But he fought for what he believed in and that meant a great deal to her. All she needed to do is get him to believe in the right things. *Yes, he could be the one*. She smiled at him.

Wess looked down at Emilen and realized he had broken the ice and gotten back into her good graces. She was a very cute little Num with a body only seen in his dreams. The ribbon he had given her was interlaced with various color threads that matched her natural flowing locks of hair. She added it to the others already tied up behind her head. Wess watched her shapely figure as they continued. *I bet she joined this trip to spend some more time with me*. He smiled back at her.

Thorik had watched as Wess caught up to Emilen and received a hug. Afterward, they laughed and talked as they reached the crater's edge and helped Ambrosius up over the rim.

Thorik peered down to see Avanda standing at his side. "I'll help clean up," she said. He smiled at her and they finished putting out the fire before catching up to the rest of the group.

The walk was still slow but faster than the day before. Several stops were made to rest as they walked farther from the river. Thorik, Gluic, and Ambrosius led the way and the rest followed.

Ambrosius was still struggling and the previous day of walking only added sore muscles to his pain. He could not give up, too much was at stake, so he employed everything he had left to continue. Gluic helped by pulling the pain out of him several times a day, and Thorik was always there to lean on and help him up and down steep hills. In addition, Ambrosius' new staff kept him balanced to make up for his bad leg. It was not the staff he had traveled the lands with for many an age, but only a limb with its branches removed.

He appreciated his helpers, but Ambrosius missed his old staff. It was a symbol of how things were when he had it. He had seen great battle victories and unions with his staff at his side. Without it, he recalled the defeats and destruction during his youth, and now his current state of helplessness. He knew that the staff was mostly symbolic and wasn't the strength of his power, but life felt empty without it, like missing an arm or a leg. He didn't feel whole.

"The grip is bad, it's cutting into my hand," Ambrosius stated as he stopped, handed Thorik the staff, and held out his hand showing the bloody palm with various cuts in it. He stood silent as Thorik quickly cleaned and wrapped his wounds. Thorik removed the leather from the staff before cutting a few slices out of the wood and then applied new skins to the hand grip.

"Here, this should fit your hand better. I'll work on reducing its weight at our next stop." Thorik firmly placed it back into Ambrosius' freshly wrapped hand.

Ambrosius squeezed his hand around it and moved his fingers a bit to modify his grip. "Better." Nodding, he began limping forward again. The trip was taking its toll on him physically and mentally. The pain increased progressively throughout the day, even after Gluic's help, and was testing his ability to focus.

Thorik was pleased that the grip was better and proceeded to lead the party along the trail to Kingsfoot. As they reached the narrows where the trail ran through a gorge, they could see that quite a bit of the walls on either side had caved in and blocked the path. The nearer they got to the narrows the clearer it was that they weren't passing through that way. Thorik looked to the right, up a precipitous slope. "This one will take most of the day."

"Why don't we stay by the river?" Wess questioned. "We'll never make it past that cliff face."

Wess' family hunted to the south and west of Farbank, so he was unfamiliar with this area. Thorik, however, was in his element. He had traveled in the mountains most of his life. He knew the general terrain, the plants, the animals, and the way the weather affected all of them. Fortunately his father had taught him about such things before Brimmelle took over as his guardian. His father had also informed him that the old trail to Kingsfoot lay above the cliff line.

"River cuts," Thorik replied.

"What?" Wess asked, thinking he had heard him incorrectly.

"As we travel farther upstream the river makes deeper shear cuts into the foothills carving out gorges. King's River Gorge doesn't open until Kingsfoot Lake. Taking the river becomes more and more treacherous with its occasional lack of shorelines." He spied what he was looking for and then continued, "Besides, see that large crack a short way up the rock face? That's our passageway through to the other side."

By this time Brimmelle, Avanda, and Emilen had helped Gluic to reach the front three. "This is far enough. We cannot climb any further," Brimmelle said as he breathed heavier than the rest. He quickly sat on a nearby rock and wiped the sweat from his forehead. Gluic was also showing signs of exhaustion as she sat next to him. Wess and Ambrosius followed suit and sat down as well.

Emilen handed around water starting with Ambrosius while Thorik pulled some rope out and began tying knots in it. He proceeded to tie the end around himself. Giving several feet of slack he then tied on Ambrosius before continuing to Emilen, Brimmelle, Gluic, Avanda and finally Wess at the far end. While tying everyone onto the rope he explained that the purpose of the rope was to catch someone should they slip along the way up the steep slopes.

Wess had cited several reasons why he should be tied between Emilen and Ambrosius while Thorik created the live chain, but Thorik used Wess' own arrogance against him by explaining that they needed the strongest people on the ends for support. Wess accepted this like a badge of honor and moved into place.

Brimmelle didn't like the idea of continuing. As he ventured farther from his village he struggled more to hold a leadership role. It also became difficult to obtain passages from his scrolls that would suggest how to handle things differently. Feeling out of place, he attempted several more times to convince Gluic that she should not travel any farther, without any success.

Gluic was too headstrong for him and often would do the opposite of what he asked anyway. Not in an attempt to be cruel, but to teach him. As Fir of Farbank, he had absolute power and in time he had allowed it to corrupt his thinking. He had never traveled to other villages or communities to experience how other Fir's have taught their students. He had become close-minded and needed to be reminded from time to time of his own mortality and flaws. There was a good man inside him, but only he could bring it out. She felt this trip to Kingsfoot would do him well and hoped he would see it through. However, if he did decide to go back, she still needed to continue on, for her task was not yet completed.

The group was soon up and moving again in an attempt to reach the crack in the mountain before sundown. It took several minutes to get used to the rope's slack between them. If not handled correctly it was easy to trip on it, which only happened a few times by Brimmelle.

With the trees slowly starting to give way to more jutting rocks, they worked their way up a long stretch of nearly vertical climbing before opening up to a series of rocky shelves which acted as a nice rest area. Thorik climbed up onto the first shelf and turned to help Ambrosius.

It was late; it had taken them longer than Thorik had hoped to get atop the cliff. The shadow of the mountain had fallen upon them and the rising full moon crested over the eastern mountain peaks and bathed them in a blue light. Ambrosius was in need of Gluic's touch and collapsed on the shelf as he rolled himself onto it.

Thorik pulled on the rope that linked Ambrosius to Emilen to help her up. While doing so, he was jabbed in the side by Ambrosius' staff. Ambrosius didn't always use the best manners when he needed water or assistance. Thorik temporarily ignored him. Instead he reached down and lifted Emilen up off the cliff to a standing position in front of him. She was as light as a feather and for a moment he held her there looking into her eyes. But the moment ended with another quick jab of Ambrosius' staff.

Thorik broke contact with Emilen and looked at Ambrosius, whose leg bandage was soaked with fresh blood. His leg obviously wasn't healed enough for this trip and it must have re-opened. Thorik kneeled next to his leg to look at the wound when he heard Ambrosius whisper, "Thrashers."

Thorik didn't believe his ears until he looked at Ambrosius' face to see him eyeing something behind Thorik's back. Thorik turned in a flash, loaded an arrow in his bow, and pointed it where Ambrosius had been looking.

It was a small outcropping of rocks with a dark cave in the center of it, not far off of the group's right. The tribe leader, a large silverhead, stood at the edge of the moonlight, eyeing Thorik. Three deep blackened scars could be seen on his forehead as one trailed below his left eye. Black hair covered the primate's body, excluding parts of the face, chest, and hands. Long muscular arms reached down to the ground as he leaned forward while standing on its shorter back legs. Within one of his large black clinched hands he held a thick bone that he slowly tapped on the ground. The eyes were the most intriguing; Thorik felt that he could see intelligence within them even in the modest lighting.

The beast showed his teeth to Thorik before moving back into the darkness.

"Wess," Thorik yelled. "Watch your back down there. We have thrashers, and they always attack from at least two sides." His father's training raced in his mind. Brimmelle and Gluic stopped climbing to look around for any attackers while Wess pulled out his own hunting bow. Avanda began grabbing loose rocks to throw.

It was only seconds before the first set of clicks came from a rock shelf above them. A howl followed behind them, in the trees, as a second set of clicks came from the cave where Thorik was aiming his weapon. "Get up here! Now!" Thorik demanded.

Ambrosius rolled back to the edge of the ledge to help Emilen pull the rope that connected her to Brimmelle. Brimmelle was much heavier than Emilen's small-framed body, and he wasn't as sure-footed. His ascent would take longer, especially now that he was panicking.

Wess loaded his bow as he saw the branches moving in the trees. He caught a glimpse of several creatures jumping from tree to tree as they moved from the lower trees to the ones above the small band of travelers. It was difficult to prepare a shot at the quick thrashers. Though Nums see reasonably well even in low-light situations, the heavy leaf coverage and the semi-darkness of night added to the challenge. It also didn't help that his footing was nothing more than a few small rocks jutting out of the side of the cliff face.

A series of clicks and a long howl came from the silverhead in the darkness of the cave causing the trees around the party to shake. The thrashers slapped their hands on the rock above, followed by one loud high-pitched howl. They attacked.

Wess began shooting in the trees as the Num-sized apes fell to the ground like rain. He had counted ten that he had shot and twice as many that he had missed.

Thorik stood on the ledge firing his arrows at thrashers emerging from the cave, only to break away periodically to fire at the ones from above. But with no one to watch his back it wasn't long before he was outnumbered. An attack from the air knocked him to his knees and he dropped his weapon. Quickly grabbing his knife, he swiveled for a quick stab into the creature's gut. With that one down, two more jumped on him. Thorik caught a glimpse of the silverhead emerging from his security of darkness before barking additional orders to his troops.

Brimmelle had just pulled himself up onto the ledge, near Emilen, as the first thrasher jumped from above and landed on him. He fell backward and off the ledge screaming in pain and carrying the beast with him. Avanda shrieked as she saw the thrashers coming from above. Ambrosius let go of the rope as he grabbed his staff and braced it on the ground to stab the next thrasher as it jumped for Emilen. Ambrosius used the creature's own momentum, now stuck on the top end of the staff, to propel it down the hillside.

Emilen had continued holding onto the rope that attached her to Brimmelle. This quickly dragged her over the edge, falling face first toward Brimmelle and his passenger.

Brimmelle and Emilen clutched onto each other as they slid down the rock with the creature in tow. Without warning the thrasher was dislodged when the rope abruptly went taut. Ambrosius now held the rope with both hands as he braced his legs against an upright rock to prevent himself from being pulled over along with them. The pain from his weak leg was causing it to tremble as it felt ready to break again.

Emilen's grip on Brimmelle broke, leaving her hanging in the air from Ambrosius' rope as Brimmelle tumbled several feet before pulling Gluic off her grip. She, in turn, fell into Avanda and Wess who dropped his weapon to catch her.

Ambrosius leaned forward to grip the rope closer to the edge. He pressed his legs against the upright rock as he leaned back, pulling the rope up. On his second attempt he heard and felt his leg quiver. Snap! It popped as it gave way. He screamed in pain as he shifted all his weight to his other leg for his next attempt to pull them up. While leaning forward for his new grip on the rope, a mouth full of sharp blackened teeth sank into the flesh of his left arm.

A few yards away from Ambrosius, Thorik tumbled with the two primates on him as they ripped through his backpack and clothes. His wooden coffer acted as a shield against rear attacks, but was a poor excuse for armor. Their speed and upper body strength easily out matched his. Grabbing the neck of the one on top of him, he began to choke the thrasher while cracking the back of his head against the face of the one underneath him. He squeezed his fingers into the creature's skin and choked him with all his might.

The thrasher's arms and legs went wild as they tore into Thorik's body. Its head tilted as the creature snapped its jaw at Thorik's arms in a chaotic manner. The raised hair on the back of the thrashers head and the folded back ears indicated that he was still in an attack posture. The creature's eyes showed no fear, only craze, only a desire to kill. Saliva from its incessant snapping covered Thorik's face clouding his vision as a third beast grabbed at his legs.

Below the ledge, Wess stabilized Gluic and Avanda for the moment. He tried to pull Brimmelle up toward them as the older Num worked his way along the slope. Brimmelle had only taken a few steps before he saw several beasts running up the hill as though it was a flat field. The creature's strong short body seemed to be made for speed in any terrain. Thrashers charged at them from several angles with their drooling mouths biting at the air in front of them, possessed with an uncontrollable rage.

Out of sheer terror, Brimmelle grabbed his chest of scrolls from his belt pouch, closed his eyes and started reciting the words he had read so often. Before his first verse was completed he was attacked and pressed against the hillside with his small chest of scrolls between him and the monster, which now had a death grip on the box with its mouth.

Emilen fell from her position trailed by a severed rope that once connected her to Ambrosius. She tumbled down into Brimmelle knocking the thrasher off him, along with his scrolls. The two Nums rolled a few more feet before being stopped by the rope connected to Gluic. Fortunately, Avanda had wedged the ropes onto a large rock to keep them from falling.

Wess waved his hunting knife in the air at oncoming attackers, as Avanda continued to throw rocks at them. Several dead bodies littered the ground as more continued to attack.

Avanda turned to see a thrasher leap into the air with claws and fangs ready to cut through her skin. Braced for the impact, she watched the body of the creature collapse upon itself and land on her with shrieks of pain. Blood and other fluids rushed out of its mouth as she pushed the dead beast off her.

Two more were at her quickly. The one coming up from below suddenly slammed its head deep into a large rock, literally cracking the skull apart. The other coming from the side landed at her feet with an arrow in its throat.

This continued a few more times before she noticed the same was happening for Wess. She peered up to see Ambrosius and Thorik standing on the edge of the rock shelf. Thorik was firing arrows faster than she could count. Ambrosius stood on one leg, propped against a rock, with his left hand holding his staff and the other making various grabbing and slapping gestures in the air.

"Climb up! They won't stop attacking while we're still here. Once we move on they will prey on their own wounded and dead," Thorik yelled down.

Despite their apprehension, the Nums turned their backs to the attacking creatures as they collected their items and started to climb up to the ledge. Bodies collapsed near them as they made the ascent, but they made it without additional confrontations.

Once there, Thorik had the group continue up the hill toward the fissure in the rock that would guide them to safety. Fortunately, it wasn't too steep and the canyon's exit was only another few minutes away. They proceeded without Thorik and Ambrosius, who continued to prevent any followers.

"I think we're okay now. Start making your way up the hillside," Thorik shouted over the screams of their enemy. But Ambrosius didn't move from his spot and continued to use his powers to crush and hit these creatures, even the ones that were no threat. "Ambrosius, snap out of it!" Thorik ordered, looking up at the focused face of his patient. "Let's go!" Reaching up, he grabbed his arm.

Ambrosius' eyes were glazed over and his face was rigid, without emotion. He swiftly turned and gestured his hand toward Thorik's chest in a squeezing type motion.

The semi-darkness of the moonlit night was making it difficult to see details but Thorik could tell that his hand was covered in blood from Ambrosius' arm. Thorik's body was now being squeezed and he reached out to Ambrosius in a plea for mercy as Ambrosius continued to tighten his grip.

Gasping, Thorik fell to his knees before his body went limp. Just before he passed out, Thorik was released. Lying there, he placed his blood-covered hand over his heart and looked over to see Ambrosius lying on the ledge unconscious.

Wess jumped down off the rock from above and asked Thorik if he could walk. Receiving a nod for a reply, Wess moved over to Ambrosius and maneuvered him onto his shoulders. He slowly carried the man onto the next ledge and then up the hill. Thorik followed behind Wess, carrying the remains of his backpack and Ambrosius' staff.

They reached the top, where the rest of the group waited for their guides, before Wess lowered Ambrosius. Wess was a strong individual but even he had his limits, and today had tested them.

"What happened? How in the King's greatness did we get out of there?" Emilen asked Thorik when he arrived.

He responded with a horse voice, "I don't know. I had just got one of them off me when the other two suddenly died. I looked around and Ambrosius was standing there waving his hand about." He stopped to wet his throat. "Then I grabbed my bow and started firing at them," he said as they worked their way through the crack in the mountainside that led to the foothills on the opposite side of the ridge.

"How will we get past them on the way back to Farbank?" asked Wess.

"There are boats at Kingsfoot. We'll take the river back downstream," Emilen answered for Thorik.

"I think there are only a dozen beasts remaining," Thorik told them. "Thrashers don't leave their dens to attack unless they easily outweigh their prey in numbers. So, I don't see them as a threat to Farbank until they breed and grow in size. We'll be back long before then." Hearing a distant howl of the thrasher leader, he added, "But for now, let's get some distance between us."

Chapter 9
Ov'Unday

After traveling a mile or so, beyond the cliff face and over the mountain saddle, Thorik's party stopped to make camp and tend to their wounds. A makeshift litter helped transport Ambrosius, as he slept off the exhaustion from the day's events.

"Unacceptable!" Brimmelle continued to rant about the battle and losing their rations. "We have but a day's food left, we're badly hurt, we've got children and women to protect, and on top of it the guest of honor can't walk, again. This journey has come to an end. Those evil beasts are within two days of Farbank! How are we going to warn everyone? We should have never accompanied this man upstream. I've told you never to trust outsiders."

"He would have died on his own," Emilen added, cleaning out the deep scratches in Thorik's sides. They were not life threatening but were deep enough to probably give him a life long scar. "It is our spiritual duty to help him."

It had become a common disagreement throughout the entire trip, background noise that they carried with them. Nothing ever resolved. No actions ever taken. No give or take. Just a continual disagreement that added a level of discomfort to everything they did.

"But not at the expense of all of *our* lives." Brimmelle reached for his scrolls to read some comforting words like he usually did; only to find the chest of scrolls gone, taken by the beast that had attacked him. Brimmelle was distraught only for a moment before becoming livid and even more irrational. "That is the last step of the king! By the words of the scrolls, we must head home to safety. This outside world is chaotic and unpredictable. We'll float downstream on logs if we must, but it is far too dangerous for us out here."

"You're fears are speaking in place of the king. The scrolls talk at length about accepting nature, for all of its chaos, danger, and beauty, and yet you avoid it at all costs," Emilen stated as she finished up with Thorik and helped him put his shirt back on.

"I accept nature for what it is, 'A chaotic struggle between life and death with no direction or goal in mind', first line of the third topic in the Nature Rune Scroll." He read from his memories. "We are above that. We do not need to submerge ourselves in this unclean environment to prove anything. We didn't ask him to come to our village, he came on his own. We owe him nothing."

"Actually, he was brought to us." Wess calmly cleaned the thrasher's blood off his hunting knife before continuing. "Dain found him and took him in." He pointed his blade in the direction of Thorik.

The focus was now on Thorik who was starting to mend his backpack and take inventory of what had survived the attack. He could feel their eyes gazing at him waiting for a response, pushing him to accept defeat and subdue him into the scapegoat for this disaster of a trip. It had all been his fault from the beginning and now it was time to come clean.

But it was a lie. He believed in his actions and would do the same again. The pain from the attack was one thing but the constant bickering was just too much. "Leave," he stated strongly and crisply to ensure that everyone clearly understand him. "I didn't ask any of you to come with me. This was my journey, my task. I was doing what I felt was the right thing to do. I talked to Gluic about it and she informed me when he was able to leave. I never involved you. I didn't ask you to disrupt your life and sacrifice it for him. But all I've heard since we left Farbank was your constant complaining. On top of that, you have blessed yourself with the power of the King's hand to determine if Ambrosius should live or die." He gazed at Brimmelle, Wess, and Emilen as he talked. "This is not your decision. You do not have the authority."

Taking a deep breath, Thorik continued, "Leave, go back home, out of danger. I agree this is no journey for children. Take Avanda back. Alert the hunting parties of what lies along the gorge rim. You should go. You must go. I will, however, continue to go on my own path despite the hardships it brings upon me, for I know that my heart is in the right place." He turned away from the campfire and walked into the darkness of the trees.

Silence fell over the camp. Brimmelle was appalled from being talked to in such a manner from his own Sec, especially in front of others. "How ungrateful, after all I've done for him. There will have to be repercussions."

Wess was without words for the first time on the trek.

Emilen crossed her arms with disappointment. "Look at what you two have done."

Thorik walked a short bit down the hill away from the campfire light and leaned his back up against a large old pine tree. Looking up at the tall straight trunk he could see a few stars beyond the top branches as he asked the air above him, "I hope I've made the right choice to help him. But how do I know if I'm doing the right thing?"

"The best way to predict your future is to create it," a deep voice emanated from around the tree, startling Thorik.

Leaping away, he looked at the tree in disbelief. "What?" He hoped to provide his ears with some validation of the voice.

"There are no guarantees your actions are right. You must trust yourself, take them, and let them play out. Take control of your destiny, follow your instincts, and be willing to live with the consequences," the voice echoed. The voice had a thunderous effect to it, not loud, but yet rumbling that gave off a slight echo.

The Num couldn't quite tell if it was coming from the tree, around the tree or perhaps above the tree. Could it be the Mountain King himself talking from the sky up above, or was this tree before him actually coming to life?

Nervous, Thorik asked as he stared up and down at the tree. "Who are you?"

"Grewen. And who might you be, little man?"

"Sec Thorik Dain of Farbank." Searching for the source of the voice in the low light, he spoke to the old tree to affix something to it.

"A large name for such a small creature."

"Actually, many tell me that it's quite short," he replied with a smirk. "What consequences do you speak of?"

"Every decision you make changes your future, even the decision not to decide shapes your destiny. You are responsible for your own actions and the fallout from them. If you accept this as truth you will lead a happier life."

Thorik stepped farther back from the tree before addressing it again. "What if others take actions that conflict with my own?"

"Blaming others for your misfortunes will only cloud your reality. You cannot control the events that happen around you. However, you have full control of how you react to them. Accept events for what they are and nothing more. To get caught in the web of others will lead you to a path of disillusion and frustration. But this line of questioning looks to be a longer discussion. Shall we move up to your campsite where it is warmer?"

"You can move?" Thorik questioned.

"Yes. And I must ask, is it customary for you to have your back turned to those you speak to?"

Back turned? Thorik looked over his shoulder to see an enormous giant standing a few yards from him, partially obscured by the areas natural thick bushes. The gigantic man stood twice that of Ambrosius as he rested his crossed arms in front of him on a thick tree branch. He looked very relaxed as he stood there with one leg propped up on an exposed root.

Thorik was horrified at the size of him. The darkness added to his fear as he trembled with shock.

"Now, this is what I'm talking about. You had no way of preventing me from looking the way I do. Your reaction to this situation is in your control and you are letting yourself be affected by it. Interesting isn't it?" Grewen mused.

"Interesting isn't the word I would use. Why did you sneak up on me like that?"

"Sneak?" Grewen chuckled at the idea of someone his size sneaking about. "Again with the blaming of others. I was resting here from my hike up this hillside when you walked up upon us."

"Us? There are more of you?" Thorik questioned looking wildly around, trying to see through the moonlit forest as he backed up to the old tree and took on a defensive position.

"Slow down little man. Are you paying attention to how you are reacting to things that don't even exist? You really need to relax."

Thorik heard Emilen scream up the hill. Looking away from Grewen, he turned from the conversation and ran up the hill as quickly as he could.

Thorik was fast and could easily maneuver within the trees as he quickly returned to camp. Brimmelle, Wess, and Emilen were huddled in the center of the opening, near the fire, as they all looked into the dark woods. Avanda stood on the far side of the fire, curious to investigate what she had seen.

Upon seeing Thorik, Emilen screamed out to him, "There's a winged beast attacking from the woods. Get over here! Now!"

Brimmelle ignored Thorik and continued calling to Avanda. He was terrified for himself as well as for her. "You're in danger, come here at once. Quickly child," he ordered. She was mesmerized by the image she had seen fly near the camp and needed to see it again. She never even heard the voices of the others.

"Where's Gluic?" Thorik asked.

Emilen suddenly remembered that Gluic wasn't with them. "She went up the hill before you left."

Thorik ran through the camp and out the other side to run up the hill to find her. He called out Gluic's name several times before finally seeing her sitting in a column of moonlight with a new array of weeds and wild flowers in her hair. Her chin was down and her eyes were closed as she kneeled on a small boulder with her open hands, palms down, floating over her stones. Spread across the flat top of the rock before her, stones and crystals were set in an artistic flowing pattern.

He had seen her do this before, but he had never disturbed her during a meditation. He approached her from the front, as she faced downhill, and placed his hands on hers to gently wake her.

Her hands grabbed his and began to pull him over the rock toward her. His legs were nearly dangling as he looked up to see her eyes open wide and with a distant look to them. Stretched and tight, her face took on a horrifying appearance.

"Find out his plans and expose him," she said in a deep masculine voice. "Many will die if he is not stopped."

Her grip was very tight and was starting to hurt his wrist. "Whose plans? Before what is stopped?" he asked before she let go of him and blinked her eyes back to normal.

Her shoulders lowered and her body became less tense as she looked at Thorik. "You've messed up my stones." Her voice had returned to normal. She lowered herself off the rock after collecting her items, placing each in their correct sack.

"Well, you see," was all that Thorik got out before a scream was heard behind him. "Let's go!" He then helped her quickly move down the hill.

Reaching the camp with Gluic in tow, he saw Brimmelle pointing Ambrosius' staff up at an angle in the air while Wess fired multiple rounds of arrows toward the trees. Emilen now had a firm grasp on Avanda to protect her as they crouched near Ambrosius.

Standing at the edge of the camp was the giant, Grewen, with a shield taller than himself. Arrows being fired shattered as they stuck the reflective metal shield. Its shiny metallic surface acted almost as a mirror, causing the fire behind the group to give off an odd light show as the giant eased his way forward.

No markings or symbols were visible on the shield. The top half of it had various waves and creases within it that resembled a large wing. The same was true for the lower half.

Grewen held the shield out in front of him as he continued to slowly work his way into camp. An arrow could be seen attached to the side of his right foot that periodically became exposed from under the lower pointed end of the red tipped shield.

"Let me see," yelled Avanda as Emilen tried to hide her from the creature entering camp.

"Stop!" Thorik shouted as he raced over to Wess and pushed his bow down toward the ground.

Wess raised it again, once Thorik let go, but discontinued the attack.

"Thank you." Grewen's voice thundered causing the Nums to increase their defensive stance. Grewen started lowering his shield and looked over at Wess. "Put that away before someone gets hurt."

Thorik nodded to Wess who finally lowered the weapon but did not remove the arrow from its position within it.

"See, that wasn't so hard," Grewen said as he let go of the shield, which began to fall to the ground. But before landing, it caught itself with a set of back legs. A tail and then a head and neck appeared as the wings folded up and onto its back. The shield had been the back and wings of a silver-scaled creature while its tail, legs, and head had been wrapped around Grewen's massive arm.

Twelve feet of intimidating muscle unfolded before them, reaching from the point of the creatures jagged teeth all the way back to his red-tipped spiked tail. It stretched out to full length as its wings folded up against its body. Reflecting the image of the camp and surrounding woods off of its silver body, it moved through the camp in an awkward and nearly crippled fashion. With arms born into the wings, long sharp claws protruded from the top front of them. This ornery beast was not made for land movement.

Its facial scales were smaller and struggled to cover the redness of his gums and dual rows of teeth that angled in various directions from his mouth. His eyes stayed squinted with his scaled eyebrows arching down in a permanent look of anger. Bright red eyelids made it appear that the creature's eyes changed from solid black to red with every blink. The Red-Tipped Silver Dragon ignored the Nums; they were of no interest to him.

Each member reacted differently to the sight. Wess instinctively raised his bow back up. Brimmelle fell backward near the fire while Emilen stood in shock. Thorik stood between the dragon and his group to keep the peace.

"Amazing," Avanda said slowly, while Gluic raised her eyebrows and smiled. "We have guests," the Elder Num announced.

"Firing that arrow at Draq will only upset him. He isn't as well tempered as I am," Grewen commented as he plucked the arrow from his foot and then walked further into camp before noticing a figure lying on the opposite side of the fire. "Ambrosius? He's alive! Excellent work, Draq. You led me right to him." In two long strides he had crossed the camp and reached Ambrosius.

Emilen and Avanda stood in front of the unconscious man as the giant approached. "Leave him alone!" shouted Emilen, while Avanda smiled in awe at his size.

Grewen reached down and gently pushed the two Nums to one side with the back of his enormous hand. "Pardon me, but I need to see if my friend is well."

Draq followed and hissed at the group, preventing them from approaching Ambrosius. Emilen tugged at Avanda, leading her to the safety of Wess.

Grewen and Draq quickly walked around the camp and gathered the items they needed as they assessed Ambrosius' status.

Brimmelle, Avanda, and Emilen stayed near Wess with his arrow still in the cocked position, trained on the two large creatures as they moved about.

Gluic stood next to Thorik as they watched. Thorik was uncomfortable about them approaching Ambrosius. He had taken such a strong responsibility for the injured man that he didn't like the idea of strangers taking over. Gluic held him back with a slight tug of his arm and assured him that everything would be fine. He trusted her ability to read people but these were creatures and he didn't know how well she did with them. So he watched, closely and carefully as the giant and dragon ignored the band of travelers.

Grewen's leathery skin made his face look old with wrinkles and the back of his bald head looked like the underside of a sack that Thorik had once made out of a banteng skin. His entire body was covered with the hairless tough brown skin.

The giant's hands were large in proportion to the rest of his body, with a thumb on each side of three thick square-shaped fingers that extended long enough to have an extra joint in them. His long face angled up past his tiny ears providing a large skull area. His body was large in every sense of the word and he wore a long brown robe that was tied above his hips with a thick rope. His feet were bare and nearly as long as Thorik's entire body.

Even with two opposable thumbs on each hand, Grewen's fingers were too large to help with the bandages. Instead he focused on gathering hot water, soaking rags, and making a comfortable bed for Ambrosius. He also added a few large tree limbs to the fire to increase the light to work by. He didn't move quickly but he was continual in his efforts to help before he finally sat down with a rumble that made everyone's footing uneasy.

Poking his thick finger at several of the packs and bags, he asked, "I'm starving. Do you have anything to eat?" Silence filled in for an answer as he continued to investigate their supplies.

The dragon seemed to take the lead role of tending to Ambrosius. Hovering over him with his back to the party, his bat-like wings were blocking their view to what he was doing. They could see his head bob up and down and periodically strain upwards as though he was pulling on something, or pulling something apart.

It looked as though the creature was devouring Ambrosius' body and Thorik couldn't sit quietly any longer. He walked away from Gluic and toward the reflective image of himself on the dragon's back scales.

"Not a wise move to sneak up on a dragon." Grewen reached over and took a log out of the fire. "Especially one as mean-spirited as Draq."

Thorik was reevaluating many thoughts at this point. Included among them was his approach on the dragon as well as his trust in the giant that now had a flaming log gripped in his hand.

He looked over to see Wess' arrow trained at Grewen while Emilen had now picked up a few hand size rocks to help protect them. Brimmelle still held the staff in a defensive manner, as he was still shocked by the entire situation.

Thorik had to think and act quickly to save Ambrosius' life without being crushed by the giant's flaming club. He saw his opening. The giant was holding the club to his side and would force him to swing it sideways to hit Thorik. If he could jump a few yards closer to the dragon and then dive out of the way before the log clobbered him, it would crush against the dragon's back instead. It wasn't much of a plan, but it's all he had.

With a few launching steps and a valiant leap of faith he made it to his intended spot next to the dragon and dove onto the dirt. He rolled slightly from his momentum and landed on his back looking up at the dragon's face that looked back down at him. Thorik had jumped too far and had rolled under the dragon's wing to his front side, where Ambrosius lay with new bandages and splints.

"Get out, Fesh!" The dragon gazing his eyes at Thorik.

Thorik complied and rolled back under Draq's wing to find Grewen scratching the bottom of his foot with the end of the flaming log.

"Oh yah, that feels good." Grewen massaged the arches of his feet with the log. Sparks of hot cinders covered both his feet as he drilled the log into key pressure points with pleasure.

Looking slightly dumbfounded as he moved away from the silver dragon, Thorik looked over at Grewen. "Fesh?"

Grewen shook his head at Draq with disappointment. "Mind your words, we're in mixed company."

Draq ignored Grewen's comments and instead answered Thorik's question. "A fesh is a low life, dimwitted creature so repulsive that one would rather kill it than see it suffer another day eating its own feces."

"It isn't something you want to be," Grewen clarified as he enjoyed the feeling of the fiery log between each of his toes. He then scrubbed the sides and bottom of his feet with it.

"Okay, I understand," Thorik acknowledged. "What kind of creatures are you?"

"They're Altered Creatures," Brimmelle interjected. "Physical abnormalities of nature created by the Notarians to fight the Mountain King. These filthy beasts are our sworn enemies, designed to kill Polenums. But they were no match for the Mountain King and his army." He ended with a slight half grin.

Grewen squinted his eyes and opened his mouth in a stretched out smile. It wasn't clear if it was the result of the Fir's statement or the digging of the flaming log on his foot. "Legends and folklore have distorted the truth," the giant said with a rhythmic grinding of the log. "We are Unday, the descendants of the Altered Creatures.

And the tales of the Mountain King War are told differently from where I come from. The victors of it are quite mixed."

Brimmelle corrected him instantly. "Mixed by you Altereds. How do you explain the building of the Mountain King statue if he had lost?"

"How do you explain three thousand years of Altered Creature and Unday rule after the war?" Grewen enjoyably tossed back. "Besides, statues are made for martyrs as well as heroes."

"You grotesque freakishly-large excuse for an overweight hairless bear!" Brimmelle yelled. "How dare you mock the King."

"Keep it down!" roared Draq, causing even the crickets in the woods to become silent.

Extinguishing the log in the arch of his left foot, Grewen tossed it back into the fire and brushed off the remaining ashes from his skin. "Draq's right. It's late." Lying down, he rested his head on an outstretched arm. "Get some sleep, we have a long walk ahead of us in the morning," he finished, before quickly falling asleep.

The dragon finished what he was doing. "You heard him, go to sleep," he ordered as he rested himself next to Ambrosius and covered him with a metallic wing.

The camp went silent. Ambrosius lay unconscious covered by a Red-Tipped Silver Dragon, a leather-skinned Mognin giant stretched out over half the camp and a group of Num's all stood and watched Thorik sit in the dirt with confusion on his face.

Bewildered over the recent events that just unfolded, Thorik looked around the camp to make sense of it all. *What just happened to our journey? Is it over? Do I hand Ambrosius over to these creatures who claim to be his friends and return home? Return home to do what? To be what? Brimmelle's Fir-Pet, as Wess likes to call it.* The dynamics of the party had changed and Thorik struggled to understand his place in it. *This was my task, my chance, my opportunity to show that I'm a leader by helping Ambrosius save our people. But how will I ever lead these new members? They will easily crush me if I stand up to them.*

Feeling desperate, he looked at Gluic for support and she nodded that it would be okay as she waved him back to her.

There was nothing to do now but keep quiet and out of the way. So, the Nums huddled near each other on the far side of the fire, away from the two uninvited guests and tried to rest.

Chapter 10
River Cut

Highoverhead, Draq surfed the wind currents as they swept over the mountain's crest. His elegance in the air was accentuated by the nature of his scales. Bursts of light reflected from each of his metallic plates, showering his body with thousands of tiny explosions.

Upon flexing his muscles, the scales flattened against his body. A solid reflection replaced the blinking star appearance, allowing him to focus the sun's rays intensely onto a nearby bird. Temporarily blinding it, Draq swooped down and captured his prey in midair for a quick meal.

Thorik watched the event, nearly forgetting about the dragon's bad temperament. "How wonderful it must be to fly," he said before looking back down at the rock he balanced on.

Jumping onto the next exposed rock, Thorik worked his way across the rushing stream. Reaching the shore, he tied his guide rope to the base of an ancient bridge platform. The arch of the bridge had been swept away long ago, but the stone steps leading up to it still remained on both banks.

A series of waterfalls were above them as well as below. Fortunately the old path had led them to an area where a flat rocky ledge had created a short stream between them that provided a good crossing. The water was perhaps waist high for a Num, and it moved quickly. Even if it was shallow, Thorik knew better than to chance traveling against powerful water currents.

The falls overlooked a mighty Kingsfoot Valley. They could see the stream run down into the King's River as the sun ignited the trees with an inferno of yellows and reds. Above the colors was a strong deep green of spruce trees that led up to the snow line. Along the far side of the valley he could see several other streams and waterfalls working their own way down to the river.

Thorik looked back to the far shore at the rest of the Nums, as they prepared to cross. Grewen moved at a slow pace up the hillside and had fallen behind, just visible through the trees. Ambrosius was still unconscious as Grewen easily carried him in one arm.

Bracing his back against the wall of the mountainside, Brimmelle recited the words from the Courage Rune Scroll. He was very nervous up on the rim of a river cut. Even with a few yards of grace between him and the edge, he continued to visualize himself falling over the hundreds of feet of the waterfall to his death. Flattening his hands tightly against the cliff, he chanted louder in hopes to drive away his own sensations of dizziness and weak knees. Never leaving Farbank prevented him from ever being higher than Sammal's old oak tree during his youth. This was the first time in his life he had experienced a fear of heights.

Wess double-checked the knot on his end of the guide rope that now spanned the stream. Emilen loosely grabbed it to provide balance. Moss covered the exposed stones, making them very slippery, although she skipped from one to the next with ease.

Once Emilen finished her crossing, she motioned for Gluic.

Gluic wasn't as agile, but that did not deter her from slowly working her way across the river utilizing the rope for balance. As she did, she could hear her son over the slapping water of the falls.

Brimmelle closed his eyes and hugged the rock wall with his back and arms. "Don't look down," he shouted to Gluic as he began visualizing her falling over the cliff. "Get a footing before you move your hands. Only move one hand off the rope at a time."

Fed up with his instructions, she stopped on the next rock and turned halfway back toward him to stop his annoying directions on how to cross the stream. The water disappeared over the edge of the waterfall only a yard in front of her.

Before she could say anything, Gluic noticed Grewen finally catching up to them. It was odd to see him run. His body wasn't made for it. Perhaps it was the fact that he was carrying Ambrosius, or was it something else? The trees. The ones from which he had just came from. The limbs were moving. Thrashers were in heavy chase.

"Everyone! Get across. *Now!*" Thorik started back across the rocks to help them. By the time he had reached Gluic, Wess had pulled Brimmelle from his safe location and onto the first rock in the stream. Thorik helped Gluic finish her final distance before turning to see Wess, who was halfway across, yelling at the Fir.

Brimmelle stood solid, frozen with fear. Staring at the edge of the waterfall, his body started to sway. He looked over the falls at the long drop beyond and envisioned himself tumbling down it. The rope slipped from his hands and he fell forward, only to be stopped as the rope lodged under his armpits. Light-headed and shaking, he leaned over the water's breaking point in horror. Grabbing the rope at his chest for dear life, his leaning caused an extreme bow in the guide rope that made it difficult for him to balance. His feet shuffled behind him for grip on the slick rock.

Wess struggled to stay on his own rock. The rope was now out to his side, due to Brimmelle, and no longer helpful. Jumping back across the rocks, Thorik grabbed Wess just as he began to lose his balance. Helping Wess to a larger flat rock, the Sec headed back for his Fir whose feet splashed in the water as he lost his footing.

Grewen pounded his way toward them, breathing hard as he lifted his heavy body with each step toward the group. He realized the error of having Draq fly ahead to look out for assassins. Danger could just as easy come from the local wildlife as well as the terrain. The giant could use the dragon's help. There was no way for Grewen to defend himself from these creatures and protect Ambrosius at the same time. The only option he had was to run for safety, not one of his strongest attributes.

Behind Grewen, the thrashers were catching up quickly. Near the front of the pack, Thorik could see the silverhead at full gallop. There wasn't time to help Brimmelle step to each stone. Something quick needed to happen. He needed to get Brimmelle across and prevent the thrashers from following them.

Reaching Brimmelle, Thorik pulled him back upright. "Close your eyes." Thorik cut the rope from the thrashers side of the stream and tied it onto the Fir's belt. A secure knot now linked the Fir to the safe side of the waterfall. Thrashers don't like water, so all he needed to do now was have Grewen remove the stepping stones.

The sudden strength Thorik felt by taking charge was quickly suppressed as he looked over the Fir's shoulder. His heart tightened and his throat went dry as he gazed at Avanda. She had been hiding from the group behind the ancient bridge platform. Still needing to cross the river, Thorik had just cut her guide rope leaving her stranded on the wrong side of the water.

"Avanda, run this way. You'll have to jump to the third rock before I can help you," Thorik yelled.

"I can't! I'm afraid of the water. I can't swim."

Panicking, Thorik needed to save Avanda's life. "You won't have to be in the water. Just run and jump. I'll catch you!"

She looked behind her to see the tribe of thrashers already attacking Grewen's legs as he ran. They would be on top of her within moments. "Promise you'll catch me!" she screamed.

"I won't let anything happen to you!" he promised.

Looking behind her, Grewen and the thrashers were nearly on top of her. She stood up and bolted out from behind the stone steps and directly in front of the giant, who nearly stepped on her.

Thorik held onto Brimmelle firmly with one arm as he prepared his footing the best he could. "Get rid of these stepping stones as you cross," he yelled to Grewen as the giant approached the water right behind Avanda.

Avanda jumped to the first one and then the second before closing her eyes and leaping high into the air, trusting that Thorik would catch her.

Still carrying Ambrosius, Grewen reached down with his free arm and started grabbing the exposed rocks and flinging them over the falls as he moved across the water. The surging stream only splashed up to his calves, making it easy for him to cross.

Thorik reached out with his free hand to catch Avanda's outstretched body. He grabbed her and in returned she grabbed him. Unfortunately, he lost his footing in doing so. Thorik fell backwards into the water, dragging Avanda and Brimmelle with him.

By the time Grewen bent down for the second rock, another thrasher had leaped onto his leg. The giant picked up and tossed the rock before swatting the creature off of him. Its flailing body splashed into the rushing water before its force quickly carried the creature over the edge and down to the sharp rocks below.

Thorik, Avanda, and Brimmelle were captured by the rushing water as well. Too far from Grewen to help, they were quickly washed over the edge and out of sight.

A moment later the rope that Thorik had tied onto the safe side of the stream went tight, knocking Wess off his feet as it shifted directions from the water out to the ledge. Emilen jumped for the rope and attempted to pull it up, but her small body was no match for the weight on the other end. Just as Wess showed up to help, the rope went limp. Their eyes widened with disbelief and concern at the thought of what could have happened. Pulling up the end of the rope, it was still tied onto Brimmelle's broken belt.

Chapter 11
Leadership

Wess moved to the ledge to look for Avanda, Brimmelle and Thorik. He couldn't see anything from his position so he jumped to his feet to work his way down from the falls and around a large rock face. Emilen yelled over the edge with no response. The noise from the falls drowned out her voice.

Grewen arrived, splashing out of the water as he kicked his bulky feet onto the dry rocks. He had seen what had happened and gently set Ambrosius down so he could help. Stepping over to the edge, he leaned over Emilen and looked down. He saw three wet Nums holding onto an angled rock. More accurately, Thorik was holding onto the rock with one hand and Brimmelle with the other while Avanda was holding onto Thorik. Brimmelle appeared to have been knocked out and he was dripping with blood.

Grewen knew that there wasn't enough footing for him to maneuver his large body down the cliff wall. Instead, he gave instructions to Wess, who was currently working his way toward them. "Brimmelle is hurt and unconscious. You need to hurry before Thorik loses his grip," he added to expedite Wess' descent.

Wess yelled back a reply that Grewen's little ears couldn't pick up over the roar of the water.

Emilen went to comfort Gluic. "I'm sure Brimmelle will be fine. They'll make it back up and we'll all be home safe before you know it."

Gluic untied a bracelet of wild flowers from her arm and wrapped them around Emilen's wrist. "You keep telling yourself that, my dear, if it makes you feel better. But truth be known, we will never see Farbank again."

"Don't give up so easy. We'll reach Kingsfoot in one piece and take a boat swiftly back to the village. We'll survive this journey," Emilen insisted.

The elder woman's face went cold and stiff. "Perhaps you don't understand, my dear. You and I will *never* see Farbank again."

Emilen never knew when Gluic was serious or teasing her. She smiled and assumed it was the latter. Channels were known for their strange ways and they had no difficulty in reminding others of it.

By the time Wess reached the fallen members, Grewen had dropped one end of the rope to him while the other was wrapped around Grewen's fingers, tightly held by both thumbs of his right hand.

Wess reached out as he told Thorik to swing Brimmelle over. Within a few slight swings Wess was able to grab his leg and pull him off to a safer place where he laid him down. Helping Avanda and Thorik off the outstretched rock, he then returned to Brimmelle to check his injuries. The elder Num was bleeding from a nasty cut to his forehead as well as his hands, which he apparently sustained in an attempt to catch himself.

Wess tied the rope securely around Brimmelle and Avanda. Once he gave a tug on the rope, Grewen quickly pulled them up and had Emilen and Gluic remove the ropes before he lowered it again for Thorik and Wess. They both tied themselves on and grabbed hold of the rope over their head.

"Thanks for helping me up there. Another second and I would have lost my balance on that rock," Wess said to Thorik.

"I'm sure you would have done the same for me," he replied.

"Let's not test that theory." He then gave that arrogant smile of his. But this time it didn't bother Thorik as much. Wess looked up and with a tug on the rope they launched up into the air and landed in Grewen's grasp.

Howling and clicking from the far side of the water continued as the apes made no attempt to enter the rushing waters. Grewen moved the group out around the bend before they sat down to rest. Emilen began cleaning Brimmelle's cuts and scrapes as he slowly started to wake. He moaned about the pain and mumbled various passages from the Scrolls of Wisdom to calm his headache.

They rested and recovered as berries were picked and eaten, as well as roots and mushrooms. The autumnal palette of the hillside was a feast for the eyes as well as the stomach.

Grewen ripped entire shrubs out of the ground. After a quick slap against the side of his foot to dislodge most of the dirt, he placed them in his mouth, dirt and all. His constant hunger was easily quenched with nearly every plant he walked past.

Gluic returned to Brimmelle with a few dark green leaves with reddish veins, as he complained about his head pounding with pain. She rubbed the leaves together between two small rocks to squeeze out the liquids from within them. After removing the solid remains of the plant from the rocks, she softly rubbed the moist rocks onto his temples.

"Pepper's mint will remove your pain," she informed him as Brimmelle blinked his eyes from the strong vapors the liquid gave off. Moments later his headache reduced, clearing his thoughts.

Thorik sat near Ambrosius with a handful of berries. "You're looking a little thin, what do you say about some Ciderberries? Ambrosius?" With concern, he placed his pale hand on Ambrosius' chest to make sure he was still with them. He was. "You've overslept and missed the high adventure. Come on now, let's see a bit of life in you."

"He'll be fine," Grewen stepped in, "but I'd suggest keeping your distance from him if you know what's good for you."

Surprised at the comment, Thorik asked, "Are you threatening me?" He took two strong steps toward the giant who had him shaking with fear just the previous night.

"No. Just stating the facts. You put your life in danger each time you get close to him," Grewen said as he watched Draq swooping in out of the sky toward them.

"And how is that?" Thorik asked as he turned back to Ambrosius just in time to be knocked down by the landing dragon.

"Get away from him, Fesh," Draq demanded.

Thorik slid on his back halfway to Grewen, before rolling back to his feet and dusting himself off. "Now you wait just a minute. We've saved this man's life more than once and we deserve the right to continue to-" He stopped as the dragon moved up and over him, leaning his head down to press his forehead against Thorik's tilted back head. Draq's black eyes stared at Thorik while he started pressing Thorik down.

"You have no right to anything." Draq defined the new rules of their journey. "You will provide food, water, and shelter for us and we will provide it to him. You will not touch him or be near him without our permission." He had pressed Thorik down to his knees. "Do you understand?"

"No, I do not," Thorik pushed back. "We don't even know you. Ambrosius has never told us about you, let alone that he is safe with you. Yet, we are expected to trust you when you aren't willing to do the same for us." His short little body pressed his head up a few inches against the dragon that was now starting to breathe hard.

"I don't have to trust you. You, on the other hand, have no choice," Draq said as he reached out with his right leg and kicked Thorik onto his back again before leaning over him and pressing his right claw onto Thorik's chest. "One or more of you may be a traitor and I cannot take the chance of him being harmed."

By this point Avanda and Emilen were furious at the situation. "Leave him alone," shouted Avanda.

"Thorik, get out of there," Emilen called, fearing for his life.

Thorik thought about how unfair this was. He had jeopardized everything to bring Ambrosius this far and now these strangers were going to take over. In addition he had lost his leadership role again. Every time he felt that he had control of what was going on it was taken away from him. *Not this time.* He continued to be pressed into submission from the weight of the dragon leaning on his chest with one leg.

Thorik glanced over at Grewen who was relaxing against a tree watching for Thorik's reaction to Draq's demands.

"You're right," Thorik surrendered.

Emilen was relieved that there would be no more bloodshed today. Wess, on the other hand, was disappointed that he had given up so quickly. He was just starting to respect the Num and felt this character flaw had resurfaced.

Draq's narrow eyes never left Thorik as he backed away and let him stand.

"You're correct. I have no choice but to trust you." Thorik brushed himself off again before glancing over at Grewen and then back at the reflective scaled face of the dragon. "You will take care of Ambrosius while I lead us to Kingsfoot."

Grewen's hairless left eyebrow rose as he looked over to see Draq's response.

"I follow no one," Draq replied standing his ground.

"Then leave us," Thorik continued. "Ambrosius asked me personally to lead him to Kingsfoot to find the truth of what happened. And unless you wish to defy his wishes, I will lead us."

"I could kill you all in but a moment's time," Draq replied.

"Yes, you could," Thorik said honestly. "And then you would need to explain to Ambrosius how you killed us for trying to protect him. I'm sure he will be grateful."

"What faith do you have that I won't kill you now and tell him that you were ripped apart by thrashers?" Cocking his head slightly as he edged it forward, "Why should I trust that you have had such words with him?"

"The way I see it, you can kill us at any point you wish. Believing that you will or won't take such actions will not help my mission to bring Ambrosius to Kingsfoot. Although killing us prior to talking to Ambrosius could cause you great issues. I don't think Grewen would lie about such things to him. So, I don't have to trust you. You, on the other hand, have no choice." He stared Draq in the eyes while his stomach fluttered from the stress of his bluff.

Emilen was bothered by the game Thorik was playing. She wanted him to stand up for himself, not to put himself in unnecessary danger.

Wess and Avanda, on the other hand, were excited to see Thorik's bravery. Their eyes darted back and forth between him and the dragon, waiting to see the next move.

Draq reached out, grabbing the Num and lifting him off his feet as the dragon's wings wrapped around, surrounding them from all outside influences. Cramped and encased inside the creature's wings, Thorik was pressed up against the silver-scaled body. Draq breathed out hot moist air and flared his nostrils down at Thorik. His large teeth began to show as the right side of his lip rose to expose the black of his gum line.

Thorik was now a prisoner, as his feet dangling off the ground and his arms were locked at his sides from the pressure of the surrounding wings. He pushed his head back to look up at the dragon's face that hovered above him. Perhaps he had taken too big of a risk. Stepped too far. Pushed too hard. He began to sweat from the hot humid air, which was hard to breathe.

Draq finally broke the stressful silence of staring Thorik down. "Don't play your games with me, Fesh. If I feel at any time that you pose a threat to Ambrosius, I will strike you down without warning."

Thorik gasped for breath in the tight environment and replied, "Same goes for me."

Draq squinted, trying to see more than what was on the surface. "You have courage little Num, and a fierce loyalty to Ambrosius. I can respect that. Just remember that you will be no good to him dead." Draq eyed him again as Thorik mustered up the strength to raise his head and eyed him back. Draq continued, "He was lucky to have found you. You may lead the group to Kingsfoot while I scout ahead for trouble."

"More thrashers?" Thorik squeezed out.

"No, Fesh." He pulled him in even closer. "Thrashers are your least concern. We need to avoid hunters."

"What are they hunting?"

"Ambrosius."

From the outside of the glossy winged cocoon, the group watched as it finally opened up and set Thorik down on his feet. He was pale and weak in the knees but stood up as strongly as he could manage.

"We have come to an understanding," Draq stated to the other Nums. "Thorik will be leading you to Kingsfoot and Grewen will care for Ambrosius while I scout ahead."

"Thorik?" Brimmelle spoke up, as he lay on the ground with a bandage around his head. "I lead this trip. I am in control here. I'm the Fir!"

"This is not a debate," Draq growled slowly and fiercely. "Thorik is in charge or you will answer to me."

No one argued the statement.

Chapter 12
Reunion of Old Friends

Avanda's playful laugh could be heard as she told Grewen of her misadventures. "And then Uncle Wess crashed into a big willow tree. It broke our wooden Runestone sled in half and nearly did the same to him," she said, finishing her story and laughing at Wess' painful event.

Ambrosius woke to find himself near a warm campfire in the mountainous forest. He couldn't believe his eyes when he saw Grewen sitting near him, chewing on a large tree root. Sitting up gave him more pain than he had expected, but he made it. "Grewen! How did you? Where did you?" Ambrosius didn't know where to begin.

"You have the name right. After that I lost you," Grewen replied with a smile. "It's good to see you, as well. It has been a long time. Fortunately for me, I ran into an old friend of ours who told me that you were in trouble." He pointed in the sky toward the reflective creature flying above.

Ambrosius looked up to see Draq scouting for any potential threats. *You did it, my friend. You brought help. I knew you wouldn't abandon me in the temple's rubble.* Ambrosius trusted no one more than Draq. Grewen was one of the few that even came close. However, it wasn't a fair comparison. Draq and Ambrosius had fought through decades of battles together. His loyal giant Mognin had fought for him in the civil war, but drifted on his own afterward in an attempt to come to terms with what he had witnessed during the Battle of Maegoth.

Grewen glancing across the camp at Thorik who was diligently working on Ambrosius' staff. "Lucky for you, you found a new friend in your time of need who has protected you until we arrived."

Ambrosius also noticed Emilen sitting next to Thorik, making suggestions for designs that could be etched into the sides of the staff. Their body language spoke volumes of their current feelings for one another as she placed her hand on his leg while they talked. Thorik moved his carving tools, that she had bumped, over to his other side. His self-confidence had grown after the run-ins with the thrashers and Emilen found that very appealing.

Brimmelle and Wess sat on a few rocks as they played a heated game of Runeage. Wess was losing and complaining about Brimmelle's strategies. Brimmelle's exceptional memory had allowed him to recall every strategy Wess had ever played against him. He was going to easily defeat the young man.

Gluic had settled herself in a clearing to meditate. After she had weeded out the limp vegetation on her own body, she placed various sticks and leaves around her. She softy touched them in what appeared to be a random sequence while sitting cross-legged on the ground.

Watching closely, Avanda was sitting near the elder Num, trying to perform the same meditation as Gluic. It was difficult to do while invariably talking at the same time, but the young Num would do her best.

"I don't know if I would call myself lucky. I am of ill health," Ambrosius replied to Grewen as he rubbed his forehead. Lowering his voice, he added, "My body and mind are weak. My powers are questionable at best. And if it was not for a gullible young Num's belief in fate and a story contrived, I would still be downstream."

"This Num takes great pride in helping you. You have deceived him?" Grewen asked.

"No, it's not like that. I told him it was fate that we met. Just because I don't believe in it, doesn't mean it's not true for him," Ambrosius reasoned. "But I can't help feel that he has something about him that makes him stand out."

"You are fortunate to be alive, fate or no fate. Draq said no one else survived. What happened?"

Ambrosius looked up at Grewen. "Darkmere has once again waged war upon us, and this is only the first wave of his hand. He will destroy anyone and anything that does not serve him. His minions are now everywhere and we can trust few. They reach beyond his sight with the help of small groups that carry out his orders. War is here and it is now up to me to gather the armies to stop it."

Grewen looked uncomfortable about what he had to tell Ambrosius but he was not going to keep secrets from him. "I don't think you will be able to."

Ambrosius was slightly surprised by the comment, especially from Grewen. "And why is that?"

"You might be wanted for the death of the Council members." He continued before Ambrosius could start asking questions. "Word is out that you called the council meeting to destroy them, giving you absolute power. This would allow you to go head to head with Darkmere without their approval."

"How could the council member's deaths be known by others so quickly?" Ambrosius questioned.

"Better yet, I came across travelers with this information *before* the council was even murdered."

"It was a trap?" Ambrosius quickly realized. "How could I've not seen it?" Thinking out loud, he continued, "Which means I was suppose to know about the upcoming disaster. How else would I get the entire council to convene?" He began playing the chain of events over in his mind. For months he'd worked to rouse the people out of their slumber. Ambrosius had single-handedly brought all of the principals of the clans and nations to their ultimate demise. "How foolish I've been. I've trusted too many and grew myopic upon my quest." He paused, as he came back to the conversation with his old friend. "The attack on the Grand Council surely will spur people to action." Ambrosius caught Grewen's smirk indicating Ambrosius was missing the point. "Regardless, few would believe that I would do such a thing," he said proudly, coming back to Grewen's topic.

"But they have seen you do such acts in your past," Grewen noted factually without criticizing Ambrosius. "They've seen you fight for the rights to your dead father's kingdom. They fought in your wars, and their families have died in your battles. And they watched as their coastline cities sank under the water of the great flood, after Maegoth." Grewen shook his head at the memories of the horrific battles that still lingered in his mind. "These same people you believe have full faith in you have watched you destroy the mightiest kingdom Australis has ever had." Relaxing his shoulders, he continued, "Changing your ways may help the future, my friend, but it does not erase your past. So yes, I can see how they *could* see you do such things."

"Grewen, you know the reasons behind that war and yet you question my motives and make me sound like a criminal?"

"No, I'm just telling you the facts. However, many others *are* questioning them. Once they realize that the Council has in fact been killed, they will question why you are the only survivor. Their thoughts will develop to the same end. Ambrosius, you will be killed once you are discovered to be alive," Grewen finished.

Ambrosius didn't know how to respond. He had worked so diligently to get where he was and then to have Darkmere pluck it from him wasn't enough. Darkmere had to make sure that no one would ever listen to Ambrosius again. He had succeeded. There may not be anyone or anyway to stop him at this point. Combing his beard with a few fingers, he said, "Was it luck that I lived or was it Darkmere's way of making sure that I suffered?"

"I wish I could just remember what had happened," Ambrosius added. "It's foggy and parts are missing."

He looked up and was surprised to see Gluic standing next to them. It was an unsettling encounter as the two realized they hadn't observed her approaching. Ambrosius looked back over to where she had been meditating only to see Avanda was still there, lying on her side taking a nap.

Gluic had overheard the conversation and had pulled out a small sack from her cloak. She emptied the contents of several smooth black stones into her hand to show them.

Ambrosius looked over at them and smiled. "Yes, they are very nice stones." His dismissive way was gentle but obvious that he wished to return to his conversation with Grewen.

"Is that volcanic glass?" Grewen asked, as he reached over to touch one.

She quickly slapped his large forefinger before he could reach it. "They have been cleansed by the moon. Your touch will weaken them."

Grewen retracted his hand and looked at the end of his finger to see how it yielded such powers.

"Thank you for showing them to us, Gluic," Ambrosius responded politely, hoping she would take the hint and leave.

She picked one of the stones up by its sides and held it toward Ambrosius' forehead. "They can help you remember what you are missing."

"I don't think your pebbles can help, but I value the offer."

She continued to hold them out in front of him as she smiled and nodded her head up and down to convince him to let her try.

Grewen grinned. "Go ahead Ambrosius. It's worth a try."

Ambrosius didn't appreciate Grewen aiding her fantasies, but now he felt locked into trying. "You need to know that I'm not going to swallow those." A bitter look crossed his face.

"No, no. You will lie down on the ground and I will build a net of energy around you." She waited patiently for him to comply.

Ambrosius gave Grewen an odd disgruntled look for getting him into this.

"What's the worst that could happen?" Grewen asked. "You lie down and take a nap for a few minutes?"

Gluic looked up to correct Grewen's statement. "Few days."

"Excuse me?" Ambrosius asked.

"It will take several days of sleep to recover from the memory reading, but you will be very refreshed upon wakening, hopefully with all your memories intact," she reassured him.

He looked over at Grewen with concern.

Grewen smiled and mocked his situation. "Did you hear that Ambrosius? You'll wake refreshed."

Gluic started by laying Ambrosius down on his back with his arms down along his sides. She placed one of the rocks on the ground near the top of his head. After adding one over each shoulder, she placed one on the outside of each ankle. Prior to setting each stone she whispered instructions to them.

Thorik looked over from across the camp to see his grandmother performing some sort of ritual around Ambrosius. Just then Gluic look up directly at Thorik and waved him over.

As he approached, Gluic began giving instructions. "Thorik, give me the Runestones for trust and enlightenment." Reaching down, she adjusted the stone near his right shoulder.

Curious, Thorik dutifully reached into his bag and pulled out a dozen before he found the two that she had requested. He quickly handed them to her.

She placed one over each of Ambrosius' eyes while kneeling next to him. Keeping his elbow on the ground she raised his left hand. A yellowish thin crystal was set in his palm and she placed his fist firmly between both of her hands. Speaking softly, she closed her eyes and began to see his thoughts while he drifted into a dream state.

It was only a moment before he had immersed himself into his memories of the past. So vivid and real, they played out as though he was living it for his first time.

Chapter 13
Hidden Memories

The city of Kingsfoot rested in a half-bowl shaped valley, which was vast in both size and life. Fall colors blanketed the lakeside while various greens trimmed the higher valley walls before giving way to the timberline and snow covered peaks, which bordered three of its sides. The area emanated peace and harmony to all the Council Members as they had crossed the valley floor upon arrival.

A two-thousand-foot high vertical slice out of the mountain gave way to a stone statue just over half the height of the cliff face. This statue of the Mountain King stood with its back flat against the cliff wall as its feet rested in the half-circle lake, surrounded by stone and crystal statues of various animals. The King looked down toward his crown, held in his hands, with warmth and kindness in his face.

The detail was greater than any had ever seen before or since. At a great distance a traveler would see a king in his flowing robes and a scar across his forehead from his war with the Notarians. If they had swum across the lake to touch the statue, they would feel each individual fiber that made up the threads of his grand clothes.

Ambrosius had walked onto the third terrace of the main garden, overlooking the lake, to find Beltrow along with many other Nums. They were all preparing the plants for the winter. The morning sun had worked its way down the Mountain King's body and now was shining on the City of Kingsfoot, which graced the area where the lake touched the vertical mountainside.

"Bless the King's travels," Fir Beltrow Ruddlehoth announced. "How many years has it been?" Short and stocky, even by Polenum standards, Beltrow had a solidness to him, which gave validity to his words. Curly light red hair covered his head as well as his chin. Small thoughtful eyes looked out from under graying eyebrows, as he smiled from behind his overgrown mustache.

"Too long, Fir Beltrow, too long. I apologize for not visiting you sooner, there is so much to be done and my youth has been lost in the wake. You however, look as you haven't aged at all," Ambrosius said.

"Maybe not on the outside, but I can feel it in my bones. For the first time in decades, my legs weren't able to make the journey south for the annual trade visit. My daughter traveled with the group in my stead." Beltrow motioned Ambrosius to come over and help him lift and flip a clay pot over the plant he was working on.

"I want to thank you for agreeing to hold the Grand Council at your Temple. It is important that no one feels at a disadvantage. It was also of great help for you to send out escorts, helping us find our way. I now understand why this valley is unknown by the rest of us in the south. Has anyone else arrived yet?" Ambrosius said, while helping with the Num's chores.

Only a handful of spiritual leaders and a small group of residents knew the location, for they lived among it as the Temple's caretakers. Typically keeping to themselves, this was a unique situation that required a secluded location out of evil's view. They had extended the offer to hold the meeting after hearing of Ambrosius' desire to revive the Council and restore peace.

"A few last night, but they asked not to be disturbed." He continued to work on his plants as he said goodbye to them for the winter. "However, it looks like we have a group that will arrive in the next few hours," he noted while motioning his head toward the lake.

Ambrosius looked to the far side of the lake and up on the valley's southern mountainside. He strained his eyes and still didn't see anything. Finally, he saw slight movements. There were several small specks moving downward below the mountain pass from Lakewood Valley. "Your eyesight is as keen as any Num I've ever met. I don't think you're as old as you claim."

Scoffing at the comment, Beltrow peered up at the Grand Mountain King statue standing in the center of the half-circle lake. "The King will have a beard of white tonight." He then finished anchoring the clay pot, which they had just set. "It will be a long cold climb up those steps in the morning. I hope I'm up for it."

"If you're not, I'll have Draquol fly you to the crown. His tongue may be sharp, but the ride will be as smooth as yakka cream," Ambrosius said lightly.

Beltrow smiled. "Draquol is here? Where? How are he and his family?"

"Draq is scouting for uninvited guests at the moment. His family is of good health and well being," Ambrosius replied.

"Last I heard, he was going to be a father. Did the hatchling survive the escape from his egg? My understanding is that most do not."

"Yes, he and Melendrol are parents of a little hell-raiser named Fraquendol who broke open that thick shell like it was parchment. He needs a lot of taming before meeting you."

"Ah, yes. I recall the first time I met Draquol." Beltrow placed a hand at his thigh and patted it a few times. "I can't say that he had a lot of restraint himself."

Ambrosius laughed. "True, but I wouldn't want anyone else at my side. I trust him with my life."

A warm smile crossed Beltrow's face. "It's good to have those in your life." Slapping his hands on the side of his pants, he knocked off the loose dirt. Reaching out with a strong two-handed handshake, he properly welcomed Ambrosius. "Welcome to Kingsfoot, my friend. My people will tend to your needs inside. I will join you later."

"I shall be looking forward to it," Ambrosius responded before leaving to stroll around the city.

The architecture was not from the Polenum culture. Nums typically constructed homes with natural plant life, which blended in with the environment. The city of Kingsfoot was not constructed at all. It was etched out of the mountain itself.

Surrounding the city was a large courtyard of carved stone and lush plant life. The ground was tiled with large hexagonal stones, each containing a rune engraved into the center. Carved stone, resembling open scrolls, lined the perimeter as they unraveled from eight feet in the air down to the ground.

Inside the outer rows of scrolls was a large courtyard filled with animal statues and then a terraced garden area containing a wide staircase in the center, connecting all three elevations. An eight-foot stone wall separated each terraced tier and on each wall the Rules of Order were written.

If it weren't for the beautiful way that it was presented, Ambrosius would have thought it to be spiritually suffocating. He couldn't walk anywhere without the enormous words of their faith staring him in the face. But it was beautiful and amazing, and without question the world's most remarkable architectural design. Each carving had exquisite lifelike characteristics, and the closer he inspected them the more detail could be viewed. It was endless.

Beltrow had neglected to tell him about the Grand Temple and the city's beauty. Ambrosius had met Beltrow during the Fir's annual summer trade visit to Shoreview, many ages ago, and the Fir had only mentioned that they lived in a small spiritual community. An area he ruled even though he did not own any of the land, for it belonged to the Mountain King. Ambrosius had assumed it was just another shabby little town.

Ambrosius walked from the top terrace, where he had spoken to Beltrow, in toward the city's exterior wall. It was a collage of animal and plant carvings. But instead of a wall with carvings in it, it was statues that acted as a wall. The great horned ibex running from a felidea, perhaps a sabered panther, was shown while a tribe of haplorhini attempted to take down a giant ursidae as it stood on its back two legs to defend itself. Some scenes could be taken as horrific views, but it was only depicting the reality of nature and the animals that lived in the King's line of sight. There were also calm depictions, such as a family of capypigs at a watering hole near a chital as well a variety of birds flying and nesting.

From a distance the City of Kingsfoot looked like a replica of the mighty White Summit which it leaned against. The entire city had been carved out of one enormous boulder. Close up, it looked more like wildlife frozen in time.

Ambrosius wandered outside a bit, marveling at the extensive size and details before he went inside. The city was filled with odd shaped rooms and walkways to give way for the structures of art, which completed the walls and ceilings in every room. One room was the inside of a whale while another was covered with insects. Every wall and ceiling looked like some type of plant or animal.

The floor was a different story, it had been carved out to depict sand, leaves, water, and rocks which Ambrosius thought amusing seeing that it was all rock. The designs in the floor were visually bold but subtle to the touch and could only be felt with bare feet or the touch of ones fingers. He was again amazed by the detail and he bent down to feel a pebble that he couldn't quite tell if it was real or carved into the floor.

"Did you drop something?" a soft voice said.

Ambrosius looked up to see a lean and voluptuous woman in a long gown of red and black as he realized he was grabbing at an etching in the floor. "No." He stood back up. "Just admiring the workmanship. Isn't it amazing?"

"Yes, of course it is, it was built by the Irluk," she said, educating him.

"The Death Witch?" he replied with amusement.

"Long before being murdered by Wyrlun, just prior to the Alchemist and E'rudite War. When she ruled Australis as the most powerful Alchemist ever. She was a god."

Before opening his mouth, he remembered why he asked the council to attend this meeting and decided to let it go, for now. "I see." He controlled his tone the best he could. "I am Ambrosius, founder of the Grand Council. And you are?"

"Megyn." Eyeing him up and down with dislike, she added, "The new Prominent of EverSpring. I have heard your name before and you are not welcome in our lands."

Ambrosius had a history of conflicts with the Alchemists and had hoped that his actions over the past several years had improved relations between them. Apparently it had not.

"All the more reason we convene in a neutral location such as this. Where is your predecessor, Bryus Grum? Has he retired at an early age?" Ambrosius questioned.

"He no longer leads us. I am authorized to speak for the guild now, but you will not like what I have to say."

"I'm sure that Bryus passed down his knowledge to you of our intent. We wish to mend old ills and build an alliance against the coming threat of war. Surely we can agree to that."

"Perhaps the approaching threat is only coming after you and your power. It might be the change that the rest of us need. Is it your fear of losing what you have that would drive us to battle and sacrifice our lives?" She didn't provide time for his response before continuing. "The changes before us are confrontational only because you and your Council have made them such. Accepting Darkmere's rule would stop all conflicts."

Ambrosius raised his voice. "I know Darkmere all too well; his treachery and his tyranny. He will only give you what you want until he needs you no more. The opportunity that you seek with him is a spell of your own illusions. Do not be fooled by your own desires."

"You're too closed minded to see what opportunities lay ahead," she said as her servant approached and whispered in her ear. Upon completion, Megyn returned to Ambrosius. "I must be leaving now. We can continue this debate at the council meeting tomorrow. I think you will find that I do not stand alone."

"Megyn," pausing to relax his voice, "Please think about what I have stated."

"Likewise," she replied and began to leave before suddenly stopping. Swiveling on the toes of her feet back toward him, she added, "I nearly forgot something. Oddly enough, Darkmere gave me a message to give to the mighty Ambrosius just in case I should ever run into you. He has a thirtieth anniversary gift for you."

Ambrosius' face became stone cold as the blood left his face. A message from Darkmere was unexpected and was more of a threat than a gift. It had been thirty years since the end of the Civil War, a time and battle he'd rather forget. Many thoughts raced through his mind. Bryus Grum, who had been one of Ambrosius' most difficult but critical converts, now was suspiciously absent from the equation. This new Prominent now seemed more entangled with the enemy than he had first assumed. Was she a spy? Not a very subtle one, if so. But what if there is a spy in the valley and Megyn is there to keep Ambrosius off-balance enough not to uncover the truth. Sounded like Darkmere, devious but not too creative. So much for the peaceful respite. Vigilance was required again.

She watched his tension with pleasure for a moment before she turned and walked around the bend of the corridor with her servant.

Ambrosius waited for her to leave before retiring for the night. Her words haunted his dreams as he struggled to sleep. He woke up early the next morning to walk with Beltrow up to the Temple, which rested inside the Mountain King Statue's crown. They greeted each other over breakfast and began the arduous task before them.

Fir Beltrow made the pilgrimage up the long stairway inside the mountain. He rested at each of the small sitting areas along the way since leaving the City of Kingsfoot's upper level. Every stop provided a glorious view from its window openings, as the rising sun warmed the stairwell with light that refracted off the window's etched glass, shining prisms of color up and down the angled hallway. The rest area also provided a chance to read the writings on the back wall, which he did each time he sat. The sounds of his readings had a musical quality, giving the words a level of grace.

Ambrosius sat with him in the window seat and listened to the lyrics of the Rune Scrolls come alive. It had been a shame that he had never spent any time learning about this culture. It seemed so rich and peaceful. His life had been filled with such significant events of far away lands and politics that he never had taken the time to sit down and observe the culture of these people.

Periodically a few other Council Members would pass them by as they sat. Often a nod would suffice as they climbed the steps, trying not to interrupt Beltrow's readings. Others never even gave them a glance.

Climbing the stairs became less of a task and more of a spiritual journey through poignant thoughts being read out loud and time to quietly contemplate each verse while ascending to the next window seat. The journey took most of the day. Ambrosius felt he had gained years of insight from it and was thankful for the enlightenment.

They rested one last time at the final complex of rooms just below the Temple. Food and drink were set out as servants calmly and quietly organized the area for the long meeting ahead.

Beltrow and Ambrosius continued to ascend the last few steps to the opening of a large glass domed room, which overlooked the entire valley. The breathtaking view was even more than Ambrosius was expecting as he walked over to the far side of the Temple. He could see the half bowl-shaped valley open up to a gorge where the winding river ran from the lake below him toward the distant Lake Luthralum.

After gazing like a child out into the valley, Ambrosius looked up and out of the glass ceiling to see the pronounced chin and face of the Mountain King several hundred feet above them. The cold autumn air had left a strong beard of white from the night's mild storm. The snow and ice on his face somehow made him look older and tired. As odd as it might seem to Ambrosius, the ice below the King's eyes made him look disheartened.

He felt a slight chill from the sight of the cold outside. Lowering his eyes, he watched one of the servants light eight large oil vats near the walls of the Temple. A second servant took a long thin rod and opened a hinged glass tile in the roof to allow the smoke to escape.

The pillars around the Temple's exterior were carved to look like open scrolls hanging from the glass ceiling. They unraveled fluidly down onto the Temple floor, sometimes extending into the room a foot or two. The scrolls listed out each of the Rules of Order facing inward toward the center of the room. The details of the stone carvings were remarkable, the rips and folds of the paper where it had hit the floor and bounced into the room suggested it had been released from above.

Making up the walls of the Temple, the pillars also were the sides of the crown that sat in the Mountain Kings open faced hands. The King did not wear the crown or hold it tight against his body to protect it. He held the crown slightly out in front of him as though he was giving it to those who wished to have it. Even with the statue's grand size it never intimidated those who gazed upon it from below.

By the time all of the Council Members had eaten and rested from their trek up the long staircase, the evening light was starting to fade. Opening proceedings would take place for a few hours tonight to voice all of the concerns that needed to be discussed over the next week.

Beltrow called the meeting to order. The representatives of most cultures and territories gathered together and found a seat at the table in the center of the temple, which resided inside the Mountain King's crown. The Council Members were a variety of several Unday species as well as humans and a single Polenum. Ambrosius sat across from Beltrow in hopes of not implying his allegiance with him. The rest began to sit as he had expected. Those with similar beliefs tended to sit together.

The Grand Council convened at the large round granite table. Carved into its surface, twelve oil vats formed a circle, providing each member with equal lighting. The flames shined evenly upon the faces of various creatures sitting around the massive stone. Many had sent their servants to their quarters, after bowls of fruit and decorative crystals had been placed on the table for the debates.

Beltrow started the meeting off. "Welcome, I am your host, Fir Beltrow Ruddlehoth of Kingsfoot." The group nodded respectfully. "Before we begin these talks, I need to impress upon this council the fact that our temple is a neutral location and no one should feel at a disadvantage. We are all equal within the Mountain

Kings hands. I hope this will reduce the apprehension that had been troublesome in prior council meetings. I commend each one of you for having the courage to attend today. This single gathering is going to be a historical event that will shape the future of Terra Australis."

The conference had begun. Beltrow sat down, motioning for Ambrosius to take over.

Ambrosius stood up from his chair with the help of his black metal staff. His graying dark mahogany hair fell down to his royal blue cloak, flowing under its own capacity. His mannerisms were refined from years of public speaking and his words were clear and precise.

"It is of these times that I speak, when alliances and a man's word have been blurred by the dishonesty and treachery of those who would see us all suffer," Ambrosius stated. "Members of the Grand Council, Province and City Leaders of Terra Australis, I implore you to heed my warnings. Darkmere is prepared to strike and this time it is not merely to conquer, but to destroy."

It was the first Council Meeting since they had disbanded the sessions a year prior due to frustration and distrust infecting its members. Servants of Darkmere had contaminated the once powerful alliance of leaders with historical prejudices. This was their last chance at unification.

After a poignant but factual oration, Ambrosius paused only a few moments. "This is our final stand. I have presented the evidence before you." Pointing to the marked up maps spread out on the table, he continued. "These demonstrate the same movements of forces that my messengers sent you earlier. Darkmere has tightened his claws around your lands. Even more so since these were prepared, so we must act quickly. Further debate only acts to delay action. We must unite against Darkmere, scourge upon our world, before it is too late." His eyes thinned on his well-aged face as he watched his audience for reaction.

"Why should we follow you?" Megyn asked. "We don't need another one of your blood baths."

Ambrosius admitted, "Many have died under my command on the battlefield, both in victory and defeat. I have a full understanding of the horrific nature of war, but I still believe that a battle for freedom is a justified cause. Peaceful slavery is no way to live."

Volnic spit on the map in front of him before standing. Blothruds were known for their bad tempers and warrior mentalities. He embraced both of these attributes as critical qualities of Del'Unday leadership. Short thin black hairs were nearly invisible against his rich dark red skin, which covered his giant seven-foot tall muscular frame. His exposed upper body was lined with various bladed spikes that jutted out from his shoulder blades, spine, and elbows. Self-inflicted scars across his chest were worn as badges of honor for successful battles and conquests. Light from the oil vats reflected off his solid red eyes, generating a glowing appearance.

Making a point, he raised his head up and looked down over his long bony face at Ambrosius. Thin layers of skin stretched out over the ridged bone structure of his hairless wolf-like snout. "I have been offered expansion to my lands with full authority over them. You have offered me nothing, and yet you would put the Del'Unday Clan on your front lines to fight for your safety." His voice was powerful and successfully filled the others with unease.

Ambrosius replied calmly, "We offer to aid you in keeping your freedom. Darkmere only offers you false promises." Keeping his intense emotions intact was difficult. He wondered why he fought so hard to save these people from themselves. Thinking beyond the diplomats at the table and to the communities they represented, he answered his own question.

Gregory Marl of the Eastland Province shook his head and commented, "You Altereds make my stomach turn. You would allow the destruction of peaceful societies for your own greed." Eastland was a human province that had seen more battles with the Unday than any other. The resentment in Gregory ran deep to the roots in his family tree.

The Del'Unday Clan was one of three main clans of Altered Creatures and was known for their aggressive ways. Blothruds tended to be the most extreme species within the Del'Unday clan. Volnic erupted with fury over the comment and quickly knocked over a servant and a few Council Members before grabbing Gregory's body and lifting it into the air. "Peaceful? I should rip out your tongue for such lies," Volnic screamed at the man's face while veins in his neck and along the bony structure of his face pulsed with heated blood. "You humans have enslaved my people for centuries and now you have the audacity to say *peaceful*?"

Gregory's pain was deep into his ribs from Volnic's grasp, but his hatred of the Altereds was too great to give in. "Only after your species enslaved us for thousands of years. You and all your filthy vile type are an abomination of nature and don't deserve any better."

The thought of a Del'Unday being subservient to a lesser creature was repulsive. Volnic threw Gregory across the room toward one of the large windows that overlooked the valley. Ambrosius reacted and used his mental abilities to stop the man from crashing through the glass and falling to his death. Instead, he fell to the stone floor with only a slight bounce.

"Volnic, this is not a place for you to wage war," Ambrosius shouted.

"But it is for you. That's why you've brought us all together. To wage war against a growing power that threatens your own, not mine. I will not be a part of your next Maegoth massacre," Volnic replied.

The comment hit Ambrosius deep, for his history with Darkmere would provide Volnic with the evidence that the Blothrud needed to convict Ambrosius of such crimes. The city of Maegoth had been in the center of the Civil War, which destroyed the Dovenar Kingdom. The battle left many tens of thousands dead and felled the once great civilization. Blood from these deaths still stained Ambrosius' hands and dreams, even after thirty years.

Ambrosius was not, however, willing to give up, knowing all too well what was at stake. He began to walk around the table as he spoke to the entire committee. "Say what you will about my dealings with Darkmere, but I can tell you that his only interest in you is to carry out his own doings."

Megyn entered the conversation. She watched Gregory being escorted out of the chamber while his arms protected his ribs, broken by Volnic's grasp. "Darkmere has approached many of us and his words come with a cost. But so do yours." Her hooded cloak showed only her beautiful face and soft hands as they extended beyond its black emptiness. Light literally did not reflect from her cloak, as though it was a hole in space.

"Agreed, my price is high." Ambrosius gave in. He ran a finger along his short beard that shaped his face without hiding it.

"The alternative price of forever living under his rule is higher. He is not what you think he is."

"Are you?" she tossed back at him.

He stopped walking and placed his hands on the back of the chair previously used by Gregory Marl. "I will not debate you on my history." Glancing down, he noticed a decorative round metal object on the floor and knew instantly what it was. Looking back up at the faces in the Council, he continued, "We are here to make a choice for our world. Do we leave here as a united front to end the attacks that have caused our people to suffer and live in fear, or do we act like cowards, give into his threats and kneel at his feet?"

"Cowards?" Volnic roared.

Ambrosius was not going to let go of his control over this discussion. He leaned down and picked up the metal disk and leather necklace before making his way back to his chair. "Volnic, I have received information that one among us is working directly for Darkmere with the sole purpose of stopping us from uniting. You seem to be an advocate for him. Where do your alliances lie? Have you become one of his minions, here to spy on us?"

The Council erupted with protest while a few members were stunned at the accusation.

"How dare you accuse me of being a servant of a human," Volnic yelled as he pounded his massive fist on the thick granite table causing it to crack in many directions.

Ambrosius turned to look at the Guild Prominent of EverSpring. "Or perhaps you, Megyn. You speak kindly of Darkmere's barbaric ways."

Megyn's emotions exploded. "We all know your feelings about Alchemists and the Del'Unday and it is not surprising that you selected us to accuse of these baseless crimes against the Council. You have no proof of such an act and you're using this premise to scare us all into agreeing with you."

"But I have such evidence. There is a traitor *here*, among us," Ambrosius responded. He held up the round brass disk he had found on the floor. It held a spherical gem in the center that was foggy and peppered with red glowing dots. The disk that held the gem was fashioned with Darkmere's symbols. His was the ancient E'rudite powers of alteration that were used by the Notarians, a forbidden power in Terra Australis.

Ambrosius tossed the item out into the center of the table for all to see. "Someone at this meeting has been spreading Darkmere's poison into our thoughts. We now have the opportunity to capture his servant as well as turn the tide on his quest of power."

"Outrageous!" Fir Beltrow shouted from the opposite side of the table. Known to be a very thoughtful and wise individual with a spiritual pureness, he normally had an easing effect on others. Believing in listening more than talking, he rarely raised his voice. This time, however, he had. And he made it clear he was not pleased. "You have used our sacred temple as trap for Darkmere's servant? You have compromised our location that has been secret for thousands of years." Standing behind his chair with his arms crossed, he had been listening to the banter and was tired of all the accusations. He understood where this was going and he would not let it continue. Not while standing in the Mountain King's crown.

The room quieted down out of respect for the Fir.

No one wished to break the silence that Beltrow had created, and an uncomfortable air filled the Temple's chamber.

Darkness had settled in, allowing the flickering lights and shadows from within the glass-domed crown to be seen throughout the peaceful valley. Inside the stone-carved crown, the Council Members waited in the round chamber for the icy chill of silence to be shattered.

Ambrosius finally broke the hush in the room. "We cannot go back and prevent what has happened. We must concentrate on where we stand at this time and what we will do for our future."

"We wouldn't even be at this point if it weren't for Challion and the rest of the Northern Dovenar Provinces," commented Megyn.

Challion defended himself. "We took the only logical action we could see." The man's short white hair spiked up like a rooster's tail, and his albino skin changed to a light pink in his cheeks from the allegations. "Blind Faith is what got us to this point. Faith has always been the issue. It breeds misinformation and fear of the unknown."

"Faith is what gives us morals and strengthens us to persevere when all looks grim," Megyn fired back. "How can you stand inside this masterpiece and not see what wonders faith can create?"

"Such as death?" Challion asked. "Most battles are fought with a flag of faith overhead. It's a façade used by corrupt individuals on the weak-minded. This great structure we stand in was a dream of faith and desire but only became reality when faith was set aside and real work was performed. No mystical powers or divine entity created this temple. It took tremendous construction and artistic skills to create such a thing for weak-minded people that need faith to survive. No reverent King's hand carved out this mountain."

All went silent. Challion knew he had overstepped his boundaries, but couldn't retrieve the words.

Beltrow was stunned, as everyone waited for a reply.

Ambrosius lowered his face into one of his hands. He knew this most likely meant the end of the Council Meeting and perhaps the last chance to prevent the pending doom.

"Blasphemy!" shouted Beltrow as he slammed his fists on the table. The table rumbled from his attack. Then the floor began to tremble. And it continued.

Everyone stepped back from the table as vibrations increased.

Across the room, Ambrosius caught a glimpse of a shadowy figure of mist and ashes. Bloodstained eyes were covered by a veil of long black hair. No flesh, only bones and veins could be seen. Burnt debris mingled in the smoke that comprised her body. She was Irluk, the Death Witch. Ambrosius knew too well what her arrival meant. There would be a violent death and she was here for their souls.

A loud crack of thunder erupted from above the glass ceiling. Looking up, the members could see the glass cracking under the quake's stress as well as from rocks falling from above. Beyond the glass something wasn't right. A fissure opened several hundred feet above them, in the Mountain King's neckline. It spanned from his left shoulder, across the front, to the right side of the neck. The gap of the crack increased and decreased as the shaking continued.

It stopped. The room went silent. The world seemed to stand still and everyone struggled to absorb what was happening. Thousands of images and thoughts rushed through their minds in that fraction of a second before the crack under the King's neck opened up and flaming red magma erupted from it.

The explosive power lifted the statue's head up and then out. The stone face tilted forward as it fell off the cliff and rushed down toward the Council Members. Red glowing molten rock trailed behind the head as it roared down the cliff face. The members looked up at the ominous sight, only for a moment, before the statue's head crashed into and through the Temple.

Chapter 14
Kingsfoot Lake

Thorik's Log: October 16th of the 649th year.
We have reached Kingsfoot Lake. I now understand why this is our
spiritual center, for no other place on earth could look this beautiful
and feel this refreshing.

Ambrosius woke up mentally relaxed and refreshed, but the visions
he had were unsettling. His memories of the council meeting were
rushed and clues to the traitor were missed or blocked out of his
thoughts. He still couldn't identify the one who betrayed them.

Thorik had successfully led the party up the old trail atop the
rim and the rest of the way to Kingsfoot Lake without any more
issues. Friendship had quickly united Grewen and Thorik along the
way, and the Num had also continued to earn Draq's trust and respect
which was more than Ambrosius had hoped. But most importantly
Thorik's relationship with Emilen had started to evolve into
something more than just friendship and attraction.

Gluic had kept to herself like always but seemed to be
spending more and more time talking to unseen members of their
group and meditating with her collection of stones. "Yes, Rummon,
we're on our way. Be patient. No, Toodles, I am not impressed," she
said while gathering grass to make herself a new necklace.

Brimmelle and Wess sat by the shore looking to the distant
shores of the half-circle lake at the city and the remains of the
Mountain King statue against the flat mountainside.

The group was relieved to have nearly completed the trip to
Kingsfoot but disappointed to find the statue destroyed. They had
hoped Ambrosius was wrong. It was a depressing sight, as they
stared at the cooled lava rock that ran down the Mountain Kings
headless body. They realized the molten rock and ash had poisoned
the waters enough to kill many of the fish downstream. The mystery
of the dead fish in Farbank may have been solved, but the destruction
of the Mountain King temple and Grand Council still raised many
questions.

The cold morning air was still hanging on as mist could be seen rising from the lake water. The chilled air made it difficult for the midday sun to burn off the vapors. The Mountain King's feet could not be seen as it stood against the vertical cliff that walled one side of the lake. The mist was still too high.

The lake was circled with large statues of various animals, all on square stone bases. Most rested on the shoreline, while some sat just above the surface of the water in the lake. All of the stone or crystal statues faced the Mountain King in natural poses, as bears stood up on their back feet and deer looked to be leaping off their statue base. Each statue had an endless level of realism that reminded Ambrosius of what he had seen inside the city.

Avanda was testing her climbing skills on the nearest statue, twice the height of Grewen. Her energy was polar in nature. One minute she was an explosion of discussion and excitement, and the next minute she would be collapsed and sleeping even through the worst thunderstorm. This was a time of activity for her, as she aggressively climbed the statue.

Above and beyond the Mountain King statue, rose a mighty snow-covered peak that could be seen from Farbank. Glaciers hugged the White Summit's sides as smoke rose from its natural chimneys. Its clouds of steam had grown and weakened over the years. Recently the pillars of vapor had been thick and dark.

Along the sides of the valley, green spruce trees ran up the half bowl shaped foothills toward the steep barren peaks that lined them. No roads or paths could be viewed, nor any buildings, other than the stone city of Kingsfoot on the far side of the lake.

Opposite the cliff face, the valley worked its way downstream, the only water output of the lake, also known to the Nums as the King's River. It wound back and forth around various foothills as it made its way to the distant Lake Luthralum.

Contrary to the lingering devastation of the Mountain King's statue, the valley continued to give off a feeling of well being that everyone could sense.

Splash!

Brimmelle jumped up to his feet and ran over toward his mother, now several steps into Kingsfoot Lake. Searching for new stones, her dress was soaking from the knees down. "Mother, get out of the water," Brimmelle ordered with no results.

She spied something under the water that gave her great interest and bent her knees to lower her entire body under water for several seconds as she found what she was looking for. A large clear crystal the length of her palm. Cylindrical in shape and as thin as her finger, it was smooth along the sides and sharp on the ends. It was a treasure to her and she turned with her dripping hair and clothes to show it off to her son.

"Please get out of there before you freeze to death," he shouted to her.

She ignored him and hid the crystal away before she cupped her hands and scooped up water to wash her face. "Good water. Warm and cleansing. It's good for healing the body and soul."

Brimmelle had taken his boots off and began to wade into the water to escort her to shore. As he stepped into the water he noticed how warm and soothing it was. Natural springs of mineral water had kept the lake at a comfortable temperature even in the current climate.

Thorik stood up and reached down to help Emilen up from where they had been sitting. He gathered his updated maps and items together and carefully placed them into his wooden coffer, which was in turn tucked away into his mended backpack.

"Em, could you please hand me my carving knives?" Thorik requested as he gestured toward the ground where he had worked on Ambrosius' staff for many more hours.

Emilen quickly gathered the neatly placed tools and handed them to him before grabbing the staff. "We should get over to the city before nightfall, it will be warmer inside," she announced as she handed the staff to Ambrosius. "I had Thorik add a few extra runes on your staff to help you during your journeys." She gave a warm smile and eyed the newly added Portent Scroll Rune.

She worked her way down to the waterfront where Wess still sat, wading his sore feet in the water. Placing one hand on his shoulder to get his attention, she announced that the rest was over. It was time for the last hike of the day, to the city of Kingsfoot.

The touch rejuvenated Wess. She had not made any physical contact with him for days, and her unexpected gesture caused him to realize how much he missed it. Wess' sense of comfort ended when she removed her hand. Not being used to losing, especially to Thorik, he vowed to get her back. *But how?*

"Avanda? Time to go," Thorik called up to the top of the huge statue of a wild cat roaring with its face tilted upward toward the Mountain King. She had been climbing and playing on it for some time now.

Looking over the edge from the top of the statue, from within its mouth, she prepared for her climb down by tossing one leg over the edge. But, without warning, she was jerked back up and out of view from the rest of the party.

"Help! Help!" Avanda cried, flinging her arms up in the air from inside the cat's mouth.

Racing to the statue, they could hear her shrieks of pain. Sweat covered Brimmelle's forehead at the thought of her danger, as Wess loaded his bow and aimed it at the statue before realizing his misguided logic.

"It's eating me alive!" she yelled by the time Thorik had climbed up to the knee of the petrified animal. "Where is my handsome hero to save me?" She giggled and then broke out laughing at everyone's emotional response. "Am I doomed to be devoured by a cat?" she called down to the group as she dramatically flung her upper body over the edge of the open mouth.

Brimmelle patted his brow dry with a cloth as he addressed her sternly, "Not funny young one. Get down here right now."

Thorik stopped climbing and chuckled. "Grewen, can you help her down please?"

"At your service, little man," he replied. Stepping up on the square base he reached up for her.

She continued to laugh as she hopped into Grewen's enormous hand so he could gently set her down in front of the group.

Slightly ashamed, she apologized with a smile. "Sorry about that, Fir Brimmelle. I was just playing."

Brimmelle dismissed her weak attempt at an apology. "Help Gluic get her items together. It's time to go."

Ambrosius slowly lifted his stiff body to a standing position using his newly modified wooden staff. "I feel like I've been in a fight with a Chuttlebeast," he said to Grewen who stood by and watched.

"Looks like he won," Grewen replied. He watched Ambrosius closely to ensure he could walk without assistance. His hand was ready to catch him, should he fall.

To both of their surprise, Ambrosius was able to walk better than he had for weeks. He quietly thanked Gluic for her help under his breath as he and Grewen began to lead the group toward the city.

"You're welcome," Gluic casually said from a distance, as she walked out of the lake with several new stones for her collection.

It didn't take long for Avanda to help Gluic gather her items, as her son and Wess waited for her.

Brimmelle, Gluic, and Wess left the resting spot and quickly passed the slow moving Ambrosius and Grewen. While doing so, Avanda followed and complained about being tired and asked Grewen if he would carry her. He agreed as she beamed with excitement while she traveled effortlessly in his arm. Avanda showed no real signs of being tired, but it didn't bother Grewen. It was no hardship for him to carry her. Ironically, the slow swaying rhythm of Grewen's walk ended up causing her to drift off to sleep.

Shortly after heading out, Emilen had stopped Thorik to point out several unique landmarks in the valley, which he quickly marked onto his continually growing maps. The two Nums fell behind the others, but could easily catch up knowing that the group could only travel as fast as Ambrosius.

Ambrosius and his escorts continued working their way to Kingsfoot, walking in the wide field of shallow grass that covered the land between the water and the woods. The steam continued to rise from the lake, as the warm water mixed with the cooling air. They reached a bridge halfway around the lake, which spanned the lake's only outlet, feeding the King's River.

The bridge was carved with the same devotion that the local statues had been. It was in the shape of a scroll that had unraveled across the river's width. Looking to be frozen in time, as though a breeze pushed the center of the paper bridge up off the water. Railings were made from the sides of the scrolled paper as it reacted to the wind and folded upwards. The bridge was flawless, except for the railing on the far right side. It had been broken and the rough stone was exposed from the top of the handrail.

Draq scouted from high above, watching the party break up into three groups. Three Nums up front, followed by his comrades, and then the last two Nums who had stopped prior to the bridge. The dragon's only concern was for Ambrosius, and he stayed within a few air maneuvers of reaching him.

Calmness made Draq uneasy. He would much rather be engaged in a fight and know where his enemy was, than to sit idle and wait for them to come out of hiding.

The Nums crossed the stone bridge and worked their way around the lake toward the city.

Ambrosius and Grewen finally reached the bridge, but stopped abruptly when they came upon the bridge's damaged railing. Ambrosius felt the rock with his right hand. It stirred up painful memories within him, but the flashes of his past were too vague to understand why. The broken stone was sharp to the touch and shards of the railing laid scattered about on the bridge and on the ground below. He slowly worked his way off the bridge and around the railing. Following the outside of the bridge he found his way back underneath it, where the river met the lake.

Grewen watched Ambrosius set his wooden staff down and reach under the bridge and grab a long black metal rod. It was his old quarterstaff. The one he had used to defeat the Sathoids of Lutin. The staff he used when he held Wilken Pres at bay during the Trial of the Humorics. It had survived, apparently better than he had. The crystal top piece sat neatly in the thin black iron rod, flaring out just above and below his hand. The grip was of the finest leather and its sister handhold was down the staff farther, for use when two handed gripping was needed. A decorative counterbalance was placed toward the bottom that could also be used as a long handled mace-like weapon. It was a glorious piece he had commissioned for himself before the Battle of Maegoth.

Grinning with contentment, Ambrosius clutched it with both hands. It revived him and gave him a sense of strength and security that everything would be okay again. Back to normal. Back to how he had made it. He felt that everything in his life would soon be heading in the right direction.

"Darkmere." Ambrosius peered up at the headless King. "You made a mistake by not killing me when you had a chance." He then grasped his metal staff tight in his fists. But Ambrosius didn't dwell too long on it as he used his newly found staff to walk his way back to Grewen who was standing at the end of the bridge waiting for him.

"It is good to see you holding your quarterstaff again," Grewen commented, as they began to distance themselves from the bridge. "You look more like your old self now." A true statement it was. Ambrosius had always been seen with this staff. It was part of his identity and charisma. As he walked with Ambrosius, he couldn't help but notice his friend stood up straighter and with more confidence.

Allowing his hand to drag near his feet, Grewen ripped a handful of grass out of the field and tossed it into his mouth while continuing to the conversation. "Is that a good thing?" he half-joked, spilling some of the grass from his lips.

Chapter 15
Hot Spring Mineral Waters

Emilen and Thorik had stopped short of the bridge while the rest of the group had moved on. Emilen continued telling him about how the Mountain King once stood proud with his hands out in front of him and how they would decorate the animal statues around the lake during festivals. Even the ones on bases that required swimming out to.

She reminisced about her growing up near the lake. "On cool days like this my friends and I would swim over to that statue of the dolphin and play for hours. We had a rope tied onto the end of its nose allowing us to swing way out and drop into the lake. Afterward we would all sit on its tail to relax." She finished and smiled at the memories.

He looked at the statue of the dolphin as it arched forward toward the Mountain King; its tail half submerged as though it was pushing itself out of the water. The statue's square base sat a foot above the water's surface like a large mat ready to catch the dolphin should it fall backwards. It was the same base that all the statues had. Some animals stood on the bases, some were stepping off of them, while this one had the tail hanging off the side and dipping into the water.

Emilen's face brightened as she spied a rope that had been left around the dolphin's lower jaw of its open mouth. "Come on, we're going for a swim," she insisted as she started removing her gear.

"What? Now? We're already behind the rest of the party." Nervous, he darted his head around to see if anyone was looking their way. Ambrosius and Grewen could be seen beyond the bridge walking toward the city while the rest were much closer to the city's perimeter. "I'm not sure that this is the right time. We need to get to the city." Watching her out of the corner of his eye, he tried not to stare as she removed her clothes and reached back to tie her hair up tight.

She turned toward him with her hands still fiddling behind her hair knot and looked at him in a questioning way. "I would suggest you undress before getting into the water." Laughing, she left her scattered clothes on the shore and walked into the warm inviting water. Sighing, she relaxed a moment before turning around.

Thorik was very uncomfortable about the situation and tortured himself with guilt as he slowly undid his shirt. As much as he wanted to just rip off his clothes and jump right in, he was conflicted by his values. Reality was, he was most concerned about getting caught.

"It's not against the Rules of Order to swim." She watched him slowly undress. "Also, the Scrolls of Wisdom talk at length about the beauty of our bodies and not being ashamed of it."

"I'm not ashamed of my body." His hands shook nervously. "Aren't you concerned about being caught?"

She looked around at the open valley. The only other people were out of sight due to the light veil of mist rising from the lake. "No, I'm not. And even if they did, we aren't doing anything wrong. We're just swimming." She smiled. "Perhaps they'll join us."

The thought of the whole party frolicking in the buff did not appeal to Thorik at all, as he removed his shirt and folded it properly before setting it square on his backpack. Still conflicted, he started with his pants until he noticed Emilen watching him. He hesitated and looked around the lake one last time for a reason not to do this. *Perhaps the party was returning to see if we're okay.*

No such luck.

His heart raced, chest tightened and emotions upset his stomach. Terrified to follow her lead, he had the same level of desire to let go of his self-inflicted inhibitions and be free. Closing his eyes, he swallowed hard and chose the latter. Turning his back to her, he removed the rest of his clothes and neatly folded them before setting them between his shirt and backpack. He made a mad dash for the water, diving head first, and returning to the surface with a sigh of relief. It felt like nothing he had ever experienced before. Freedom, openness, total relaxation. He couldn't describe to himself how great it felt to conquer his anxieties and be free of his fears.

After floating in the warm water for a bit he wondered if he had ever truly relaxed before today. This was a new feeling for him and he soaked it up. The lake was more than warm water; there was something special about it. Something spiritually uplifting. He began to take notice of the pleasant tingling sensations around the souvenirs left by the thrashers.

"Enjoying yourself?" Emilen asked with a chuckle as he floated on his back with his arms straight out to his sides. He smiled without opening his eyes for his response. She laughed at his reaction to the warm water. "These waters will prevent your wounds from souring and will even heal our bodies if we stay long enough. We'll revive ourselves for a bit before we enter the city."

Grabbing his hand, she led him toward the statue. They parted from each other halfway there and began to swim the remaining distance due to the depth of the water. Emilen quickly out-swam Thorik and headed around the side of the dolphin's statue, out of sight. He slowly approached the dolphin and worked his way around, holding onto the base to help him move along. Thorik was not as agile in the water as he was on land and was a little out of breath.

As he rounded the second corner he saw her lying on the statue's giant half-submerged tail that had a slight cupping on both sides. This gave her some privacy without preventing her from seeing the Mountain King side of the valley. She folded her hands behind her head as she leaned back in the tail fin, far enough down so that her body was still mostly in the water. She was a vision of beauty with skin that looked of silk. Her soul-markings fell from her neck and down her chest before splitting under her breasts and then behind her back. The misty sunlight glistened on the clear water as it warmed her exposed neck and arms with each passing wave. She was so calm and natural in her present state that it also put Thorik at ease.

Working his way over, he lifted himself onto the giant tail next to her. He also put his hands behind his head as they both looked up at the headless Mountain King Statue, across the lake, towering over the valley. It was sad, actually, to look upon it in its current condition. The King looked so helpless and betrayed, and yet it couldn't break the overwhelming feeling of harmony of the valley and the lake.

Emilen sighed loudly as she gazed up at the statue and then rolled over and snuggled up to Thorik. "You know what's sad about this?" she asked, resting her head on his shoulder and her knee on his abdomen.

He couldn't think of anything at the moment. He had never felt so peaceful and relaxed in his entire life. So he stayed mute to listen to her answer.

"I never really appreciated seeing the King while I lived here. He had always been watching over us and I guess I assumed he always would be. But now it's gone and I never really treasured it." Her heartfelt tone helped set the mood.

Thorik listened while running his finger along her arm that rested on his chest. Starting from the soft skin of her shoulder and working his way down to her fingers, outlining each one at a time as he looked at the King. "How could you not see the magnificence in it? Even now it's overwhelming and is by far the most impressive monument to our faith that has ever existed. I don't understand."

She lowered her eyes and traced his chest with her fingers as the warm water and mist covered most of their bodies. "It's like seeing a cloud out your window every day of your life. Never a day without it. It becomes lost in the background and you just assume that it always is going to be there," she paused to look up into his eyes, "Haven't you ever had that happen?"

"Yes." He gave it some thought. "But the only thing I can compare it to is my parents. I suppose I had assumed that they would always be there for me. So I never truly cherished what I had while they were alive." Just talking about them saddened him as he inhaled deeply and pulled her in tight.

"I'm sorry to hear about your parents. You've never told me what happened to them." She then rested her head, this time on his chest.

Thorik swallowed at the thought. "It was an accident that nearly killed all three of us. My father had befriended a traveler. A man named Su'I Sorat, who told of great riches in the mountain's valleys. He had ancient maps of the valleys and canyons but no references on how to get there." Thorik noted, "That's how I became interested in mapping."

He continued, "My father was a skilled hunter, far better than I am. Mum had a keen eye for tracking. When I was little I would often join them on hunts, learning the trade. By the time I was of age, I was able to hold my own. Yet, my parents wouldn't allow me to travel with them when Sorat was there. Instead, I had to be watched like a hatchling by my Uncle Brimmelle in Granna Gluic's house."

"It was during one of their travels, we had a big storm in Farbank. Biggest one I had known. Thunder woke me from a nightmare of my parents in trouble. Somehow it seemed more than a dream, though. I don't know why, but it was so real to me. However, Brimmelle refused to believe me and escorted me back to bed. I couldn't help believing that my parents really were in danger. So, it wasn't long before I quietly snuck out from their house and ran home to grab my gear. I had spent so much time looking at Sorat's maps; I knew them by heart. I also knew that my father was planning to check out a valley across the King's River past Spirit's Peak. So off I went in the middle of the night to find them. Fortunately the rain began letting up enough that I could find my way. After crossing the river, I walked hard all through the night, the next day and into the next rainy night before I reached the valley." Thorik paused and looked into the missing face of the Mountain King.

Waiting for an answer, Emilen asked, "Did you find them?"

"Yes." He took a long deep breath. "But I was too late. There had been a rock and mud slide during the storm and had flooded the valley and littered it with mud and tree limbs."

Continuing his story, he added, "I saw some of their gear in the mud when I first arrived, so I began searching. The rain was against me as it began to pour hard on my efforts. Eventually I was able to find my mother unconscious. But during the removal of the rocks to free her, a wave of mud roared down the valley toward us causing the canyon wall to give way. I was swept away in a river of debris. Grabbing a still rooted tree, I clung to it as I reached for the safety of a nearby rock ledge. It was still too far for my weakened body to reach the mud-free canyon walls. I couldn't pull myself out. I just didn't have the strength. My parents had been killed and washed away and I feared that it would be the end of me as well."

Thorik straightened up and finished his memories. "That's when Brimmelle reached down and saved my life. He had figured out where I was going and followed me up the mountainside, and had just caught up with me. He was so angry, I'm not sure he will ever fully trust me again. He didn't talk to me for days as we recovered my parent's bodies and buried them nearby. He didn't even say goodbye to them as I set up stone markers so I knew where to visit. I think he was as angry with them as he was with me."

Thorik sighed and remembered his parent's faces. "I sure do miss them. What I wouldn't give to have one more day with them. Just one more." Tears of sadness and happiness of the thought ran down his cheeks.

"I'm sorry, I didn't mean to upset you." She starting to pull away to give him some space.

He didn't allow her to go far as his arm behind her stopped her from leaving. "No Em, its fine. I'm okay. It's just that this is the first time I've talked about it." His other hand started to gently touch her face as he stared into her gorgeous, big green-blue eyes. They were the same color as the lake and gave him the same calm feeling as the water. He continued to look deep into her eyes as he softly traced the lobe of one ear.

"We don't have to talk about it anymore if it upsets you." Knowing that after all they've been through lately, he was emotionally tired. So, she changed the subject. "I think you will like my parents. My father is a Fir, but is nothing like Brimmelle. And my mother is a lot like me." She smiled, hoping to get on a more pleasant conversation.

"*Your* parents?" Thorik squeaked out, wondering how they would feel about their daughter and him holding their naked bodies together less than a few hours walk from them. Within eyesight of the city itself.

She could see that he was anxious again and realized that it was time to leave. "It's okay Thorik, we can go. Thank you for talking with me. I feel like I haven't been able to do that with anyone for a long time." She started to roll away again.

Thorik realized how important this was for her and softly nudged her back to him. "Em, we can talk a *little* longer before we have to go." Not even his anxieties could shake him from this dream, as he held her tight in the water, resting on the tail of the dolphin, looking out at the Mountain King.

She smiled and cuddled up to him in the warm lake water as she talked about all the things she and her friends used to do around the lake while growing up. They continued to talk another half an hour before making the short swim back to land. They proceeded to dry off and get dressed before heading to the bridge.

Once at the bridge, Thorik noticed an area on the right side railing that was damaged and went to investigate. He looked at the debris and tried to determine what could have caused the destruction of the railing. Peering over the edge he looked down and saw Ambrosius' wooden staff with antler trim, the one that Thorik had worked so hard on to make sure it supported all of his needs. But obviously it didn't and it was not needed anymore as it lay tossed against the rocks like any other branch that had been washed up on shore.

Emilen looked to see what was so intriguing and quickly realized what it was. She placed a hand on his shoulder and comforted him. They left the stick lay and moved on toward the city. It didn't matter anymore for this journey was coming to an end anyway.

She placed her hand in his and held it firmly to comfort him. "We should keep moving. Now that our group has reached the city, my family will be out looking for me." Trying to distract him from the thoughts of the staff, she held his hand and led him off the bridge.

Neither her words, nor the walk, relieved his disappointment.

High overhead, Draq arched his long scaled neck as he made a quick turn to the left while flying over the forest beyond the lake. He had been scouting for several hours in search of signs of danger but found the valley to be peaceful. His trained eyes worked their way back and forth to ensure he had not missed anything before he turned to head back.

Once he made this decision he straightened out his body and leaned his head slightly down, increasing his speed. His wings flapped hard several times before tucking them in back to stabilize his flight as he shot like an arrow across the valley. The angle of his descent had him heading near the bridge at the mouth of the river. He was uncannily fast and could hardly be seen by an onlooker, if there happened to be one.

From the air, it would have looked as though Draq was to crash into the river just before the bridge as he rapidly approached it. With ever increasing speed, he pulled up just far enough to rocket his way under the bridge and out over the lake where he glided mere inches from the calm water, maintaining his great pace.

Craning his neck to improve his streamline shape, he lowered himself into the water. The massive speed and his aerodynamic features allowed a smooth entry into the water with nothing more than a ripple.

Flying underwater was slower than in the air, but Draq was just as graceful. Turning and gliding like a giant manta, his only limitation was how long he could hold his breath while searching for food. Fortunately he didn't have to test his endurance as he spotted a three-foot long toothfish. It darted quickly to the side as Draq flew by him on his first pass. The chase was on.

Diving down after the fish, Draq performed an underwater ballet of twists and turns, racing around ancient columns and arches. Frightening away schools of smaller fish during his pursuit, he turned quickly to avoid parts of the Mountain King Statue's face, as it rested on the lake's bottom. It was at that point where he captured his prey and bolted to the surface for air.

Thrusting his body out of the lake with his meal in his strong jaws, his wings quickly shed their water. Spreading his wings back out to full length, he flew up toward the headless Mountain King, finally landing and eating his dinner on the empty neck of the statue. He was able to view the entire valley from this vantage point and watched Ambrosius pass the boat docks near the city.

Gluic was up front by this point along with her son and Wess as they approached the city's outer barrier. Brimmelle stopped at the series of perimeter statues in amazement as he saw his beloved Runestone Scrolls spelled out in massive stones. Every passage and every verse were exactly as he remembered seeing them every morning and evening during his readings to his village. His blood raced as he slowly approached and touched them, tracing the etched letters with his finger.

The scrolls had been carved in granite to appear to be unraveling from an invisible holder eight feet in the air. Each scroll was cascaded down to the ground and rested on a large hexagonal granite slab with a rune symbol in its center. These stone carvings had a detail that became more obvious as Brimmelle inspected it closer. Imperfections in the parchments had been added, as well as eloquent waves in their journey to the ground. Each scroll was carved in unique ways as they rested back to back, one facing out to the party as they approached and another scroll facing in toward the city. Between each set of scrolls was an opening to allow entrance onto the city's property.

Wess moved between the scroll pages and emerged inside the perimeter where scattered animal statues stood on a grid of hexagonal granite slabs, as if protecting the city. Past them lay a wide stairway leading up to three levels of garden area. Several chunks of dried magma had landed in the open gardens from the destruction of the King's head. These black rocks were jagged and smelled of sulfur causing the entire area to smell of rotten eggs. "Is this place safe?" Wess asked.

Gluic walked past Wess and noted, "Don't worry; there's nothing to fear until nightfall. Build a campfire near the entrance of the city." She pointed to the top tier.

Wess agreed before thinking about what she had said in such a dry tone. "What is there to fear *after* nightfall? And where is everyone?" he responded with more of a nervous touch in his voice than he had wanted. But she did not answer as she walked up the stairway.

Ambrosius finally arrived at the outer row of scrolls with Grewen as they met Brimmelle reading his favorite verses from the courtyard side. Brimmelle's glee at the monuments to his faith came through his loud reading of the words, which awoke Avanda from her nap.

"Grewen, will you let me down?" She wanted to investigate the new area on her own.

Grewen set her down and she stood weak legged, rubbing her eyes. Once her vision cleared, she stood up straight before rushing off to see everything she could with the remaining light of the day.

"Stay close to Brimmelle," Grewen called out to her, as he attempted to hand off responsibility to Brimmelle before leaving. Brimmelle nodded his head to the comment but never looked up nor stopped his readings.

Following Ambrosius, Grewen turned sideways to work his way between the large stone scrolls, into the courtyard and then up to Wess' roaring fire at the top of the stairs near the entrance of the city.

The city looked so empty compared to the last time Ambrosius had visited. "The survivors must have abandoned the city," he mentioned as he looked around for traces of them. Everything looked in order as though they left without any provisions. "Although there doesn't seem to be enough damage to warrant that."

Wess passed Ambrosius and Grewen on his way down the stairway as he went for more firewood. "Where is everyone?" he asked in passing. He only received a shaking of the head from Ambrosius implying he didn't know.

Upon reaching the top tier, Ambrosius and Grewen rested on a bench as they watched the last two Nums work their way around the lake toward them. "Keep your eyes open my friend, we may not all be what we appear to be," Ambrosius quietly commented to Grewen.

"It would seem unlikely these little ones are anything but what they seem. Are you sure you aren't just becoming paranoid after this last incident?" Grewen calmly replied as he reached over to grab a flaming stick out of the fire and began using it scratch between his toes.

"I'm not sure who I can trust anymore."

"You must trust those that have earned it," Grewen added as he wrinkled his face with pleasure from the toe cleaning.

"I'm not sure I can do that."

"What's your other option? Live on your own, always fearing that everyone will back-stab you? That's no life. That's self-inflicted torture," he concluded as he started on his other foot.

They quieted down as Wess returned. "Where's Gluic?" Wess asked the two outsiders.

Grewen and Ambrosius looked at each other in question before looking about the open gardens. They soon surmised that she must have entered the city. The evening light was fading and dark would set in soon, so Grewen removed the flaming stick from between his toes, "Grab a torch, it looks like we're heading in."

Wess still had a lot of distrust for the two, but he did as he was told and followed the other two into the city in an effort to find Gluic.

Chapter 16
Abandoned City of Kingsfoot

Astonished by the city's design, Thorik walked toward the perimeter scrolls. Brimmelle was now resting on one knee reading the runes in the center of one of the many granite tiles with his eyes and hands as the light diminished.

Avanda came running up to them and grabbed Thorik's hand. "You have to see this place. It is so different from Farbank." She pulled him past the scrolls and into the courtyard. "Look at all of these animal statues. I counted over thirty that I knew what they were."

Thorik brushed his hands along the stone animal statues as he accompanied Avanda and Emilen to the inside. "This is amazing, Em. What a wonderful place to grow up." Looking around and seeing most everything in perfect shape, he added, "Why was it ever abandoned?"

Panic struck her face as she looked about for signs of life. She ran across the stone courtyard and up the stairs. Not exactly understanding her actions, Thorik and Avanda followed as she ran past the campfire and into the city yelling various people's names.

Thorik yelled up to her while in pursuit, "I'm sure your family is fine. They must have just left because of the damage or went someplace safer."

It was all he and Avanda could do to keep up with her as she darted from one winding corridor to another in the limited light still emanating from the windows. She rushed into several rooms only to find them empty of life. By the time Thorik and his young student had entered behind her, she was already pushing past them on the way back out. This continued until Thorik decided to wait outside in the hall for her to return from each room. This approach worked much better until she didn't return from one of the rooms.

With very little light left in the hall Thorik and Avanda peered into the room expecting to see her resting with exhaustion, but instead they found a storage room with an open door on the far side. He quickly ran over to it and looked both ways down the new pitch-black hallway without seeing or hearing any sign of her. "Em?" he called down one way and then the other without any response. "Now what?" he asked, knowing they were lost at this point regardless of direction. The last bit of light had diminished from the storage room and left Thorik and Avanda lost in the dark.

Feeling her way about the room, Avanda opened a cabinet engraved with decorative designs. Inside she felt cloths, a chalice, ornamental objects, and other ceremonial items. She stopped at a familiar object. "Thorik, I think I found a full oil flask."

"Excellent," he replied. He had found a lantern.

He located his flint in his backpack and filled the lantern with oil before lighting it. Their eyes adjusted and started to focus on the room. It had turned green from the oil's flame.

Humming could be heard, soft at first, then growing in strength. It was familiar and vibrated from every direction. Not from behind the walls, but from the walls themselves.

The walls and ceiling quickly pulsed to life as they saw bees covering every inch of them.

Avanda stood still, watching in amazement.

Chills ran down Thorik's spine. He grabbed Avanda's free hand and pulled her out the nearest door, into the corridor where Emilen had exited. He slammed the door behind them and rested his back against it while catching his breath. Struggling to understand why they hadn't seen or heard any bees until that moment, he fought off Avanda's pleas of curiosity to investigate it.

Instead, he selected a direction and started down its path with the lantern out in front to show the way. Avanda ran her fingers along the carvings of plant life on the walls as they continued. She could almost see the plants move from her touch. It seemed so life-like.

After a sharp turn in the corridor, the plant life became covered with carved cobwebs. Thorik strived to walk quickly in an attempt to catch up to Em. Although in reality, he was slowing down from an uncomfortable feeling about the place. The corridor was very wide at this point as they walked along the right wall. The cobwebs had turned to stone spider webs and were now covering all surfaces. Out of the corner of his eye he saw the webs shake and stir. He became tense and nervous.

"Avanda, stop touching the wall," he instructed.

"I'm not. It's moving on its own," she replied with renewed interest in it.

"Just stand on the other side of me, so you're not accidentally brushing up against it."

"Why? Isn't it amazing? The stone is actually moving!"

"Yes, amazing. I'm sure it's just a trick of our eyes. We are tired and not used to the lantern's light yet. Now please walk on the other side of me," he instructed.

"I'm not tired," she said. "It's really moving. They're alive, watch," she announced as she stopped and plucked a few spider webs with her fingers. It vibrated for a moment before subsiding.

"It's stone, Avanda. Stone carvings don't sway or move. It's our eyes or something. Just because you can't explain it, doesn't mean that the stone has come alive."

Disappointed in the response, she challenged him. "If it's just stone, than you wouldn't be scared to touch one of the carved spiders, would you?"

"Avanda, we don't have time for this."

She smiled in the green light, giving her an eerie look. "Hold your finger up against a stone spider and prove me wrong. Then I'll drop it, forever."

Thorik sighed. "Avanda, please. We need to find Emilen."

"The Runestone of Bravery says…"

"All right, that's enough. I get that plenty of reminders from Brimmelle. Pick a spider so we can get this over with."

Her lantern lifted toward the stone wall that displayed layers of webs and periodic palm sized spiders in the center. He moved closer to the one she pointed at. It was about eye level.

He reached out to touch it. But before he did he retracted his hand and lowered it to the web below. He wanted to prove to himself that this was still a carving before touching the spider itself. Thumping a web caused it to move. "It must be some kind of twine made to look like stone." He plucked the web a few times with his fingers. Each time, getting a bit closer to the center of the web, near the spider. "This is a waste of time," he muttered, stepping back from the wall.

He looked over at Avanda. She was smiling at his inability to prove her wrong.

"Fine, here is your answer." He took the lantern from her so he could get better lighting on the wall image. He stepped toward the wall and placed his first two fingers squarely on the spider carving. He could make out the tiny hairs on the spider's back. The detail was amazing. He stood there relieved with his fingers still pressed against the stone wall for a few more moments. He had conquered his fears and was now ready to move on. If felt good. It felt fulfilling. It felt like the spider just moved out from under his fingers and was now climbing on his hand. Looking down, his eyes agreed.

Avanda screamed as the spider ran up his hand and under his sleeve.

Thorik's left arm was occupied with a lantern, preventing him from swiping at it. Instead, he tried to shake it off. But it was too late and it was already crawling up his sleeve. Startled, he tossed the lantern to Avanda, while removing his backpack and shirt. He felt a bite on his upper arm as he screamed from the pain. He ripped off the rest of his shirt as the spider ran onto his back where it couldn't be reached. Thorik panicked and slammed his back against the wall to squish it. He felt the creature crack behind him and looked down to see it fall to the floor.

Avanda quickly stomped on it. She then attempted to kick it off to the side only to find that it was only a carving in the floor.

Success was short lived as Thorik realized that his back was now stuck to the wall carvings of webs.

Looking around for support to peel himself off, he noticed several more hand-sized spiders moving toward him from all directions on the wall. He pulled his chest forward, the granite webs stretching as they held onto his shoulder blades.

Avanda began to pull his arms as he pulled his body forward. Small pieces of his skin ripped off and dangled from the wall carvings. Excruciating pain from ripping of flesh increased as one of the spiders jumped onto the back of his neck while another leaped onto his head. Fear increased and adrenaline rushed though his body, giving him the will power to rip himself free of the granite illustration. Portions of stone web clung to his back while the wall had claimed segments of his skin. It was an even swap that Thorik had no interest in checking at this time as he stumbled away from the webs.

Avanda could see two more spiders on his back and grabbed the only weapon available, Thorik's backpack. She swung the pack as hard as she could to crush or at least knock off the spiders. She failed, however, to warn Thorik of the upcoming attack.

"Awww!" Thorik shouted as she knocked him down to his knees.

"It's okay," Avanda notified him. "I got one off. Just one more on your back to go."

Thorik rolled out of the way of Avanda's overhead crushing blow with the pack. It smashed against the floor with the sounds of his items breaking.

"Avanda, stop! Trust me, I've got this," he told her as she prepared for another strike.

Reaching up, he grabbed the spider that was now biting the back of his neck and threw it off into the distance. The other burrowing in his hair was more difficult. It clung to his hair as he tried to remove it. He was only able to lift it an inch from his head and he knew that his time was limited. The lantern displayed light on several more spiders making their way toward him.

He pulled his hunting knife out of his belt holder with one hand as he continued to lift the spider from his head. With one quick swipe he cut just below the spider, removing its legs and a large section of his hair. The spider was now extracted and was tossed down the hall.

Thorik grabbed Avanda's hand and the lantern before running down the open corridor as quickly as they could. Noticing a set of closed doors, he crashed through them and quickly turned to shut them once Avanda was in as well. Closing the doors tightly he looked at the edges of the door and the floor beneath it to see if any were coming through. It looked as though they had outrun them.

He breathed deeply as he rested his hands on his knees. His back was bloody from the webs as well as the spider bites on his arm and neck. The scratches and bruises from his backpack didn't help any either. He could feel drippings of blood running down his skin and grabbed a cloth out of his worn backpack to clean some of it off before returning his shirt.

The pack was ripped and stained from broken canisters and items. His coffer was intact, but it had crushed many of the other items. Disappointed, he looked over at Avanda's innocent face.

She brushed herself off and softly smiled. "I told you they were alive."

Putting on his torn shirt, he noticed movement from within the new room. Stone murals of a tropical forest bordered the grand sized chamber and trees created a canopy overhead. Although the light from the lantern wasn't particularly bright, its beam carried for quite a distance, allowing Thorik to see a door on the far side of the room.

Turning to the nearest wall and raising his light higher, he looked out past the wall's foreground bushes for some sign of life. He placed a hand on a carving of a bush in front of him in an attempt to look past it. Remarkably it worked and he could see the leaves move when he pushed it to the side. Thorik wondered if he was hallucinating or whether the stone actually was behaving in this very unstone-like manner.

A slight movement under the next shrub caused Thorik to go on the defensive. "Back up, something is out there."

"Out where?" she replied, confused at what was happening. "You mean inside the wall?"

He nodded.

Backing away, she noticed a sound, and then an object moving toward her. She fell onto her backside, away from the wall, as a creature jumped from its coverage and entered into the room at her feet. A clear crystal, long-eared hare hopped past Avanda quickly before disappearing into the adjacent wall.

"I'll take a few crystal hares over granite spiders any day," he chuckled before hearing a large catlike growl from the wall he had just investigated. They froze. His heart missed a beat. *Not again, what is this place?*" he thought as he gently helped Avanda to her feet.

Keeping an eye on the wall illustration, he could hear the breathing of a large animal following their slow movement into the room. His experience with large cats in the wild had been enough to know to keep his distance, and also not to act like prey by running. It didn't help with fresh blood on his back. He grabbed one of the broken jars from his pack and threw it in the direction of the sound, attempting to scare it off. The glass jar traveled deep into the flat carving of the forest and shattered against a tree near the hidden creature. It had no effect. Thorik's depth perception struggled as he tried to focus on various distances within a carving that was no more than a finger's width deep.

Placing his pack on his back, he grabbed a dagger. Taking Avanda's hand in his free hand, he continued working his way out into the center of the room, toward the far door. The cat moved along the wall with him, hidden from their sight.

The hunt lasted until the cat had an opportunity. It leapt out of the wall at Thorik, pushing the Num to the ground and knocking the dagger from his grip. Landing past Thorik's fallen body, the black marble panther circled quickly before jumping onto the Num. Fleeing was unlikely, the cat easily outweighed him. Stretching and grasping a sharp piece of glass, which had fallen out of his pack, Thorik stabbed the sharp edge toward the cat's stone leg. Unfortunately, the cat grabbed the Num's arm in his mouth, preventing the strike.

Avanda attacked from behind, swinging the lantern at the panther's head. It hit, breaking the lantern and removing all light from the room. Everything went quiet. She had only one way to know if she had succeeded in frightening the cat. She reached out with her hand into the darkness to see if anything was still on Thorik. The silence added to her hesitation as she reached out her arm closer to where she thought they had been.

Her hand landed upon Thorik's arm and then chest, before she felt the stone claw of the panther still resting on him. She knew there was no escape. Avanda screamed.

Chapter 17
Speak of the Dead

A large rib cage arched upward over Grewen's head. Each bone acted as a column in the corridor, as though Ambrosius, Grewen, and Wess were walking inside the body of a giant creature. Several doorways exited the corridor along both sides, blending in to keep the carved atmosphere.

The ribs met in the center, high overhead, and a muscular structure could be seen on the walls between them. Grewen stood up straight as he walked down the hall and ran his fingers on the textured ceiling overhead. He held up his torch to see all of the imperfections that had been purposely carved in great detail. "Amazing. The last time I've seen this level of craftsmanship was on the Tower of Lu'Tythis," Grewen commented as he noticed a small symbol carved into the end of one of the ribs. It was a glyph of some type that he didn't recognize, perhaps an artistic signature. Three overlapping circles, each with a single rune within it.

Ambrosius had walked ahead while Grewen conducted his investigation and Wess cautiously peered into several rooms on the sides of the hallway.

"Grrrrrrr." The sound echoed in the long corridor.

Wess felt an overwhelming desire to hide near the giant. Trust or not, the Ov'Unday was more comforting than the beast making the odd growling and rumbling. Bow and arrow ready, he had backed up against Grewen and tossed his torch before him, hoping that this new unknown would leave.

"Grrrrrr," the gurgling of the growl was more apparent this time.

"Show yourself." Wess spoke out into the darkness.

Grewen reached down with his free hand patted his stomach. "Oh, sorry about that," the giant commented about his stomach rumblings. "I'm so hungry I'd consider eating meat." Glancing down at Wess he compounded the Num's uneasiness. Grewen chuckled at Wess' reaction to his joke until he heard Ambrosius asking for him.

Ambrosius was standing at the end of the hall in a large doorway that held two thick wooden doors, opened into the corridor. Beyond the entrance was a room, round in shape with a domed ceiling. In the center it hosted a large granite table with many chairs around it.

"It's the Temple," Ambrosius said.

Leaning down to get through the doorway, Grewen stood back up to observe what Ambrosius was describing. "It appears to be in better shape than you let on," he jested.

Wess walked in behind them much more nervous than the others. "I don't think we should be in here. It smells of death." He still didn't fully trust either one of them, but at this point he was more concerned about the odd feelings he was getting from the carved-out rooms.

Ambrosius walked farther into the room and looked about. "Gluic?" he asked as he spotted her sitting on the floor beyond the table, placing stones in a large circle around her, with various patterns on the inside.

She looked up only for a moment as she continued to work. "Oh good, you're here. We're almost ready."

Ambrosius shook his head with a smile before his attention returned to the room. He touched the back of the chair that he remembered standing at when the Mountain King's head came crashing down through the glass ceiling. "It is very similar, but it is not the same. These statues of Polenum warriors now stand where the windows were, and the ceiling is stone instead of glass."

Grewen reached up to touch the carved ceiling and knocked his knuckles on it several times. "Sounds like stone." He walked over to sit on the large granite table to rest. "So, why the duplication of rooms?"

"It's a Mori Site," Wess said plainly. The other two looked at him and then each other in question before Wess continued. "A Mori Site is built for the elders that can no longer make it up to the spiritual sites on top of the valley walls. It allows them a chance to atone for disrespecting the Rules of Order. We have one in Farbank. I assumed everyone had them."

Wess realized that he had captured both of their attentions. He was not going to lose this opportunity to be in control for a while. Rolling up his sleeves and placing his hands behind his head, he sat down and relaxed in a chair. It was at this point that he began to enlighten them about his culture and himself as well.

This continued for a short time before two short figures approached the doorway.

Thorik limped into the Mori Site and saw Wess sitting at the table telling Grewen a clever little tale about his past, while Gluic talked to one of the many statues in the room. Ambrosius had his back to the group as he investigated one of the stone warriors. Avanda followed Thorik; carrying the lantern along with some the items that had fallen out of Thorik's ripped backpack.

Thorik's clothes were bloodstained and his backpack was torn and dragging behind him. Wess and Grewen stared in question as he sat, falling into a chair near Wess.

"Nice hair, Dain," Wess said of Thorik's self-inflicted haircut. The last time Wess had seen Thorik he was talking to Emilen prior to the bridge. Since then, the rest of the party hadn't had any conflicts, so this appearance of a dishelved and bleeding Thorik was unexpected. He grinned as he assumed that Emilen had rebuffed Thorik's advances with hostility. "Where's Emilen?"

"I don't know. But I'm fine, thanks for asking," Thorik replied to Wess before addressing the rest of the group. Ambrosius and Gluic were busy and didn't pay him any attention. "We followed her into the city and then she lost us. I was hoping she was with you. She knows her way around the city, but we should still go look for her. I don't like the idea of her being alone."

Grewen's bald eyebrows crunched in the middle of his face. "What did you run into, or should I ask what ran into you?"

Wess was suddenly reminded of Gluic's warning that they had nothing to fear until after dark. It was definitely after dark and Thorik's wounds instantly alerted his senses. His face gave a nervous twitch as he waited for Thorik's response. It most likely would be something hideous.

Thorik motioned his head to Avanda.

She walked over and set the damaged lantern on the table.

Thorik pointed to the bent object. "This is the cause of my pain."

Wess chuckled. "Dain, you may want to practice fighting torches before you move on to lanterns."

Grewen's eyebrows relaxed at his answer. "The lantern attacked you?"

"In a way, it did. Would you like me to demonstrate?"

Grewen looked over at Wess who was confused at Thorik's answer and still nervous about what really could be out in the dark. "Wess, you better stand behind me before he releases that lamp, it looks of foul temper."

Wess began to move out of his chair before realizing that Grewen was playing with him. Irritated that he was on the wrong side of the joke, he sat back down and folded his arms across his chest. "Okay, Dain, release your lantern of terror."

Gluic interrupted, as normal, on a completely different subject. "Ambrosius, we're finished. They are here now and prepared to talk to you."

"Who wants to speak to me?" Ambrosius asked.

"Those who died in the temple. They are here among us," she continued as she reached out into the air as to hush a voice that only she could hear. "They are speaking of the killer of the Council."

The rest of the party looked about for something to happen, but it didn't.

Ambrosius looked at her strongly. "Thank you Gluic, this is what I came for. Ask them who destroyed the temple and killed the Council Members."

"They don't wish to talk to me. Ask them yourself." Gluic was apparently having a conversation with someone else and didn't appreciate being interrupted. "He'll find it and bring it to you. Be patient." She continued her conversation with her unseen friend as she walked out the doorway into the large ribbed corridor.

Ambrosius looked around for something to speak to. He finally walked up to the statue that Gluic had spent time with and asked, "Who did this to you? I need to know to prevent others from your same fate."

There was no response.

Frustrated, Ambrosius called out to the other statues, "If you wish to speak, now is the time." No response. "Who did this to you? Come alive and talk or we shall leave here with no direction to take justice."

"Are you sure you want them to come alive?" Thorik asked.

All attention turned to Thorik as he opened a small glass door on Avanda's lantern.

Ambrosius stepped over to the table and braced himself against it. "Thorik, I need to know who did this. If you have some way to help, you need to do so."

Thorik lit the oil wick in the semi-functional lantern and sickly green dancing light painted the room. The green light kissed the decorative walls and statues providing them with a birth of life and freedom to move about.

One of the statues began to move. First its eyes and then its fingers and mouth. Wess gasped and jumped up from his seat. Intrigued, Grewen scanned the room to see all of the activity, while Ambrosius stepped back from the animated statue.

All of the statues had to come to life and moved inward toward the group. Wess took a defensive stance with his back to the center of the room. Thorik ushered Avanda under the table for safety.

"Why has the slayer of the Council returned?" the statue in front of Ambrosius asked.

Ambrosius corrected their statement. "He has not. However, I have returned to discover who your assassin is, so I may vindicate your deaths."

Another statue repeated the question. "Why has the killer of the Council returned to Kingsfoot?"

All of the statues now had their weapons and shields forward and were ready to start fighting. They independently moved inward from the outside walls, each restating the phrase at random times with slight variations.

"No, you have it wrong," Ambrosius announced. "I didn't kill you; I'm a victim of this as well." He firmly stated to the statue in front of him, whose speed was increasing as his spear rose toward Ambrosius' head.

Eight statues surrounded the group, each with weapons in hand and steps away from attacking the travelers. All were chanting the same accusation over and over again.

Ambrosius stood firm and shouted, "Stop! You have made a mistake." Each of his words came out strong and clear. Controlling his temper was becoming strenuous. Thorik could see the side of the man's face become rigid and menacing. "I command you to stop!" Ambrosius demanded.

It was too late. Wess picked up a thick wooden chair and crashed it into the statue closest to him. Wooden splinters and debris showered the area, while the force of the impact knocked the statue over. It landed hard and shattered into pieces across the floor.

One of the statues swung at Thorik. The Num ducked and rolled to the far wall to escape the blow. By the time he got back up, he could see Wess on the back of one of the statues while Grewen calmly held two of them at bay with his huge hands.

Oblivious to Wess' and Thorik's challenges, Ambrosius easily held off several statues with his own powers as he tried to understand what was happening.

A statue grabbed Wess off the back of another stone warrior. Tossing him to the ground, it prepared to stomp its granite foot onto the Num's head.

Avanda jumped out from under the table, reached for the lantern, and then blew out the flame, returning the yellow light from the torches. All unnatural life had ceased once the wick had been extinguished and the green light had faded. Much like when the large cat in the other room had attacked Thorik.

Wess squeezed his face out from under the statues boot. A second later and he may not have had a face at all. Rolling away, he pushed himself up onto one knee to catch his breath as he pointed at Ambrosius. "I knew it!" Wess claimed as he worked both legs under him and stretched his back. "You killed all those people. You destroyed the Mountain King Statue. You *are* behind this."

Ambrosius sat down in disbelief. "Why would they blame me?"

"Because it *was* you," Wess said.

Thorik stepped in. "He's not the kind of person who would kill others for power. He's just not like that."

"Oh, you would be surprised. He's clever, but Brimmelle and I were right all along about him."

"Wess, why would he ask us to help him come all the way here if he had killed them?"

Wess thought quickly and replied, "Because he came back for something. Something he didn't have time to get last time but now with everyone out of the way he can find it."

"Like what? What have you seen him take? You've been with him the entire time."

Wess was a little puzzled by the questions but it didn't stop him. "Perhaps he hasn't found it yet." He gave a slight pause before he smiled and continued. "Or maybe he has already acquired what he came back for."

Wess walked over and grabbed Ambrosius' metal staff, as it leaned against the table. "Thorik, where's the walking stick you made for him? I don't recall him having this quarterstaff while he was in Farbank."

It was a sensitive subject for Thorik, but he didn't let that change his mind. "Finding his staff doesn't make him a murderer. You have to trust me, he didn't do this."

"How do you know for sure? Tell me, what should we believe? His words or the words of those he has killed? The ghosts of his victims have pointed to him," Wess added.

Ambrosius sat and scratched his beard while ignoring Wess, trying to figure out why the spirits of the Grand Council were accusing him of such crimes. "Frustrating," he acknowledged. "This hasn't helped us discover any clues as to who is working with Darkmere. Without this lead, we will have to go directly after Darkmere himself," he mumbled.

Thorik responded to Wess' comments, "We don't even know what those things were. Were they indeed spirits? Or were they controlled by someone else? There are a lot of questions to be answered before accusations can be made. Besides, don't you think Ambrosius would know if he did this or not?"

Wess, dismissing Thorik's logic, was quick on the offensive again, "Lets say for a moment that he's not lying to us. Maybe he's still missing some of his memory from when he got hurt and ended up in that crater. He could be telling us the truth that he doesn't remember, and yet still have killed them." He turned and looked directly at Thorik. "Remember when Trumette fell and knocked his head against the village well? He lost two days of memory and swore he hadn't been in Sammal's tree house, didn't he?"

Thorik argued the point, "Trumette loses two days of memory every time his wife makes him take a bath. Ambrosius' memories were restored by Gluic. He recalls exactly what happened."

"Maybe Wess is correct. Perhaps I am missing some facts," Ambrosius spoke up. "I keep having dreams of the destruction and what happened afterward but I lose the specifics by the time I wake. Gluic helped regain some of most of my memories, but not all of them."

"There, I knew it," Wess proudly acclaimed as he pointed the black iron staff in judgment toward Ambrosius.

Thorik thought for a moment before responding to Ambrosius. "There is a way to find out and end this discussion. Gluic, can you restore the rest of his thoughts?"

The lack of response reminded them all that she had wandered off again.

Thorik quickly put his items together in what remained of his backpack, grabbed a torch, and headed out the doorway to find Gluic. "Come on Avanda, we still need to find Em as well."

She grabbed her lantern and its flask of oil before following him out of the room.

Wess slowly positioned himself between Ambrosius and the doorway with the quarterstaff gripped for combat. He bent his knees slightly and hunched forward in case Ambrosius made a leap for him.

Instead, Ambrosius leaned farther back into his chair and continued stroking the path of his mustache that led to his beard. He tilted his head and looked at the ever so quiet giant. "Grewen, what do you suppose they meant? If these statues were indeed speaking for the spirits here, they could not have been referring to the actual destruction of the Temple, as I was there with them. Do they blame me for bringing them here in the first place?"

Oddly enough, Wess was startled as he had forgotten about Grewen. He was so large and still that he almost blended into the room. Wess moved his way behind Ambrosius and pulled out a hunting knife and held it in a threatening manner. "Grewen, keep your distance or Ambrosius' blood will be on your hands. This murderer is in my custody until we can get him to a higher authority."

Grewen ignored Wess and answered Ambrosius. "The spirit's questions are vague. But if it is true that you don't recall what happened, how can you honestly say that you didn't kill them?" Wess nodded his head in agreement with Grewen.

Ambrosius, slightly disappointed at the response, acknowledged, "I suppose I, at least indirectly, am responsible for their death."

With more confidence now that Grewen was on his side, Wess stepped forward and placed the sharp blade of his hunting knife against the side of Ambrosius' neck. "We've had enough of your lies and games. Tell us why you have destroyed this Temple, killed these people, and then returned here." Wess stood as though he was going to sever the older man's head from his shoulders if he didn't get the answer he wanted to hear.

Grewen lowered his head into one of his large palms in disbelief. The giant could only hope that Ambrosius wouldn't get angry at the Num's actions.

Wess only had a moment to look up and see Grewen's response before he was knocked off his feet by an invisible force that lifted him up, high in the air. The impact of the Num's body against the stone surface knocked the wind out of him and causing him to drop his blade. Pinned to the ceiling, facing down, a mixture of fear and confusion crossed his face as he looked at the two outsiders.

Ambrosius moved only one eyebrow. This level of his powers was like brushing away a fly when he lifted Wess up. Ignoring the annoying Num, he continued his conversation with Grewen as though Wess had never been in the room. "Though the implication was that I had planned it. Why would I create a Council to unite Australis only to destroy it? I'm trying to rebuild our world, not overthrow it."

"The Del'Unday would disagree with you. So would the servants of Darkmere." Grewen also ignored the body above them. "It is well known that you have been displeased with the Council's progress over the past many years and have been pushing for a more aggressive response to Darkmere. Because of this, you were seen as a threat to the Council's power, and likewise the Council was a threat to you."

"Disagreements that have been blown out of proportion." Ambrosius dismissed them with a wave of his hand. "The Council did not understand Darkmere like I do. His words of friendship are laced with poison thorns."

Grewen added to his analysis of the situation. "The fact that your conflicts are publicly well known will make it difficult to persuade others to believe that you are not behind this disaster. In addition, your history of conflicts with Alchemists, Del'Unday, and in the Dovenar Civil War has crippled your persona in many ways."

"And you Grewen, where do you stand on my character?"

"I believe you are a man of many challenges and responsibilities. I fought along side you during the Civil War and have killed for your cause. I have watched as you have taken justice into your own hands when others would not. You are a man who has had everything and yet has nothing to show for it. You are my friend and an honorary Ki-Ov'Unday family member. I see no reason you would lie to me. So I will continue to trust you until it is proven otherwise."

"Thank you, my friend."

"But be aware that the evidence is starting to stack up against you," Grewen continued. "You have nothing but your character to stand on at this point. And there is still the issue of your memory. Truth be known, you haven't even proven to yourself that you didn't destroy the temple in a fit of rage."

Ambrosius took a deep breath and slowly let it out as he thought about the comment, before looking over to see Thorik and Brimmelle stepping into the doorway.

"Brimmelle," Wess managed to get out as he gasped for air.

Brimmelle jumped back a step and grabbed the door-frame with one hand. "By the Rune of Reason, what is the meaning of this?" Brimmelle shouted.

Ambrosius looked up and lowered Wess to the stone floor. Floating down, Wess tried to look in control by holding Ambrosius' staff before him. Once on his own feet, he backed up toward Thorik and Brimmelle.

Wess explained what he had heard to the other two Nums behind him, "He's made many enemies and killed before. This isn't his first time. He confessed to these crimes."

"Perhaps you'd like to spend some more time on the ceiling." Ambrosius eyed the spot where Wess had been. He was already in a bad mood about being accused of the murders and his patience was getting thin with Wess' incessant accusations.

Wess backed up into the doorway as he told Thorik and Brimmelle, "We're getting out of here before he kills the rest of us." Glancing over at Grewen, he continued, "Or we get eaten by that one."

"Nah, I don't really care for Nums. Too stringy." Grewen smirked, picking at his teeth as though something was between them.

Thorik grabbed the iron staff out of Wess' hands. With that, Wess bolted down the hallway followed quickly by Brimmelle.

Thorik walked over to Ambrosius and leaned the dark metal staff against the table near him. "This is yours." He then turned to leave the room. Stopping on his way out, Thorik stared into the corridor as he said, "I hope you found what you came for." Standing up straight with his back to Ambrosius, he pulled his shoulders back and clasping his hands together. He added, "We found Emilen in her old living quarters, *if* you are curious to know her fate. She and Gluic are now preparing our beds for the night in the main hall. We all will be heading home at sunrise." And with that, he left the Mori room.

Ambrosius looked at Grewen with grief over the giant's last comment. "This is not a good time for you to be joking around."

"Maybe you're right," he replied. "Nums take things so seriously. Are you sure they aren't related somehow to the Del'Unday?"

"Nor is this the time to continue our debate over the lineage of species." The pressure from the day was getting to him and he rubbed both eyes with the thumb and forefinger of his right hand. "I need to get the word out that the Council is destroyed and call a meeting of the remaining leaders. We must address this threat from Darkmere before he attacks again."

"Perhaps you don't understand. The first sighting of you will probably create a mob that will hunt you down. You may very well be an outlaw. A wanted criminal. Already convicted and sentenced by all the northern provinces."

Ambrosius shook his head in disbelief, "It can't be that bad. I have been a Head of State or Council Member my entire life. They wouldn't dare accuse me so quickly without any proof. I think you underestimate the following I have."

"And I think you underestimate Darkmere's ability to influence others. Perhaps you should know that he is scheduled to speak somewhere in Woodlen."

"Denrick Copperman won't let it happen. His loyalties are with me."

"Denrick invited him."

Ambrosius was disheartened. His face went cold and his eyes searched for an answer. "We need to go there and confront him."

"You're going to confront Darkmere during his visit? How do you intend to find out where he will be? Woodlen is a large province with several cities. You can't just show your face around there to ask questions. And last time I checked, Unday's were only allowed as slaves or gladiators." Grewen's fist hit the stone table a few times to add emphasis to his last few words. The pounding echoed out the doorway and down the hallway.

Ambrosius stood up and grabbed his staff, which he raised and pointed up toward Grewen's large face. "I don't know how I will find out where he is, but I must," he yelled back. "I have nothing to lose at this point, do I? Darkmere has destroyed everything in my life up to this point. I will not sit back and let him win."

"Win? Is this about you winning? Is this just a continuation of the Civil War to you? Or worse, some out of control rivalry?"

"No, that's not what I meant." Ambrosius lowered his voice and weapon. "I mean win, as in him taking over Australis in a cruel dictatorship. If he succeeds everyone will give up their own independence and beliefs in order to follow his. You know this."

Ambrosius sat back down. "I can understand how people hate me for the things I've done. I also have had great friction with many cultures. But I have never forced them to change their ways to follow me. I've only asked them to understand and accept other beliefs."

Leaning forward onto the table, he looked at the giant's leathery face. "I need to confront Darkmere head on."

"Again I will ask, how will you walk freely inside the Dovenar Wall of Woodlen to find out where he will be? You are too well known, and will be captured immediately. I'd help, but Ov'Undays can't enter the land. Only humans and Polenums are free to walk about."

Ambrosius shot a quick look at Grewen who returned a slow look back to the man's calculating eyes.

Grewen leaned forward and softened his deep powerful voice the best he could, "They left here with ill feelings and they are heading downstream in the morning. How do you plan to turn that around?"

"I don't know. But I must. Too many lives are depending on me."

Chapter 18
Turning Point

Draq nested on the neck of the Mountain King statue for the night. A small cave had been created when the head had fallen off, and steam was continually rising out of it. It was a warm spot to sleep for the night with a perfect view to see any intruders arriving.

He looked down to his right to see the campfire light outside the main entrance of the city. Memories of past crusades with friends tempted him to go down, but he no longer was one to socialize, nor did he like being inside. He felt confined and helpless when he entered buildings or tunnels. He had comparatively little way of defending himself against those who would threaten him or his friends. He needed space to fly, to glide, to swoop, to strike.

He missed the days of battles and returning home after the victories. It had been a long time since he and Ambrosius had a victory to celebrate. It had also been a long time since he had been home with his family. He didn't see that changing any time soon.

Draq coiled up near the steam vent and rested his head over the edge of the statue's neck so he could view the valley at all times. After the long road Ambrosius and he had traveled, the dragon no longer could look out and see such a valley as beautiful. Instead, all he saw were hiding places that others could be using before they attacked. The world was now a large continuous battlefield.

The Num's campfire sat in the center of the first huge hall of the city while the original fire could be seen just outside the main doorway flickering in the cold breeze. Snow was starting to accumulate in small drifts just inside the doorway.

It looked frigid and dismal to the group, as they kept warm near the second fire. It was not the cold of the winter storm that caused them to stay silent; it was the chill of emotional conflicts.

Emilen was cuddled up against Thorik under a shared blanket, her eyes sad and wet from weeping. Thorik leaned his head against hers to comfort her in her time of need. "I miss them."

"I'm sure they're safe. Perhaps they went downstream to Farbank or Longfield," he replied. "I'll help you find them."

"Thorik." She looked into his eyes. "You're very sweet, but they could have traveled across the mountains to Shoreview for all we know." She placed her finger up to his mouth as he began to respond with some heroic comment. But she did not want it. "Just hold me. If the Mountain King wishes for me to see my parents again, then it will happen. I will not waste your efforts, if it is not what he wishes for us to do." Smiling at him, she brushed her fingers against his cheek and softly nodded her head, telling him that it would be all right.

Thorik felt a surge of love toward her, which he hadn't anticipated. He didn't know if it was from the soft strength in her voice or from the warmth of her hand against his skin. Removing the hood of his cloak, he held her hand against his neck and closed his eyes. He took a deep breath and leaned toward her.

Wess sat with Avanda, jealous of Thorik's relationship with the redhead. They sat on the opposite side of the fire from Ambrosius. Wess kept his eyes focused on the elder human, while sharpening his hunting knife. The rhythm of the grinding metal was nearly hypnotic as it echoed off the walls.

Grewen sat with his feet up against the lapping flames of the fire as he wiggled his toes to get the flames between them. He sighed several times as the heat touched just the right spots.

Brimmelle tried to get Gluic to sit down and warm herself under their blanket, but she was busy placing various stones near the fire.

"Mother, please sit down before you catch yourself on fire," he told her.

Ignoring him, she pulled another small river-rock out of her pouch and held it near her lips, speaking quietly to it for a short time. She traced it with her finger as she nodded; listening to what it had to say. Afterward, she gently placed the stone in a specific place up near the fire with the many others that were already warming. This ritual continued until she had nearly thirty stones and crystals laid out in various groups and distances. It wasn't a particularly uniform placement but somehow it was organized in a naturally pleasing sort of way.

Grewen looked over at the stones as Gluic returned to Brimmelle and got under his blanket. "Why the grouping? Wouldn't they warm faster if they were evenly dispersed?" he asked.

She looked at the stones with a puzzled look on her face before she responded. "I'm not sure. I would guess that they work better in groups than individually spread out." She continued as she enjoyed the patterns made by the rocks, "Or perhaps some of them just don't get along with others. I just put them where they tell me to."

Grewen's right eyebrow rose as he turned toward her with his smile. "Well, that's very nice of them to take the pressure off of you in having to decide their resting spots," he said slightly sarcastically.

Gluic nodded. "Yes it is," she concluded in a serious tone. "It's a lot like us." She nodded in agreement with her own statement. "We all make our own choices as to where we sit and who we like and dislike. I wonder if we're as smart as the stones."

Silence fell back on the group as they listened to the crackling of the fire and the wind blowing through the distant front doorway.

Ambrosius finally broke the silence with a question. "Thorik, do you believe in your heart that I killed these people?"

Thorik answered in a slow thoughtful manner. "I believe that it is in your nature to do whatever it takes to succeed, regardless of who gets hurt. Your focus is so strong that you might forget about the cost of your victory. You are much like Wess in that manner."

Wess straightened up and looked offended, but Thorik continued before he could defend himself.

"I also believe you are doing your best to help our world become a better place. And sometimes it takes fighting for what is right and fighting those who would hurt you more in the long run. Do I believe that you killed the Council and that you destroyed the Mountain King Statue? I don't know anymore. I want to believe you, but it's difficult. It also shouldn't matter to you if I believe you or not. After daybreak you will never see me again."

"But it does matter, Thorik. It matters to me because you are what I'm trying to save. You, your family, your village, your way of life. There are people like you all across this land that will no longer be free to enjoy life anymore if I don't help them by stopping Darkmere from conquering the free lands." Ambrosius sighed at the thought. "I am not fighting for my personal gain. I am fighting for the freedom of others."

Thorik absorbed his comments and then noted, "Good, I'm glad we could be of service to your cause and I hope we helped. May the King's vision help you foresee trouble and his sword give you the strength to win your battles."

"I can't do this alone," Ambrosius added. "I need your help to stop Darkmere."

"My help? Why my help? Surely you have more powerful friends at your call. You don't need us. Gluic has healed you enough that you can travel without her. We are tired and want to return to home. It's over. What more could we possibly give you?" Thorik concluded.

"Your friendship," Ambrosius stated. "It is more powerful and reliable than the mighty Spear of Rummon. It's not about powers or strength; it's about attitude and desire. Real power comes to those with a drive to accomplish a goal. Real power is within you, my friend."

"Where is this headed?" questioned Thorik.

"I need your help in leading my people."

"Into war? I'm not the person you think I am."

"No, not to war, to freedom." Ambrosius continued, "It is quite simple. I need your help in finding out where Darkmere is so I can stop him from his oppressive takeover. He has many that follow him because they have no one else to trust, until now. Thorik, you have a gift. They will trust you. They will listen to you. And you can help them understand what he's really trying to do."

"I don't know if I can live up to your expectation," he responded.

"Do you remember when I told you that you looked familiar?"

Thorik nodded.

"I've recalled where I've seen your face before. It was here, up on that mountain. Your face is the same as the Mountain King." Ambrosius paused to let it sink in. "Thorik, I believe you are a descendant of the Mountain King."

Brimmelle began to choke on the water he was drinking. Spraying a mist toward the fire, he struggled with the water as well as Ambrosius' words.

Thorik smiled. "And seeing that the head is gone, I am supposed to just believe it to be true."

Ambrosius thought about his lack of evidence as Brimmelle struggled to contain himself. "True, I have no proof. Although, Emilen could most likely tell you better than I."

Emilen looked into his eyes. "It is true; you do look a lot like him."

The words made Thorik feel good, but again there was no proof. "It is very nice that I have facial features similar to the Mountain King, but that does not prove that I am related in any way. Ambrosius, perhaps you were not aware that our scrolls say he died in the Great Emancipation before he had any children. Therefore, there are no descendants."

Brimmelle nodded his head as he began to gain control over the water he had been choking on.

Ambrosius played his last game piece on the table. "Understood. But you did promise me that you would see this through. Surely you're not going back on your word."

"I did nothing of the kind. You asked for help to get to Kingsfoot. I have fulfilled that."

Ambrosius answered back in a softer tone to defuse Thorik's new edge. "Actually, I told you that I was heading upstream to Kingsfoot. I asked you if you would help me find the ones responsible and prevent their next attack."

"You played your words on me," Thorik protested, realizing Ambrosius was correct.

Brimmelle laughed at Thorik. "I warned you about this. Outsiders can't be trusted. You would be a fool to follow him now that you know that he has a tongue of a serpent."

Emilen voiced here opinion, "I think we should go. We can do this. If we can help in some way to save lives, then we should. You could be a great leader, Thorik. I can feel it."

Her comments were quickly followed by Brimmelle's rebuttal. "He's no leader. A leader must take charge and make decisions that may not be popular. He doesn't have it within him. His heart is too soft. He cares too much about how his orders will make others feel. He is now, and will always be, a follower."

Brimmelle glared at Ambrosius. "I've had enough of you and your stories. It's time we set our sights on Farbank before winter fully arrives. You've fill the boy's head with ideas which will get us all killed. Leave him alone and go about your business. And for the record, the rest of us made no commitment to you, nor your quest to save the world."

He looked back over at Thorik and ordered, "You're no descendant of a king, you're not a leader, and you're not capable of turning the tide of some war, and you know it. Don't let this man entice you into believing that you are more than you really are. You're a Sec and you used to be a hunter, a questionable one I might add. And the only reason you hold the position of Sec is because of me." Lying down, he got comfortable for his night of rest, "You're lost without my guidance."

Thorik stared at Brimmelle and thought about his words before looking back to Ambrosius to speak, "I'll go with you."

Ambrosius was relieved at his answer and was thankful that Thorik still trusted him.

Brimmelle, on the other hand, was outraged. "How dare you disobey me! After all I have sacrificed for you. You miserable ingrate, you will never become a Fir now." Suddenly aware of his surroundings, and his lack of control within them, he stopped his rant and gave Thorik a disappointed fatherly look before rolling over and turning his back to him. "I won't be there to save you this time," he mumbled.

Emilen smiled at Thorik. "I will be there for you." Her words put any criticism from Brimmelle out of his head so he could get a good night's sleep. For the first time in his life, Thorik felt liberated.

Wess had been watching Thorik and Emilen. Their relationship had been getting steadily stronger since the river-cut crossing, and if it wasn't broken up soon he may never have a chance with her. All he needed was to wait for an opening. And if he knew Thorik well enough, Thorik himself would cause that opening. Hopefully it would happen soon, prior to them being separated.

Thorik's Log: October 17th of the 649th year.
Emilen and I have joined Ambrosius, Draq, and Grewen to travel to Woodlen in an effort to prevent the destruction of the kingdom by Darkmere. I hope I won't regret this decision.

Morning came and a light fog had covered the valley. The freezing mist attached itself to the city's external walls and the statues in the courtyard, coating them with a thin layer of ice.

Thorik and Emilen had said goodbye to the other Nums during breakfast and were leaving the city and following Ambrosius and Grewen by a few stone throws. The two Nums held hands while listening to the cracking of frozen grass under their feet. They headed around the lake as Draq continued to watch from the Mountain King's neck.

Emilen turned around and waved at Avanda, Brimmelle, and Wess as the three loaded their gear into one of the several rowboats that rested at the slippery docks, just outside of the city.

"Uncle Wess, I don't want to go back without Thorik and Emilen." Avanda struggled with the idea of leaving.

"I know. Nor do I. But it looks like we missed our chance."

"Our chance for what?"

"Nothing." He realized he had been caught in an emotional moment while looking at Emilen. Wess waved back to her, disappointed that his chance with Emilen had just ended. He turned and prepared the boat for the downstream voyage, following orders from Brimmelle with a voice loud enough to carry across the lake.

Finishing loading the boat, Brimmelle realized that Gluic wasn't around. She had run off ahead to show Ambrosius and Grewen her new stones and nuggets of gold.

Brimmelle yelled for Gluic several times before he raced his stocky body from the docks toward her, slipping on the ice and falling twice along the way. At his pace, it took several minutes to pass Thorik and Emilen and reach his mother. He was out of breath. "Mother, we're leaving."

"Yes we are, I didn't think you were coming," Gluic said to her son before she continued to explain what each of her stones was used for. "These red rubies help energize and motivate you, and this pink crystal removes emotional debris from your heart," she informed Grewen.

Brimmelle caught his breath enough to speak again. "We're not going to Woodlen, we're leaving to go back home to Farbank."

Gluic stopped and kissed his cheek. "You have a safe trip and button up that shirt. I don't want my son to catch a cold while I'm not around to help." She buttoned up his shirt for him while talking.

"No, Mother, you're coming with us to Farbank."

"I can't right now dear, but I'll meet you when we get done." She proceeded to catch up to Grewen; leaving Brimmelle confused and frustrated.

"Wess!" Brimmelle yelled back to the docks. "Unload my things. I'm going to Woodlen." Slumping his shoulders, he began his walk back to the docks, passing Thorik and Emilen again.

"Yes! Here we come," Avanda sang out from the dock's edge.

Not overly surprised, Wess unloaded the supplies while the group moved out of visual range. He again had a chance with Emilen. All he needed was the right opening.

As Wess and Avanda approached the Fir with all of the gear, Brimmelle questioned, "I said just unload *my* things, you two are still going back to Farbank." Avanda looked down, disappointed.

Wess took Brimmelle aside, "I know, but what if Ambrosius is the man *we* think he is, you're going to need all the help you can get."

Brimmelle thought for a moment. "True. But we still have to warn Farbank of the Thrashers and outside the valley is no place for a child."

"We can send a boat down river with a message. The current should get it caught in the pond, like everything else that floats down the river." The 'pond' was actually an eddy in the river near Farbank that had widened the banks such that debris riding the river often would get caught and circle there for days before continuing downstream. "If it should make it past the pond, it will get caught in the Longfield fishing nets and they will send someone upstream to warn Farbank. And as far as Avanda goes, she's in no more danger with us than trying to get past thrashers along the river bank."

Brimmelle sighed as he saw Wess' reasoning and welcomed the thought of an ally on their journey. "All right," he finally said. "Send the note and let's hope it finds its mark. We're going to Woodlen," he commanded, as though it was his idea.

Avanda's face lit up as she raced ahead to tell the rest of the party. Brimmelle followed her while Wess returned to the dock and prepared the boat for its own journey downstream.

As the five leading members approached the bridge, Ambrosius stopped at its mouth while the other four continued over it. Grewen, Gluic, Avanda and Brimmelle stopped halfway across to wait for Ambrosius, who had disappeared from their sight for a minute, only to return again from alongside of the bridge's entrance.

Thorik and Emilen approached the bridge as Ambrosius rounded the corner to make his way up onto the deck of the bridge. Thorik realized immediately that Ambrosius had swapped out his original metal staff with the antler-crowned hazelwood one that Thorik had made.

Ambrosius glanced over at Thorik and then at his staff. "New beginnings." With a soft grin, he turned back toward Grewen to move forward onto their destination.

Chapter 19
Frozen Slopes

The group rounded the lake and walked up the mountain's foothills that were covered in sheets of ice, which increased in thickness the higher they climbed. Several layers of clothing were donned to fight the chilling wind that raced down the mountainside toward them.

Bundled and cold, the members slipped several times on the icy slopes. They had been walking the better part of the day and were only a little over halfway up to the pass. Frost built up on faces and exposed skin while backpacks and supplies stiffened like bricks. Their fingers began to burn from the freezing temperatures to the point that they were of little use anymore.

All of Gluic's decorative feathers and plants had frozen or blown off. Survival was the only concern at this point.

Although he had not been in this part of the King's valley, the general terrain was familiar to Thorik. He was able to keep them on the buried trail.

Ambrosius had been using his powers to create a shield of energy. It held off most of the wind, but hours of sustaining this level of focus exhausted him and the shield was shrinking in size and strength. It had been too long to continue such a task. Ambrosius began slowing and stumbling. Thorik moved to his side for support.

Reaching the pass before nightfall was not going to happen. Everyone was tiring out with each painful step, as feet began to feel more like blocks of ice, and toes lost total feeling and movement.

Brimmelle, who had been complaining most of the day, finally yelled out, "We're going to die on this mountain unless we turn around and go back to the city of Kingsfoot. It's our only hope."

Grewen disagreed. "It's too far." He looked at Gluic and Emilen struggling to keep their legs moving. His eyes lowered to Avanda, who was curled in a ball between Grewen's massive hands and arms. "We'll never make it back and I don't think we can go on."

Ambrosius intensified his powers to block the mighty winds. "Pushing forward is our only option."

"No," Thorik yelled over the wind. "We will have to find shelter here, right now, if we wish to survive. This entire mountain range is filled with small caves. We just need to find one for the night."

The group continued to walk for another painful half-hour as they looked for such an opening in the rocks.

"Over there," shouted Thorik as he pointed to an angled crack in the mountainside. "I'll bet there's a cave in there. We should stay the night in it, if there is." He began walking toward it and stopped at a tree near the entrance to remove a few layers of bark before entering the opening.

Nobody argued or commented. Physically and mentally drained, they followed Thorik into the temporary shelter.

Ambrosius, Gluic and Brimmelle were exhausted and immediately dropped onto the rock floor inside the crack in the mountain. The cave was not large, but it provided substantial shelter from the wind. It had a moderate sized opening to the outside, room enough for Grewen to crowd into.

"Grewen, break off a few limbs and then move that large rock in front of the cave so it blocks the wind, but leave a gap at the top," Thorik directed.

On a normal day it would have been an easy task for Grewen, but with hands trembling uncontrollably from the cold, it would be difficult. "I'll see what I can do." He set Avanda inside the cave prior to trying.

"Do your best." Thorik turned to see his shivering party sitting in the corners of a small triangle shaped cave. With shaking fingers of his own, he removed a flask of oil and some flint from his backpack.

"Wess, pull the weeds and dead brush out of the ground and stack them over there," Thorik ordered, pointing at the wall near the entrance. His upbringing prevented him from telling Brimmelle and Gluic to help, so he continued without them, "Emilen, grab a few of your hair ribbons and start fraying the ends."

Wess looked around at the brush near the entrance and began his duties while Emilen worked with Gluic to unravel the cloth.

Ambrosius used his weakened powers to help Grewen move the boulder in front of the cave. Afterward, Grewen began breaking down the limbs for firewood as Ambrosius used his depleted energy to hold off the cold winds from blowing into the cave.

Thorik made a clean area to work and prepared the piece of bark that he had stolen from the tree. He placed the unraveled cloth into the now curved bark holder. He sprinkled some oil on the wood to help it get started.

With his hands still shaking from the frost, he struck the flint to create a spark over the oil stained cloth, but instead caught his finger in the process. The numbing pain shot through his hand and he wrenched away in agony. His nearly frostbitten fingers were already sensitive and this process was becoming too much for him to handle. Clutching the flint in his unsteady hand he tried again in vain to get a spark.

After Thorik's break from Brimmelle's years of domination, a new found determination had welled within him. By the time they had reached the cave, he was fully in charge of the party. He was also fully responsible for their lives. Thorik had to succeed. He had to save everyone. He had to prove that he could be a leader when a leader was needed the most.

Again and again he tried, but his inability to control his exposed fingers made it impossible. He refused to give up as he continued his effort, even though his fingers and knuckles took a serious beating. The burning sensation of the frostbite had already started.

Wess reached over and grabbed his wrist. "Its okay Thorik, let me have a go."

It was the first time Wess had called Thorik by his first name. Thorik realized Wess actually was sincere and that leading was as much about giving directions as it was about knowing when to ask for help.

Reaching out with stiff clawed hands, Thorik dropped the tools into Wess' hands. Wess had been warming them inside his clothes for the past several minutes and they were much more flexible.

After a few quick strikes, the shower of sparks lit the fire. Wess blew on it. Small at first, cupped in the bark tray, they slowly added more fuel until they had a controlled fire with the smoke leaving by way of the gap left at the entrance. Smiling at his accomplishment, he winked at Emilen. She nodded in appreciation.

Ambrosius had released the wind shield once he was comfortable that the fire was strong enough to fight it on its own.

After warming up a little, Grewen broke the rest of branches to be usable as firewood. As he snapped them down to size, Wess stacked them along a wall.

Thorik located a dozen fist-sized rocks and placed them near the fire, along with all of his Runestones.

"Not you too?" Brimmelle commented. "Now she has you cleansing stones." Glancing at Gluic, he shook his head.

Thorik finished with his work, ignoring Brimmelle's words, and allowed the rocks to absorb the heat of the fire. Reaching over with a mink skin, he grabbed the first rocks that he had placed near the fire. He handed a few to Avanda, Gluic, and Emilen. "Place these between your layers of clothes and in your boots to warm you up. Then place your hands near the area as well."

After taking care of them, he handed warmed stones out to the rest of the party before enjoying a few for himself.

As the stones lost their heat they were set back near the fire and replaced with a hot one. The rotation of rocks went on all night as they slept for an hour at a time.

Chapter 20
Del'Unday

Ascending the remaining mountainside consumed most of the following day. That afternoon, they exited the crevasse that linked the Mountain King Valley to southern Lakewood Valley. It was a welcoming sight. The wintry storm had not passed over the crest of the mountain range as the snow and wind was captured within the northern valley. South, the sun was shining among the scattered rain clouds onto green slopes and land beyond.

The entire southern lands could be seen for hundreds of miles in a panoramic view that took the Num's breath away. Never had they assumed the world was so vast.

Thick rich forests and distant mountains covered the east while scattered lakes and hilly woodlands covered the land just southeast of the mountain pass. The southwest had more mountains as well, but with less vegetation on the upper heights which abruptly sprung up from the low flat lands. Soft wisps of smoke rose from two distant twin mountain peaks.

To the south and southwest was a great lake that had no end in sight. In the far distance, perhaps on an island, stood a tall slender line. Its height was even with their own.

"What is that?" Thorik asked.

Ambrosius looked over at the vertical black line in the landscape. "Lu'Tythis."

"What is it?"

"It is a tower."

"It can't be. The top is as tall as a mountain."

Ambrosius agreed. "That's a fair estimate. The large crystal in its pointed top sits several thousand feet high. You will see the crystal's rhythmic light display at night, high in the sky. It's very soothing." Turning his attention away, he focused on the southern valley.

"Before us lies the Lakewood Forest. See that thin line running from east to west along the Cucurrian River?" Ambrosius questioned while facing southeast and waited for an answer. Not receiving one, he looked at Thorik who was fixated on the tower.

"Thorik, keep focused." Ambrosius raised his voice. "The line," he repeated and pointed back in its location.

Thorik shook it off and looked to see the thin line that ran between lakes. "Yes, I see it."

"Good. That is the Dovenar Wall that borders the entire Dovenar Kingdom. This section protects the province of Woodlen. We will travel down to the entrance gates at the city of Pyrth. You will go into Pyrth to determine if it is safe for my arrival. You'll have to start conversations and overhear others. Perhaps you can find out something from the local pub or market place."

Grewen added, "Also keep your ears open for someone who goes by the name of the Terra King, I would very much like to know where and when he will be speaking to the people."

"Exactly what kind of conversations are we listening for?" Thorik asked as he found himself staring again at the black vertical line of Lu-Tythis Tower in the background.

"You're looking for information about the murder of the Grand Council. Grewen has heard that I may be a suspect, so we need to know how prevalent that rumor is, in order to determine our next step. Your best source of information will be the Gentry, but I do not think they will talk to you, so you will need to talk to the Plebeians for information."

"Gentry? Plebeian?" Thorik was confused.

"Simply put, Gentry have the power and Plebeians do not," Ambrosius summarized.

"How will I tell them apart?"

"If not by the attitude, look at the clothing and jewelry," Ambrosius mused. "You also need to stay clear of the Alchemists. They have great powers and will read you like an open scroll."

"Alchemists?" Thorik asked.

"Yes, you know. Wizards, mages, witches, sorcerers and the like. They wield powers they claim are 'magic' in nature."

"Is that what you are?" Thorik asked.

Filling his mouth with a handful of local weeds, Grewen smirked and eyebrows rose as he waited for Ambrosius' response.

Ambrosius was slightly shocked at the question but attempted to downplay it. "No, I am an E'rudite," he said proudly and humbly.

"What's the difference?"

"We are students of true nature, not just of what you see, hear and feel, but of the fundamental fabric. Over time, this allows us to be closer to the very structure and make up of all life. One result is we can, if needed, manipulate many of the threads of this fabric, such as energy, gravity, time, space, and the elements. It is a studied art that requires many years of discipline and guidance to be responsible for such great knowledge. It can take a lifetime to master a single natural art. To be an E'rudite, one must understand the forces of nature to such great degree that those forces become an extension of oneself."

He continued, "Alchemists, on the other hand, have a spiritual belief that guides them to natural energies which they utilize. They use and mix these energies together to create various reactions much like a recipe to make a cake. They do not understand why it rises and tastes the way it does, only that it will when ingredients are mixed in the correct manner. This, they call 'magic'."

"Often these 'magic' recipes are complex and sensitive to variation. They struggle to control these reactions. So, the Alchemists often enchant objects for later use. Enchanted objects can then be activated in a number of different ways depending on the substance and enchanter. Some have verbal or physical commands such as breaking the object or getting it wet. This allows others who have even less understanding of these forces to be able to use them." Ambrosius sighed. "Ignorance and power are dangerous bed-fellows."

Thorik scratched behind his ear in thought. "So it's kind of the same but just different ways to get there?"

"Close enough."

"So why don't you like the Alchemists?" Thorik injected.

"Because they do not understand it for what it really is and they don't have the discipline to use it correctly and responsibly, causing them to be reckless."

"None of them?" Thorik questioned.

"Most of them. Magic is dangerous; you would be well advised to stay clear of it."

"So, are E'rudites more powerful than Alchemists?"

"Not always. It isn't that simple." Ambrosius was tired of the line of questions and ready to move down the mountainside once Draq gave the signal from the air.

"Did the E'rudites create Lu'Tythis?"

"Enough questions for now, my curious friend." Ambrosius looked back at Thorik who was again staring at the tower.

"Thorik." Ambrosius raised his voice again. "There are a lot of things in this world that will be new to you. If you stop to dwell on them all, we will never get anywhere. You must learn to focus."

Thorik apologized, "Sorry, you're right. We will pass the Woodlen gates and inquire around a bit in the city of Pyrth. If your name is still in good standing, we will find out. We'll return with our findings, make our plans, and then determine who destroyed the Mountain King Statue."

"Excellent." Ambrosius looked up into the sky. A solid glare of reflected sun interrupted the shimmering from his Draq's scales. "Draq has given us the all clear. It's time to travel down into Lakewood Valley and the safety of the forest below."

"Then let's be on our way," Gluic said, standing next to him, ready to head down into the valley. She had already donned a headdress of local weeds as she began stuffing a feather in one of the holes in Ambrosius' leather vest.

The days travel down the mountain was much easier than any other day during the trip. A fire-free camp was established that evening to prevent any potential assassins from locating them. It was a cool night for sleeping without a campfire, but they would enjoy it much more than sleeping in the frozen cave on the other side of the mountain.

"Thorik." Emilen gazed up into the southern night's sky.

He turned from his camp duties to follow her line of sight. Above the trees, semitransparent sheets of green, blue and red waved in the sky like flags in the wind. These misty banners flapped in the windless breeze as they decorated the night's black pallet.

Thorik walked up behind Emilen and wrapped his arms around her waist, pulling her in tight. "Beautiful. This must be the light display from Lu'Tythis Tower." He recalled his conversation with Ambrosius.

They stood, holding each other, watching the event for what seemed like hours before retiring for the night. Upon waking, the colored waves had been banished by the rays of the morning sun.

There wasn't much of a trail as they traveled down the foothills into heavier woodlands. A week or more had passed before they reached the scattered lakes. By doing so they lost sight of Draq and assumed all was well until he came swooping in to alert them of a small army of Del'Unday Warriors.

"How many?" Ambrosius asked.

"A few hundred with spears and launchers," Draq replied.

"What kind of close range weapons are they traveling with?"

"Nothing special, just standard hand to hand combat items."

"No rams or bores?" Ambrosius questioned.

"No."

"Odd, why would they attack the wall without any weapons to get inside it?" Ambrosius wondered. "There must be another target for their attack. Where are they located?"

"They are camped in a river basin downstream, out of your current path. You should be able to pass through without having any confrontation with them," the dragon said.

"That doesn't sound like the Draq I know." Ambrosius grinned at the thought. "Lead the way. I want to see what they're up to. It may be a small lead to a larger plan."

The party continued in the direction led by Draq while Brimmelle complained that he thought this was a bad idea. With his protest falling on deaf ears, they eventually reached a rim looking down into a river basin filled with creatures.

The Nums gasped at the many Del'Unday species that existed and how fierce most of them looked. When asked, Grewen was indulgent enough to answer the Num's questions about the various species.

A few tall red skinned and eyed Blothruds walked along barking orders at the rest of them. Hairless skin stretched over their long snouts, exposing lower and upper teeth. Armed with spiked knuckles and elbows that naturally grew out from their skin, they only carried a side saber on their belt for battle. Jagged angled blades grew out of their back spine, undoubtedly for rear attacks. Two large hairy wolf-like legs supported razor-sharp claws and thick pointy spikes. Shoulders back and standing tall, it was easy to see that they were in charge of this battle campaign.

Hunched over, the two-legged Krupe appeared to be the common military guard and soldier. They wore sharply cut dark metal armor and were equipped with various weapons. Fully covered with metal, it was impossible to see the color of their skin or the shape of their face. Only glimpses of eyes could be seen from within the slots of the helmets. Krupes carried out the orders of the Blothruds without question and kept the site in order. In fact they never spoke. They were silent as they went about their chores. The unknown spooked the Nums.

Several Brandercats wandered the camp on all fours in search of their next meal. When standing on their back legs, these lizard-skinned cats were as tall as the Krupes. Crouching down and sitting quietly, they waited for opportunities to eat. While idle, their scales would quickly change colors to match their surroundings causing them to vanish from sight.

During a delivery of raw Fesh'Unday meat, a Brandercat leaped from its hiding place and snatched a hundred pounds of the uncooked food with its dislocating jaw and multiple layers of teeth. In the few seconds that it took for a Krupe to catch up to the Brandercat, over half of the meal was consumed. The cat laughed in a human tone about the event. Running for cover after being poked sharply with the Krupe's spear, it swore bitterly back at it.

It took the Nums by surprise to see an animal of such speak.

Avanda pointed at a dragon, less than half the size of Draq, with dark coal colored scales. "That one looks like Draq, but I can't find any that look like you," she said to Grewen.

It was Ambrosius' turn to widen his eyes and raise his eyebrows as he waited for Grewen to respond to Avanda's question.

"That's because I am an Ov'Unday, not a Del'Unday."

"What's the difference?" she replied.

"Delz are bred for war and conquest. We on the other hand are at peace with nature and accept what we have." Grewen taught his class of one.

Brimmelle entered with an assumption, "So, Ov'Unday are good and Del'Unday are evil?"

"No, life is not that black and white," Grewen explained. "They justify their actions with their beliefs, teachings, and traditions. What seems evil to us is not an act of evil in their minds. Also remember, history is written by those who are victorious. When the Delz conquer lands they record themselves as good and the destroyed civilization as evil. Most aggressors do the same."

Brimmelle voiced his thoughts, "I don't trust any of them. Filthy Altereds are all alike."

Grewen flinched at the term. "We prefer to be called Unday. Altered Creatures are things of the past. Slaves of a race long gone."

Thorik entered to the conversation with Grewen. "Draq is a Del'Unday but you get along with him."

"Rare as it is, sometimes Del'Unday and Ov'Unday can coexist. The Delz also have been known to take Fesh'Unday as pets and laborers, something we Ov'Uns typically do not do."

Seeing Avanda's questioning face, Grewen decided to answer it before it was spoken. "Fesh'Unday are the wild creatures such as wolves, grazers, thrashers, bushdogs, and Faralopes."

"Quiet," Ambrosius ordered. Several of the Del'Unday infantry marched toward their position. Fortunately, they marched by without issue. After veering off, they were soon out of sight.

Looking out at the camp, it seemed odd that they were not preparing for battle.

Ambrosius looked at the water system being built along the small river. "They plan to stay for a while. They're spending a lot of time making shelters instead of sharpening their blades."

"Perhaps they are training," Grewen suggested.

"Or they are waiting for more reinforcements to arrive." It just didn't look right to Ambrosius.

"Why attack now?" Grewen asked.

"Maybe they have received word that the Council has been destroyed. They lost some of their key commanders too and could be seeking retribution. Also, they know there is no longer any power to hold them responsible for such an attack on Woodlen."

Ambrosius' lips tightened as he thought about his prior statement. "But how would news get all the way to Ergrauth in time to prepare an army and have it travel this far within a cycle? I think whomever was feeding the information you intercepted has also informing Ergrauth. Who else has received this information before the incident even occurred? This net of deception is far wider than I had imagined. We must proceed even more cautiously."

"I say we leave before we get caught." Brimmelle's visions of the creatures were making him uncomfortable.

Ambrosius nodded. "I agree, we must depart before dark. There is no more to learn here without putting ourselves at risk."

With that, they cautiously left the Del'Unday area and were back on their way to Woodlen.

After traveling several more days, they camped overnight in a small clearing encircled by thick trees and brush to hide their location. A small stream ran through the camp, providing a pleasant sound for sleeping. The plan was set for the Nums to head south to Woodlen after breakfast.

Chapter 21
Woodlen Province

Leaving the other three at camp, the Nums followed the stream through the woods as it mated with other sources of fresh water and gradually grew in size. It wasn't long before it was as wide as Draq's wingspan, never reaching more than knee deep.

They continued downstream until the water ran under an old wooden bridge with three of its four light posts broken off. After flowing under the bridge, the stream merged with a rapidly moving river, far too deep to walk through. The bridge connected a wide dirt road that followed the river from its path upstream to their left, across the intersecting shallow stream, and then downstream for as far as the eye could see to their right. The route was old and its maintenance poor as it slightly curved back and forth to follow the main river.

Just beyond the rushing river rested an old stone and mortar wall, whose height reached just above the treetops. Pursuing the same course as the river and road, it failed to weave back and forth in as natural a fashion as the waterway. Along its top, guards could be seen walking and peering over a short protective block barrier.

Bright yellows and greens colored the guard uniforms and several hanging flags, which stood out against the blue sky. The overly bright colors appeared out of place on the ancient degenerating wall.

Pausing for a moment on the dirt road, the group looked in amazement at the height and length of the wall. Never had they seen one so large. Why would anyone need a wall of such magnitude?

Gluic was the only one not impressed. "It's a shame the people on the other side of the wall don't get to see the river." Reaching the fast paced river, she placed a hand over it. "Strength and energy. They have locked out what they need most."

After the initial amazement to the wall's size wore off, they began looking both ways to determine how to get past the barrier and inside the province. A few people could be seen in the distance, downstream.

Emilen looked over the bridge to the right. "I believe the entrance is downstream."

"Why do you say that?" Thorik asked.

"When my father was ill, I took the summer trade visit for him. I'm pretty sure I traveled across this bridge."

Thorik looked up and down the long road that followed the river and wall. "It all looks about the same in both directions. It could have been any bridge that you recalled." He then heard voices up on the wall. "Let's ask someone."

Thorik looked up at a guard sitting on the short ledge of the wall above them, eating an apple. "Hello up there," Thorik yelled but didn't receive any response. He cupped his hands on both sides of his mouth and tried again. "Excuse me, we could use your help down here." Still no response. "Please sir, can you tell us how to get on the other side of this wall and enter the Woodlen Province? We're looking for the city of Pyrth."

The guard looked down at the Nums before calling another guard over. Upon arriving, the first guard pointed down at Thorik and commented to the other to which he received a nod of his head. With that, the guard wound up and flung his apple down from above toward Thorik with full force. Even with a quick dive out of the way the apple still hit hard and exploded on the back of his leg.

Looking up at the guards as they laughed and pointed, Wess instinctively grabbed his bow and loaded it.

"Put that away!" Thorik screamed at Wess as the two guards had grabbed their own weapons and were being joined by several others on the wall.

Wess looked up at the ever-increasing number of arrows and spears pointed at him from the wall's topside. He slowly lowered his weapon and placed it back over his shoulder in hopes of defusing the situation. "Well done, No-soul." He was irritated at himself as well as Thorik. "We need to leave here."

"Next time, I would appreciate it if you would listen to me," Emilen said with a verbal stab.

Wess began to walk toward the bridge, the direction Emilen had suggested. He hoped that this was the chance that he was looking for to start getting close to her again. "I don't see how you put up with someone that doesn't trust your judgment." He received no reply from Emilen.

As his party supported his decision they were mocked from above as various objects were tossed down at them. Ale and old stew lightly rained down onto their heads as rotten fruits splashed at their feet. This continued for several minutes until the guards realized that the Nums would not respond to their taunting threats. Returning to their duties, the guards finally ignored them.

Cleaning the food from his clothes, Wess scowled over his shoulder at Thorik. "That will teach you not to listen to Emilen," he said loud enough to make sure the petite redhead would overhear.

Emilen finished cleaning her hair of trash and tied it up tight. "He's so set in his ways, he couldn't tell friend from foe."

Thorik's walking slowed slightly from the comments.

Brimmelle looked over at Thorik in another disappointed moment. "You won't listen, will you? The world is filled with evil and you need to learn who you can and cannot rely on." Brimmelle lowered his thick wild eyebrows and looked straight at Thorik. "You can't trust anyone but your own kind. You can only trust Nums," he said, thumping his finger against Thorik's chest. Brimmelle turned and walked up front with Gluic.

Again, Thorik slowed his pace.

Avanda walked along side Thorik for a few moments before taking his hand in hers. "I believe there are good and bad in every type of people." Remembering Grewen and Draq she added, "Or creature."

Thorik didn't reply as they continued to walk along the road avoiding the mud puddles from recent showers that accumulated in the wagon wheel grooves. The warmth of holding Avanda's hand made the travel less depressing.

It wasn't long before they reached an area of the wall that jutted out slightly on both sides of a gated entrance. The wall turned at a right angle and continued into the Woodlen Province from both sides of the exterior overhead gate. It continued into Woodlen for approximately forty feet and stopped at a second similar gate. The catwalk above the wall continued over both gates with many more guards posted than anywhere else they had seen. A large solid metal door hovered horizontally overhead, hinged near the first gate. A simple pin removal would allow the door to swing down against the wooden seal, preventing any attacks in a moment's notice.

Wess led them under the first gate after eyeing the guards up on the wall. "Dain, want another apple?" He smiled and chuckled to himself as they all fell in line behind others entering the walled land.

At the front of the line was a creature-pulled wagon of goods. It had traveled a quarter of the way between the two vertically lifted gates before stopping to be inspected. The wagon was followed by three fishermen carrying the day's catch and then the Nums. While waiting for the guard to finish talking to the wagon owner, Thorik moved up in front of Wess to lead them into the province. Brimmelle and Wess pulled him back behind them to make sure he didn't say anything they all would regret.

"Where's your slave permit for this Fesh?" asked the sergeant on duty about the creature harnessed to the front of the wagon. "Fesh'Unday are not allowed in Woodlen without proper permits unless they are dead and will be used for skins and meat, especially here in the city of Pyrth."

An elderly man sat on the front of his wagon holding the creature's reins. "I have recently captured this Unday and have not had a chance to register it."

Stepped up to the creature, the sergeant looked it over. Large hairy hooves braced two large back legs under its heavy center while the long tail acted as a counter weight to its wide and stubby neck and head. Covered in thinned, coarse, white hair over black skin, the Fesh'Unday looked over at the military official who was now standing next to it.

"Wild Faralopes are untamable creatures that are dangerous and outlawed." The sergeant raised his gauntlet and touched the creature's back. "You will not receive a permit for this type of a Fesh unless it is for the Melee Matches." Reaching over, he grabbed the creature's mouth with both hands to hold it closed as he used his thumbs to check its teeth and gums. "Looks like we've got a nice one here, she might be entertaining to watch in a fight against Foresc Blox's new gladiators."

"She's not for sale nor for fighting," the wagon owner noted. "I need her to haul my goods. The law states that I have one day to register her. Now leave her alone."

Releasing the Fesh'Unday, the sergeant walked over to the man. "Listen up Plebeian, don't you tell me what to do. I'm Sergeant Borador. Here in Pyrth, I *am* the law. I could kill this beast right now and throw you in prison for talking back to me and still sleep well tonight." Grabbing the reins from him, the sergeant began to whip the weak man with them. "You need to think twice before disrespecting Gentry."

The old man fell to his side from the lashings, causing the sergeant to reach farther with the reins. The tugging caused the Faralope to rear backwards, losing control and slamming her way free of the wagon's arms. Spooked, it ran wildly.

"Gates down," commanded a guard from above. The metal rods of the gates were thicker than Thorik's thumb, and were separated at a hand width apart. Hanging by chains that coiled around large spools on the far side of the wall, guards released the locking lever that held the gates vertically up in the air.

Both mighty gates came crashing straight down. The first set separating the men Nums from the women Nums. Thorik looked at the downed gate and realized he was fortunate not to have been crushed under its tremendous weight.

His thankfulness for a lucky break came to an end once he realized he was trapped between the two gates with a crazed rampaging creature. The three Nums ran behind and then under the wagon for safety. It was short lived as the Fesh'Unday soon made its way behind the wagon as it began to lap the caged area.

Arrows and spears began to fly from above as everyone except the sergeant ran in madness. An arrow shot into one of the fishermen's legs making him fall, only to be trampled by the beast on its next loop. Several spears broke through the wagon's deck nearly catching the three Nums that hid under it.

Sergeant Borador watched the mayhem for several moments before grabbing one of the thrown spears out of the ground. Waiting for the creature's next lap around the temporary pen, he positioned his weapon over his shoulder and behind him, ready to release it with all of his might.

Racing with fear in her eyes, the panicked Fesh moved out from behind the wagon only to receive the blade of the sergeant's spear in her chest. She fell to the ground in a cloud of dust as additional arrows shot from above to ensure the sergeant's safety.

Coiling up the chain, the gates lifted, allowing several guards to enter the area.

"Take it in for butchering and push that wagon out of here," the sergeant ordered his men before addressing the old man again. "If I ever see you trying to enter my gate again I'll be sending *you* in for butchering."

The elderly man and his wagon were taken out to the dirt road and dumped.

With their day's catch flattened into the ground, the two remaining fishermen carried their injured friend into Woodlen to get him some medical treatment.

Emilen, Avanda, and Gluic caught up to their party as they began to walk past the sergeant's watchful eye. He seemed to like the quiet and obedient Nums with their heads down and eyes lowered, and he let them pass without issue.

Once inside Thorik could see that the wall which lined the province was wide enough at the top for two or three men to walk shoulder to shoulder. Halfway down the Woodlen side of the wall, the thickness doubled with an additional walkway that provided ramps and stairs to the upper level as well as the ground.

Beyond the walls and gates was a large common area for military personnel, including blacksmith shops, armories, a mess hall, sleeping barracks and stables. Beyond this area was a smaller defensive wall that entered into a commerce area just past two large open wooden doors.

Looking into the stables they could see several Unday chained up against the walls. They appeared to be intelligent as Thorik watched them having subtle conversations with each other. Those with muzzles communicated with eye movements and head gestures.

"Do you suppose they are Ov'Unday? They look more docile than the Del'Unday we've seen," Thorik asked the group.

Brimmelle grumbled with disgust, "It doesn't matter, they are all the same. Wild, dirty, and dangerous, like the one that just about killed us at the gate."

"I don't think they are all like that. How about Grewen and Draq?" Thorik asked.

"Draq is without a doubt dangerous. I think Grewen can be as well, if provoked. And he's definitely dirty. Either way, none of these creatures should be trusted." Brimmelle ended the conversation by turning away from the stables and toward the market place.

Thorik and Avanda looked at the despondent faces of the enslaved creatures chained to walls and to the fronts of various military carts and wagons. One creature was seen tied to a post as it was being whipped in punishment for some wrongdoing. Thorik didn't agree with Brimmelle on this point but realized that there was nothing he could do to change his mind.

Thorik felt terrible about how they were being treated and extremely guilty about not doing anything to help them. "This is wrong. We can't just leave without trying to help."

Brimmelle fired back over his shoulder, "Leave it alone, Thorik. Every issue in this world is not our responsibility to fix. We're over our heads as it is, so unless you plan on taking on the entire military single handily, I suggest you pay attention to what we came here for."

Feeling uncomfortable at the Fir's agitated tone, Avanda moved up toward Gluic and the rest of the Nums that had continued walking.

Slowly following Brimmelle, the sight of slavery hit Thorik hard; he wouldn't give the issue up. "Ambrosius wouldn't stand by and allow such things to continue. He would take action and make a difference. He would change things."

Brimmelle turned around and stopped Thorik in his tracks at his disobedient tone. "Change? Ambrosius has corrupted your mind. Change is not what he has led you to believe. What has it done for us?" His voice now raised, he was lecturing his nephew firmly. "We were nearly killed by thrashers, living statues, a freezing winter storm, and a racing Fesh'Unday. For what I ask you, for what?" Ending with a huff and a glare that weakened Thorik's legs. The Fir was at his limit.

Thorik heard the words and struggled to answer. "To save others. To prevent another attack."

"What attack? As far as we know, Ambrosius could have caused the first one on the council. And even if he didn't. To save who? These people?" He looked at the military and their enslaved Unday. "Why is it our responsibility to take care of their problems? Shouldn't they deal with it themselves? When have we ever asked for outside help?" It was a rhetorical question, but he waited for Thorik to absorb the obvious answer. "I don't trust outsiders."

Thorik countered his claim. "That's not true. How about Emilen? She didn't grow up in Farbank, so technically she is an outsider."

"She is a Num, born in our spiritual city of Kingsfoot. It's completely different."

Thorik felt he had figured out the truth. "This is about other species more than being about outsiders. What is it about them that you fear?

Brimmelle rebelled against the questioning with a roar that put Thorik back into his place. "Don't you take that tone with me, Sec Dain. You owe me your life for more than one occasion. The least you could do is to show me some respect." Quiet fell as Brimmelle straightened his clothes and puffed out his chest while looking at Thorik's browbeaten response. Softening his voice to a stern fatherly level he added, "What is so wrong with keeping things the same? Don't you like our life in Farbank?"

Thorik cast his eyes down to the ground. "Yes, very much so."

"So, why would we risk changing it by deluding our minds with their thoughts? The Mountain King has provided us with rules to live by, and as long as we do, he keeps the crops strong and the fish plenty." Brimmelle looked at Thorik's lowered head and knew he had captured the obedient boy he once knew. "Let us stop this march across lands that are not ours. We need to take everyone home. This is not our fight, nor our responsibility. Our obligation is to Farbank. We should be making sure that *our* people are safe." Brimmelle was finally comfortable that he had won his case and they would soon be home with things back to normal.

Thorik looked over at Avanda and Emilen and realized the danger he had put them in. Nodding his head a few times, he admitted Brimmelle was right. "Yes, we need to bring them home to safety. But not until we finish this last request for Ambrosius."

Brimmelle was not pleased about Thorik's last comment, but before he could say anything, Thorik continued.

"I made a commitment to Ambrosius to find out if it was safe for him to enter the province and I intend to live up to it. The Mountain King's words in the Responsibility Rune Scroll state-"

"I know what the scroll states," Brimmelle interrupted. He wasn't going to fight the words of his teaching. Besides, he had won. They were going home, very soon.

Thorik and Brimmelle quickly caught up to the others as they reached the open gates leading out of the military area.

Entering Pyrth's market area, Thorik noticed that all of the vendor stands were on raised tiled areas, several inches above the vine-infested street of worn and broken flat stones. Unlike the tents of Farbank, these were solid structures with overhangs that routed rain away from their patrons.

The other obvious difference was how they conducted business. Bickering and loud haggling back and forth took the place of pleasant conversations and updates on family members. They also did not exchange or trade goods. Instead customers provided metal pieces much smaller than his Runestones to pay for their items.

Respectively leery of humans in this city, they found a Num selling her fruits and vegetables. Produce seemed so much larger and vibrant back at the Harvest Festival, but they were famished and wished to eat.

Greeting the fellow Num with a cheerful attitude, Thorik hoped to start up a pleasant conversation. Periodically he would stop in hopes that she would join into his dialog. Perplexed, she stared at him waiting for his selection of items.

He finally realized that she was not going to add to the conversation, so he chose the items they required. Once completed she requested payment.

"I have no metal pieces. Will you accept a mink skin?" Thorik asked and received his answer in her impatient facial expression.

Gluic stepped forward, looking down into her open bag of gems and gold nuggets. "Maybe I have something she would like?"

"Mother, she doesn't want your river rocks." Brimmelle pulled her back and had her put the pouch of stones away.

Thorik had to come up with some form of payment. They hadn't eaten in a few days. Thinking for a few more moments, he pulled out his sack of Runestones. Pausing, he questioned his options one more time. Emptying a few into his palm, the vendor's eyes lit up.

"They look authentic. Where did you get those?" she asked.

"From the Mountain King," Thorik replied, as she took one from his hand. "Would you take one as payment?" he asked, and yet he hoped in a way she would say no.

She inspected it closely. "These are the real things? How did you come by these?"

Thorik nodded. "Most of them have been handed down from generation to generation."

She looked the group over and then returned her attention to Thorik. "So you must be a Fir. I apologize for my rudeness. I know that the Terra King has several groups of spiritual leaders that journey for him. I just didn't realize that you were one of them."

Brimmelle nearly fell backwards from the shock of Thorik being called a Fir. "Wait just a minute. I am Fir Brimmelle Riddlewood the Seventh of Farbank," he corrected her. "These are my followers." He had established their significance with his words as well as with a change of his voice. Suddenly feeling important again, and in charge, he knew things would soon be getting better. It had been a long time coming.

"Joyous," the vendor said. "And I am Mira Shovell of Victory. I have so enjoyed your master's resurgence. It has been inspirational to us as of late, seeing that we are under constant threat of being attacked by the Unday." She continued her conversation as she loaded up several items into a sack for them. "Ever since the Prominent of Pyrth left for the Grand Council, the Terra King has been here to help keep our hopes up."

Engaged in her comments, Thorik couldn't believe his luck. "He's here?"

Looking a little confused Mira asked, "Of course, aren't you a part of his core spiritual leaders?"

Emilen thought quickly. "Yes, however we have just returned from a lengthy special mission for the Terra King and haven't seen him yet. Could you tell us where he is?" Emilen smiled and used her natural charm in hopes that the lady would accept the story.

"At the theater. Today's resurgence will start soon, but as you know, it's lengthy, so take plenty of food," Mira replied while handing Emilen the sack of fruit and vegetables. She looked back at Thorik and held up the Runestone that she had taken from him. "I'll take this one as payment."

Thorik parted with the object and tucked the rest back in his sack before tying it off and storing it away. "Where is the theater?"

Mira pointed down the main street and explained some simple directions as she watched Thorik get out a blank parchment to start drawing a map of the area. He was quick and accurate but left out many details for now that he would fill in once he had time to sit down.

Brimmelle finished his meal before nudging Thorik. "Put that away and eat something. We all need our strength." As ordered, Thorik returned his notes to his scuffed up wooden box and grabbed a pear to eat as they started walking down the main road.

The road was filled with large two story houses and shops that peddled everything from jewelry and clothing to house goods and foreign wares. A bright glazing of color and fascia boards covered ancient buildings in hope of looking fresh and new. But once Thorik looked past the exterior glamour he saw foundations cracked and walls struggling to support ceilings, while watermarks on the walls exposed prior rain leaks in the roofs.

Wess did not see any of those things; instead he ingested the energy of the city with all of its hustle and bustle of the busy streets. The color of signs and clothes exploded in a vibrant collage everywhere he looked. "This is amazing. I never knew there was so much life and excitement outside of Farbank."

"It's not real, these people are living a fabrication of their own making," Thorik responded as he saw many people wearing old and dirty clothes under their crisp and clean robes and coverings.

Emilen looked over at him. "You sound more like Brimmelle every day. Why are you picking it apart? Just enjoy it."

Wess couldn't resist adding to Emilen's sting. "She right, Firpet, you need to be less critical. Start enjoying life like these people do." He used the opportunity to once again get between Thorik and Emilen, by stepping in front of him, causing Thorik to slow down.

Thorik fired back, "We have a specific task to get done here. We aren't on a holiday."

Wess turned around and walked backwards, keeping pace with Emilen. "*You* have a task, not us. We didn't make any commitments. Besides, who said you can't enjoy yourself while performing it?" Once completed, he spun around on the ball of his foot to keep up with Em.

Thorik let the conversation end. For years he had heard Wess' speech of letting go of rules and responsibilities to enjoy life. Right now he was more interested in finding out more about the Terra King and overhearing any comments about Ambrosius. In doing so, he isolated himself from his group, like he usually did when in deep thought. He fell behind the other Nums as they continued toward their destination.

Stopping periodically to look in the large picture windows of the shops, Wess and Emilen enjoyed seeing the foreign items for sale. They pointed and laughed as they moved from shop to shop, guessing what the use was for many of the unknown objects. Feeling right at home in the city they greeted oncoming traffic with waves and smiles as though they were locals themselves.

Thorik was jealous of Wess and Em's easy rapport with the locals as well as each other. He felt threatened and inept as he walked down the road behind them, pondering his dilemma. *Now is not the time to take issue with it. Now is the time to get information and get back to camp. I will deal with this later.*

He felt several taps on his hand before looking over to see Avanda trying to wake him from his own world. "What is it, Avanda?"

She grabbed his hand before replying. "Did you see that lady back there with the three large feathers for a dress? How about the man walking on sticks as tall as Grewen? Or the kids with the blindfolds trying to run across the street without getting hurt? These people are crazy. Isn't it great?" She was beaming from ear to ear.

Avanda had several reasons to be pleased. First of all, they were in a fun place with a lot of new things to see. Second of all, she was happy to see Wess and Emilen spending time together again. She didn't want Thorik's feelings hurt, but she had wanted her uncle to meet someone soon so he would be happy and Avanda could have cousins to play with.

Thorik smiled at her unusual appetite for the insane as they followed the rest of the Nums down the crowded road.

Brimmelle and Gluic led the group around the corner to the right and toward the gathering. Stopping, she searched the ground for a moment. "There are no good stones here."

"I'm sure they are the same here as they are in the King's River Valley."

She knelt down a few times as they walked and picked up a few small rocks. "No, the stones here are dead. They don't speak."

"Well then, it's a good thing you brought your own stones to talk to." They turned again to the right where they saw thousands of people lined up to enter a large open amphitheater.

The crowd was starting to flood in. Brimmelle and Gluic were quickly swept up in the tide and were washed to the far side of the theater before sitting down. They watched as the rest of their group was moved into seats near the entrance.

Cramped already, additional audience members continued to push their way in on the sides until there was no room left on the long arched stone benches that surrounded the lower stage. Standing room along the sides quickly filled as Brimmelle started to feel claustrophobic.

The remaining four members of Thorik's party only made it as far as the seating near the entrance before they were blocked by others. Split into two groups on far sides and one row behind, Thorik was just happy that they didn't get separated even more before sitting down.

Looking down to the front, Thorik could see several red cloaked guards as they kept the front seats open for the Gentry. These people were the upper class and apparently had better privileges. They wore nicer garments and jewelry and seemed to walk stiffer and slower than the rest. He also noticed that all of the Gentry were humans, whereas the Plebeians were a mixture of human and Polenum races.

"I heard that the Terra King will be granting healings today," a member of the crowd behind Thorik commented.

Another added, "He is also supposed to select his new core spiritual leaders."

Thorik looked confused and then wedged his body sideways to turn and ask the two men behind him, "What happened to his last core of leaders?"

"They were sent off on a quest. Now he needs a new group for another important task," one answered back.

Thorik worked his way back forward to see several large wooden hexagons with rune symbols being moved onto the stage followed by large signs painted to look like scrolls with large text for the audience to read. The stagehands finished placing the props on stage as Brimmelle read the scrolls from afar. He was instantly upset as he noticed missing words and passages.

Thorik also noticed these right away and made comments to Emilen and Wess.

"They couldn't write down everything on the scroll and still expect us to read it." Emilen tried to calm Thorik. She was still energized from the excitement of the city and the current crowd.

Thorik looked over across the way to see Brimmelle upset and having many words with other audience members near him. The dispute went on for a short time before Gluic ordered him to sit down and be quiet. He was obviously not happy, but sat down anyway.

Chapter 22
Terra King

With a striking of a hammer to the enormous hexagonal gong, everyone in the audience cheered as a tall thin man walked out into the center of the stage in white flowing robes that covered his feet and dragged behind him. His hands were together in front of him, hidden by the robe's long sleeves. The hood of the robe also covered most of his head, allowing only his long white beard to be seen.

Without saying a word, he raised his right hand with his palm out to the audience to silence the applause. His appendage was thin, pale, and bony with several age spots. All went quiet as the white robed man waited for all attention to be on him.

"Before the Age of Man, and the prior Age of Altered Creatures, there was the Age of the Notarians." The man had a strong commanding voice for all to hear. "This was the age when men and Nums created the Rules of Order and the words of the Runestones in an effort to free themselves of the Notarian torturous rule and to stop the devastation of Australis. This is not Num folklore. It was the beginning of the strongest unification of our people in history."

Motioning toward himself with his right hand he continued, "I know this to be true, for I was there. I *was* the Mountain King." He paused, and the audience gasped. "My body has been reborn, but my soul and spirit are the same. I recall the paradise we had lived in prior to the destruction brought on by the Notarians."

"Threatened by the movement for freedom from myself and my allies, the Notarians created the Altered Creatures to destroy all human and Polenum life. A hundred thousand creatures were created from the depths of evil to wage war, and so they did. But in doing so they not only destroyed our civilization but the creatures went wild and turned on the Notarians as well. I was killed during the final battle and my thoughts and energy set adrift."

Brimmelle was shocked at the concept. Sitting motionless, his anger grew over the misrepresentation of the rune scrolls. "This is obviously a hoax," Brimmelle said to his mother. "The blood of a Polenum runs through the Mountain King's body. A warrior, a leader, born of grace and honor. Not a human who hides his face and blurs the words of the ancient stones."

The Terra King signaled one of his red cloaked guards, who swung a hammer hitting the gong again. This time two Unday appeared, one from each side of the stage. The crowd gasped and screamed at the sight of these oddities of nature. One resembled a large wolf with long muscular tentacles thrashing about as small lighting bolts emanated from the ends. The second creature slithered onto the stage with its knee-high slug-like body as it spat acid from extendible spouts, which covered the boneless body.

Ignoring the deadly creatures sneaking up on him from behind, the Terra King calmed everyone down. "After my death, the Altered Creatures and Unday ruled Australis for nearly four thousand years as our people lived as nomadic tribes or as their slaves."

Girgling and twitching its body, the giant slug turned from a dull brown to a bright red before shooting a stream of acid onto the back of the man's leg. Instantly his cloak dissolved, followed by layers of flesh from his leg. Bleeding on the stage, he was fortunate enough to have most of his muscle still intact. In great pain, he withheld his scream and stumbled a few steps to the side, pointing at the creature. "*They* tortured us and entertained themselves by having us fight to the death. When we could do no more, they ate us raw and still alive."

The crowd shuttered in horror while listening to the tale and watching the creatures surround him for the kill. It somehow justified the current reverse scenario that took place, where all three types of Unday are forced to kill each other for the sport of men.

The Terra King removed his hood. His bald head and thin face were plain, causing onlookers to focus on his large solid white eyes, recessed in pools of shallow gray skin.

Crouching away from the two beasts, they had him cornered against the back of the stage. "And although the Age of Man has arrived, it still has not fulfilled itself. Instead of removing the Altered Creatures from our lands, we cower behind walls like rabbits hiding in their holes. This must stop." Stepping forward he slapped his palm onto the slug's body, causing it to liquefy. Starting at the place of contact the soft mass of the creature turned into water and splashed onto the stage. "We cannot continue to live in fear from them any longer. Why would we hand a cowards legacy down to our children. It is an outrage to procrastinate on such an issue."

The mutated white wolf curtailed his advancement after seeing the watery grave of the other. Growling, he stood his ground and looked at his options to attack.

Turning, the Terra King walked toward the Del'Unday wolf and pointed at it. "We have made attempts to work with these beasts, these deformities, these aberrations with no honor. But we continue to pay the price. Three hundred years ago, the last Dovenar Wall was built, stopping the expansion of men and Nums. Peace was formed, until we were attacked in Eastland time and time again. And here in Woodlen as well. Unprovoked! Unwarranted! Inexcusable! We gave them no threats." Touching his own leg, the flesh grew back into place to everyone's amazement, including the wolf-like creature. "Our only crime was not torching them and returning their ashes to the soil from which they were created." Retreating, the Del'Unday backed off and lowered its head to admit defeat.

The crowd jumped to their feet, yelling death threats to the Altered Creatures. Raised fists and daggers showed signs of anger and desire for revenge. It took several minutes for the Terra King to regain control. While doing so, he waved the creature away as his guards escorted it behind the stage curtains.

"Caution, my friends. The winds are changing and the creatures are gaining ground. We could easily lose everything we have and return to the Age of Altered Creatures. It is at your doorstep right now, as we speak. You must make a choice to help our cause, or die under the ruling of beasts."

He paused to get a sense of the crowd, who were violently agitated at the creatures as well as themselves, for not taking action. Yelling protests against the creatures, the crowd was nearly out of control. Those without anger in their eyes, pleaded to the King for help against these beasts. Their body language showed him that he was getting the response he wanted.

The Terra King continued, "But all is not lost, for there is still hope. Actions can be taken to help us against them. With the guidance of the Rules of Order and the words of Runestone Scrolls we shall take back this land which is rightfully ours. And those who help will live forever as the Grand-Firs that saved Australis."

He paused allowing the audience to cheer and scream in support. Soaking it in, the King allowed the crowd's energy to become contagious to those still in question. Even Emilen and Wess had been swept up in the shouting as the King continued. "Some of you have the strength to be the new hero's of this age. Legends will be written about you and lyrics will be sung about your courage. You know who you are, in your heart down deep. You know you can make a difference if given the chance. But I cannot take you all, so be sure you will commit to carrying out your forefather's dreams before standing and joining my core of spiritual leaders," he ended on a very enthusiastic note.

The crowd cheered and applauded enthusiastically.

Em stood up on her seat and raised her arms. "I will join you!"

Thorik was shocked that she had been caught up in the excitement of the speech and forgotten what they had come to do. "What are you doing? Get down before someone sees you." Red robed guards were moving toward various people that stood up. Thorik spotted one guard making his way up the crowded stairs toward her.

Emilen spoke to Thorik as she gazed at the Terra King. "Don't you see, Thorik? This is our way to help revive our beliefs. We finally have the help we've been looking for to spread our words of wisdom." She looked down at him and reached out her hand for him to take. "Come with me. We will spread the glory of our faith across the land. We will be heroes and we will be honored. You've been looking for a way to be respected. Here it is, take it."

"No, this is wrong," he replied as the guard moved closer to them. "This is not how we learned our faith."

"Maybe we weren't told everything we needed to know." She stepped down off the seat, grabbed both of his hands and looked deeply into his eyes. "Please Thorik, for me. I want you to come with."

He clutched her hands tight and tears swelled up in his eyes. "No, I can't. Please don't leave."

"I must," she said as the guard reached them.

"Just you?" the guard asked her.

"No, I'm joining also," announced Wess, quickly stepping forward and placing an arm around her to ensure they wouldn't be separated.

"Wess!" Thorik and Avanda choked out at the same time.

Wess looked over his shoulder as the guard began to escort them down to the stage. "Sorry Dain, I'm taking my opportunities when I can find them. Take care of Avanda for me," he said to Thorik before looking over at his niece. "Enjoy every moment in your life, little girl. Thorik will bring you back home to your parents. Tell them about my heroic contribution to society to save the world."

Laughing, he walked down the steps holding onto Emilen, before yelling back to Thorik, "And good luck with your quest."

Avanda had tried to leave with him but Thorik wouldn't allow her to go. He held onto her tightly as she cried for her uncle to return.

The crowd showed their support with overwhelming approval as the new core of leaders stood before them. The Terra King asked each one to announce their name so that all could hear who the saviors of destiny were. As each one did so, the Terra King placed a leather necklace over their head. Hanging from the leather was a decorative brass disk with a small crystal sphere in its center.

Thorik's heart broke as Em announced her name, and then churned when Wess called out his.

Avanda clung tightly onto Thorik. "Don't leave me, Thorik. Promise that you won't."

"I won't leave you, Avanda. I promise," Thorik said softly as his anger at Wess' irresponsible action grew. He looked over at Brimmelle who was just as furious at their actions.

After the new group of leaders had announced their names, they were all led off the stage to begin final teachings that were needed to reach these levels of wisdom. It was announced that isolation from all others would be required for an extended amount of time to prepare the new recruits for these tasks.

Thorik now sat with Avanda, wondering what he could do. *What were they thinking? We have a promise to keep for Ambrosius. They have a responsibility to Avanda.*

He finally turned back to the people behind him that seemed to know a bit more about this process. "Where are they taking them?"

"Don't know. No one knows. Many people have tried to stop their husbands, fathers, and other family members from joining but have never found them. You would think that they would just be proud of them for their contribution."

It wasn't the answer that Thorik wanted to hear.

Time felt as though it was running fast and standing still all at the same time for Thorik. His mind was spinning with questions of what to do next. He couldn't leave Brimmelle and Gluic at the resurgence and the crowd was too tight to make his way over to them, so he sat idle as it continued.

The Terra King walked over to one of the large wooden Runestone mockups. It was the Health Rune. "As the reborn Mountain King, I have the responsibility and burden to provide all of the Fir with proper instructions of how to interpret the Words of Wisdom."

Brimmelle couldn't believe his ears. "Firs are not told how to interpret them. The words are sound, solid, and speak for themselves."

The people around Brimmelle tried to get him to quiet down.

The King continued. "With this burden, I also have my original abilities to carry out their true powers. This Health Rune, for example, means more than internal and external health. It holds the secret to physical repairs of the body. A broken limb or burns can be healed with it. Come to me if you have ailments and I will demonstrate."

Several people stood up. The guards directed them to Brimmelle's side of the seating area before heading down to the stage.

Brimmelle stood up and shouted, "This is an outrage. The Runestones are not to be used as some spectacle in a theatrical show. They are a belief system of words and the meaning of them. You don't learn the true nature of what these rules and scrolls were created for by being entertained." He looked sharply over at Thorik who was watching him with more interest than ever before. "You have to read them with your own eyes and come to your own understanding," he finished with passion in his voice that he himself did not know he had.

Brimmelle turned to Gluic, to see her reaction, only to find her gone. In her place, two red guards grabbed him before they dragged him out of the event. While doing so, he looked toward the stage to see Gluic standing in line to be healed by the Terra King.

He began to panic. Never in his adult life had anyone ever physically restrained him. The thought of it wasn't even in his mind until after it was being done. He suddenly realized that he could be in danger by authorities with higher power than himself. A terrifying concept he had only begun to understand.

What would come of him? More importantly, who would take care of his mother? The situation became even graver as he realized that his mother was in danger and he would not be able to help. Not now, perhaps not ever again. *What have I done?*

"Where will he be taken?" Thorik asked the now familiar people behind him.

"The Southwind mines are where most protesters are sent." He was uninterested in Brimmelle's fate.

Thorik's world was quickly falling apart and then to add to that, Gluic was now walking onto the stage as the man in front of her reached the King.

Gluic smiled and waited patiently in line as others were being healed by the touch of the Terra King. As usual, Gluic had her own agenda that occasionally crossed paths with everyone's goals. It was always a question of *how* her actions would help later, more than *if* they would.

"My leg was crushed while logging and had to be removed." The man displayed the wooden replacement below his knee.

"I can see that," the Terra King said. "Do you believe in the Rune of Health's healing powers?"

"Yes sir, I do."

"Do you believe in my power as the Mountain King?" Placing his hands onto the man's wooden appendage, he used his powers to alter the makeup of the material into flesh and bone, veins and arteries, fat and muscle.

"Yes, I believe," the man shouted.

"Again." The Terra King continued the manipulation of matter from wood and air to living tissues. Everyone sat in silence as they watched in awe.

"I believe in your powers and in the words of the Runestones."

Lowering his leg down to the ground, the Terra King removed the man's cane. "Walk."

The man stood on both legs and took a step forward and then another.

The crowd went wild.

Gluic was next in line as she smiled at him while walking over to center stage. She grasped a thin crystal tightly in her left hand. Its powers would come in useful.

"I have stones," Gluic told to the Terra King in a serious manner.

"And how long have you had them dear lady?"

"For many years now."

"Show me where you hurt and I will lay my hands upon you so you will be healed."

Gluic smiled and reached out for his hands. "I will guide your hands to the spot."

He allowed her to take his hands. A sudden shock ran though his body. His chin wrenched down into his chest and his legs buckled, knocking him to his knees. Spasms shook his body as she held his hand tight within hers. Continuing to shake, he collapsed to the floor.

Kneeling on her left knee, she looked into his white eyes as she tightened her grip. *Do you hear me?* She thought while her face tightened.

Shaking uncontrollably, he stared into her eyes and responded. *Yes.*

Good. Now, what's behind this deception? What are your plans?

A flood of thoughts began to pour into her head. The images of violent deaths and suffering were overwhelming. Battles of creatures against the humans were seen as well as a flood wiping out a city and people drowning in horror. She saw his past and his plans for the future; slavery of humans and a Del'Unday kingdom of great power. Trying to wade through all of his hatred, she focused on his thoughts of his current plans and she saw them. She then saw his silhouette standing above her as she lay dead.

Her mind link had been broken. She looked down to see new life in his eyes and he smiled from the visions he had just given her. She quickly placed the crystal in her side pouch as she tried to stand.

But, it was now Gluic's turn to suffer as he grabbed tightly onto her remaining hand. She froze in her tracks for a few moments before she began to fall to the ground. Her flora decorations quickly began dying and tumbling off her. She reached over with her free hand and grabbed his wrist. She channeled her pain back into his hand, which had a hold on her. Squeezing his wrist she prevented the pain from deluding itself up his arm. His hand turned dark as heat blisters formed and his fingers began to thin.

Everyone was speechless as they watched the two struggle back and forth on stage.

The Terra King shouted in pain as his hand burned from the acid that oozed out of the blisters on his hand. He released her, and she did the same.

She stumbled a few feet away while regaining her balance. Turning toward the audience she pointed at the King and announced, "This is-" Nothing else came out.

The Terra King stood up slowly as he watched her. He had used his powers of alteration to change all the air around Gluic into a poisonous gas. She could not breathe.

Gasping for air, she tried to make it off the side of the stage. She needed to get away from him before it was too late. A guard stepped in her path, stopping her escape. A second guard stepped in between her and the Terra King to prevent her from returning. Both guards began to choke from the poisonous gas, which extended from the Terra King's hands and surrounded her body. She fell to her knees, then to her side. Then calmly and quietly, Gluic died.

Silence came over Pyrth's amphitheater while the Terra King worked his way back to the center of the stage. As he caught his strength, one of his servants ran over to show him a document and whisper in his ear.

Thorik was physically and mentally numb. He didn't know how to react to the sight of his grandmother lying dead on stage. He couldn't even feel Avanda holding onto him and burrowing her face into his chest while crying. He couldn't hear or feel anything.

"We are under attack my friends, my patrons." The Terra King broke the odd air about them. Pointing down to Gluic's body, "This was a servant of Ambrosius. Sent here to kill me."

"And it continues to get worse. Our Grand Council has been destroyed and our final attempt to bridge this species gap has ended. Ambrosius, a long time supporter of the Altered Creatures and their Unday descendants, has destroyed the Grand Council. Desire for corruption and his personal agenda has removed our only remaining chance for peace." The Terra King knew how to play the crowd with a dramatic pause. "He has been spotted today north of Woodlen traveling with several of these perversions of nature. He has come for you and your children. He plans to destroy everything you have in order to get what he wants, a return of power for the Altered

Creatures. For he, my followers, is a Notarian E'rudite, a servant of the original Notarians."

Over half of the crowd stood up to flee the theater. Thorik debated his options. Grabbing Avanda's hand, they headed for the exit along with many others in the audience. However, their reasoning was to save their families, not to alert Ambrosius of his sighting.

"Be seated my children. You are safe for now. We have dispatched several of my best enforcers to bring him to justice and the guard duty at the gates are being tripled."

A few of those on the ends of the rows had already left, including Thorik and Avanda, as the red guards regained control and ordered the audience to sit back down to continue with the long ceremony.

Chapter 23

Vengeance

"**I** loathe hiding," Ambrosius shouted as his current situation was getting the better of him. "I struggle to believe that I cannot show my face inside the Dovenar Walls. The land that I fought my entire life to protect and save." He frequently spiked the end of his staff into the ground in anger, while stomping around the temporary campsite.

The camp was far enough from the Dovenar Wall to evade detection. The open area was hidden with thick brush and had a few logs to sit on next to the small passing stream. They had selected this location to wait for the Nums to return with information because it was off of the main roads and the Nums could follow the stream back up from Woodlen.

"Relax, Ambrosius," Grewen responded as he rested on his back. Taking a bite from one of the fire logs, he chewed on it while watching the large white clouds pass behind the thick green covering of leaves. With a full inhale of the fresh air, he closed his eyes to take his own words to heart before letting the air out with a slight whistle of his pursed lips. "If the Nums come back and say it is clear, you'll walk right in. This is just a precautionary measure. Think of it as a temporary exile before your triumphant return." Grewen smirked and he opened one eye to see Ambrosius' reaction.

Ambrosius did not react to his words.

Perched on one of the larger logs, Draq watched his friend pace back and forth. "I could fly over to see where the Nums are. Perhaps they have the information you need and I can fly back with it to save time."

"If there are truly assassins looking for me, your current flying may have already placed us in jeopardy. And if it is not true, Del'Unday's are still captured for being near the Dovenar Wall. You'll end up fighting a Chuttlebeast or some other Unday at the next Coliseum Event," Ambrosius replied.

"I'd like to see them try. I have no fear of them," Draq softly replied with a challenging manner.

"I don't want you to take that risk. I need you to care for Ericc if something should happen to me."

Draq lowered his posture a bit. "Your son is safe with my family."

"Son?" Grewen's little ear stubs perked up. "Why congratulations my brother, why didn't you tell me you had spawned new life?" Grewen leaned onto his left elbow and reached over to pat Ambrosius on the back with his right hand. "So how old is the little guy?"

Ambrosius nodded a thank you to Grewen with sadness in his eyes. "He's fourteen," he said slowly. "But I haven't seen him since he was six."

Grewen was shocked at this news. "For the love of Trewek, why not?"

Draq realized that Ambrosius would struggle with this line of conversation and intruded into it. "Stay out of it, Grewen. You don't understand what it takes to be in his position."

"What I don't understand is how you could not see your son for eight years," Grewen replied.

"It's for his own safety." Draq worked his way between the two.

Grewen could no longer see Ambrosius behind Draq. Looking for an answer he reached forward and grabbed the dragon around the neck with one hand and moved him to his side so he could see Ambrosius. He held the dragon out of view with the same level of emotion he would have with moving a rock. It was just an annoyance, nothing to get upset about.

Draq did not enjoy his emotionless removal from the scene, and he began to thrash about. Grewen's grasp was too tight to break free but it wasn't enough to cut off the airflow. Draq's tail violently slapped the ground, his wings flapped, and his claws scratched in an effort to break free of the Mognin's hand.

"Ambrosius. What's going on?" Grewen asked as Draq swung his spiked tail and lower claws up onto Grewen's outstretched arm. Grewen's skin was thick but Draq's razor sharp points impaled him and began to draw blood. Draq tightened his claws with all of his strength.

"Ouch!" Grewen yelped. Releasing his grip, he tried to shake the dragon off his arm.

Draq finally let go. "Don't ever touch me again," he snarled. Lifting off the ground with his strong wings he flicked the blood off his claws down at Grewen before he flew off into the woods, out of view.

Draq was one of the meanest and nastiest Del'Unday he had ever met. Short tempered and violent in a fight. Grewen knew the only reason he didn't attack him with full force was because of Ambrosius. Draq was many things, but most of all he was loyal. He would never abandon Ambrosius in his time of need.

"He'll be fine once he has some time to himself," Ambrosius advised the giant.

"Tell me about your son," Grewen requested again as he started to bandage the claw marks on his arm.

"After the Dovenar Civil War and the Battle of Maegoth, you left to find inner peace. I had my own similar journey. I went to seek guidance from the Third Oracle in the Northern Wastelands. He helped me understand my role as a leader and the need of a council of peers from every part of Australis. Returning to the six remaining provinces, I began the Grand Council."

"I know about the Council. But what does this have to do with your son?" Grewen asked as he finished tending to his bleeding wounds.

Ambrosius ignored the question and continued with his story. "During the third year of the Council I met Asha at the Greensbrook conferences, and we quickly fell in love. The Grand Council had begun to unite and make important steps forward. Life was good."

"My success must have struck a bad vein with Darkmere as he began to stir the hatred within the city of Corrock toward those who followed the Council. His legions of Del'Unday would try to stop everything we put in place. But it was me he wanted, not the Council. So, I resigned my position and began a family hidden away from the public's eyes. My son, Ericc, was born in secrecy and was never told of his heritage. The less he knew about my past, the less likely he would be pulled into my affairs."

"Darkmere must have redirected his forces to search for us, for all was quiet during my absence. Asha and I were able to evade them, often moving just before they arrived to kill us. It was aggravating to always be hiding and living in the shadows, never knowing who our enemies were."

"Our luck ran out while we lived in a small shack on Ki'Volney Lake, just east of your birthplace, near Lagona Falls. I returned home after a day of fishing to find that Asha and Ericc had been taken." Ambrosius fought off the vivid memory as he talked his way through it.

"I followed the tracks of the Del'Unday captors northwest to Corrock where I found my wife strung up onto the city's locked gates. Her arms and feet tied secure and her dress ripped and bloody from their torturing of her. They had let her hang there, starving. She hung from the barred door for days, mocked by locals, staring out across the landscape waiting for me to save her, but I never came. She was dead before I arrived. The Death Witch Irluk had taken her soul and left an empty shell of a body. I had failed her."

Ambrosius stopped only a moment to take a sip of water before he continued, "After lowering her from the gate and saying goodbye, I turned my attention to finding my son. I was furious as I tore the gates apart and entered the city looking for him. I tortured and murdered many Del'Unday before I was told that my son was to be ceremoniously killed by Alchemists in an attempt to prevent Darkmere's premonition of my son killing his own. I left the devastated south entrance of Corrock with Asha's lifeless body, to bury her properly and begin my search for my son."

"I searched for months until I got wind of the location where my son was to be sacrificed for Darkmere. During the Eve of Light, in the Alchemist's Temple of Surod, I found him and I would have never gotten out of there with my son if it weren't for the help of Draq, Chella, and Bovel. Unfortunately, Chella and Bovel did not make it out alive."

"Darkmere and his people have been hunting for my son ever since. Being constantly recognized from my past I had two options. Hide away from civilization with my son or hide him until I could stop Darkmere. It was then that I asked Draq to take Ericc to his home and raise him with his own son and wife. He agreed and has done so ever since. I don't know where he is, for I do not want my own thoughts to betray me. I only know that Draq will keep him safe until he is of mind and strength to protect himself."

Ambrosius looked at the sad face of Grewen before concluding his story, "And now here I am again, hiding. I am getting too old for this game, but I refuse to live my life in fear."

"Fear will do you no good, old man," said an unexpected voice from the woods behind him.

Ambrosius used his staff to quickly get on his feet before swiveling to see a man walk out into the small clearing. Middle-aged with short, straight black hair, he wore a red and gold cloak, colored with magical symbols that lined the bottom as well as around the neckline. He held a mere stick of a wand before him in one hand and several strings of beads in the other.

Ambrosius quickly looked around and recognized several Del'Unday species moving in the woods as they surrounded the two. He motioned for Grewen to watch his back as he placed his attention on the Alchemist who was approaching him.

Grewen stood up to his full height of over twelve feet, hoping that it would intimidate them and prevent an attack. In addition, he smiled as though he was looking forward to a good fight. His huge leathery hands slapped together with a crash that made everyone stop in their tracks before he rubbed them together to loosen up his wrists and fingers.

Grewen had no intent on hurting anyone; he had vowed not to offensively attack anyone after the Massacre at Maegoth. Regardless, he understood that the majority of warfare was mental strategies more than brute strength. This game he was willing to play.

Ambrosius was not one to be intimidated. He quickly took charge of the situation and demanded information from the uninvited guests, "Speak your business quickly, for I am in no mood for games."

"Your game has ended today." The unknown man nodded his head at one of his Del'Unday on his right.

Without taking his eyes off the intruder, Ambrosius could see a hairy hunched-back Del'Unday move forward into the clearing to his left. The creature limped from old battle wounds as it dragged something toward them. It stopped, leaned down to grab the item, and threw it into the camp.

Thorik was tossed to the ground. He rolled to a stop near Ambrosius, only to quickly jump back to his feet in defiance. He had several scratches and bruises but quickly regained his composure and dusted himself off. "His name is Sharcodi," he told Ambrosius. "They ambushed us halfway upstream."

Ambrosius glanced over at Thorik in disappointment before returning his gaze back at Sharcodi.

"Don't blame the Num, he actually was of little used to us," Sharcodi commented with an arrogance that came across in his body language. "When I found them, they wouldn't have seen me even if they were standing next to me," he said with cocky display of his thorn bush wand.

Them? Ambrosius questioned to himself. Not knowing if Sharcodi had all of the Nums or just a few more, he kept his question silent. "Invisibility spells to sneak up on Nums is not impressive. A wizard worth his weight would have easily found a Mognin in a forest from the pounding of his enormous heart. Yet, you prefer to capture and interrogate defenseless Polenums."

"I told them nothing," Thorik defended himself. "I promise."

It made no difference to Ambrosius. He had given no information to the Nums that could leak out and harm him. He was much too wise for that. Ambrosius was more interested in knowing where the rest of the Nums were, but knew better than to ask in front of their company. Perhaps one or more were hiding safely.

"He's quite correct, you know." Sharcodi's smug attitude was thicker than tar. "He wouldn't even give up his own name. Really, it was quite improper, especially for a Num. But the fact is I found you easily enough without his assistance."

Sharcodi nodded to his strongmen again, who this time brought out Avanda. She was kicking and biting as the Unday attempted to keep hold of her.

"I thank you for the safe return of our companions. But we really must be on our way," Ambrosius stated to Sharcodi. He presented himself very casual and unmoved by the intrusion of the Alchemist and his Del'Unday horde.

"I'm afraid I did not come here to reunite you with old friends. I came here for you. Your young one here will stay with us until I am comfortable that you have been properly detained."

The Del'Unday pulled out a long deformed blade and held it to Avanda's throat. The blade appeared to have been bent and hammered back out many times in the past, but the edge was still sharp. Battle-beaten points across the blade pressed against her skin.

Thorik screamed, "No, don't hurt her!" If it were not for Ambrosius holding onto the back of his cloak, Thorik would have made a run for her. As it was, his actions made the Del'Unday pull the knife up, creasing Avanda's skin.

"What is it that you seek of me?" Ambrosius said without emotion.

"I seek many things from you. First of all I want to hear you apologize for the Civil War destruction of the Dovenar Kingdom. And surely for the collapse of Surod Temple, where I personally used to live before your wrath." Sharcodi looked at a few of the Del'Unday that had surrounded the camp and continued, "Then apologize to these fine Del'Unday for crushing the buildings and innocent families in the forth district of Corrock. Some of them had families that died in that attack from you."

Sharcodi stepped toward Ambrosius and Thorik feeling pretty confident about his situation as he continued his speech. "You also owe your Num an apology for destroying his spiritual Temple, the Mountain King Statue." He patted Thorik on the shoulder and gave him a wink to imply that he was helping him out.

Thorik listened to the speech and was again questioning what other secrets of his past Ambrosius may have hidden from him.

"But before I forget, I want to thank you for the destruction of the Grand Council. It has allowed us to take back that which is rightfully ours. Now that the Council is out of the way and marshal law has taken over each city, we can quickly fix those things that aren't up to our standards." Sharcodi smiled as he finished.

Ambrosius stood calm as his senses monitored Sharcodi's movements walking about the camp. His concern was more for Thorik and Avanda at this point. As dangerous as Sharcodi was, he was no match for Ambrosius. At least he wasn't the last time he saw him eight years ago in Surod as an apprentice. It had taken a while, but Ambrosius finally recognized the name, the voice, and the egotistical Alchemist want-to-be that fought along side his master, the High Wizard Noreldi.

"Typical," Ambrosius said. "You want me to grovel to make you look superior to your small army of misfits."

"Oh, dear no," Sharcodi replied with a caviler wave of his hand. "I already know I'm superior to you in many ways. While you were out trying to run Australis with your council, I was working on my craft and perfecting it over the years for just this meeting. You see, you are a relic of what was and now I am the vision of what will be."

"You're delusional, just like your old master Noreldi," Ambrosius calmly remarked with a lack of fear. The calmness was starting to bother Sharcodi, but the use of his prior master's name pushed him to the edge of anger.

It was obvious that he wanted to make Ambrosius squirm and ask for forgiveness, but he would not get any of that on this day. Ambrosius had been broken and struggling for many weeks now and had little patience for this man's futile threats.

"Delusional, am I?" Sharcodi turned his back on them and walked toward the woods. Facing Avanda, he smiled at her as he began to speak quietly. Raising the string of red beads, he moved one bead at a time over his finger to the other side.

Thorik looked to Ambrosius for direction, only to see him tilt his head slightly and squint as though he was trying to listen for something. Moments later, Thorik looked up to see the tops of the trees starting to blow in the wind and a large dark cloud approaching overhead.

"If you leave now, I will let this intrusion pass," Ambrosius announced. "But I warn you, if you provoke me, my retaliation will be swift."

The wind immediately picked up causing Thorik to separate his feet for traction against it. He struggled to keep his balance as the wind shifted directions and pulled him back and forth.

Grewen didn't react to the wind as branches and sand blew against him. However, even he had to shield his eyes a few times as the blowing dirt was getting so thick he could hardly see the trees around them anymore.

Ambrosius stood firm as his cloak and tunic flailed in the gusts while he stared at Sharcodi who was turning toward Ambrosius with his beads at chest height. His fingers were fumbling with the beads as he softly chanted to them. He opened his hand enough to drop a string of red beads to the ground.

"Look out!" Thorik shouted as he pushed Ambrosius to his side just as a fiery rock missed Ambrosius' back. A shower of flame had begun to strike the group of three with flaming liquefied rocks, the size of a Num's fist.

Ambrosius had fallen to his knees. He was stuck several times on the back causing him pain, keeping him from standing. The fiery rocks also had lit his clothes on fire. Regardless, he continued to make his way to his feet until he was struck in the head, knocking him back down to the ground.

Thorik had his arms over his head as he tried to protect himself and make it over to Grewen. The sand continued to get into the Num's eyes while the wind knocked him over twice more. A falling flame smacked him in the right shoulder, just as he reached Grewen's leg.

The rocks pounded on Grewen's back and head as he started on his way to find his friends through the cloud of swirling dirt. He reached down and picked up Thorik and shielded him from the falling balls of fire, before making his way over to Ambrosius. The back of Grewen's robe had started on fire and it was starting to spread across his back.

Ambrosius could feel the burning of his hair and skin as the fire quickly overtook him. The wind fanned the flames in every direction as he yelled in pain.

Grewen heard Ambrosius scream and quickly plucked him from the ground only to toss him into the small stream that ran through the camp. Following him to the water, he knelt down over Ambrosius to protect him from the onslaught of burning hail.

Ambrosius raised himself slightly out of the stream and spit out the water that had rushed into his mouth. Taking only a moment to shake off the chill of the water, he sat up next to Thorik who was also being protected under Grewen's large body.

Sharcodi's sinister laugh could be heard as the sand continued to blow at their faces and the fire rocks beat against Grewen's back as he arched over them. "This is the reason I have been looking for you. I have come to slay the mighty Ambrosius. I came to pay you back for the destruction you unleashed on this land, for all the lives you have taken." Sharcodi walked closer to the threesome and smiled as the chaotic weather avoided his own body.

Thorik looked about, seeing several Del'Unday creatures coming out of hiding and into the camp. Thorik and his friends were surrounded by dozens of vile looking beasts. Most with horns, fangs, or claws ready to strike the small group of three.

Grewen's robe was bursting with flames across his back as he continued to protect his two friends. It did not bother him. In fact, he enjoyed the heat and the pounding. He could have stood there for hours if it weren't for the other issues at hand.

"You will suffer greatly, but I will not kill you. Darkmere wishes you to be alive to watch your son's death." Sharcodi slightly lowered of his wand which reduced the wind noise. He wanted Ambrosius to hear him loud and clear. "Perhaps you are not aware that your son has been spotted by Darkmere's dominion. They will soon have him captured."

Ambrosius' blood boiled as he heard the words, raising himself out of the water with a single purpose in mind. He stood up, walked to Sharcodi, and held his staff out to his left side as he lowered his eyebrows and focused on wizard. "Where is Darkmere?" he demanded.

A slight flick of Sharcodi's wrist caused the storm to intensify and Grewen pulled Thorik farther under him to protect him from the increased frequency of raining fire. The wind was becoming so severe that even Grewen had to brace himself with one arm.

Ambrosius was furious and stood firm while the sand and fiery rain continued to increase directly around him. Even at this great intensity, it never reached his body as it was deflected a short distance before hitting him. "Where is he?" he demanded again to the Alchemist.

Sharcodi looked concerned that Ambrosius was not affected by his magic and lifted his arm and wand directly at Ambrosius as he chanted a few unrecognizable words.

Ambrosius looked at Sharcodi's outstretched arm and reached out with his mind to snap the middle of his forearm backwards. A loud crack was heard over the howling wind. The end of Sharcodi's forearm was lifting into the air for a moment before falling. It hung from the rest of his arm like a possum from a tree limb.

Sharcodi looked on in shock and horror of his useless arm as Ambrosius used his powers to quickly break a series of bones in the same outstretched arm, working from the initial break toward his shoulder.

Before Sharcodi could react, the upper arm snapped in half with a loud crack and fell downward, hanging from the flesh on the remaining stub of his arm past his shoulder.

As quickly as it had started, the wind and fire ended with no traces of ever existing. Thorik looked at his burns disappear. "What happened?"

Grewen looked at Thorik; his burned clothes began to repair themselves. "It appears to be a masterful illusion."

"I asked you a question," Ambrosius said through his tight teeth. He approached Sharcodi to look him eye to eye.

Upon seeing this, the Del'Unday launched their attack on the small group. Several ran at Ambrosius and were quickly knocked back into the trees by his powers. With a glance at Avanda, he used his powers to crush the Del'Unday's hand, hoping to force the knife out of his grip. His attention to that specific Del'Unday was only momentary as he returned his anger toward Sharcodi.

Grewen grabbed two of the Del'Unday and held them out to shield himself from the oncoming attacks. His enormous hands fit around the back of their waist with an unbreakable grasp. Oncoming Del'Unday swung weapons at Grewen's hands to release them, only to hit their own clan member time and time again. The Del'Unday, which were held in Grewen's grasps, began to fight back and block the oncoming attacks of swords and spears.

Concerned for Thorik's well-being from an oncoming Brandercat attacker, Ambrosius utilized his powers to lift Thorik up out of the way and onto a large tree branch.

Thorik was startled by the aerial flight, but quickly stabilized himself on the branch and loaded his bow. He pointed the arrow down at the scaled cat only to find that it had disappeared. Thorik searched everywhere near the base of the tree and found the same results. The cat was gone.

More Del'Unday left their hiding places to join the attack.

Ambrosius' E'rudite powers crushed Sharcodi's ankles, preventing the spell caster from running away while he addressed the new wave of attackers.

Unable to stand from the broken ankles, Sharcodi fell backwards and scattered his magical items across the ground. They were now out of his reach and he was temporarily without power.

Ambrosius turned around to see eight more Del'Unday attacking. Spears and arrows were in flight toward him as well as one of the Krupes who had leaped at him.

Ambrosius raised his staff in front of him to shield himself from the multitude of attacks from every direction. Just as the invisible shield began to form, the earth from below him fell inward, allowing the attacks to continue forward. He fell and landed on his back at the bottom of a ten-foot deep hole. A giant Del'Unday Terragrub had dug the hole and was on one side of Ambrosius, showing its five-foot round mouth of spiraling teeth. The Del'Unday from above began to jump down on him.

Thorik peered back and forth looking for the Brandercat along the ground. His weapon cocked and ready to fire. His focus was only interrupted as he saw Ambrosius fall into the ground followed by many Del'Unday jumping in after him. It was at this moment that the Brandercat jumped from an upper branch onto Thorik, knocking him to the ground.

Thorik quickly rolled to his feet and ran into the woods away from the cat.

The feline purred loudly with pleasure as it ran to catch him. "Good. Run. The chase adds to the taste of the meal. Your raised heart-beat fills your flesh with hot blood, sweet and juicy."

Thorik darted in and out of the thick woods faster than ever before in his life. He knew of no one that could keep up with him, until now. The creature was not only keeping up with Thorik, but he was gaining on him.

Thorik looked over his shoulder to see the creature closing in on him and then fade off. It had blended into the colors of the terrain. Still visible, it blurred and became unfocused.

Thorik could not stop and look, he only had fractions of seconds to peer back and the creature was no longer visible to him.

Not knowing what to do, Thorik heard the crunching of leaves and sticks under the Brandercats heavy paws. The sounds approached closer and closer until there was a sudden quiet. Thorik darted to the right, assuming the creature was airborne and couldn't make the turn.

He was correct; the Brandercat skidded to a halt and turned to run after Thorik back toward camp.

Nearing the campsite, Thorik was exhausted. Splashing his way across the stream, he turned around and fell to his knees. Aiming his bow at the empty forest on the far side of the water for several minutes, he waited for some sign of the creature.

The Brandercat slowly moved across the water just downstream of the Num. It moved one foot at a time, slowly in and out of the water, trying not to disrupt the water flow. Success would have been his if it were not for the exceptional eyes of Polenums.

Thorik noticed the small changes in the water downstream and didn't think twice before shooting.

The arrow flew toward the creature as it tried to jump out of the way. But it wasn't fast enough. The head of the arrow lodged deep into the right shoulder, piercing the chest, causing it to fall with a splash and reveal its location.

The creature's natural brownish green scales came back to life as it stood up and limped to shore before falling again.

Thorik armed his bow with another arrow from his quiver and walked toward the wounded cat. "Don't move!" Thorik shouted.

The fallen creature coughed and laughed back at Thorik. "You fesh don't have what it takes."

The adrenaline from being chased was still hot within Thorik. He raised his bow up to put the creature out of its misery. Staring down at it he realized that his goal was not to kill it. Instead it was to preserve the lives of his friends and himself. "I've done my part with you. The local Fesh'Unday can finish you off." He then turned away.

Blood poured out of the wound of the Brandercat as it gasped for breath. "You coward. Kill me or the next time we meet I shall eat you alive," it shouted as Thorik ran back to the battle.

Reaching the campsite, the ground began to rumble. The hole where Ambrosius had fallen was emitting shockwaves of trimmers underground. More Del'Unday had arrived to surround Grewen. Thorik realized that there were too many Del'Unday and they would eventually overtake them. Even with that said, he had to leave Grewen and Ambrosius to defend themselves. He needed to find Avanda.

With a screech that nearly pierced Thorik's ears, Draq rocketed out of the woods, through the open area, and back into the woods on the far side, picking up one of the Del'Unday in his passing. His speed was so fast that nobody even saw him. They wouldn't have even noticed him if it hadn't been for the sound, and the breeze that followed.

His time away from Grewen had cooled him off, but his return to camp to find them fighting heated up his blood with excitement and the thrill of taking out his victims.

Draq did not slow down as he released the Del'Unday, slapping the creature hard against a large tree, killing him instantly. Turning around for another run, he blasted his way between the trees back to the opening. Once there, he corrected his course and grabbed his second victim with his claws, launching it off its feet without warning. This time Draq arched his back, bolting his way above the trees and beyond before releasing the creature in midair. He raced the falling creature back to earth with great pleasure. Draq enjoyed this far too much and made this into a game as he passed by his falling victim on his way to the next.

Thorik rushed out of camp in the direction that he had last seen Avanda. Upon entering the woods he found the jagged dagger that had been used against her. It lay in the dirt covered with blood. His heart raced at the thought of her being hurt, or worse.

A trail of blood weaved its chaotic way amongst the ground, bushes, and tree trunks. Thorik frantically followed as the fresh blood droplets to a tree. He stopped and looked for the next clue to their direction.

A high-pitched scream was heard from beyond the next grouping of red-thorn bushes. He raced around to find her sitting with her back to him, legs crossed, and hunched forward.

He stopped to look for the Del'Unday that had captured her. Not seeing it, he slowly stepped closer to her. He noticed blood on Avanda's clothes. She wasn't moving.

Looking back into the woods for her attacker, he quietly spoke, "Avanda? Are you okay?"

She sat up and turned her head toward him. Blood splatter covered her face and shirt. Tears ran down from her eyes and past her cheeks. "I'm fine." After placing the last few odd shaped items into a red and gold pouch, she sniffed and wiped her face with her left sleeve. She had found Sharcodi's purse of magic and was intrigued by its contents, but knew better than to show an adult who may take them from her.

Still very leery of the situation, Thorik kept his eyes on the woods while helping her up. "You're covered with blood, are you sure you didn't get hurt?"

"It's not my blood," she stammered and sniffed. "That deformed creature's hand exploded." Twitching at the memory replaying in her mind, she continued. "After dropping the knife, he chased me into the woods."

"So you lost him. Well done. But he may return," Thorik finished as he cautiously led her back to camp.

"Oh, I don't think he'll bother us any longer," she commented. During her fight with the creature she had thrown several objects at him from within the found magical pack. To her surprise, his body shrunk to a mere tenth of his original size and was last seen being chased by a hawk.

She knew her tale of adventure would surely have the purse of magical items taken away, so she placed it under her cloak to keep it in hiding until she returned to Farbank and showed her friends.

Back at camp, an enormous ground quake lifted Grewen and the Del'Unday off their feet before they fell down to the still quivering earth. A moment of absolute silence blanketed the woods.

Just as everyone started getting back up, a second ground blast occurred. This time several Del'Unday were thrown from the Terragrub hole, landing in nearby trees and in the stream.

Ambrosius slowly climbed out of the hole. Cut and bleeding, he had finished off the multitude of attacks. Tired and in pain, his business was not yet completed. The ground was littered with Del'Unday. Some dead, some unconscious, while others groaned in pain. But Sharcodi was still alive and held valuable information.

Thorik and Avanda had just entered camp and ran over to help their E'rudite friend out of the hole.

Ambrosius glanced over at the remaining Del'Unday. Not a word was spoken as they gained their footing and rushed out of the camp, into the deep woods, away from the E'rudite.

He returned his gaze to find Sharcodi, who by this point had dragged himself into the woods. Ambrosius walked over to the spell caster as Sharcodi got on his knees to beg for his life.

"Where is my son?" Ambrosius demanded one last time.

Sharcodi groaned as his ribs cracked from Ambrosius' power. "I will not betray the Terra King's orders." He hadn't given up yet. With one last effort of strength he used his remaining arm to reach for powder within a small side pouch and throw it at Ambrosius' face. The E'rudite quickly used his powers to redirect the unknown red dust back at him. The powder hit Sharcodi's face and launched a series of events that ended with his head slowly dissolving away in a gruesome fashion.

Ambrosius took the end of his staff and pushed the headless kneeling body over before looking around at the camp. By this point Draq had the trees littered with creatures and Grewen still held a few battered, but alive, creatures out in front of him.

"Terra King?" Thorik asked as he moved toward the middle of camp. "He's the one that killed Gluic, and his men have taken Brimmelle to a mine in Southwind."

Grewen turned his attention to Thorik, "Gluic's dead? By the hands of Darkmere? Where?"

"No, not Darkmere, the Terra King. And it happened in Pyrth's amphitheater."

Grewen dropped the unconscious Del'Unday that had been used as his shields. "Darkmere and the Terra King are one in the same," he informed Thorik.

Ambrosius declared, "We are going to Pyrth," as he headed past them, following his own orders.

Thorik and Avanda quickly moved around the camp picking up arrows and placing them in his quiver for future battles.

Grewen's face saddened before continuing, "I'm sorry to hear about your grandmother's death and your uncle's capture. We should be able to cut through River's Edge to get ahead of them and free him in Pelonthal. Where are Wess and Emilen, are they safe?"

"I don't think so, it's a long story. I'll tell you on the way," answered Thorik as they rushed downstream to keep up with an angry Ambrosius.

Chapter 24
Frontal Assault

By the time the small group neared the Dovenar Wall, surrounding the province of Woodlen, Ambrosius was more furious than ever. He had played back every one of Darkmere's attacks on him and his family's life over and over again. Visions of his wife and her death flashed in his mind, as well as the battle to save his son. He recalled various arguments of their youth and how they escalated into a Civil War that ended with the horrors of the Battle of Maegoth. Memories of the day when Darkmere killed the King caused Ambrosius to tighten his fists. An endless line of death and pain existed every time he thought about his nemesis.

He had instructed Draq to fly home to see if the claim of his son could be true, but Draq would not leave Ambrosius on the eve of battle. Protection of Ambrosius was his primary reasoning, besides he never turned down an opportunity to enjoy a good fight.

"It's conceivable that Ericc has been seen," Draq admitted.

Already furious, Ambrosius snapped back at Draq, "How is that possible? You have him protected away from civilization."

"He has run off twice before, but we have located him with my son's help and brought him back. No harm was done," Draq responded.

Ambrosius' voice deepened as he addressed the winged beast. "No harm? If he has been seen and identified by any of Darkmere's vultures, his life is in danger along with your family." Fuming over this new information, he asked, "How could you let this happen?"

"Ericc loathes being confined and refuses to follow anyone's rules but his own. He's much like his father in that regard," Draq spit back with a chilled tone as he distanced himself from the E'rudite and flew over the treetops.

The dragon's words only added fuel to the E'rudite's anger as he stomped through the forest.

The walk toward the Dovenar Wall had given Thorik and Grewen time to think clearly. Walking into the city of Pyrth was not a good decision for any of them. Their attempts to convince Ambrosius of this were wasted as he had already made up his mind.

Draq flew high overhead to warn them of traps, but apparently no one had planned for a frontal assault by an E'rudite, a dragon, a Mognin, and two young Polenums. Draq had not led them down the winding stream that Thorik had taken. Instead, he gave them a more direct route to the front gate.

Ambrosius approached the Dovenar Wall gates as the locals moved out of the way and the guards approached. It was an odd sight to be seen as a well known dignitary, now outlaw, walked up defiantly with a huge Ov'Unday and two little Nums in tow.

Emotions were high as the guards loaded their arrows in their bows along the upper catwalk of the wall. A small group of military personnel broke up a quick huddle as the leader motioned for a squad of men to stand on each side of the gate's entrance.

Avanda held onto Thorik's hand and couldn't believe the level of focus everyone was giving them. She had been the center of attention before, but never by such a tense group.

Thorik looked at Grewen for reassurance that they wouldn't be sent to death for this. Grewen responded with a shrug that informed him that he didn't know what would happen.

They both continued in their attempts to talk Ambrosius out of this approach all the way to the gate, which was now lined across the top with guards and a few dozen more on the ground in his way. In the center, Sergeant Borador stood with his hand raised to stop Ambrosius. Thorik recognized him from his first crossing into Pyrth and was not looking forward to meeting him again.

"By the local authorities of Pyrth and the province of Woodlen, you are hereby ordered to surrender yourself for crimes against the Dovenar Kingdom," the sergeant ordered.

"Then it is crimes against myself, for I am the Dovenar Kingdom authority." Ambrosius commanded, without affecting his stride. "Now get out of my way!"

The sergeant asked again for Ambrosius to stop with no results. "Prepare to fire on my command!" he shouted at the rows of archers on the wall in hopes of making his point clear to Ambrosius. It did not, and the sergeant was not going to allow the most notable criminal ever known to just stroll through his gates. "Fire!" he finally shouted. The sounds of bowstrings twanged as they released their arrows.

Grewen quickly leaned over the Nums to protect them from any arrows coming their way. It wasn't needed, for halfway through their flight the arrows took a sudden turn away from Ambrosius and went instead toward the guards in front of him. The military group panicked and tried to get out of the way as the arrows shot into their legs and arms during their escape. The E'rudite powers of Ambrosius were stronger than they had been in some time and they were charged with energy from his anger at Darkmere.

Sergeant Borador stood firm in the center of the two gates waiting for Ambrosius. He had easily evaded the oncoming arrows with a few quick turns of his body. Sliding the broad sword out of its sheath, he grasped it firmly with both hands. "I will enjoy this." He pointed the end of the sword directly at the approaching fixated man.

The rest of the guards ran or crawled to safety behind the second open gate as Borador gave his next order to them. "Lower both gates," he said once Ambrosius was past the first one.

Both gates came crashing straight down, locking Sergeant Borador and Ambrosius in a cage.

Grewen saw the falling gate but was unable to reach it before it had hit the ground. The gate was quickly locked into place with many metal beams preventing Grewen from lifting it back up. Once he realized this, he grabbed the gate's thick iron rods and tried to pull them apart. Welded horizontal rods provided extra strength to the gate making his attempts very difficult.

Grewen pulled with all of his might as the bars slowly bent. Snapping of weld joints could be heard over the creaking of metal as he slowly increased the size of the opening.

Thorik yelled through the gate, "Ambrosius, there's too many of them on the wall. Get out of there."

Ambrosius walked toward Sergeant Borador and glanced at the outstretched shining metal blade in front of him. He stopped as he heard the rumbling of guards, preparing for their own assault on him from the catwalk above.

Sergeant Borador had him within his snare of fifteen-foot thick walls topped with heavy armaments and thick rod iron gates on each side. At his call, a hailstorm of spears, arrows, and boiling oils would flood down on top of Ambrosius. His captive was trapped. The E'rudite was his.

"I was told to take you alive, but I can live with the consequences of your death," Borador spoke as he raised his masterful sword over his head to attack the silent prisoner.

Ambrosius abruptly raised his arms out to his sides. His fingers fanned out in his right hand while he grasped his wooden staff in his left.

Fractions of time felt like long frozen moments as everyone began to feel the enormous power building within the E'rudite.

"Fire!" Borador shouted, causing a launch of a hundred projectiles toward Ambrosius from above.

It was at that moment, the walls in both directions of the E'rudite's outstretched arms exploded with fury, shattering the individual blocks into small shards of flying debris. The gate and catwalk behind the sergeant also erupted away from them sending sharp broken metal rods into the distance.

The guards that once stood on the wall had been catapulted a great distance with the wall fragments; some landed on roofs of buildings while others were crushed from tumbling blocks. Limbs and clothes were ripped from many guards at the time of the detonation. They flew through the air and struck other military personnel that happened to be in the area.

The devastation to the walls and the surrounding area was immense. Dust from the eruption of power started to settle on the traumatized environment. Every structure in the vicinity had taken some level of damage from the blast, as the survivors began to slowly move about in confusion.

Sergeant Borador stood, paralyzed with fear, as he realized the grand force that had just been wielded. He no longer stood in a cage of strength, but instead he was encircled with waist high rubble. The strong hold he had on the sword, still over his head, began to weaken under his own trembling.

He moved to the side as Ambrosius started his walk forward again, but had a last second burst of courage and took a large swipe with his weapon at the passing man.

The sword struck at Ambrosius' back only to be stopped by an invisible shield, just prior to hitting him.

Ambrosius glanced over at a large piece of wall that had only fallen twenty yards from them. He enlisted his powers to pull it toward them at a great speed, as though it had been kicked by a giant.

Just missing Ambrosius' back, it grabbed Borador in its flight and struck a building on the opposite side.

Ambrosius never looked back to see Grewen bending the gate apart, or Thorik and Avanda screaming at him to stop before it was too late. He only focused on what was before him.

He had been in Pyrth enough to know exactly where the amphitheater was located. The most direct route would be through the market place and then a line of government buildings.

Draq screeched into the dysfunctional military courtyard with air acrobatics and assaults on armed soldiers and guards along the walls and rooftops. Ensuring not to steal Ambrosius' thunder, he had waited intently for the first explosion before starting his attack. Flying just feet over the wall's catwalk, guards jumped off both sides to find safety. Those that didn't jump were grabbed during his passing and tossed over into the river.

The archers fired rounds of arrows and watched in vain as they could not penetrate the dragon's scales. However, if any of the large arrows that the ballistae shot at Draq were to hit, he would have been knocked out of the air. Fortunately for Draq, his speed and agility prevented their ability to properly aim such weapons.

A good battle rejuvenated Draq. Natural and instinctive in every way, it was what he was born to do. He teased the rooftop soldiers with false injuries as he plummeted toward the ground only to pull up at the last second causing them to jump from their perches. He enjoyed seeing the fear in their eyes.

Ambrosius firmly walked forward forgetting about his friends as Grewen continued to bend the bars on the remaining outside gate. Ambrosius' thoughts were primarily on his son as well as the destruction and death he had seen over the years, all caused by Darkmere. *It must stop, and it must happen today.*

Storming forward he reached the closed wooden doors that led to the commercial market area. The few guards that tried to defend the city were quickly disposed of as he advanced toward the heavy wide oak doors. With a flick of his wrist the doors exploded away from him sending missiles of splinters in every direction but his own.

Empty bent door hinges clung to the block wall as he entered the next area that was covered in wood chips, splinters, and dust. People screamed and ran from the destroyed doors.

Merchants and patrons rushed out of Ambrosius' path while he worked his way across the large market area toward the steps of the old and decrepit Taxation building. Never veering from his course, he removed shacks and toppled wagons that lay before him. Nothing stood long which suggested him diverting from his route. Approaching the series of government buildings, he vaguely recognized some of the officials scattering from the area. His mind only saw one last obstacle in his path between Darkmere and himself. Reaching his arms out and squeezing his fists, the ancient vine covered building imploded, crumbling before him and sending a dust cloud into the air as rats and roaches scurried for new hiding places.

Ambrosius stepped up to the top of the rubble as the dust cleared and the ringing in his ears, from the destruction, began to subside. Once it did he began to hear screaming voices of men, women, and children. Thorik and Grewen could also finally be heard from the market. They had broken through the gate and were running up to him.

In a nightmarish sensation, he looked behind him to see his friends as they approached, begging him to stop. Past them he saw a market place in ruin as injured people made their way to safety. Children cried while blood dripped down their bodies from cuts and deep gashes caused by flying wooden splinters.

It was a terrible sight of innocent people bloody and broken. A tornado of anger had caused pain to everyone in its path. Nearly a third of the market buildings had been severely damaged as arms reached out from under rubble in a plea for help.

Avanda had stopped to help a small child out from under a collapsed wooden roof.

"What have you done?" Thorik screamed at Ambrosius.

Ambrosius came out of his loathing trance, looking at his trail of destruction all the way from the front gate. It was horrific and he was distressed in his realization that he had done this to the people he was trying to help.

He turned back around as the dust settled to see the amphitheater filled with injured people from the devastation he had caused. Beyond the crowd was the stage where Darkmere stood, posing as the Terra King.

"I told you he would come for you! Rise, my family, and take him down," Darkmere commanded, pointing at Ambrosius.

The audience members quickly turned into a mob as they stood up on their benches, blocking Ambrosius' view of Darkmere. Picking up stones from the destroyed building, they began throwing them at him as they crowded around.

Stones were easily deflected, but Ambrosius had to choose how many more lives he was willing to put in danger to kill Darkmere. At the same time, he had come this far and to stop just feet away from this barbaric killer would be a waste. How many lives would he save by killing him on this day?

He continued to hear Thorik and Grewen yelling for him to stop. But the damage was done and he began to push forward toward the stage as the mob was pushed back against his invisible powers. All he needed was a clear view of Darkmere to incapacitate him, so he continued to press forward as best he could without causing any more injuries.

The mob continued to grow in size as they screamed and smashed rocks against his protective shield. It had no effect on Ambrosius, or his shield. His mind was focused on Darkmere.

Additional people arrived from the direction of the market place as they surrounded Grewen. They turned into a second mob as they approached with weapons and ropes. Military forces had shown up with large nets and shackles to capture the Ov'Unday. Grewen turned his back to Ambrosius to deal with his own immediate threat.

Draq landed behind Grewen in an attempt to scare off the gathering of humans and Nums. "Ambrosius will take out that other group before he goes after Darkmere. You and I can take out this one." Draq was clearly enjoying the chaos and battle. His Del'Unday roots were showing through his impenetrable scales.

Grewen's choice to fight would cause the death to these frail humans and Polenums. His opportunity to escape had been closed off with lines of archers along the wall that separated the market place from the military courtyard. He realized that he had been trapped and that surrendering was the only way to survive without killing someone. "This fight will have to take place at another time. I will not harm these people."

Thorik looked at him in despair. "No, Grewen. Don't give up. Run for it. Get out while you can."

Grewen looked over at Draq as the crowd moved toward them. "Take Ambrosius to safety, and then go to Pelonthal to save

Brimmelle. They will have to use the River-Green Road to get to Southwind. If I can escape I will meet you there."

"I will not let these Fesh take you into slavery." Draq began to move toward the crowd to attack. His eyebrows lowered and his teeth began to show, in a successful attempt to intimidate the locals.

"No more death today, my friend. No more." Grewen extended his arm to his side, preventing Draq from charging them. "I will be okay. Save Ambrosius." He nodded to Draq, indicating that it would be fine and to do as he asked.

"See you in Pelonthal." Draq lifted off to fly over to Ambrosius.

Grewen looked down at Thorik. "Disappear and blend in. You will be difficult to find in this city. Men think all Nums look alike." He gave a halfhearted grin as he nudged him back into the crowd.

The mob attacked. Grewen stood still as shackles and chains removed his freedom of movement. He looked up from his newly applied metal neck braces and watched as Thorik found Avanda in the back of the crowd that cheered the capture of this twelve-foot beast.

Ambrosius pushed his way forward and opened up a gap to see the stage again. This time it was empty with no signs of Darkmere's exit. There were too many options to check them all as Ambrosius looked around for a clue. But it was too late, for Darkmere had escaped.

The Terra King's followers continued to tighten around him as the ones in front were being pressed against the invisible barrier. He watched as several of them gasped for air from the pressure of the crowd. Finally one passed out and fell, only to be replaced by another body being pushed to the front.

Ambrosius realized that even by standing still he was hurting these people. Civilians that were doing nothing more than protecting their families from the obvious threat, himself. *Attempting to explain to them that the Terra King is the threat would be wasted energy after what I have done. What have I done? I allowed the end to justify the means, just as Thorik had said I would.*

Draq flew overhead. "Bust out of this Ambrosius. Where to next?"

Ambrosius was starting to feel sick with regret and disappointment. "Can you lift me?"

"For a short distance." Draq looked up at the row of stores behind the back of the stage. "I can easily get you over the buildings for you to continue your pursuit."

"No," he replied and looked back toward the front gate. "Back to the woods."

"I don't understand. We haven't caught Darkmere yet." Draq looked at the mob around his friend. "And I know you can get out of this situation. Why leave now?"

"Can you or not?" he asked again.

"I can," the reflective dragon responded, frustrated that the attack was over without a victory.

"Then do so." He raised his staff horizontally above him.

Draq reached down and grabbed the staff, lifting Ambrosius off the ground. He looked down to see the vacuum of his absence cause a wave of people to flood into the center.

As they lifted over the market place, Grewen could be seen chained up by the second gathering with the support of many brightly colored military uniformed men. Thorik and Avanda on the other hand were nowhere to be found.

"What have I done?" Ambrosius asked Draq as he looked at the destruction that he had caused.

"You were trying to save them from Darkmere's impending wrath," replied Draq who was working hard to keep them in flight.

"At what cost? At the cost of those I'm trying to save?"

Arrows shot from the ground and tops of walls as they escaped the city limits. Those that hit Draq's scales bounced off with no effect. The same could be said about those hitting Ambrosius' energy shield.

Although they were not fast, they were able to fly into the woods far enough to find temporary safety. It would take some time for the men to cross the rivers and streams to catch up to them.

Ambrosius commanded Draq to fly home and find out if his son was missing. He needed to know if he was chasing a ghost in another one of Darkmere's games. While he did that, Ambrosius would work his way down to Pelonthal before Brimmelle was lost forever in the Southwind Mines.

"Meet me in Pelonthal with good news of my son." Ambrosius raised his hand to signal farewell to his companion who was flying away.

Lowering his hand back to his side, he sighed. "Grewen, dear friend, what harm have I put you into?" He began to walk toward Lake Luthralum as he continued his conversation with the giant, who was now many miles away. Grieving would have to come later, for Ambrosius needed to sustain his hope. It was still up to him to prevent the next major attack, which would happen in just five weeks. Everything rested on his shoulders to find out where it would happen and to prevent it.

"It will be up to Thorik now to show his valor and wit to save you. The Num is special, you will see. He will rise to the occasion. Yes, it is his time to shine," he told his friend silently into the breeze, hoping the giant would be safe.

Chapter 25
Coliseum

Thorik's Log: November 13th of the 649th year.
After a week, I believe we have found Grewen. The locals have told us that all Altereds held in captivity fight to the death in the games. We hope they are wrong.

Bouncing back and forth from the crowd on all sides, Thorik and Avanda tried to keep up with them in the darkness of the night. Streaming around corners and up steps with the flow of the other patrons, they finally made their way to the inside of the coliseum where the lanterns and flaming vats lit the way to seats.

It had been a difficult weeklong travel to arrive at this event on time, and the two Nums were exhausted, dirty, and hungry. Fortunately, they blended in with the crowd.

The coliseum was enormous and sat tens of thousands of people in multi-tiered circles that surrounded a sand filled base. Four significant areas could be seen from Thorik's vantage point. At the bottom was the sandy arena filled with various white marble statues and large bowls of burning oil. The walls around this level were decorated with additional statues depicting scenes of battles and celebrations. Doorways were blocked by thick rod iron gates.

The next level up was for the Gentry and other nobility, decorated with flags and banners of many color combinations. Situated along one side of the coliseum, it was comprised of several rows at twice the height difference of everyone else's seating. It also supported its own entrance from one side.

The Plebeian section was dull in comparison, crowded and poorly cleaned. It was the largest area of the complex and provided multiple entrances for multiple levels. Filled with various races of humans and Nums, seating was tight and viewing was not always the best.

Caged sections of the coliseum filled in as the fourth unique part of the coliseum. Thorik could see two such sections from where he sat but assumed that more could be hiding from his view. They branched off from the sandy arena floor level with iron bars that covered the walls and ceilings of corridors and rooms. It looked out of place with the white marble backdrop of the rest of the architecture which was coated with lush green plant growth.

Thorik opened his battered coffer and grabbed a few of his drawing supplies as he began to record the coliseum's layout, while they waited for the Melee Matches to begin. Bumped several times by excited viewers, Thorik protected his work from their spills of drinks and food. He sketched out each of the areas to the best of his knowledge with the view that he was given. Adding more detail later, such as the floor statues, caged rooms, overrun ivy walls, and flaming vats for light, he was nearly finished by the time the event started.

"It's been awhile since we've seen Grewen. I hope he isn't injured," Avanda commented.

Thorik looked at her concerned face. "I'm sure he's fine. They wouldn't allow him to fight in the games tonight if he wasn't well."

"Are you sure he's going to be fighting tonight?" she asked.

"We have to just hope the information we gathered is correct."

"And if it isn't?"

Thorik didn't like the line of questioning. He knew that the information could be wrong and Grewen could be on the far side of Australis by this point. "If Grewen were here with us right now he would say, 'Worrying about it doesn't do any good. It is what it is'. So we will have to just wait and see."

Avanda crunched her face at Thorik. "You don't do a very good imitation of Grewen."

Thorik chuckled. "Sorry."

She added, "And if he *was* here to say that, we wouldn't be worrying because we would know where he was."

Thorik opened his mouth to explain what he meant and then decided not to bother.

Spectators roared as several high level officials walked out to their seats in the Gentry section, signally the onset of entertainment. Thorik and Avanda watched the best they could as people frequently stood up in front of them to cheer.

A large man walked out into the base level and kicked the sand around a bit as he practiced a few jabs of his sword with one of the statues. He was taller than any man Thorik had ever seen and with arm muscles the size of tree trunks. Blue colored cloths were waved above many audience members' heads as they chanted his name. "Asentar, Asentar," they continued as the man's muscles rippled with each practice maneuver.

"For the first match tonight we have Doven's champion of champions, the supreme knight of the Dovenar Kingdom, Asentar, who will single handily fight off a tribe of thrashers," a man in bright green and yellow robes announced using a large horn.

The crowd cheered again when they heard his name and began to clap randomly at first. After a short time everyone fell into sync. Clap, clap, clap. The beat from the audience was strong and intoxicating as each clap was accompanied by part of his name. "As-en-tar, As-en-tar." It was hard not to get caught up in it.

Asentar worked his way past several statues to the center of the sandy stage. Once there, he bent his knees in a wide leg stance with nothing more than a short sword in his left hand and a thin long sword in his right. Slightly hunched over, ready for the attack, he looked over at the announcer and nodded his head.

The thrashers were released from several entrances into the arena and they made their way toward the muscular man. Some jumped from statue to statue as they made their approach from the air while others galloped straight for him.

The sight brought back frightening memories for the two Nums as they wondered how this single man was going to fight off over two dozen of these beasts.

A few of the thrashers turned and started to climb the walls in an attempt to attack the audience. The first of these climbed up the wall a few rows in front of Thorik and pounced on the man in front of him. Clawing at the man's arms, which protected his face, the creature jumped to the man next to him. It continued to leap and attack until a few guards were able to catch it in a net and carry it off.

Bleeding slightly from their injuries, the crowd seemed to dismiss the assault as nothing more than an accident. Thorik was surprised at how quickly the attention was back to the battle with Asentar.

A second off-course thrasher climbed up the wall below the Gentry seating area. This one was quickly shot by several nearby guards prior to the beast harming anyone.

Thorik watched as Asentar spun his swords around and sliced at the attackers with an unexpected grace. Using both swords, he moved his body in complete rotations as he fought them off. He stopped momentarily and repositioned himself when time allowed, but never looked overly challenged in his continuing battle.

Over twenty creatures lay at his feet as he spun the swords in the palm of his hands while walking over to the remaining ones devouring their own dead tribe members. Not missing a beat in his steps, he slashed the last few creatures without an issue.

Asentar walked over to the Gentry and bowed as they politely applauded for him. The mighty warrior turned to the Plebeians and waved his sword in the air as they cheered and praised his name.

"I heard that he once killed a Chuttlebeast with his bare hands," a member of the audience said enthusiastically.

His neighbor relied, "I heard it was two Chuttles."

Eavesdropping on their discussion, Thorik didn't know if they were speaking the truth or if it was the ale talking. Then again, he didn't know what a Chuttlebeast was, so it really didn't matter.

Wagering on each fight increased the excitement for the audience as bright yellow clothed men walked up and down aisles taking bets before each battle. Coins were exchanged and sides were selected as they prepared for the coming event.

Some matches included several humans against various Unday, although most of them were strictly creature against creature. Avanda quickly picked sides for each match as she cheered them on. Somehow it didn't seem real to her as she sat in the stands, becoming caught up in the excitement.

Cataloging all the names he could, Thorik struggled to watch the matches themselves due to the bloody content. He even had difficulty watching thrashers being slaughtered, and felt slightly sorry for them.

It was difficult to tell the Del'Unday from the Ov'Unday, but the Fesh'Unday were pretty easy to recognize. They acted on pure instinct and had limited communication. A pack of wolves barked and growled together as they fought a family of tigrons. Both appeared to be Fesh'Unday with minimal intelligence.

Melee after melee continued until the final event, late into the night. The tired spectators regained their excitement as the anticipation of this ultimate rumble was about to start. The yellow clothed men were surrounded by betting patrons in hopes of cashing in big.

Thorik watched the insanity of people being entertained by watching creatures fight to the death. If he could have left, he would have done so long ago. But he couldn't abandon the possibility that Grewen was still going to show up.

"And now, what you've all been waiting for, the Tri-Unday Midnight War," the announcer said and tried to control the cheering and yelling of the Plebeians so he could continue. "As you know, before Victor Dovenar built the first wall and safe heaven for men, the Altered Creatures ruled Australis." The crowd hissed at the remarks. "As the expansion of the Dovenar Wall continued, Men and Nums were no longer threatened by them. The remaining unwanted lands were shared between the three clans of Altered Creatures until a war began. A fight for dominance."

"Tonight we will reenact their final battle for you. You will see the reason why men cannot trust these evil creatures and why your taxes go to protect our great walls." The announcer paused for the applause and looked over at one of the lead Gentry who nodded back at him.

"Place your bets on which Unday will win the Midnight War," he shouted as the crowd scrambled for their last chance to bet.

Thorik and Avanda watched the chaos as they were elbowed and jabbed several times as people made their way toward the sides to bet on the winning Unday clan.

Once completed, Thorik could finally see the arena again. White, black, and gray flags hung behind the announcer on a wooden tree stand for all to see. It was a score tracking system of some type.

The arena's iron gated entrances also had these same colors hanging over them, although Thorik could only see the white flagged entrance and gray one. The black-flagged entrance faced toward the Gentry, not viewable from Thorik's location.

Thorik watched as audience members waved various colored cloths over their head like they had done at many of the previous matches. The only difference this time was that more flags were waved and that three colors were in play. It was almost even between the gray and black flags with a small scattering of white.

Trumpets sounded as the gates opened and the audience sat on the edge of their seats waiting for the match to start.

A rumbling could be heard as creatures trampled the hard dirt below their feet on the way out to the arena. One by one, creatures appeared from each gate, many at a full run as they headed toward the center.

Under the gray flag came out the wild creatures, the Fesh'Unday. They were disorientated, angry, and looking for a kill.

"I hope they weren't fed anything for a few days. I want them hungry," a man waving a gray cloth yelled to his buddy over the crowds cheering.

His friend waved a black flag as he watched the creatures enter from below their seats in a much more calm and ready for battle manner. "Yes! I have a Blothrud," he shouted back. "You don't have a chance now."

The Blothrud stepped out into the arena several yards before stopping and eyeing the Gentry leaders. Within the Gentry seating area, several Alchemists stood up to make their presence known to it. The on-looking Del'Unday stood up like a man with dark red skin and long powerful wolf-life hairy legs. Bladed spikes extended from his shoulder blades and down his massive spine. A large scar on his back could be seen at a distance, running from his upper left shoulder blade down below his belt on the opposite side. Whatever had caused it had also broken several of his angled spikes on his back. A symbol on his right shoulderblade had been branded by a hot iron.

Turning his head to the left to watch the Fesh enter the arena, the Blothrud's long bony face resembled a mix of dragon and wolf features. Sharper and less fleshy than both, his lips struggled to cover its mouth full of glazed teeth. His eyes were solid red and shimmered in the flickering light of the fiery vats. Wearing no more than a few ripped cloths around his waist, he stood up straight and defiant.

The other Del'Undays kept their distance from the Blothrud and instinctively so did most of the Fesh'Unday as the towering creature stood his ground, surveying the new landscape. He was not nearly as tall as Thorik's friend Grewen, but he looked a lot more intimidating.

Thorik listened to the two men next to him as they named off the creatures fighting on their sides. Every once in a while they would make a comment about the white team of Ov'Unday but never with much interest.

"Oh, no!" shouted the second man. "You have a Chuttlebeast!" He shook his head in disappointment while his friend stood up on the seat and cheered.

The Chuttlebeast charged out from under the hanging gray flag with its large cube-like head. Long clumped and matted wool covered this four footed thick-legged creature. It was nearly as wide as it was tall as it stood eight feet to the top of its shoulders. This clumsy looking animal apparently only had one strength, to charge and bulldoze anything in its path. It ran straight for the center crushing other Fesh'Unday and marble statues in its way. If the initial striking of its flat face didn't kill its victims then the trampling of its massive hooves would.

The Chuttle raced around the arena hitting anything in sight, as it clobbered several creatures while they stepped into the arena from the entrances. Recessed eyes were covered by the thick wool and could have been part of its misguided head-on attacks. As it continued to charge and run into the side walls, Avanda realized it had less to do with the wool and more to do with lack of intelligence.

The beast ran past her location, flooding the area with a pungent, vile, acid-like smell. The crowd had been prepared and held their breath while it passed. Avanda and Thorik breathed in the vapors, not knowing any better. They instantly felt the fumes burn the inside of their nasal cavity and spike a quick and powerful headache that lasted only a few seconds. The creature and smell were gone as quickly as they had come.

Thorik listened to the two men continue as creature after creature was released.

"Shane, look over there," expressed one of the men. "The white team has a Mognin."

Grewen stepped out from under the white flag and looked around at the chaos in the arena. Fresh cuts and whip marks were visible on his body as his ripped shirt hung down from his waist. He had been beaten severely and not cleaned up afterward. A large branded symbol could be seen on his right shoulder blade. In spite of the injuries, he stood up straight with dignity. It easily made him the tallest creature in the arena.

"He's huge," said the other. "I've never seen a mog that big before. Is it too late to change my bet?"

Thorik looked over to see Grewen standing on the sand looking around at the audience cheering him on. White flags suddenly waved harder as they realized what they had.

Avanda screamed with excitement, "Thorik, he's here. You were right!"

Thorik was torn between being correct that Grewen would be here and mortified that his friend was now a slave and gladiator. "Now all we need to do is free him," he said softly as he looked at everything he was up against.

Grewen stood motionless as he watched creatures of all types waging war. Thrashers were jumping about while bears stood on their back legs trying to scare off creatures approaching them. It was pandemonium. Over a hundred Unday were now packed into the walled sandy pit.

A tigron leaped at the Blothrud with full force nearly knocking him over. Holding back the tigron's head with his hands, the Blothrud reached down with his own mouth and made a large bite into its neck, crushing and killing the smaller creature instantly. Releasing the tigron from his bloody jaws, he tossed the dead carcass up into the stands.

The announcer removed one of the gray flags from his three-branched score tree. Several flags had already been removed and the white team was not doing well.

The Plebeians screamed and yelled as creatures were killed and flags were removed. The fierce thrashers spent most of their time eating from the ever-increasing dead bodies. One by one the numbers dwindled down until only a few creatures were left.

Grewen had survived mostly because of his size. Most creatures wanted nothing to do with him, fearing his strength. The same could be true about the Chuttlebeast and the Blothrud.

The Chuttlebeast continued to run amuck destroying everything in its path. During its last tour around the outer wall it wiped out two Del'Unday, one Fesh'Unday, and four Ov'Unday before seeing Grewen.

The Chuttlebeast charged with full force at Grewen who was still on Thorik's right side. The crowd had been waiting to see this for a long time and they stood up with excitement. Thorik couldn't see and grabbed his pack to move up to the front.

"Avanda, it's time." Thorik softly nudged her.

She grabbed her belongings and followed him.

People were standing everywhere as they waved their cloths for victory, allowing the two small Nums easy maneuvering between them.

"Do we have to use it all?" Avanda asked him as they continued.

"Yes, we can't take a chance. We don't know how much will be required."

Thorik reached the front stone railing to see the Chuttlebeast collide with Grewen who had his hands out ready to catch the beast's cube shaped head before it slammed into him. His braced feet slid in the dirt as the creature pushed Grewen backwards. He held onto the Chuttle with one hand on its flat boned nose and the other at his ridge over the left ear. Grewen held his breath from the vapors it gave off.

The Mognin grappled with the creature and pushed with his mighty legs to slow it down. But the weight and momentum of the Chuttle continued to push him back toward the Blothrud, who was now seeing an opportunity to attack Grewen from the back as he skidded toward him.

The black and gray team supporters yelled and cheered in delight as they saw the last Ov'Unday prepare to die.

Thorik could see that Grewen had no idea he was about to be attacked from behind and realized that it was now time for action. In addition, Grewen's head was starting to nod forward as the beast's vapors were starting to knock him out.

"Hand it over," Thorik said.

Avanda reached into her sack and removed the flask of oil. "Not all of it. I want to save some. It may come in handy."

Grewen's backward slide was reaching the two Nums.

"Avanda, there's no time." Thorik voice was more stern than normal.

Looking at her friend Grewen's dilemma, she quickly handed the glass flask to Thorik.

Thorik looked at the Chuttle pushing Grewen backwards directly in front of him. He threw down the flask into one of the nearby large vats of burning oil. Upon shattering on the shallow base of the vat, it released the oil that they had taken from the city of Kingsfoot.

The flame quickly changed from a yellow to an odd green that coated the inside of the coliseum. The statues within the arena and along the walls suddenly came to life, just as they had done in Kingsfoot. As the mystical oil continued to work in the arena area, the wall sculptures behind the audience of the Plebeians and the Gentry emerged from their hibernated state. Slow at first, each newly living being emerged from the hanging vines and from behind tall ferns.

The crowd began to panic as the threat of this magic became all too real. Stone they were, but they acted like the wild animals they resembled.

Confusion ran everywhere as the stone structures began to have a life of their own while interacting with the crowd. Gigantic prehistoric creatures moved from their resting places and stepping on those in its way, while stone spiders, snakes, and bugs were released among the crowd.

The Gentry were trapped. The only exit from their seating area was now blocked by several moving statues. In an attempt to escape they started lowering themselves over the wall near the Ov'Unday entrance.

The Blothrud noticed the escaping Gentry and then looked back at Grewen, still sliding backwards. He jumped at Grewen, knocking him off his feet. Both of them rolled to the side, out of the Chuttlebeast's path.

"Get on your feet and run this way," the Blothrud shouted at Grewen, while he got back on his own wolf-like legs and began to run.

Grewen obliged out of sheer confusion at the scene he was now viewing. He didn't understand why the Blothrud had saved his life but this was no time to ask. Standing up, he followed the Blothrud at his own lumbering fast pace.

They ran past several animated statues as the Blothrud knocked a few over with his swinging forearm. Grewen looked back to see that the Chuttlebeast had turned around and was charging behind them.

"Get ready to jump when I give the word," the Blothrud instructed. He watched as the Gentry leaders made their way down the fabric of the white flag to the sandy arena and gated entrance. One of the Alchemists said a few words and pointed his wand toward the locked gate. It unlocked and opened for the Gentry as Grewen and the Blothrud stormed toward them, followed by the Chuttle.

The Gentry and the two spell casters raced inside, closing and locking the iron gates behind them just as the giant Undays arrived. The Blothrud slowed down to allow Grewen to catch up to him with the Chuttle just steps behind them both.

The Gentry and one Alchemist raced down the caged corridor. The second spell caster was a witch who held her ground while watching the two tall creatures run at her, side by side. She knew the gate would hold, but didn't want anything thrown through the rod iron gates that could hurt her companions. The witch pulled out a small object from her cloak and said a few magical words. In a blink of an eye she transformed her body into a rock wall just behind the gate.

At the last second the Blothrud yelled, "Jump!" and pushed Grewen to the right as he jumped to the left, allowing the Chuttlebeast to race between them into the locked iron gates. The bulky beast crashed through the entrance at full force. The gate snapped off its hinges as the massive face of the Chuttle charged forward. A momentary scream could be heard as the Fesh'Unday hit the rock wall, exploding debris in every direction, trailed by droplets of red blood. The beast continued to race down through the corridor after the remaining Gentry and Alchemist.

The Blothrud stood back up and looked over at Grewen who had fallen face first into the sand. Pointing at the Mognin, he said, "You owe me one, Mog." He turned and headed down after the Chuttle to finish his attack on the Gentry who had imprisoned him. He would now take out his revenge for the years of torture that they had given him.

Grewen finally stood and looked around to find Thorik lowering Avanda and himself down the black fabric over the Del'Unday entrance. Grewen hurried over to them, avoiding the still animated statues.

Avanda greeted him with a hug to the giant's leg. "Grewen, I was so afraid I'd never see you again."

Looking down at the little Num on his calf, he replied, "You worry too much, little one. It never solves anything."

Thorik smiled at Avanda over Grewen's comment. Perhaps he had rendered a better impression of Grewen than she had given him credit for.

Respectfully, Thorik looked at the blood and dirt covered large friend who was giving advice on not getting stressed about life.

Grewen was always a source of calm for Thorik regardless of the situation.

Looking around at all the chaos in the coliseum, Thorik commented, "Let's get out of here and save Brimmelle in Pelonthal if it's not to late."

Grewen agreed. "He would have had to have been processed in Doven and then catch the next prisoner wagon to Eastland before they take him through Pelonthal. We should be able to get in front of him."

The three entered the Del'Unday tunnel to make a quick escape from the coliseum, Pyrth, and the province of Woodlen.

Chapter 26
Shoreview

Tall thick grass arched from the breeze rolling in off Lake Luthralum. The grasslands ended abruptly at the edge of the bluffs. Dramatic breaks from the rolling fields and mountain foothills were common along the northern shores of the lake.

The grass had begun to turn brown from the fall temperatures and had gone to seed. On the top of each enormous blade of grass was a fluffy bright white bedding, containing hundreds of grass seeds. Wind blowing off the lake scattered the seeds in the air, giving it a wintry blizzard appearance.

Ambrosius softly parted the tall stalks of grass in his path to see where he was going. The floating seeds clumped onto his clothes as he headed against the wind toward the lake.

The grass before him finally parted to show the edge of a bluff and a large oak tree. The tree was one of few that dotted the hills. The grasslands had become so thick that few other plants had a chance to grow. This tree must have come of age before the grass had taken over the landscape.

Ambrosius stopped at the tree. Its roots gripped the edge of the bluff as though it was hanging on for its life. Long thick roots worked their way down the rock walls and into cracks. Nearly a third of the tree's base was hanging over the edge.

Reaching over, the E'rudite touched the old tree with great respect. He understood the tree's daily struggle to fight the strong winds that wished to push it over while the ground underneath it slowly eroded away with each rain.

The long walk from Pyrth had given Ambrosius time to think about what had happened over the past few months. His life had been turned upside down. His mistakes had amplified as his anger got the best of him, perpetuating the issue. Again, a vicious circle of his own making.

"Ambrosius, you fool. How did you let yourself get to this point?" he asked himself.

He could feel the energy flow from the tree into his hand. It was massively strong and rejuvenated his own strength to carry on and to make things right. Patting the tree like one would pat the back of an old friend; he looked down over the edge of the bluff at the city of Shoreview.

The city was in a shallow beach area surrounded by the bluffs on three sides. A large system of buoyant platforms supported streets, homes and stores. Nearly half the city was floating on the water, while the other half kept it anchored to the land. The thriving city was land-locked and grew in the only direction it could; out into the lake.

Ambrosius stood near a trail leading down to the city. The windy path snaked its way past cliff dwellings randomly carved into the bluff walls. Wooden ladders and walkways connected the dwellings vertically and horizontally in a chaotic maze, working its way down to the dock-like city below. People flooded the wooden walkways as they went about their daily chores, while children played on the interlocking system of bridges and poles as though it was a giant play area.

The city itself was built over a sandy beach and on top of a sturdy and elaborate docking system which acted as streets. Businesses and homes were built on the dock with multiple levels to compensate for the lack of the city's potential to grow inland. Thin long flags flapped in the wind above every home with colors and crests of the families who lived within them.

High tide was starting to creep in under the city and would fill the entire area with several feet of water before it was over. The beach would soon be a watery coastal cove, rising nearly to the dock pathways before it began to recede and expose the sand again.

Ambrosius worked his way down the trail. It led to a wooden walkway and then to a ladder and then to another walkway before going down one more very long ladder and down several flights of stairs. Stepping out onto the street, he knew there was a less physically challenging way down but he couldn't recall it. Every time he had visited Shoreview, the path had changed. The city was dynamic in nature and seemed to redesign itself every few years.

The humans and Nums of the city politely greeted him as he passed. A few Ov'Unday could be seen on a distant street, while curious children followed him in a game of discovery with the outsider. The city, for the most part, felt as he had remembered it to be.

With his feet firmly on the ground, so to speak, he walked across the raised street and out onto the floating section of the city. Stopping several times to gain his bearings from his last recollection of the town, he finally stopped at a shop. The sign out front read, "Dare to Trade."

Trying to enter, he found the door to be locked. Pulling his staff before him to knock on the door, he heard a snort from behind the door. A second snort and a cough followed.

Ambrosius walked to the side of the store and looked at an open window hanging over the water several lengths from the storefront. Two boots extended out the window, one resting on the other, toes up to the sky. A fishing pole also extended from the opening and a line had been cast into the water below.

The snort was heard again as the owner of the boots shuffled his feet slightly. A pause of silence was broken with light snoring.

Ambrosius grinned at the opportunity.

Using his powers he slowly unbuckled and then lifted one of his boots off the owner's foot and lowered it to the water. Raising the end of the fishing line, he attached the boot to the fishhook and placed it back into the lake. A firm pull of the line with his E'rudite powers startled the person in the window.

The remaining boot and the tattered sock disappeared from the windowsill as an unshaved chunky man leaned out of the shop to grab his fishing pole, which had slipped from his grip. Upon grabbing the tool, he reached his thick hand out to pull the line out of the water. His hopes were high as he licked his lips and gazed down into the lake for some sign of his catch.

Unfortunately, his desire was quickly dashed as he saw a boot instead of a nice meal. Leaning out of the window, he pulled the boot up to him, unhooked it, and tossed it back into the water with a grumble. Just as he let go of the item, he recognized the clasp on the boots side. Pulling himself back into the store, he looked down and realized he was missing his boot.

Back at the window, the hairy-back shirtless man rested his weight on the sill. Bewildered, he looked in the direction he had tossed his boot.

"Looking for this?" Ambrosius said from the opposite way of the man's view.

Swiveling his head and body, he saw the lean man standing on the dock platform pouring the water out of his boot. "Ambrosius!

You son-of-a-Krupe!" he jested. "Best respects. When did ya get in town?"

"Only now."

The man disappeared from sight and heavy footsteps pounded their way to the front of the store. The lock was quickly released and the door swung open, exposing the filthy inside of the shop and letting out a nasty odor.

The man in the doorway was a hand shorter than Ambrosius but weighed twice that of the E'rudite. Shirtless, his large hairy stomach hung over his pants and was coated with leftovers from several meals. Less than a beard and more than stubble, Dare's face looked dirty and unkept. He had limped into the doorway from an old wound to his hip, which he offset by using a large Fesh'Unday leg bone as a cane. The thick and dirty bone had battle scars and engravings. Fresh blood coated an area toward the bottom of the cane where gray rat fur still clung.

"Dare, it is good to see you." Ambrosius held his breath a few seconds afterward while the smell dissipated in the breeze.

"And I you," he replied, before noticing the burn marks down Ambrosius' face and neck. "What happened to yur face?"

Ambrosius had completely forgotten about his physical scars. It took him a second to realize what Dare was asking about. Touching his tender skin, he said, "The Grand Council has been destroyed, and nearly took me down with it."

"You be at Kingsfoot during the purification?"

Stunned, Ambrosius asked, "How do you know what happened at the council meeting, let alone where Kingsfoot is?"

Scratching his chest before removing a few unwanted items from the hair on it, he replied, "Know of Kingsfoot, but not where it is. Beltrow was one of my best customers. Came down from the mountains every summer ta trade. Good man, he was. I knew somethin' was amiss when no one from Kingsfoot came down for the annual trade this year."

"You said 'he was'. How do you know of his death?"

"A flock of them faith-followers came through 'ear after the destruction. They stated their scrolls called it a 'purification' to start over. Said their valley's air went sour and they had ta leave. Talked General Stickwell into trading one of his boats for some gems. As quick as they arrived, they set sail for some place called Elysian. Odd that I never 'eard of it."

Ambrosius absorbed the new information, before nodding and saying, "It has been some troubling times, my friend."

"Better days ahead with you back, I think." Dare rubbed his thumb and finger together over an imaginary coin.

"My last purchase from you filled your pockets full," Ambrosius commented. "Times should have been good to you with such wealth."

"Aye," Dare replied. His eyes shifted as he thought about his reply. "Sweet Nectar of Irr, she is a troubling wench. Her vile grasp drained me by inches in torment and left me dry."

Ambrosius looked at him shamefully. "You traded your full purse for a taste of spirits? Nectar of Irr, no less. You've never been able to stop once you start drinking. You know better."

"I does now. Have no more taste for her. The thought sours my mouth as we speak."

"I hope so." Ambrosius looked around the busy street he added, "May we talk in private?"

"At your service. Come aboard." Dare allowed Ambrosius to enter his store of odds and ends.

Before shutting the door, he noticed two young Nums spying on his affairs and pointed the bloody end of his cane at them. With a loud stomp of his foot onto the street deck, he yelled, "Begone, ya snooping tadpoles!"

The curious children ran off as Dare limped back into the shop and slammed the door behind him. "Shouldn't 'av used the foot without my boot," he grumbled to himself while shaking off the pain under his torn sock.

Piles of abnormally shaped objects were along every wall. Mostly junk left over from when his shop was filled with exquisite items from all over the land. These items were what didn't sell and had been collecting dust and insects for a long time.

It took Ambrosius a few minutes to get used to the thick air from the decaying musk of dead rats in the corner as well as Dare's own sweaty clothes that lay about. "I am in need of your services."

"What tis ya wanting?" Dare asked. He rummaged through the junk piles and lifted his remaining valuable items up to show his customer. "A rack of a three-horned estoo?" he asked, but quickly read Ambrosius' facial expression. Kicking a large fanged rat out of his way he collected several other objects. "Cloth fashioned from the webs of Kiri Desert Spiders? Moon Lake gribson peddles? Ergrauthian spices?" All were answered by Ambrosius' deadpan expression.

"Information," the thinner man explained.

"Ah." Dropping the items on the floor, he used his cane to walk right up to him. Leaning his hairy arms against Ambrosius' chest, he moved his face close and looked up at his patron. With over exaggerated mouthing of his words he said, "My specialty."

The stench coming off the man's body was nothing compared to the death vapors released from his mouth. Ambrosius turned and walked to the window where Dare had earlier been fishing in his sleep. Clutching the sill, he leaned his body on his straightened arms and took a deep breath of the air from outside. "No games this time. I have to know some critical facts. Do *not* appease me with half-truths to support your purse."

"Misinformation, I swear. I didn't know it had been tainted." The fat man scratched his backside as he thought. "Never on purpose. Never to my favorite customer." He gave off an uncomfortable trustworthy smile to persuade Ambrosius to trust him.

Collecting one last breath of fresh air from outside the window, Ambrosius turned around and leaned lightly on the windowsill before addressing the pathetic looking man in front of him. "Where is Darkmere going to strike next?"

"Darkmere?" He voice gave away his surprise. "Ain't been 'ear for ages. Last I 'eard he vanished into the east."

"He is often disguised and goes by the alias of the Terra King."

"Terra King you say? Name plucks my cobwebs. Again, not through these parts, but within the Dovenar Walls he makes his mark." Dare taxed his brain. "I know of the ill and his sickly followers."

"Good. Tell me what you know."

"Not so fast, friend." Dare ran his dirty fingers through his balding hair to act more businesslike. His hair ended up sticking at an awkward slant while a fresh coat of thick natural grease covered his hand. "What we be talking in payment?"

"Saving your life."

"Not like ya to threaten me. What's come over ya?"

"No threat. The information I am looking for will allow me to stop Darkmere from his next attack. If I am unsuccessful, he will likely take over these lands. He eventually will catch up to you."

"There ain't never been a prison I can't escape," Dare boasted. "Proved that to Darkmere himself."

"Who articulated anything about him sending you to prison? After what you've done in your past, I don't see him keeping you around long."

Swallowing hard, Dare agreed. "Truth it be. But my purse runs dry. Surely it is worth something for my efforts."

"I will make good on my account. But the price will depend on the information given."

"Heave ahead." Dare rested his bone cane at his hip and extending his oily hand out to Ambrosius to lock the deal.

"Agreed." He reached out to shake the man's hand.

SLAP! Dare slapped his hand into Ambrosius' causing a squishy popping sound from within the grip. Holding tightly to the taller man's hand, Dare placed his other hand onto Ambrosius' forearm and held it firm as he shook it hard. "Like times of old it is." Releasing his grip, he turned away.

Dare walked over to a table and cleared it of all objects with one swipe of his cane, crashing the collection to the floor. Grabbing a map from a wall rack, he unscrolled it onto the now empty table. "Terra King been racing up'n down the outer wall like a feline after a Sandrat." He pointed to various cities on the map of the Dovenar Kingdom. "Avoids the lake like the plague. Fear of water after the Civil War, I venture." Chuckling as his own joke, his raspy voice caused it to almost sound like a cackle.

"Has there been any pattern to his movements. Any location that he visits more often?"

Dare tried to put the sightings he had heard about into some type of order. Scratching under the roll of his stomach with both hands, he said, "Paces like a caged tigron, it seems. Back and forth, north and south. Never still for long. Only in one place long enough to shout his anger at them Altereds. Lands, loud, and leaves he does."

"Is there anyone he has befriended along the way? Any leads we can follow?"

"Friends? Nay. Fear keeps them closer than stink on Chuttles." Looking intensely up from the map, he scratched his backside once more. "Promises immortality fer joining his cause.

Collecting corpses is more like it. Never seen again are they who join him in crusade. Taken in by the words of the Mountain King to do his bidding."

Looking back to the map, Dare continued, "No battle field I see for his next attack."

Ambrosius was disappointed. "Keep working on it. Perhaps you will recall more with time."

"Doubt that, I know what I know. That's all there is," Dare admitted. "What else ya be needing?"

"Transport to Pelonthal."

"A ship and a crew ya say?" Dare stood up straight. "Costly request. Coins needed up front for provisions."

"I have friends here that I can obtain the funds. How soon can we sail?"

"Ship I have, Captain I be, but a crew and supplies will take a few days to rustle up."

"Fine, we sail in two days."

Chapter 27
Dead Waters

"**H**ow did you meet Ambrosius?" Thorik asked his giant companion as they walked along the edge of a shallow gorge. The summer had dried up most of the water at its base, leaving only a small stream until the spring rains would refill it.

The open dry landscape was colored with patches of short golden grass. Splashes of purple added color to the O'Sid Fields from hard little seeds that clung to the stems of the local govi-weed. The land was dreadfully hard and flat, except for the dry waterbeds and the termite mounds.

They had been walking for days outside the Dovenar Wall without the fear of being attacked by humans. Of course, walking in the open Fesh'Unday land was not the safest way to travel.

"It was a few years before the Civil War." Grewen moved Avanda's sleeping body from his left arm to his right to prevent it from stiffening up.

"Ambrosius had come to Pelonthal after it had been invaded by the Ov'Unday," Grewen added.

"I thought Ov'Unday were pacifists. Why would they invade a human province?" Thorik returned.

"It's complicated, Thorik." Grewen walked over to one of the thin tall mud mounds.

"Everything about Ambrosius seems to be complicated. The facts that I continue to learn seem straight forward, and so far support Darkmere more than Ambrosius."

"Like I said, it is complicated." Grewen made a fist with his free hand and slammed it deep into the mud mound before stirring it around inside.

"It appears simple enough to me. The Unday continue to attack men and Nums. Darkmere is fighting for the men while Ambrosius is fighting for the creatures."

The Mognin pulled his hand free of the mound. Giant biting termites coated his fist as they attacked his thick skin. "Don't always believe what you hear." Sucking the insects off his hand, one finger at a time, he pushed a few trying escape back into his mouth.

"I don't have to. I've seen it with my own eyes. Ambrosius destroyed the Grand Council, we both heard the ghost of the Council. Ambrosius destroyed the buildings of Pyrth and killed many of its residents; we both saw that, as well. His friends are Ov'Unday and Del'Unday. What more proof do I need?"

Licking the remaining termites from his palm, Grewen looked down at the little Num. It appeared that Thorik was struggling with his own argument. "So why is it even *you* don't believe it to be true?"

"I don't know, maybe that's what bothers me the most. My heart is not agreeing with my eyes."

They continued walking in silence for a short time.

"Thorik, did you fight along side Ambrosius and me against the Del'Unday and the human Alchemist, north of Woodlen?" Grewen asked.

"Of course I did. You were there."

"Do you consider me your friend?"

"I tracked you down and saved you in the coliseum Melee Matches, didn't I?"

"So, are you against Del'Unday and humans working together for peace?" Grewen asked.

"No, what kind of question is that?"

"The evidence would imply it. You befriended an Ov'Unday and then fought Del'Unday and a human. Even though these facts are true, they are obviously not complete. You are accusing Ambrosius of the same thing. Seeing his battles and my friendship has given you facts but not the entire story, and yet you are using them against him," Grewen stated with no response, so he continued. "Do you consider Draq your friend?"

"I don't know yet." Thorik gave off a concerned smile.

Grewen nodded his head in agreement. "Me either," he said with a grin.

They both lightened the serious mood with a long overdue laugh.

Thorik's smile lessened a bit. "I wish I knew where I fit into all of this."

"What do you mean?"

"What's my purpose here? I feel that I can make a difference in this world, but how? And who am I to become?" Thorik took a deep breath while reflecting on his own questions. "Following Brimmelle's words of wholesome tradition fills me with comfort, but Ambrosius' conviction to change things for the better feeds a fire within me that I feel destined to follow. I struggle between the security of Farbank and the adventure over the next hill." Looking up at the gentle giant he asked, "I want both, and yet neither of the extremes. How do I find out who I am and what I should believe?"

Grewen warmly grinned and tilted his head toward the Num. "My dear little friend, life shouldn't be about finding yourself, it should be about creating yourself."

Thorik pondered the words and looked back at the path before them. It would take some time to digest Grewen's comments.

The friends headed south over the O'Sid grasslands that slowly turned to sparse vegetation and Kiri Drylands, always keeping the Dovenar Wall just within sight to their west. Bands of Del'Unday and Fesh'Unday were occasionally seen. Hiding from them slowed down the trip often to a snail's pace. Grewen taught Thorik and Avanda what plants and roots were edible as they stopped frequently to fill Grewen's rumbling stomach.

Avanda made several attempts to catch a horned toad before she was successful. "I'll call you Ralph," she told the critter who rested in between her hands. Its capture was short lived as she dropped it and wiped her hands off. "Yuck! It peed on me." She then started the chase again.

Thorik had finished eating and began working on his maps and notes again while Grewen continued to search for enough food to fill his large body.

Chewing on various plant roots, Grewen asked Thorik, "What made you decide to become a Sec?"

"I really didn't have a lot of choice." Thorik stopped and looked over at his friend.

Grewen's face shifted as he looked confused. "What do you mean?"

"After my parents died, I was too young to live on my own so my Granna Gluic took me in to live with her and Brimmelle. He didn't appreciate my moving in, feeling I was too unstructured and childish. I lived with them until I turned sixteen, this past spring."

"Surely he could remember what it was like to be a youth."

"No, I don't think so. His father trained him to be a Sec since he was seven. Then he passed away when Brimmelle was only eleven, handing over the Fir status to him. He quickly became the leader of our village with no time to be a child. I think he has always held that against me; the fact that I still choose to enjoy life instead of giving into being an adult."

"Becoming an adult doesn't mean giving up your ability to have fun and enjoy life," Grewen replied.

"To him it does. And I have failed in doing so. During my long three years living with them he trained me endlessly to become a Sec. He still insists on it, but I frequently let him down."

"Why do you let him get to you? He's your uncle, not your father."

"He's the closest thing I have to a father. He has saved me from myself on more than one occasion."

"According to him or to you?"

Thorik looked confused. "What do you mean?"

"He has convinced you that you need him. From what I have seen, you do not."

Thorik became defensive. "He's done a lot for me and has looked after me when I needed it."

"Don't get emotional, little man. I was just saying that you have proven on this journey that you can handle yourself. His words should be used more for guidance rather than orders to be taken."

Thorik sighed. It was easy to say, but he couldn't ever see himself stand up against Brimmelle. Just the thought made him uncomfortable.

Avanda returned to them, displaying her newly caught common brown-back snake. The two-foot-long snake coiled around her wrist and hung its head down looking for insects as Avanda tried to feed it grass. "Thorik, would you like to meet Ralph?"

"Ralph?" Thorik questioned. "I thought the horned toad had that name."

"Yes, it's easier to remember their names if they are all the same," she added. "Here, you can hold him?"

Thorik instinctively stepped back. "No thanks. We need to get going soon. You should put your friend back with his family."

"All right. I think I saw about twenty of his brothers and sisters near here earlier. I'll see if I can find them again," she responded.

Thorik took a quick survey of the ground near him to make sure none of Ralph's family had dropped by to visit.

Grewen smirked. "It's only a snake."

"I know. I was just looking around to make sure we aren't forgetting anything."

"You're a terrible liar, Thorik." Grewen chuckled to himself as they prepared to leave the site.

Slightly embarrassed, Thorik looked up to see the endless horizon of the desert. "How much farther?" he asked Grewen.

"Well, we passed the Woodlen Province, so we probably have a day before we finish passing the province of Doven and arrive at River's Edge."

"Is River's Edge a nice place? I would assume that they allow Ov'Unday, if they are going to allow you to cross," Thorik surmised.

Grewen looked a little set back at the question. "It wasn't Para'Mathyus, but it was very nice. Like all provinces, the Dovenar Wall surrounds it to prevent Unday from entering. In River's Edge, the wall lined the province along the crest of the shallow river valley bluffs. The entire province is only a few miles wide but it follows the river for probably eighty miles upstream from Lake Luthralum."

"You said it 'was very nice', does that mean it was destroyed by the Del'Unday?"

"It means that it was once a rich valley of growth and prosperity from both a natural and economical way. It was caught up in the middle of the Dovenar Civil War and became the final battle point between the North and the South."

"Who won?" Thorik asked.

Grewen shook his head at such a black and white thought. "Neither. During the final battle, a great wave from Lake Luthralum came ashore and destroyed all lakeside cities. River's Edge was hit the hardest as the wave rolled up the low river valley all the way to the end of the province, only to be stopped by the Dovenar Wall, near Ki'Volney Lake."

"Once the water receded did they rebuild?" Thorik asked.

"Interesting enough, the waters didn't recede. They stayed at the higher levers. However, the majority of all humans and Polenums at that time lived on Lake Luthralum's shores and were destroyed by the wave. What you have seen outside your valley is the starting over of a new civilization. You were one of the few totally isolated from these major events of our time. Consider yourself lucky."

Avanda released the reptile, returned and gathered her things so they could start heading south again.

The next day the landscape became barren and opened up to sand dunes just before they reached River's Edge's exterior province wall. It was built much better than the Woodlen Province wall with large thick blocks, each taller than Thorik. The blocks were accurately cut and showed no gaps between them.

No guards were seen on top of this wall as the three friends made their way over to a sand dune leaning halfway up the wall. Once they were on top of the dune, Grewen lifted Thorik high enough for him to grab onto the roof and pull himself up.

Thorik reached back down to help Avanda up as Grewen pushed her as far as he could. It was enough to get her on top of the wall with Thorik.

"Now what?" Thorik asked, looking to the east and west without seeing the end of the wall in either direction.

"Find something that can help me climb up."

The top of the wall had been sanded smooth from the desert winds. Only periodic metal brackets were present and looked to have been designed to hold down equipment. On the inside of the wall several staircases made their way down into the water. The water itself spanned the entire distance to the far perimeter wall on the south side of River's Edge. It was over a mile across. No land could be seen within the walled lake. However, several objects protruded through the water to the west.

"I think I see something." Thorik called down from the wall before walking west with Avanda for a few minutes.

As they walked, Avanda stared at the water and its distant shore. "I can't go in there. We'll have to go around."

"You'll be fine."

She shook her head quickly. "No. You don't understand. I am *not* going to get in the water."

"One thing at a time. I need to get Grewen up on the wall first before we even have the option of crossing the lake."

"I'm just letting you know that I won't do it." Shaking her head, she ended the conversation.

Grewen followed Thorik from below the wall and then relaxed on top of the nearest dune where Thorik stopped.

"It looks like the top floor of a building." Thorik removed his pack and outer clothes, before folding them and handing them to Avanda. "I'm going to swim over to it and see if I can find something to help us."

Thorik finished removing his boots and valuables before walking down the steps and lowering himself into the water. It was cooler than the water of Kingsfoot Lake but warmer than the water that ran along Farbank's shores. He swam across to the landing where he raised himself to walk inside the upper level of a submerged building.

Inside he found a bedroom with a staircase down into a water-filled lower level. Walking over to the stairwell, he noticed several items gently floating within it. Spotting a rope floating in the back, Thorik lowered himself down the flooded stairway until he was swimming again as he grabbed for the ropes end. Grasping the rope, he pulled it to him only find out that it was the strap to a robe of a person that had died wearing it. The corpse rolled upward in the water and landed its remains on top of Thorik.

Thorik screamed as the dead body fell apart in his hands while attempting to push the body away. He turned to swim the short distance back to the steps as he felt something grab his foot and pull him under. The dark and murky water made it difficult to see as he reached down to free his leg. During his attempt, the now disrobed corpse parts sank and floated down onto him. An arm bone landing on his stomach and a rib cage covering his head was all that Thorik needed to send him into a panic. He tried to push the parts away. Bending down to free his trapped ankle, the skull floated down in front of him with its mouth wide open, laughing at Thorik's predicament.

In a state of frenzy, Thorik broke free of whatever caught his leg and made his way up the stairs and out of the water, where he struggled to regain his composure.

Grewen enjoyed his time basking in the warmth of the hot desert sun as he sank his exposed feet into the hot loose sand of the Kiri sand dune. He missed this kind of weather that reminded him of his days as a youth collecting sandcrabs along Ki'Volney Lake.

He sat on the top of the dune and leaned back on the wall, closing his eyes and wishing for simple days to come. Daydreaming of past and future events, he was struck in the face with a heavy wet cloth.

He looked up to see Thorik looking over the edge of the wall at him.

"Sorry about that. I lost control of it." Thorik struggled to pull up the chain of beddings that he had dragged through the water and up the stairs of the wall.

Thorik pulled the rest of the chain up and looped it four times down to Grewen and back up through the metal brackets on top of the wall.

"Is this going to hold me?" Grewen asked.

"Yes. As long as the fabric is strong enough and the knots hold tight."

"Sounds good enough for me," Grewen chuckled.

"And if these metal brackets are still strong enough. I can only vouch for the knots. Everything else is out of my power."

"Thanks for the vote of confidence," Grewen added as he held the four loops of linens in his hands. Using the different height loops for footholds and pulling hand over hand, he scaled the wall within a few minutes. The hard part was still to come as he tried to pull his body up onto the ledge while Thorik and Avanda attempted to help the giant at least twenty times their own weight. But pull they did, as they finally rolled his exhausted body onto the top of the wall.

"That was easy enough," Grewen said between breaths. "When is this trip going to get rough?"

"You should be fine for a while as long as you can swim." Thorik looked out across the better than a mile swim in front of them. Not getting a witty remark back from Grewen he asked, "You can swim can't you?"

"Not one of my strongest attributes, little man."

"Well, I forgot to bring my boat on this trip. So unless you have one hidden under your clothes, I think you need to learn quickly."

Grewen smiled at the candor and wit of the remark. "It's good to see you found your sense of humor. How hard can it be? If fish can do it, I think I can figure it out."

"Oh, by the way, Avanda will be riding on your back. She doesn't know how to swim either."

Avanda's ears perked up. "I'm not going to ride on him. He'll sink."

"I'm inclined to agree with Avanda on this one. Mognin's sink like a rock," Grewen said.

Thorik looked at them both. "Grewen, is crossing these waters our only chance to catch up with Brimmelle before he goes to the mines?"

"Yes, as far as I know," he answered reluctantly.

Thorik continued, "Avanda, do you want Fir Brimmelle to be lost forever in some mine? Never to see Farbank again? Is that the fate you wish upon him?"

"No," she replied.

"Then we need to get past our fears and cross this waterway." Thorik finished and led them to the water before they could think of a reason not to go. Truth be known, after the incident in the stairwell earlier, he was not excited about getting back in the water either.

After working their way down the steps to the flooded valley, Grewen slowly stepped into the water and found out that it only came up to his thighs at this point. "Perhaps I'll just walk across, want a ride?" he asked.

Backing up to the wall's staircase, Thorik climbed onto his back and straddled his neck as he held onto his large head for support. Avanda stepped onto Grewen's large palm before sitting down for the ride.

Making their way toward the center, the water continued to work its way up Grewen's body until Thorik's feet were getting wet and making him nervous. Memories of the recent skeleton kept him wary of these waters.

"What's the matter Thorik? I thought you knew how to swim." Grewen chucked as he kept lifting his hand higher to prevent Avanda from getting wet.

"I do, but when I went into that house to find a rope I had a strange experience."

Grewen chuckled at the skittish nature of Nums. "Did you get attacked by a ghost or something?"

"Grewen, how did you know?" Thorik asked in surprise.

"I was just poking fun, Thorik. Legends of the waters being haunted by Irluk and the drowned souls of River's Edge are just folklore."

"Your folklore grabbed my leg and pulled me under earlier," Thorik rebutted.

"Come on, now who's pulling whose leg?" Grewen chuckled as the water reached a new level that came up to Grewen's chin. "The only haunting of River's Edge is down by Lake Luthralum, where Maegoth used to stand. The rest of the river is safe, as far as I know," Grewen added and winked at Avanda.

She played along. "You're not scared, are you Thorik?"

"No, Grewen's words have given me great comfort," he said with dry sarcasm. Thorik lifted his feet out of the rising water and grabbed his backpack to set it on Grewen's head. "I hope this is the deepest part of the valley."

Grewen step fell a little deeper. "I don't think we have even hit the original river yet, so we will need to start to swim for it soon."

Thorik began to get his gear ready for the swim as Avanda eyed several poles sticking out of the water. She was very nervous and willing to try anything before having to swim. "Grewen, that row of lamp poles to our right. Perhaps that is a bridge over the old river base." A sparkle of hope was in her voice.

"It's worth a try." Grewen agreed and moved over to it. "Your eyes have done it again little one, we have found a bridge. I hope it's intact all the way across."

They were now moving very slowly as Grewen walked on his toes and paddled with his free hand. This continued for nearly an hour as he tried to maintain his balance so he wouldn't spill his passengers or their supplies into the water. They crossed the bridge and made their way toward the far wall without any issues.

Finally the water level began to recede down Grewen's neck to his chest.

Relieved, Thorik sighed. "Smooth sailing from here. I'm glad that's behind us."

"See, you were worried about nothing," Grewen added to the comment.

Avanda laughed at both of them. "You both were so scared."

"Ouch!" Grewen expressed. "Something just bit my leg."

Thorik laughed. "I'm not falling for it, Grewen."

"I'm serious. That really hurt."

"Fine, I'll have a look at it when we get to the wall."

"Ouch!" Grewen jerked forward to pull his foot free, nearly knocking Avanda out of his hand. It didn't help. "Something has a hold of me."

Grewen was slowly being pulled backward by one leg while attempting to stop himself with the other leg pressing against the muddy lake bottom.

"What's happening?" Thorik asked.

"I told you, something has a hold of my leg. It's dragging us back into deeper waters." Grewen clenched his large jaw as he made another attempt to pull free without any success. "You two need to jump off and swim the rest of the way while I try to free myself."

Thorik pulled out his hunting knife. "I'm not leaving you again." He then tied Avanda's and his items together. He tossed one sack on each side of Grewen's neck for safety. "Stay still and I'll swim down and cut you free from the plants you most likely got caught in."

Second-guessing himself only for a moment, Thorik jumped into the water and swam down in the thick murky waters. Even with no cloud cover, it was difficult to see anything as he followed Grewen's body down to his captured leg.

Expecting to see some aquatic vine wrapped around Grewen's foot, Thorik was terrified to find an army of skeletons pulling on him. Remnants of flesh and mud covered the animated bones as they worked together to pull Grewen into darker waters.

Blood could be seen spilling out of Grewen's leg from what appeared to be bite marks. Thorik didn't take time to think as he reacted to the situation. He reached down and grabbed Grewen's thick leg for balance and used his own feet to kick off as many of the skeletons as he could.

Three of the semi-flesh covered dead floated forward and grabbed Grewen's other leg, causing the giant to lose his balance. Avanda splashed into the lake as he was forced to use both hands to stabilize himself.

As his mighty hand reached over to grab her, she was pulled under the murky water, out of his sight.

"Avanda!" he yelled and plunged both arms under the surface to find her. His huge limbs swung back and forth in his attempt to grab her body.

After a few quick passes he clutched onto her and raised his hand above the water to investigate. To his surprise he found an animated corpse in his hand instead of the little Num. He tossed their bones into the distance before submerging his massive hands for another attempt.

Thorik held onto Grewen's leg as the large limb thrashed about. He continued to kick the skeletons off Grewen's body one by one. However, it wasn't long before a few of them began attacking Thorik's grasp with series of bites and clawing at his arms and hands.

Feeling another hand on his leg, Thorik reached down to remove it. But upon touching it, it felt more flesh than bone. He grabbed the wrist and pulled it off his leg before raising it toward him. It was Avanda, and she was in a state of horror.

She screamed in fear as her remaining breath escaped from her mouth and floated upward.

Thorik pulled her toward him just as a fleshless face looked over her shoulder at him. This latest skeleton was armed with a rusty sword as he prepared to shove it through Avanda's back and into Thorik's chest.

Thorik let go of the security of Grewen's body. Kicking hard at the bony arm that held onto Avanda's leg, Thorik pushed Avanda up toward the surface with all his might as the skeleton's weapon made its way toward them.

The water erupted with bubbles in front of Thorik as he waited to feel the rusty blade penetrate his chest. Instead, a large hand reached out and grabbed Thorik around his chest and shoulders. He was instantly raised above the surface to see Avanda in Grewen's other hand.

Grewen was violently kicking at the attacks on his legs. He laid the two Nums over his shoulders and began to swipe at the skeletons crawling up his sides, out of the water.

Thorik and Avanda held onto Grewen with their remaining strength as they both gasped for air. They spit and sputtered as the water was removed from their bodies.

Grewen removed the clinging skeletons from Thorik and Avanda's bodies as he headed for the wall. Once there, he set the Nums down on the wall's lower dry platform and sat down to remove the stragglers hanging onto his own legs.

Thorik choked his way back to life. "Folklore?"

"So I've heard," Grewen replied as he tended to his own wounds.

Chapter 28
Myth'Unday

The three friends had climbed out of River's Edge by passing over the southern Dovenar Wall. They walked toward Pelonthal, along a dirt path that followed the province's wall to the west. They were again dry from the day's sun but now wet from their sweat in the heat.

After several long hot days, they had made it past Solann Ridge. The temperatures had begun to lower and the foliage was much more pleasing to the Nums. Lightly wooded areas along soft grassy hills and meadows greeted them.

Grewen could tell the Nums enjoyed this climate much more than the dry heat of the desert. "Welcome to the edge of the Mythical Forest," he announced. "Home of the Myth'Unday."

"There's another Altered Creature clan?" Thorik asked.

"Not exactly. Myth'Undays were created by the Great Oracle to bring joy to Australis as well as to entertain her. Instead of being an alteration of other animals and creatures, they were created from the energy that exists in the forest."

Avanda's curiosity kicked in and questioned him before Thorik had the chance. "What do they look like?"

"I'm sorry to say that you most likely will never find out."

"Why not," she replied.

"Because they may not wish to be seen," Grewen continued. "They would rather play with you."

"How can they play with me if I can't see them?"

Grewen smiled. "Have you ever walked through the woods and heard noises like someone else is there, but they are not. Or have you seen movement out of the corner of your eye but it stops before you can focus on the area?"

Avanda nodded her head. "Yes."

"That would be them. They live in most forests, but this one is their home. The Floral Faeries, Brush Brownies, Leaf Pixies, as well as the rest of the inquisitive Myth'Unday species, all originated from this forest.

Thorik listened to the tale. "Sounds much better than living corpses." He smiled at his young student. "Avanda, if we are lucky, maybe you'll get to see one."

Grewen cleared his throat and shook his head to Thorik. "I don't think you want to meet any Myth'Unday."

Thorik looked confused. "Why not?"

"Many have come into the timberland to see or catch a Myth'Unday, and most never returned. The few that have were changed for life. Always looking over their shoulder and afraid of their own shadow," Grewen cautioned. "No, I wish not to see any Myth'Unday during our travels."

As darkness approached, they stopped just off to the side of the road by a small spring to stay the night. A canopy of light green leaves overhead acted as a blanket to keep the warmth in the campsite.

"Grewen, are we going to be safe here from the Myth'Unday?" asked Avanda in a timid voice.

Grewen waved her over to him as he lay on his side. "Come over here little one. I won't let anyone harm you."

Avanda came over to him and cuddled up against his chest. He covered her with a blanket before placing his hand just above her to keep her warmth in and any night dew out.

Thorik lay down and relaxed near the spring. "How much farther until Pelonthal and the River-Green Road?"

"The River-Green Road follows the inside of Pelonthal's Dovenar Wall. It runs from River's Edge to Greensbrook, and we have less than a day's walk to get there."

"Shouldn't we be walking all night to make sure they don't get ahead of us?" Thorik asked.

"No. They will have to go all the way around River's Edge, through Eastland, before traveling all the way back to Pelonthal. They will have to pass us on this road to pass us at all."

"Why wouldn't they take a boat or ferry across?"

"Some legend seems to scare them away from crossing over River's Edge." Grewen looked down and winked at Avanda.

She smiled and closed her tired eyes.

"Aren't we going the wrong way? Shouldn't we be heading to Eastland to free Brimmelle when they leave the Dovenar Wall's gates?"

"Eastland has been the center-point of conflict between men and Unday for many centuries," Grewen answered. "I'm not getting any closer to that province than I have to."

Grewen stretched his neck and looked down to make sure Avanda was comfortable. "Trust me Thorik, we're headed the right way. Now get some sleep."

Thorik looked up at the stars between the trees for a bit, thinking of the events along his travels. Thoughts of Emilen crept back into his head and he began missing her. How he wished she was with him snuggling up under the blanket. For a moment he thought he could smell her scent and feel her touch. Holding onto these feelings he soon drifted into a deep sleep as he dreamed about his memories of her.

Thorik woke up from a pleasant dream about Emilen, but lost his thin smile when he looked over to see Grewen wrapped up with glowing threads that danced in various colors. Glistening sparkles appeared, floating in every direction. Thorik adjusted his eyes to see hundreds of little shiny dots flying around them.

He lay on his back and looked about at several small beings playing and frolicking around the campsite. Singing songs and dancing to their own light and airy music, they tried to wake Grewen by teasing his feet and face as he laid in his constraints. Neither seemed to faze him.

Bending his knees, Thorik pushed his body up with his arms to find a petite girl sitting on his left knee with two red oak leaves for wings. She was no bigger than his finger as her reddish glowing body shined bright like a flame.

"What kind of game is this?" Thorik asked, still half asleep.

"A game? What a great idea. Let's play a game!" A male voice had responded from the natural spring behind Thorik. "What kind of game do you like to play?"

Thorik rotated his body and looked over to the small pond, scaring the winged girl away. The water had a slight blue glow about it that brightened the underside of the tree coverings. It also illuminated the grass and rocks that lined its shores.

On one of the rocks a frog was sitting upright, holding a fishing pole whose line sank deep under the water. He wore an odd hat made of some sort of shell of a nut, although somehow it looked normal on him. Around his neck he wore a blue ribbon fashioned like a scarf. He looked very dapper and strangely normal.

Thorik leaned forward and squinted to see if his eyes and ears would work better at less of a distance. Surely he was seeing things.

One of the frog's legs dangled over the rock's edge while the other was bent, allowing for his foot to be flat against the top. "It's a wonderful natural dock. I bet you wish you had brought your fishing gear."

Thorik was confused. He wasn't sure what bothered him more, the idea of a knee-high frog talking to him or what he had to say. Everything was oddly familiar and yet barely understandable. Blinking his eyes to wake himself up did no good.

"Mr. Theodore J. Hempton, at your service." The frog tipped his hat with his free hand. "And who might you be, my boy?"

Thorik leaned back to a normal sitting position while watching in amazement at the frog talking. It seemed awkward not to reply, even if he didn't believe his own eyes.

"Sec Thorik Dain of Farbank," he responded, still confused at the possibility of frogs talking.

"Well of course you are. That sounds like a ripe good name for such a lad as yourself." The end of Theodore's fishing pole began to tug down a few times. Gripping the rod with both hands he began to back up on the rock to pull his catch out of the water. "So, do you like a taste of the unknown in your games?"

"What?" Thorik replied.

"Your games," he continued. The fishing line pulled hard causing Mr. Hempton to fly forward and land very close to the end of the rock before stopping himself. He didn't allow his fishing to interrupt the conversation. "Do you like livin' a little on the edge? Peeking in the neighbor's windows, if you know what I mean?"

"No, of course not," Thorik replied offensively.

Mr. Hempton pulled back his foot-long fishing rod as it bowed in a strained arch. "No, No, obviously not. Right you are. Who would?" The line in the water thrashed about before heading out toward the center of the natural spring pond. "But don't you ever wonder what it would be like to lose your restrictions and inhibitions and just do what feels right?"

"Sure, I suppose."

"Good, now we're getting somewhere." He continued to struggle with his footing as the line kept pulling. "What would you say to a little game?"

Thorik looked over at Grewen who continued to have movement confinements placed on him and now apparently over his mouth. Avanda was secure under his arm, but for how long? "Tell them to let my friends go first."

"Heaven's no. That would spoil the game. They are the prize you know."

"What?"

"Well, you have to have a prize at the end of a game, otherwise it's not worth playing, I always say." Mr. Hempton pulled back on the line with all his might but struggled to make any headway. "Be a good lad, and hold onto the pole for me while I grab a net."

"I'm not helping you."

"Come on, be a sport. Grab the line, we'll play a game, and then we'll be off with you. Simple as that, no harm done." Mr. Hempton suddenly fell forward from the pull on the line and grabbed hold of the sides of the rock with his back feet as his body hung over the edge.

Instinctively Thorik grabbed the rod to help out. "What kind of game is this?"

"Hang on."

"Hang on? Never heard of it. How do you play?"

"You hang on." Mr. Hempton's smile made Thorik's heart sink.

Thorik was instantly pulled from the grassy shore into the shallow pond only to find himself deep underwater still holding onto the short fishing pole. Looking around, he felt the current taking him away deeper into the water. He was no longer in the natural spring near Mr. Hempton, but instead he was in a moving river.

Afraid to let go of the rod, he held on for dear life as he descended into the water's depths. Holding his breath the best he could, he saw one, and then several, flesh deprived bodies in his route. The fishing rod line pulled Thorik toward the center of a crowd of partially skinned skeletons, who had suddenly realized that he was drawing near.

Thorik knew that if he let go now, they would easily overtake him. His only other option was to hope the speed of his moving catch, at the other end of the fishing line, continued or sped up. Perhaps he could just race his way past them before they got hold of him.

Several bony fingers grabbed at his arms and legs while he advanced past the first group, only to find his hooked fish had stopped running from him. The fishing line went limp. Groups of full and partial corpses surrounded him as he looked about for his options. Above him, he spotted the light of the sun and a way to escape. He began his swim to the surface in an attempt to reach it before the dead caught up with him.

The half-flesh bodies effortlessly moved their way toward him as he closed in on the surface. The water began to clear and the sun's warmth could be felt through the top of the water.

Just as his left hand breached the surface his other hand was tugged down by the fishing rod. His air wouldn't last much longer. The only chance available to get away from the swimming dead was to let go of the rod and swim to shore. It was the only logical decision, but it didn't feel right. It wasn't within the rules of the game. It had been called "hang on" for a purpose and he wasn't going to jeopardize Grewen's and Avanda's life by messing this up.

It was only moments before the bony fingers grabbed his ankles and then his legs. He held onto the little rod with all of his might as one of the skeletons bit into the back of his right hand.

Thorik's underwater scream came out as a large bubble of valuable air that he needed, and he watched it float up and burst onto the surface as the dead pulled him down. He continued to fight them off but there were too many of them, and it was difficult to do as he held onto the fishing pole whose line was now tangled around and through his attackers.

As he was about to give up from lack of oxygen, the fishing line went tight snapping several boned bodies and launching Thorik in a new direction. He reached over with his left hand to hold onto the rod just as it started to slip out from his right.

The water drove hard against his face as he raced against time before he nearly passed out, and then it stopped again. The line went limp again and he looked up to see a green light from above. With a few small strokes of one arm he reached the surface and gasped for air.

He breathed heavily for a few minutes, trying to regain control of himself. Thorik looked around realizing he was in a large granite room with one door on the far side. In the center of the wall on his side of the room was a fountain that sprayed into a small shallow stone pool. Numerous vats of burning oil displayed a green flame as the wall and floor carvings began to come to life. Spiders, bees, panthers and other creatures pulled away from their stagnant hibernation and started moving toward the pool where Thorik sat.

Holding the tiny fishing pole in one hand, he made a dash for the far door. Heavy water-soaked clothes weighed him down, making it difficult to run directly for the far doorway. Rays of soft blue light peeked out from underneath the closed door.

Halfway across, his path was blocked by a white crystal Brandercat. *I only have one chance at this. I can't stop.* He leaped up and rolled over the back of the cat. Landing back on his feet, he never looked back as he continued running toward the door, which opened for him under its own power. A column of blue moonlight beamed into the room, washing out a section of the room's green light.

Black marble bees began to swarm around him, stinging him violently. He slowed as he tried to protect himself from them. Swatting at the ones near his face, he looked about to see what else in the room was coming his way. While doing so, the door began to close again.

Larger creatures broke themselves free of the walls, slowly making their way toward Thorik, while the smaller ones quickly attacked. Spiders of ruby crystals lowered themselves from the ceiling, while granite beetles ran up under his pant legs.

"NO!" Thorik shouted in defiance. Turning sharply back toward the doorway, he focused on his destination and ignored the pain that the animated attackers were inflicting upon him. Charging for the door he accepted every bite and sting along the way. It was the price for freedom, and he was willing to pay it.

The door began to open again as he approached its archway with new strength and attitude in his shoulders. The room exited over the center of a small pond within a lightly crowded forest. Mr. Hempton waited patiently for Thorik to arrive.

Numb to the ongoing attack, Thorik reached the doorway and entered the moonlight. The stone animals that entered the light with him began to petrify and harden. The rest of the creatures stopped their approach at the edge of the blue light. At last, he was free.

The fishing line went tight.

Thorik grabbed the pole with both hands and looked back at the line as it led to the fountain on the far end of the room. It began to pull him out from the archway, back into the green light. He turned to see Mr. Hampton, who was waiting for Thorik's reaction.

"Not this time." Thorik's voice gave him an aggressive posture. He leaned back toward the pond and began to pull on the string. It was a struggle, as he lost his footing only once. But this time *he* was in control. Pulling hand over hand, the fishing line coiled near his feet.

"What kind of catch are you?" he asked, as the line stopped. It was stuck. "Oh, no you don't. I've come too far to not finally catch you."

Pulling with all his might, the line finally gave way, knocking Thorik onto his back, landing on the ledge of the doorway before it dropped off to the water below. He began to reel up the loose line as he stood up.

He looked into the room to see what type of fish he was dragging across the floor, past the idle stone creatures. But the string was not tight as he coiled. Either he had lost his catch or it was moving toward him.

Jumping out from over the top of the animated statues, a thrasher roared as it attacked the Num with his snapping jaw and clawed hands. The fishing line was wrapped onto the primate's hand as it landed on Thorik, knocking him backward, through the doorway and into the natural spring below.

Grewen snored away as various colored flickering pixies and faeries entertained themselves on top of his huge sprawled out body. They bounced on his stomach, put flames to his feet, played hide-and-seek in his robes and even opened his eyelids in an attempt to wake him up. All with the goal of teasing him more. Remarkably none of this woke the giant up from his slumber and the Myth'Unday lost interest in their games.

Thorik emerged from the pond with a splash, still holding onto the frog's little fishing pole. Quickly realizing that the thrasher was gone, he stood up to walk out of the shallow spring toward land.

His legs struggled to hold his weight as they shook under his body with each step he took. Walking to the edge, he fell onto the green grass where he had been sleeping before all this had started.

Mr. Hempton sat on the edge of his rock with his thin legs crossed and his hands folded politely in front of him on his lap. "Good show dear boy. Well done."

Thorik reached over and handed the twig of a pole back to him.

Mr. Hempton looked it over to ensure it was in good shape. "That was fun. I do so love games. You're quite good yourself. Would you like to play another?"

"No." Thorik rolled over onto his back to rest. "To what purpose would you put me through such a thing?"

"Purpose? It's just a game, lad. Not everything has to happen for a purpose."

The statement irritated Thorik for it went against his mother's favorite saying. "That's not true. Everything happens for a purpose."

"You'd like that to be true, but even you have doubts about it. That's why it bothered you so much when I said that. Just like you have been questioning the purpose of your adventure with your friends."

Thorik shook it off and went back to the original questioning. "Why did you put me through such a horrible torturous game?"

Mr. Hempton looked at Thorik with intrigue and smiled. "Dear boy, it was *your* game."

Still breathing hard from the underwater experience he asked, "What? I don't understand."

"You made up the game, the rules and the challenges out of your own fears and desires."

"You read my thoughts and used my fears against me?"

"Goodness, no. You used them against yourself. Just like you do in real life. The only difference is when you are with Myth'Undays, your thoughts become more real to the senses. Take me for example. What am I?"

Thorik was still trying to digest this new information as he answered. "A frog, of course."

"Am I now? The last person that saw me thought I was a Tree Nymph." Mr. Hempton adjusted his hat and winked before continuing. "You see, everyone sees things differently. That does not make you right and them wrong."

"Does it make me wrong and them right?"

"No, neither have to be false to make the other true. They both can be correct and yet see two different things. Lad, things can exist differently for different people."

"So, is there nothing to believe in? Nothing to fight for? Is everyone right just from different perspectives?"

Mr. Hempton laughed. "Don't fool yourself. There is plenty of wrongdoing in this world, and you usually know when you are a part of it. The challenge comes when you are so focused on what you know is right that you refuse to even listen to other perspectives. This can be just as dangerous.

Thorik sat for a short time thinking about the conversation and the pain he had caused himself in the game. "So, what's my prize?"

"Pardon me?" Mr. Hempton replied slightly surprised at the question.

"My prize for holding on to your fishing pole while I was attacked by all of my fears. What is it?"

Mr. Hempton looked perplexed. "I'm not sure. You're the first one to win. At least that I know of. Well played, by the way. Bravo," he said with polite clapping of his hands.

"Your prize was to have Grewen and Avanda if I lost." Thorik turned and looked over to see the little flying Myth'Unday untie him as he slept. "What's my prize for winning?"

Mr. Hempton gave the question some serious thought before responding. "Where are you traveling?"

"What does that have to do with it?" Thorik replied, annoyed with the games.

"Entertain me for a bit more, won't you?"

"We are in route to meet with others on a journey."

"To do what, may I ask?" the frog questioned.

"My uncle has been captured and is being sent to the Southwind Mines. We've come to save him while they transport him along this road. After that-"

Mr. Hempton interrupted Thorik in mid-sentence. "There's your prize, you silly Num. And a grand prize it will be. Of course it's not much of a prize to me if I were to win. Or for most people for that matter."

"What are you talking about?" Thorik asked.

"I will free your uncle," he said with a smile and a wink.

Thorik thought about his offer and gave a wide grin. *Perhaps things do happen for a reason.*

"A fine game this is, and although it has strategic qualities, it lacks the excitement of survival," Mr. Hempton commented to Thorik as they played another game of Runeage. "Perhaps if a player were to lose a toe or finger with each tile surrendered."

They continued playing as the other Myth'Unday creatures sprinkled sleeping dust over Grewen and Avanda.

"Is that absolutely necessary?" Thorik asked again. "Grewen could really come in helpful with stopping the guards to free Brimmelle."

"If they wake and see me, they must play a game. And I can't guarantee that they will win." Mr. Hempton took a moment and set down his next rune tile.

"So, no one can see Myth'Unday without playing a game?" Thorik asked.

"Not true in the slightest. How did you ever win our game in the pond?" Mr. Hempton asked to himself before continuing. "Young children can see through our illusions, but who will believe the words of a child? In addition, I ask for payment to see me in the form of a game. Some do nothing, but many others require a great deal more. You're quite lucky you ran into me. My sister would have ripped out your eyes for gazing upon her. She's extremely vain you know. The arrogant twit will never let me live down the day I broke her mirror. 'Get over it already,' I says to Raython. 'Look in a mud puddle. It reflects your face better.' I added." The frog laughed at his own memories.

Thorik gave a confused look as Mr. Hempton's story led to his personal memories. "So, Avanda should be able to see you without playing a game."

"Don't be so sure about that. Kids grow up fast now days and innocence is quickly lost. As much as I'm up for another game, I think we'll have our hands full in a very short time."

The sun rose and turned the sky light shades of blue before a leaf winged Myth'Unday flew down from a tree to notify Thorik of an approaching wagon.

Thorik climbed up into the tree and watched the wagon work its way to the apex of a hill before going back down into the next shallow valley.

He called down to Mr. Hempton. "I see a wagon and several riders approaching. It looks like Darkmere's guards." He climbed out of the tree and hid behind some bushes.

Mr. Hempton looked over at a Tree Faerie wearing an acorn for a hat and a pinecone for clothes.

The Faerie nodded back to Mr. Hempton and went right to work. It ran out into the middle of the road and stopped before it began spinning around like a top. It gathered more speed as it spun and eventually drilled itself into the ground.

All was quiet for a few seconds before the ground began to rumble. Earth began to push up from the center of the road as a tree started to quickly grow up out of it. Limbs formed and the tree's height increased as well as its width.

Once its branches were long enough to span the road, it stopped. A slight pause was taken before a series of eruptions, near the tree, exploded dirt into the air. Thick roots pushed their way out of the ground in every direction. They pulsed and grew until they were easily over a foot thick.

The oncoming wagon would not be able to pass this obstacle.

Thorik was tugged and pulled into hiding by the Myth'Unday, as the wagon approached. He still was in awe of seeing a tree grow in a matter of minutes.

The wagon arrived over the hill and came to a stop before the tree. Two soldiers sat on the front of the wagon. It was being pulled by a four-legged Fesh'Unday, long and thin with tan hair. Six guards road the backs of Faralopes and other similar two-legged species. Two of the riders took the lead, followed by the wagon and then the other four riders.

The wagon itself was a cage on wheels and contained a dozen human and Polenum captives. Thorik immediately saw Brimmelle sitting in the back corner, hot and depleted from the trek across the desert. He did not look well.

Once they stopped, the first two guards got off their beasts and started discussing how they could cut out the roots for the wheels of the wagon. One grabbed his battle-axe from his mount and walked over to chop at the roots blocking the path. He swung the axe with full force as it cut deeply into the root. Pulling it out for another swing, he stopped when he noticed blood on his blade.

The guard next to him noticed it as well. They both looked down at the root to see blood pouring out of the wound.

As they looked upon the root with disbelief, the tree limbs from above attacked. They grabbed them both and lifted the two up, stripping them of their weapons that fell back to earth.

It was at this time that the Myth'Undays attacked like a swarm of multicolored fireflies. Several large blankets were flown over from the woods and placed over the prisoner's cage. It was held down to prevent those inside from seeing the Myth'Unday.

Glowing threads began to wrap around the guards as sleeping dust was sprinkled in their faces.

The guards fought back and shielded themselves the best they could. One guard near the back grabbed one of the faeries out of the air and held it tight in his fist. The glowing Myth'Unday brightened her intensity as the guard gazed upon streams of light shining out between his fingers before feeling the flesh in his palm starting to burn. He opened his hand quickly and began to blow on his palm to cool it down as the faerie sprinkled dust in his face.

Other guards made futile attempts to swing swords and maces at the tiny creatures, resulting often in their own injures. This continued as the Myth'Unday teased and tied up the guards who were now falling off their rides.

Chaos around the wagon quickly subsided as each of the guards fell into the Myth'Undays bindings. All but the wagon driver were tied up and moved into the woods, out of view.

Mr. Hempton hopped up onto the front of the wagon and then onto the captive driver, stopping on his shoulder. He showed the man his fishing rod. "I hope you're up for a game, or two."

It was impossible for Thorik to know what the Guard saw when he looked at Mr. Hempton, but it was obviously something that struck fear into him, for he screamed at the sight of him.

He was quickly bound and removed from the visibility of the prisoners.

Thorik ran out to the road and grabbed a fallen battle-axe near the tree. Looking down at the bleeding wound in the exposed root, he asked, "Are you going to heal?" Looking up he saw nearly a hundred little acorns suddenly grow and then fall to the ground. Each of them sprouting legs, arms, and heads moments after they landed. They all quickly scurried into the woods as the tree itself decayed before Thorik's eyes. Tree limbs drooped, then fell, before the entire plant turned to dust and swirled softly away in the breeze.

"Thank you." Thorik then wished the Tree Faerie farewell.

Moving to the back of the wagon, Thorik pulled off the blanket and busted the lock apart with his new double bladed weapon. He swung the door open, freeing the captives. They all looked drained and thin from lack of food as well as burned from the desert's hot rays.

Reaching into the cage, Thorik began helping people out of the wagon and down to the road. In his haste to help, he almost didn't notice his Grandmother. "Granna Gluic? Is that you? I thought you were dead."

"My death was over exaggerated." She then held up her sack of stones.

Thorik hugged her tighter than he had ever done before. He had missed her greatly and suddenly realized how much he enjoyed her company. He never wanted to let her go again.

"She was unconscious for a few days." Brimmelle followed her out. "But I nursed her back to health with my readings of the scrolls."

Still hugging Thorik, Gluic commented softly into his ear, "It was my stones."

The prisoners stretched their legs and bodies as they walked toward the natural spring. Near the water sat a bountiful feast of fruit for the eating. They quickly enjoyed the gift of food and thanked Thorik for it time and time again.

"You're welcome, but it wasn't me. The Myth'Undays gathered it for you," he would say but no one seemed to listen.

Grewen and Avanda woke to the sight of the group enjoying their feast. There was more than they could eat, but perhaps less than Grewen could.

"Hello?" Grewen sat up from behind bushes that hadn't existed when he had fallen asleep.

The crowd stood in fear at the sight of the giant Mognin.

"It's okay," Thorik announced to the recently freed people. "He's our friend."

Taking some time to calm everyone down, Thorik gathered some food for Grewen and Avanda.

Thorik loaded his new battle-axe onto his back as several people asked how he had saved them.

"I had help from some Myth'Unday's that I befriended," Thorik said. "I won a game with Mr. Hempton, he's a tall frog." He smiled as he used his hands to show everyone how tall Mr. Hempton was. "And for my reward he helped me free you."

"How did these frogs help you?" one of older men asked.

"No, there was only one frog. The rest were little forest people with mystical abilities. Some had wings, some could glow, others dressed themselves with leaves and nuts," Thorik explained.

The group laughed at his far-fetched story of magical little people and dismissed it as they thanked Thorik again for the rescue and food.

Keeping the celebration short, they wished to start their return trip to see family and friends. The group boarded the wagon and mounts to head back toward Eastland in a state of jubilation.

Brimmelle and Gluic said their goodbye to the group as they rode away, before the two turned back and visited with Grewen and Avanda. Avanda and Brimmelle quickly began telling their own adventures as the two stories bounced back and forth on top of each other.

Thorik leaned against a nearby tree watching his friends, as he noticed something move out of the corner of his eye. "Thank you."

Mr. Hempton stood on a branch and leaned on the trunk. "No, no. Thank *you* my lad. You play a fine game. Just remember, you always control the game until you stop believing that you do."

"I'll remember that, next time I meet another Myth'Unday."

"Lad, I was talking about your games outside the Mythical Forest."

Thorik understood and nodded.

Theodore Hempton gave Thorik a wink before hopping off the tree and over to the hidden and bound guards, to find his first challenger.

Thorik smiled as he watched the frog hop away before turning to see Grewen packing up all of the supplies and the remaining food. It was time to leave.

Chapter 29
Pelonthal

Thorik and his party made their way along the River's Edge southern perimeter wall toward Pelonthal. The farther west they traveled, the climate became more hospitable with lower temperatures and comfortable humidity levels. Grass turned greener and pockets of timber continued to increase in size, as they continued to skirt the northern edge of the Mythical Forest.

At the top of one of the many rolling hills, the Pelonthal Dovenar Wall could be seen running south from the River's Edge Province. With each hill they walked over, the wall became more defined and details of the gate's opening came into view.

Getting sidetracked, again, Thorik questioned the wall acting as a dike. "Grewen, what holds the water inside River's Edge? Wouldn't it run out of the gates into the land beyond?"

Chuckling at Thorik's ever-inquisitive mind, he replied, "Only if they were open. The solid protective metal doors can be dropped, closing them tight from the inside to prevent any kind of attack. The pressure from the water continues to force them into a tight seal."

"Let's focus on this gate right now," Brimmelle suggested as he pointed forward. He was very nervous as they approached the entrance with an Unday as part of their party. Flashbacks of the Woodlen Gate Faralope incident kept popping into his head. "I don't like this."

Grewen noted, "It's fine. The only purpose of the guards at Pelonthal's gate is to keep out war mongering Del'Unday or Fesh'Unday that may eat the local crops or livestock. Ov'Unday have been living in Pelonthal for decades."

Few words were spoken as they approached the beautifully designed wall. Decorating the outer wall, patterns of trees and hills could be seen at first glance, while plants and animals were seen with more effort. The wall was not carved out like the objects in Kingsfoot or the Woodlen Coliseum, instead they were artistically placed colored rocks that created various scenes of nature across its entire length.

The road led to the gate. From this vantage point, Thorik could see both north and south walls of River's Edge with the lake in between them, as well as several building tops which could be seen above the surface near the center. Many more buildings existed in this location than where Thorik had crossed. He assumed it most likely meant more dead souls rummaging around as well.

Thorik commented to Grewen, "The River's Edge Lake looks wider here, and there doesn't seem to be a straight path across without going through a building. I can see why no one passes here."

"Looks pleasant enough." Brimmelle was unsure what all the fuss was about as they stepped up to the open gates.

Thorik smirked at Brimmelle's words before he looked up and began to wave at one of the guards on the wall.

The Fir pushed Thorik's arm down. "You don't learn, do you?"

Thorik smiled. Brimmelle's comments somehow didn't dig quite as deep as they used to.

Thorik cupped his hands on either side of his mouth as he spoke to the guards. "Gentlemen. How are you on this fine day?"

A guard walked over and peered down at the group. "All quiet, as usual. How are the roads toward Eastland? We heard of a devastating storm that blew out many bridges and towers in Southwind and the winds were heading northeast along the Southern Mountains. Did you get any of it?"

"No sir, perhaps we left before it hit," Thorik replied.

"Praise your timing. She sounds like a mean witch."

The guard uniforms were of blue and white, uncomplicated and functional with no frills or lace. None the less, its simplistic look gave more of a clean and genuine look than the uniforms of Woodlen.

"What be your business on this day?" the guard asked.

"We come to visit friends."

"What part of Greensbrook?"

"No, in Pelonthal."

The guard looked perplexed. "River-Green Road runs through the heart of the forest, straight to Greensbrook and then on to Southwind. There are no side roads to the lakeside cities in Pelonthal. Never been a need."

Grewen realized the potential confusion of the Nums and entered the conversation. "I used to live here and still have family in the capital. I know the way." Looking at the sun as it lowered in the west, he knew they wouldn't be able to make the trek through the forest before nightfall. "Do you have lodging for the night?"

"Stables are large enough to hold you, as long as you get along with Faralopes and Uderipes," he answered as Brimmelle flinched at the word 'Faralope.' "That should keep you dry and safe until morning. But even with daylight, you don't want to get lost in the forest or the Myth'Unday will have at you."

A second guard came out from below, at the gate entrance. "There'll be a fee for the lodging and you'll still have to pay the same toll even if you're not following the entire length of the road."

"Accepted. Thank you," Grewen said as they walked under the hanging gate, which the giant had to bend down to get under.

Gluic walked over to the toll man and emptied a few gold nuggets into his open hand.

He shook himself out of his boredom as he gazed at the precious tender provided.

Grewen smiled at her. "That should be enough," he said before she doubled the already high price she had paid.

Once inside, the road turned sharply to the left and followed along the inside of the wall for as far as they could see. The path was made of flat stones wedged together in a skillful manner. Over the years the odd-shaped stones had lost their luster and grass formed in the seams, but instead of looking old and unmanaged, it gave the road character and a charisma of its own. It felt comfortable and relaxing like Thorik's path from his cottage to Farbank.

They stayed the night without issue and followed the River-Green road first thing in the morning. They traveled south for several miles with the wall on their left and the thick forest to their right. The wall and road cut straight through the middle of the Mythical Forest with a forty-foot thick opening.

"Here it is. This is the way." Grewen had turned abruptly from the road and started walking toward the trees.

The Nums looked around for some kind of sign.

"How do you know?" Thorik asked.

"It's the seventh double-root tree we've seen since we entered the province."

Skeptical, Brimmelle looked into the dark forest and at the double-root tree, which were actually two trees that grew together in various twisting fashions. "Are you sure?"

"I think so."

"And if you're wrong?" Brimmelle asked in his commanding Fir voice used often on Thorik.

"Then I'm wrong, and we'll miss the city and have to sleep in the forest. Hopefully I got it right." He entered the forest.

Brimmelle did not like the response, or the fact that Grewen walked away without providing the Fir with an opportunity to argue the point. Now he had no choice but to follow the giant to continue the discussion.

Thorik entered the dark woods, followed next by Avanda, Gluic and then Brimmelle.

The forest was thick with ferns and trees with exposed roots on land that never seemed to flatten out. Small creeks and streams sporadically appeared from ground springs and ended under rocks and vegetation. The ground was covered with a soft red mud and clay that clumped onto everyone's boots as well as Grewen's feet. It made the constant up and down hike slippery and dangerous.

The wind rustled the upper leaves of the trees and gave off a soft whistling sound, much like music. It was followed by soft voices in the background that could not be understood. Motions in the forest were seen out of the corners of their eyes but never where they were directly looking. The group had an uncomfortable feeling that they were being watched.

Grewen kept his senses on alert. "I have the feeling the Myth'Unday are toying with us."

Brimmelle looked up at the enormous man. "You mean the little forest folk that Thorik was telling us about earlier? I'll keep my eyes open for any flying frogs," he sarcastically replied. His uncomfortable laugh was an attempt to block the noises in the woods.

"Thorik never said the frog could fly." Avanda glanced over at the other Num. "You didn't, did you, Thorik?"

Thorik smiled at Avanda's attempt to defend him. "No, he didn't fly. But I don't think these Myth'Unday know of my good relations with Mr. Hempton. They may not take so kindly to our trespassing."

Thorik's apprehension about the odd noises and soft voices that he heard was stiffening his stride. He tried to relax. Mr.

Hempton's game had taught him that his fears were his worse enemy. It wasn't easy, but he needed to control it.

Grewen's small ears didn't catch all the sounds that the Nums did. Unlike the rest, Gluic chatted away with the unseen guests. Then again, she had been doing that for years. Thorik wondered if she had been talking to the Myth'Unday all that time.

After his taunting of Thorik was over, Brimmelle became edgy with each new sound that he heard. "Did you hear that? I heard footsteps following us." He turned and walked backward as he scanned the terrain. It wasn't more than a few steps before he fell from his haste and clumsiness. He crashed through a fern, down a small slope and into a muddy puddle with a loud splash.

"Perhaps you're right. I think I just heard something myself," Grewen teased.

Brimmelle's backward fall had coated the Fir's backside with thick clumps of wet red clay. But instead of lashing out in anger, he became alarmed from his great discomfort in the area. "We are not alone. There must be Del'Unday out here with us." His heart quickened as the soft voices became louder while sounds of snapping branches and heavy footsteps increased in frequency and volume.

"It's not Del'Unday, Brimmelle. It's the forest folk," Avanda replied. "Oh Thorik, do you think I'll be lucky enough to see a Myth'Unday."

"Keep your eyes open," Thorik said kindly, hoping that they wouldn't run into any. He had no desire for another Myth' game.

Brimmelle continued to panic. He was seeing movement in every direction, but couldn't focus on any of it. The snapping of sticks and slushy foot falls in the mud continued to get closer to him. "We need to get out of here!" he shouted.

Of course, they had not seen or heard nearly what he had.

Avanda looked back at him and smiled. "I thought you didn't believe in them."

Thorik shook his head, cautioning her not to tease. Brimmelle was having a hard time in this forest and they needed everyone to keep their wits about them.

With fresh flora crammed in her hair, Gluic walked back to Brimmelle. "Take these." She placed two black spherical smooth rocks in his hand. "Hold them tight and they will calm you down."

"Your river rocks will not save us from the spirits in these woods." Then Brimmelle placed them in his side pouch.

"Yes they will," Thorik added. "The Myth-Unday have obviously chosen you to entertain them. They play on your thoughts and your fears. What you believe is real, is real, at least to you."

Grewen stopped and looked back at Thorik. "Nicely spoken little man." Turning back, he led his friends farther west, hoping they would see the city soon for the evening was not far off.

Brimmelle followed behind as he continued to look at the trees that began to bend from their own power instead of the wind. He stopped in his tracks as the large double-root tree in front of him looked to be waiting for him as the other party members passed it by. It stared him down, from unseen eyes.

The outstretched arms of the tree curved its end branches toward him. A knot in front opened as a mouth. Brimmelle was frozen with fear for several seconds before he realized he was sinking in the thick mud. Attempting to lift his feet was useless as he sank even deeper.

"Help!" Brimmelle screamed. "Come back," he shouted. But the rest of the group was long gone, out of sight.

Mud covered his knees as he struggled to free himself until he saw the large double-root tree step forward, dragging its root system out of the ground. Earth around it popped up in the air in small chunks as the roots lifted from beneath it.

Watching the tree make its way slowly to him, Brimmelle spotted a brown squirrel running toward him from his right. It made tracks across the mud and onto Brimmelle's shirt, leaving a trail of tiny footprints. The squirrel came up onto his shoulder and looked him square in the eyes before squeaking out various chattering sounds.

"Go away, leave me alone," Brimmelle demanded of the rodent.

It replied back to him with an open mouth of large dangerous teeth and a violent scream, chilling Brimmelle to the bone. Only inches from his face, the squirrel continued to bare its teeth at him. Brimmelle attempted to slap it away, only to find his hands were stuck at his sides.

Looking down he saw several roots from the oncoming tree had already wrapped themselves around him. Moving ever so closely, the tree purposely broke off one of its own limbs. The Fir was certain that the sharp end of the limb was to be used for thrusting into his chest.

The squirrel ran down and bit his wrist, causing his reflexes to move his arm forward within the restrictions of the roots. Moving to his front, the critter opened one of Brimmelle's side sacks, which was no longer covered by his arm. It grabbed a few items out and raced back up to his shoulder.

Screeching at Brimmelle, in its high pitched terrifying sound, it almost bit the Num's nose off before it ran back down his arm. It placed the two round black stones, which it had stolen from the sack, into Brimmelle's hand.

Brimmelle grasped the items tightly as the tree reached down and picked him up out of the mud and into the air. Dangling like a lifeless sack of rice in its two largest limbs, the tree's mouth opened. It was large enough to take him in with one bite.

"Are you with us?" the tree's thunderous voice asked.

"What?" Brimmelle responded.

The squirrel ran along the ground next to him and asked, "Brimmelle, do you feel any better?"

"That sounds like Thorik's voice," he commented and looked around for the boy.

"He's coming out of it," the tree said in Grewen's voice.

Brimmelle's eyes widened as he beheld a hideous Del'Unday Krupe walking toward him. Its black sharply cut armor covered everything but the glowing eyes that stared at Brimmelle. It spoke, "You just couldn't keep the stones in your hand like I asked, could you?" Sounding a lot like his mother's voice.

Brimmelle tried to understand but couldn't. Sounds and sights blurred and faded in and out. He tightly held his mother's precious stones, which the squirrel had given to him. Closing his eyes, he hoped that it would all go away.

Thorik's voice hit Brimmelle's ears clearly this time. "It's just a hallucination caused by the Myth'Unday. Your own fears are betraying you. Pull yourself out of it."

"We've lost a lot of time, we need to hurry if we plan to make it out of here before nightfall," Grewen said. "It's not wise to stay the night in the depths of the Mythical Forest, especially if you have a chance not to."

Brimmelle slowly opened one eye to see Gluic, Thorik, and Grewen standing over him. "How did they do this to me?"

Grewen lifted him to his feet. "It's their forest. They can do what they want. Entertaining themselves by making your nightmares come alive is what they enjoy, especially at night. So, let's hurry so we don't have to sleep here."

"Look everyone," Avanda yelled, standing a few yards from Grewen. "I caught one of them. I have my own Myth'Unday."

Thorik and Grewen's eyes widened and hearts sank at the thought of the potential issues to follow.

"You what?" Thorik said back.

She smiled as she stepped up to the group with her hands cupped, top and bottom, around her prisoner. "I jumped around a tree and surprised her. She had just started to fly away when I caught her."

Grewen looked around for an attack from her Myth friends.

Gluic moved closer to Avanda. "Let us see her. Show us her beauty and her magic."

"I don't want her to fly away," Avanda said. "Can we put her in a sack to keep safe?"

Thorik stepped behind her and placed his hands on her shoulders. This was just like he used to do in class in Farbank, when he wanted the students to think deeply about something before speaking to the class. "Avanda, I want you to think about the Runestone that you are wearing around your neck. How does it apply to this situation?"

Avanda thought about it and nodded in agreement. "We have a responsibility to all life. Only take what we need and give back what we can," she recalled from his teachings.

She took a deep breath. "Goodbye little winged lady." She opened her hands to reveal a colorful butterfly. It flapped its wings a few times before it left Avanda's palm.

"It's beautiful!" Gluic was obviously delighted.

"But that's not what I caught," Avanda explained, as the winged insect circled around Avanda's head several times before leaving them. "Honest, it wasn't."

"We believe you." Thorik was happy the way things turned out.

And the group hurried off. Up and down the small folds of land and through periodically dark shaded areas, from heavy tree growth, until it opened up into an airy slope leading to a city near the lake. The last bit of sun was falling as they made their way down.

Night had fallen before they reached the city. Lanterns lined the streets and buildings with a glow of energy about them. Music and merry-making could be heard while passing the first row of odd shaped homes. No exterior boundaries or walls protected the city as the gradual increase of houses led them toward the city that sat along the water's edge.

Thorik heard horns and flutes playing exciting new tunes while drums and string instruments supported them. Each instrument played its own melody that complimented all the others. This organized chaos was relaxing and uplifting at the same time.

They rounded the corner to see a cobblestone open area along the lake, filled with artists of all kinds. Painters and pot makers crafted their wears as sculptors and ironworkers showed off their latest creations. The well-lit lakeside festivities included musicians, chefs, acrobats and more. Jewelers developed custom designs for waiting customers who were already wearing a ridiculous amount of accessories. Flaming foods were served to patrons as they watched glassblowers create wonderfully colored glassware.

Grewen sighed with relief. "Pelonthal City, the last safe heaven for mixed blood."

The area teamed with life and vitality as all races and species coexisted together enjoying each other's company. A young Mognin played tag in the streets with a Clupper and Num while a large bird-like man used his own feathers to paint on a canvas of flattened bark.

Clothing styles varied as well as the fabric used, but for the most part the theme was loose fitting and relaxed. No guards were seen and no walls loomed over them as the people enjoyed life along the docks. It was hard to believe this was in the same kingdom as the other cities they had passed through.

Thorik walked along the boardwalk looking out at the boats swaying back and forth from the shallow waves. A light breeze blew off the lake into town, cooling off the sun baked brick streets and buildings. It was a perfect evening to unwind from the grueling experiences over the past few weeks. The air had the smell of the beginning of fall when the first rush of mountain-air cooled off Farbank after a warm sticky day.

Walking past artwork of wood, clay, and metal they stopped frequently admiring the ingenuity and creativeness that was required to make the objects evoke such emotions. Shiny brass and metal sculptures of abstract ideas were on display, as well as statues of known animals.

Thorik sat down on the side of a large fountain decorated with metal animals, some in the water while others were mounted along the outer wall. Turning his back to the fountain, he watched his friends and family enjoy what the city had to offer. He only wished that Emilen were there to enjoy it with him.

"Don't turn your back on me, Fesh," said a growling voice from behind Thorik.

Thorik whipped around to realize that he had mistaken Draq as one of the metal sculptures. "Draq? Is that you?" he said softly to the unmoving metal dragon perched on the fountain's edge.

"Yes, why are you whispering?" he asked.

Thorik was surprised and relieved that he wasn't hearing things again. The Mythical Forest had him questioning everything.

"Draq!" Grewen announced as he walked across the open area toward them.

"Grewen," he replied back. "Good, you broke free. I knew they couldn't keep a hold on you."

"Actually, Thorik freed me." He looked down at the young man. "I am in his debt."

Politely, Thorik added, "Actually Avanda helped also."

Skeptical, Draq looked at the little Num and began to make his compliment to Thorik. "So you saved– Gluic?" He had interrupted his own sentence with the sight of the elderly Num.

"What?" Thorik questioned.

Draq continued in a controlled voice, "Gluic, you're alive?" Lowering his eyebrows and looking back over at Thorik, he added, "Thorik told me that you were dead."

"Oh, I was, dear. But I never let that hold me back before," she replied.

Draq shook off his perplexed look from her answer before continuing. "I suppose Thorik saved you as well," he remarked with dry sarcasm.

Gluic shook her head. "No, there were too many guards. Thorik's friend, the frog, and his butterfly companions saved us." She was absolutely sincere in her statement.

Draq looked up to Grewen for a real answer.

Nodding his head while mouthing the word "frog", Grewen used his hands to show the small size of the frog that had helped them.

"I don't want to know," Draq returned in an attempt to end the confusing conversation.

Brimmelle stepped up to the group, holding onto Avanda's hand. "We are here also," he alerted Draq of his freedom.

"Good," Draq replied with little interest. "Ambrosius' son, Ericc, is no longer at my lair but we have no evidence that he has been captured by Darkmere. If he has been, Darkmere will want to be present before the Alchemists attempt his assassination. So, we need to find Darkmere. To do that, we need to determine where his next target will be. Unfortunately we haven't found any leads yet."

"We know where he is going." Gluic started digging for something within her many pockets.

"How is that possible?" Draq asked. His interest was peaked, yet he was skeptical that these Nums could accomplish a task which an E'rudite and dragon could not.

She pulled out a large cylindrical crystal, the one she found in Kingsfoot Lake. Smiling and nodding, she held it out in front of them. "In here."

Draq's head drooped as he realized that she didn't have the information he needed and they were no closer to finding Ambrosius' son today than a week prior. "I don't think Darkmere is in your crystal."

"No, but his thoughts are trapped in here," she told him.

Draq lowered his head toward Gluic's open hand and eyed the crystal. "How is that possible?"

"Darkmere gave them to me when we held hands." She gave a quick wink. "Go ahead, touch it and see."

Draq backed off. "I don't touch anything having to do with Darkmere unless it involves his death."

Grewen reached out his hand only to retract it at the last second. "Last time I tried this you slapped my finger and told me I would suck the energy out of it," he jested before he opened his palm for her to place it.

"That's true," she reminded herself. "They still haven't forgiven your species. Amazingly vast memories. They never do forget." Turning to Thorik, she left Grewen slightly stunned by the comments.

She set the crystal in the center of Thorik's palm and closed his fingers around it. Gluic placed one of her hands on top of his fist and the other below. "Close your eyes. What do you see?"

Visions of horrible acts flashed through his mind. Torture, pain, beheadings, mutilations, and more. Visions of Darkmere and Ambrosius in battle, crushing waves from the lake, sacrificing a child at an altar. He was obviously disturbed by the images and tried to turn his head away. "So much evil. So much hatred. I can see so much pain in his life."

"Where is he headed?" Draq barked.

Thorik focused for a few seconds as he mentally asked the same question to the crystal. A room came into view. A man, Darkmere, stood at a table looking at a map. Pointing to the western coastline of Luthralum, a thin mountain range came into view. A break in the range exposed an arched line and words describing the location. "Australis Weirfortus," Thorik responded as his eyes opened wide, breaking the trance-like state, which held him. "What's a Weirfortus?"

Grewen and Draq looked shocked as they turned their heads out to the lake, looking into the moonlit horizon.

"He wouldn't dare," Draq growled.

"To what end," Grewen replied. "What possible purpose could he have?"

Draq clinched his jaw. "If this vision is correct, this will be the end of Australis."

"As we know it?" Thorik questioned hoping for clarification of changes they may see.

Grewen shook his head. "It could mean the end of our land and the end of all life that lives on it."

Chapter 30
Friend or Foe

As instructed by Grewen, Thorik led the Nums along the shoreline street toward the Crab Pot Inn. Glistening sheets of color danced high in the atmosphere extending from the Lu'Tythis Tower. They had seen the distant flowing lights every cloudless night since they had left Kingsfoot. The locals thought nothing of it, but Thorik was always captivated by the beautiful light show. He recalled the first time he had seen the tower after exiting the pass. Memories of Em revealed images of them cuddling together as they watched the tower's lights. It seemed so long ago. Only a month or so had passed, yet he felt he had experienced a lifetime of adventures. *She would have loved to have see them this close to the tower*, he thought.

Reaching the Inn, Thorik opened the front doors, which led them into a grand room supporting dining and drinks. Thick wooden beams arched up the walls to the peak in the center of the ceiling. A large open fireplace was the primary light, with scattered lanterns attempting to back it up. Wet fishing nets dried on large rusty hooks and crab baskets hung from the walls along with several trophy-sized crab skeletons. Some were larger than Thorik and had pinchers the length of his arm.

The room smelled of seafood and ale. Pungent, but not to the point of being unbearable. The dozen or so diners didn't seem to complain as they broke open crab legs ripe with meat.

Ambrosius sat at one of the tables along the far wall from the fireplace. It was poorly lit and isolated from the patrons who sat among the other tables. He was quiet and reserved, bringing no attention to himself as he kept his face in the shadows.

Thorik walked over to him, but wasn't sure how to start the conversation. The last time they had seen each other Ambrosius was destroying the northern Woodlen City of Pyrth and its residents along with it.

Ambrosius looked up and noticed the group approach him. He smiled and rose to his feet. "Welcome to Pelonthal City my friends. I am glad to see you are all well. Especially you, Gluic. I had heard that you had passed away."

She smiled at the sentiment. "Who's to say I hadn't?"

Ambrosius wasn't sure how to take her comment, so he redirected the conversation to Thorik. "Your travels have been long and far. It is good to see you have saved Gluic and Brimmelle. What came of Grewen's fate?"

"Avanda and I broke him out of the Coliseum Melee Matches. He is here with Draq, currently visiting family to arrange for transportation."

"So the stories are true. I heard word that the Coliseum attacked its attending audience with a life of its own. I could only hope that it was your doing in saving Grewen. You have done well, my friend."

The words bothered Thorik. He turned to his grandmother. "Gluic, can you and Brimmelle please secure rooms for us and put Avanda to bed. I need to talk to Ambrosius."

Avanda protested as Gluic pulled the child from the table and to the innkeeper before heading up to their rooms.

Brimmelle stayed at the table for a moment shaking his head at Ambrosius. "I have nothing to say to him anyway. He's the cause of all our problems," he said to Thorik in a fatherly way. The Fir was exhausted from the day's travel and didn't have it in him to argue any further. Wishing to clean the dried mud and clay from his clothes, he turned and went up to the rooms with Gluic.

Thorik looked back at Ambrosius. "Get this straight." He leaned forward onto the edge of the table. "I have not 'done well'. I have done nothing but what I had to, because of *your* attack on Pyrth and on helpless innocent people. We wouldn't be here right now if it weren't for your uncontrolled anger and reckless disregard for others in your pursuit to take revenge on Darkmere."

Ambrosius was solemn in his response as he sat back down. "You don't understand Thorik, it is very complicated."

Thorik's fists flexed. "I am tired of being told it's complicated. It's an easy way out for you to defend your actions. In your mind, the end justifies those who get hurt. But you don't want to be held responsible for those details. You want the recognition of the final result, hoping that everyone in the end will forgive and forget what it took to accomplish it, as well as those who died in your wake."

Ambrosius kept his voice low, hoping to encourage Thorik to do the same. "That is not true."

"Oh no? Then what are you doing here?" Thorik's voice had raised instead of lowered. "Brimmelle's captors would have rolled right past this province toward Southwind while you sat here in this inn. You made no attempt to save him!"

"It wouldn't have done any good to save him if he and tens of thousands of others would die just a few weeks later from Darkmere's attack. Now lower your voice," Ambrosius said sternly while keeping his own intensity at bay. He didn't like the attention they were gathering from the nearby diners.

"I will not! Not until you provide me with an answer of substance." He stood up straight and continued, "I trusted you. I fought for you. I believed in you."

Ambrosius glanced back and forth at the other tables, concerned about what might be overheard. He then returned his gaze back to Thorik's eyes. They looked stronger than before, more assured of himself and less apprehensive. "You have grown during your travels, my friend. I was correct, you know. You will make a great leader someday." He pulled out the chair next him and motioned to it. "Please sit. I have put you through great dangers. I owe you an explanation."

Hesitating at first, the Num sat down at the table while Ambrosius waved the barkeeper over to order drinks. After the drinks had been served, Ambrosius began his story.

"I was born a prince to the Dovenar Kingdom. My twin brother Tarosius obviously had the same fate. It was our responsibility to keep the Kingdom strong and prosperous. I was educated in the fundamentals of finance and legislation. My brother was educated on military tactics with the desire for him to protect the Dovenar Walls from invasions."

"Ru'Mere, the King's advisor, taught us in the ways of the E'rudites. A skill that has been forbidden in Australis for thousands of years. He had been born an E'rudite and had managed to conceal it throughout his years."

"Tarosius embraced his powers of matter alteration and eventually traveled to Corrock for more advanced training by Deleth, the Dark Oracle. I stayed behind and continued my training of gravitational control by Ru'Mere, who taught me massive powers and the responsibility that accompany them. He was a great mentor, leader, and friend."

"Tarosius returned years later from his distant training to regain his position and become the next King of our land. He had changed his name to Darkmere, a name Deleth had crowned him with. It wasn't long before he and King Gorren began to dispute. Ultimately Darkmere killed the King, followed by many of the King's faithful supporters."

Thorik tried to absorb this information as quickly as it came at him. "The Terra King, which is Darkmere as well as your brother, killed your father?"

Ambrosius raised a finger to stop the interruption. He knew that this line of questioning would derail him from saying what he needed to. "Darkmere quickly took strength in the military and began a campaign to rule the Kingdom. Ru'Mere advised our mother, the Queen, to crown me as the new king, providing me with the power to stop Darkmere. When she did, my brother was furious and attacked city after city that supported my throne. Eventually cities followed him out of fear and a separation was created between the northern and southern provinces.

The capital city of the Dovenar Kingdom at that time was Maegoth. It sat in the middle of this conflict and was constantly being fought for. A battle of horror rampaged the earth at Maegoth as the final battle of the Civil War. Prominent Alchemists joined Darkmere's forces and had cast spells of eternal life and mind control onto their warriors, but forgot to grant them freedom from pain."

"Darkmere's strategic moves were well played and his army was strong, but we surpassed their efforts with sheer heart and desire to win. My army of men and Ov'Unday quickly took control of the battle. However, after realizing that the enemy was not defeated we began to kill the same warriors time after time as they screamed in horror. They began begging for death as they were forced to continue their battle against us. Out of mercy, we dismembered their bodies and decapitated their heads to remove them from this life, but they would not die. Those incapable of fighting anymore stared at us in desperation to end their life, crying in horrific sounds that still haunt us in our nightmares. It was the most unsettling massacre that has ever taken place."

"Even some of the Alchemists had a change of heart and began granting death. Darkmere quickly found out about the spell reversals and swiftly killed those Alchemists for such treason."

"It took the Great Wave from the lake to rise up and wash the blood from the earth to end the battle. The battlefield, along with the city, now resides underwater in the mouth of River's Edge."

Thorik thought out loud, "Those were the living dead in the river we saw."

"Yes. The battle ended thirty years ago on December 13th. We are less than three weeks from this anniversary."

"He's going to finish the war on the day he left off," Thorik surmised.

Ambrosius nodded to confirm Thorik's words while taking another sip of his ale.

Thorik's face still looked puzzled. "But what caused the Great Wave?" he asked.

"We did. Darkmere and I are at fault. I used to blame my brother, but with age I have come to realize that it was both of our stubbornness that drove Ru'Mere to do whatever it took to stop us from killing everyone. Ru'Mere released a wave of water on our battle and was willing to sacrifice both of us and the coastal cities in an effort to save all of Australis."

Ambrosius continued, "Darkmere was defeated and retreated to Corrock. There he fought for leadership and slowly gained his army of Del'Unday warriors and assassins."

"While he trained his military machine, I sought out guidance from Oracle of the North, Feshlan. He instructed me to establish a great council of all creatures. One that would unify the land and bring peace back to Terra Australis after four thousand years. I traveled the land in search of all races, beliefs, species, and clans. Excluding Corrock and Ergrauth, most were willing to at least listen to the idea. Four guilds of Alchemists joined as well and three families of the Ov'Unday clan. The two Del'Unday clan cities joined to keep abreast of our talks. One member from each of the six remaining Dovenar Provinces also attended."

"Great strides were taken over the years to bring peace to the land. A decade later, the societies of our people had begun to blend and mesh. Borders began to seem vague and fears started to drop."

"Darkmere resisted the movement and sent his vile serpents to uproot our work. However, years of attacks only led to unification and strengthening of the council as they worked together to fight him. He quickly realized his errors and focused on coming after me, knowing that I was the catalyst in organizing his defeat."

"I went into hiding and Darkmere faded from the people's view in his pursuit for my family. He eventually murdered my wife and is still in pursuit of my son. He intends to stop the prophecy which states that my son will cause the death of his son."

"Time passed before he returned to his primary mission of total dominance. But this time it would be different. Darkmere discovered a new way to fight the Council. Instead of head on, he would poison them from within. He changed his physical appearance and took on the persona of the Terra King, evading those looking for Darkmere. Through the use of the ancient Mountain King spiritual beliefs, he acquired small bands of locals to infiltrate their own lands and cause pain. He deluded them into believing his interpretation of the scrolls and appointed himself as their new King with the power to carry out the Mountain King's words."

"With this newfound power he used his followers to remind their citizens of the terrors and fears of the past. Mistrust led to prejudice and intolerance. Small scale attacks provoked retaliation of larger ones, only to be returned again. Humans and Altereds parted ways as anger and fear erupted across the land."

"The Terra King preached to humans and Nums with words of courage and safety while his alter ego, Darkmere, quietly played the Del'Unday on their banishment from the Dovenar Kingdom."

"Allegations of bigotry climbed all the way up to the Grand Council. Key members that spoke openly against each other began to mysteriously die. This validated that members of the council couldn't be trusted. No longer was there a safe-heaven to hold meetings, and so it was disbanded."

"Authority over individual cities was splintered and marshal law took hold. Chaos ruled in areas of weak military powers. Humanity was quickly being lost and kinship among species seemed doomed. The Unday were expelled or enslaved in every province except here in Pelonthal, and parts of Southwind and Greensbrook. Humans and Nums were treated no differently in the Del'Unday cities. Our civilization had stepped backward several centuries."

"Once I heard of the abandoned council, it took me nearly a year to find a safe location and hold a new meeting. I was able to get a message to Beltrow's annual trading party while visiting Shoreview. They in turn responded to my contact with a date and location to be escorted to the Temple. It was our last chance to right Darkmere's wrongs. But again, he circumvented our goals and put an end to peace by destroying the entire council."

Ambrosius changed his tone as he stepped away from the story to talk directly to Thorik. "What I did to those people in Pyrth was unfortunate and I will never forgive myself. They were going about their lives in peace, free to live how they wished. But understand my friend; either Darkmere or freedom must die. They cannot coexist."

"Unfortunate?" Thorik's face tightened at Ambrosius' attempt to not fully apologize for his actions. "How do you justify your actions as unfortunate?"

Ambrosius relaxed slightly into his chair and looked straight into the Num's eyes. "There will come a day when you must make choices and take actions that may seem wrong to your closest friends, and even yourself, but you must do them anyway for the better of all mankind. If I had stopped my brother on that day, I could have saved hundreds of thousands of lives. Now they are all still in jeopardy."

"But you hurt others in your failed attempt. I don't believe that I would have made the same choices as you have," Thorik replied.

"And that may be your weakness. You try too hard to please everyone. In doing so you may be putting them all at risk."

Thorik didn't know how this conversation changed to his own flaws. He took a quick sip of his drink and moved back to Ambrosius' challenges. "So, if you are the Dovenar King, take charge of your land. Re-unite your people to fight Darkmere. Performing this by yourself only pits them against you. It is not the way for a king to rule."

Ambrosius took a moment to wet his own dry throat. He also took the opportunity to look about for others listening to the conversation. All was clear. He leaned forward and talked softly.

"I am not the rightful king. I am an E'rudite. I have not enough human bloodline to support it. You see, just before the battle of Meagoth, I discovered that for us to have E'rudite powers, our parents must have them as well. My mother didn't, nor did the King. It was Ru'Mere who claimed this ability and therefore was our true father. Our mother, Rubecca, and Ru'Mere had fallen in love prior to her being forced to marry Gorren Prey. She was pregnant at their wedding, but early enough along to assume we were Gorren's children. To give up this information would have caused the deaths of Ru'Mere, Tarosius, myself and our mother. So everyone remained silent."

"So there is no rightful king?" Thorik asked.

Ambrosius stroked his beard. "There is another Dovenar family line that gave birth to a royal child. But that young man is not ready for the throne."

Thorik questioned his thinking. "Your mother was still the Queen, why can't you rule? Why does your E'rudite blood scar over this option?"

Ambrosius realized Thorik's misunderstanding and looked for a way to put it into perspective for him. "Fir Brimmelle has absolute power in your village of Farbank and look at how it has affected his relationships with others." He raised his hand to prevent any protest from Thorik. "Hear me out on this."

"Imagine if he also had the power of an E'rudite. Fear and resentment would begin to brew by those he ordered. Eventually his powers would have to be used to stop those that would see him overthrown. Use of his powers would only perpetuate the issue. He would eventually have to rule as a god or be killed. He would have no choice. There is no middle ground to stand on."

"My brother and I should have never been given the Kingdom in the first place. It has disrupted the entire land. The time of the E'rudites is over and we should not exist any more. The Alchemists have lost strength every generation since the master book of spells, Vesik, was lost in the Govi Glade. They too will be a thing of the past."

"I am the only one that can stop Darkmere from taking over Australis. I must do this to allow the land to evolve naturally. It will soon be time for the rightful king to take the throne and for men, Nums, Ov'Unday and Del'Unday to live together."

Thorik cocked his head slightly. "Who is the rightful king?"

"I cannot say without putting his life in danger. He is out among the people and gaining allies as we speak. He will be ready once Darkmere and I are gone. All that is left for me to do is to find Darkmere before December 13th."

Thorik folded his napkin into a perfect triangle and set it up against the corner of the table as he watched Ambrosius quench his parched mouth after all his talking. Adjusting the napkin to line it up with the table's edge, Thorik asked, "Did you believe it was fate that I found you on the Kings River shoreline, or was that just a lie to get me to help you?"

Ambrosius' face saddened as he set his mug down. The smell of ale filled the table as he exhaled deeply. "Obviously it was a lie, my friend." He lowered his eyes. "Otherwise we would have found Darkmere in time. But with no leads and only a few weeks to go, I don't see how this can be accomplished." Raising his eyes back up to meet Thorik's, Ambrosius said with all sincerity, "I am sorry."

Thorik smiled. "Thank you for being honest with me. But you are wrong, it was fate. For I know where Darkmere is."

Ambrosius wasn't sure what to make of the response. "Don't toy with me."

"He is traveling to Australis Weirfortus," Thorik noted.

Ambrosius' face sank in disbelief. "Then he has found out how to get in."

Chapter 31
Luthralum Tunia

Thorik helped Grewen load the boat just as the first light of day crested over the distant mountains. The cool moist air felt good as it drifted off the lake into Thorik's face. "I'm glad your nephew was willing to lend us his boat."

"He doesn't use it anymore now that he's settled down with a family."

The long rowboat was wide enough for Grewen to sit in. Toward the back on both sides, stabilizers were connected by angled beams to make sure that they were not in the way of rowing. It was sea worthy and functional but not fancy. No markings or trim to add any class; however, the design was smooth and pleasing to the eye.

Thorik turned to see Brimmelle running after Gluic as she raced down the street wearing nothing but her undergarments. She was free like always, enjoying life wherever it took her. She reminded Thorik of his mother and how she never seemed to let things get her down. She could roll with whatever came at her as she enjoyed the ride. Somehow he felt he was starting to lose that part of himself.

"Thorik?" Grewen asked. "You with me?"

Thorik snapped out of his daydream and answered, "Yes, what do you need?"

"Round everyone up so we can leave."

Thorik did just that. He walked off the dock and back onto the cobblestone way, informing Brimmelle and Gluic that it was time to leave before heading toward the Inn to inform Ambrosius and Avanda.

He met the two halfway to the Inn. The hood of his cloak hid the E'rudite's face as he walked with the Num youth.

"And then I caught a Myth'Unday in my hands," Avanda told Ambrosius as they walked along. She had been explaining all of her high adventures ever since they left the Inn. "You should have seen it. She was so adorable with her little wings. And then she changed into a butterfly and flew away."

"Why hide?" Thorik asked Ambrosius, once Avanda finally took a breath. "These people aren't looking for you. You're safe here."

"You are mistaken. I am not safe any place at this time. Safer, perhaps, but not safe."

They walked to the boat where they met Brimmelle and Gluic climbing aboard the large rowboat. Circling overhead, Draq waited impatiently for the group to leave.

Grewen was the last to get on. Sitting in the center to help balance out the boat, the Mognin pushed off from the dock. Grabbing the paddles, which were attached to the boat with metal pivot joints, he turned the boat around to head away from the shore.

The giant slowly began to row the boat between the many obstacles in their path. Chimneys and roof peaks covered the watery landscape, looking like tombstones floating on the misty lake. Branches of forgotten trees scraped the bottom of the boat, like fingers of those who had been lost in the great flood. The old city of Pelonthal rested under the water. It was a constant reminder of the Civil War's destruction.

Snacking on seagulls in midair, Draq flew overhead and helped guide his comrades toward a small island chain filled with palm trees. It was a welcome rest on their journey across the water, but it was only temporary and the boat soon cast off again to reach Australis Weirfortus before Darkmere did.

Brimmelle took a nap after rigging up a blanket and equipment to provide a small area of shade for his fair-skinned face.

After many hours of watching seagulls fly overhead, Thorik opened his coffer and pulled out his maps and notes to update them.

Thorik's Log: December 5th of the 649th year.
We have set sail and are in a race against time. We have but a week left to cross the lake of Luthralum Tunia and stop Darkmere, assuming he is there at all.

"Where did you get that wooden box?" Ambrosius asked.

"I've had it for years."

"How come I've never noticed it before?"

"Brimmelle doesn't like me wasting time writing in my journals, so I keep it tucked away. Why?"

"Never mind. It's too unlikely." Ambrosius realized that he was growing impatient with the slow pace of the boat. He knew Darkmere was about to destroy the kingdom, while he sat there doing nothing. Little things were starting to agitate him. "Don't be hiding things."

"I'm sorry. I didn't realize you hadn't seen it before."

Ambrosius stopped himself and placed a soft hand on the boy's shoulder. "No, I'm sorry. You did nothing wrong."

While weeding the limp plants from her clothes, Gluic had watched the discussion and turned her attention to Ambrosius. "What's on your mind?"

"It's what's not in it." Ambrosius sighed. "I still don't understand how Darkmere found and destroyed the Grand Council. Each member had to be shown the way. I don't think he knew how to get there. And yet I'm certain he was behind its destruction."

Gluic removed one of her small sacks of stones from her belt, "We never finished regaining your memories, now is as good a time as any."

"I would like that. In fact I *need* to know what happened. If for no other reason than for myself."

There was just enough room in the boat for Ambrosius to lie down and receive Gluic's help. She began the same as before with the placing of the stones and then her hands. It wasn't long before his mind drifted off to a far away place and a memory of the Mountain King, the Temple, and the Council.

* * * * *

Ambrosius tossed Darkmere's disk to the center of the granite table, for all to see. "Someone at this meeting has been spreading Darkmere's poison into our thoughts."

The Grand Council erupted with anger and accusations against one another.

Beltrow put a stop to all conversation as he hammered his fist on the table. "Blasphemy!"

Ambrosius felt the floor below him shake as he saw Beltrow still standing with his hands on the table, frozen with frustration.

Across the room, the E'rudite caught a glimpse of Irluk, the Death Witch, waiting for her new arrivals.

A thunderous crack from above caused him to look up and see the neck of the statue begin to crack and fall. Irluk had disappeared from sight and Ambrosius raised his staff in the air. Using his E'rudite powers, he pushed with all his might against the on-coming mountainside. He pushed up into the air against the falling face as it rocked back and forth between nature's gravity and his powers. What felt like a lifetime to Ambrosius was only seconds to those in the temple as they started to panic.

Streams of glowing fiery red lava shot from the now larger crack below the King's neck. It was too much for even Ambrosius to hold up any longer. The giant face came screaming down at him with the light of the flaming rocks surrounding it. There was no time to run or escape.

Time slowed as Ambrosius watched his friends and partners run for cover inside the chest of the statue, but time was not their friend today. He stood alone on the far side of the entrance to the temple while the rest pushed their way out.

He braced for the impact in the fraction of the second that was given by raising his staff, in both hands, above him and creating a shield of energy around himself. But time wasn't on his side either as molten rock crashed through the ceiling and struck the side of his face and chest, knocking him to the floor just as the face of the Mountain King breached through the glass ceiling.

All went silent for Ambrosius as he felt himself being crushed by the rock face. His energy shield pushed against his body and then snapped him out of the Temple, tumbling through the air. Wind fanned the flames of his burning flesh as he was hurled across to the far side of the lake.

He landed with a crash into the side of the bridge that spanned the river. Sending stone fragments of the railing in every direction, he bounced like a limp doll down to the ground underneath the bridge. Ambrosius had lost control of his powers long enough during the impact to feel his legs slap against the stone before he landed and rolled on the ground toward the lake.

Lying on the shoreline of where the lake met the river, he was in extreme pain. It was overpowering, unlike anything he had ever felt before. Lungs crushed from the crash, he gasped for air. The side of his face and chest were burnt and he couldn't move one of his legs.

Ambrosius struggled to roll over to look across the lake at the Mountain King. It was a horrific sight as the steaming glowing blood of the mountain poured out of his neck and down the front of his body. The staircase windows extruded lava as it worked its way down to the city. He lay there watching for quite some time, realizing the horror of what just occurred.

Incapable of getting up, he pondered his fate until a cloaked figure in a small rowboat pulled up to shore. The person helped him into the boat and covered him with a blanket. They headed under the damaged bridge and then downstream. Ambrosius fell in and out of consciousness as the river ran down the center of the gorge before opening up to periodic wide shorelines and rapids.

As they continued, the rapids picked up again and tossed the little boat around in circles until it finally capsized, ejecting both of them into the fast moving water. Still in pain, Ambrosius attempted to swim with his arms as he watched the other person swim toward the boat that was quickly moving out of Ambrosius' reach downstream.

With the cloak now off the other person's head, the E'rudite could see the face of the one who saved him. It was a servant of the Mountain King's Temple, the one who had been knocked over during Volnic's outburst. Her eyes reached out to him as she grabbed hold of the boat and watched Ambrosius sink under the water.

He struggled to make his way back to the surface as he fought with everything he could against the undertow. He lost his bearings until he cracked his head against a large object. Finding the rocky shoreline, he climbed his way out of the water and onto a large smooth boulder. He looked back to see that the cloaked figure and the boat were gone.

* * * * *

Ambrosius woke with a jolt, soaked in his own sweat. Looking around he realized he was back in the Mognin rowboat. They had run aground on a small island to take a break from rowing on Lake Luthralum. Thin tall columns of rocks pierced the sky from the tiny island, which only had a few safe sandy beaches to land on.

Everyone stared down at him, quietly waiting for him to speak. Draq could be seen perched on top of the rock pillars surveying the ocean landscape.

Ambrosius organized his thoughts and realized that his pushing of the Mountain King statue's face caused the rocking of the giant stone head and the final tumbling onto the council. "It was I," he exclaimed. "I was the one that destroyed the temple and killed the council."

Chapter 32
Australis Weirfortus

Thorik walked through the story with Ambrosius. "Are you saying that you pushed the head of the Mountain King up, causing it to crack at the neck in the first place?"

"Yes, that is now my belief."

"Why would you do that?" Thorik questioned.

"I thought it was falling down toward us. I was trying to save everyone."

"What made you think it was falling? Didn't you say the quake started before you looked up?"

Ambrosius thought again about his memories. "It was Darkmere's disk. The gem in the center must have been enchanted with a spell of great illusions," he realized. "It was on the table for all to see. All that needed to be said was the proper word for its spell to be cast on everyone present."

"What word?"

"Blasphemy."

Thorik looked shocked. "Fir Beltrow?"

Ambrosius nodded. "That is when the illusion started."

Brimmelle was not going to listen to them talk badly about a Fir such as Beltrow. "Impossible! No Fir would plan to kill others, let alone destroy his own temple and people. I don't believe it," he protested.

"Nor do I, my friend. Nor do I." Ambrosius' words surprised Brimmelle as the E'rudite stroked his beard. "But that was the word that activated the enchantment. So, if he didn't know, then someone else knew him well enough to gamble on him saying it."

The group thought about his comments as they launched off the sandy beach and continued across the lake. Grewen's rowing provided a respectful speed across the sometimes choppy waters. However, this day was providing very little resistance to their travels and they soon began to see an ominous wall in the horizon.

The Dovenar Wall paled in comparison to the structure before them rising out of the water. This new wall stood taller than the Mountain King Statue and bridged a distance of such great lengths that Thorik could only speculate on its size. It was as if the earth had been turned up on its end, protecting them from falling off the edge.

Closing in on the great wall, they could see slight seams between the massive blocks stacked from deep below the water, and all the way up to the clouds. The sun worked its way into the clear water showing the unending depth of the wall.

"What is it?" Thorik asked in utter amazement.

"This?" Ambrosius gazed at the overwhelming size of the structure with great respect. "This, my dear friend, is what allows us to exist. It gave birth to our land, and allows life to spring forth. This is Australis Weirfortus."

Confused, Thorik asked the obvious question, "How does this wall do all of that?"

"It protects us. If this were not here we would have never been born, for there would not have been any land to be born to."

Thorik pushed for more clarification. "I don't understand."

"This is not just a wall. It is a barrier that holds back the ocean from regaining this inlet which we call home. If this dam should break, a mountainous wave, thousands of feet high, would rush in and consume everything you have ever seen during your life time." Ambrosius glimpsed at Thorik's worried face. "And yes, that means Farbank as well."

"Who could build a mountain of stone blocks?" Thorik asked.

"Notarians, along with the help of E'rudites, the Altered Creatures as well as men and Nums. At one time they all worked together to create a paradise called Terra Australis, a few thousand feet below sea level. Weirfortus was built and the ocean waters were removed from the sea inlet to make way for fresh water and new life. But something in paradise went wrong and a battle ensued, killing most of the humans and Nums while leaving only a few E'rudites and Nortarians."

Ambrosius stretched his back and continued. "The remaining Notarians are known today as the three Oracles; Ovlan the Great, Deleth the Dark, and Feshlan the Lost. But even they stayed at odds with each other, which is how the Unday took over Australis for thousands of years. Finally humans came into power, allowing for great strides in advancement. But they also began to fight amongst themselves as well as against the Del'Unday and Ov'Unday. It was at this time that the discovery of the Weirfortus water reservoirs was made. Shortly after that, one of the reservoirs was opened causing a great flood wiping out all coastal living."

Thorik opened his coffer to take notes. "The Civil War Flood?"

"That is correct, Thorik. And that was only one reservoir. There are many more, and they continuously fill themselves back up while pulling the salt out of the ocean's water."

"How do you know this?"

"Because after the flood, I was the one who found and then closed the Weirfortus reservoir doors."

"But why would Darkmere wish to flood the valley?"

Ambrosius thought about the answer before giving it. "I have been asking myself that same question ever since we left port and I don't think he would. I see no reason for him to destroy everything when he already removed the Council and myself from challenging his authority. But I do believe he will open at least one reservoir to raise the waters higher."

"How high?" Thorik asked.

"Only to the top of the Dovenar walls," Ambrosius answered. "Walls have two possible uses. To keep things out or keep them in." The E'rudite stroked his beard as he spoke. "Disguised as the Terra King, he has scared men into believing that the Del'Unday are on the move. They have all returned home to take refuge behind their tall strong walls that surround Lake Luthralum. The water he releases from Weirfortus will fill in the human provinces, just like it did in River's Edge at the end of the Civil War."

Thorik looked at Ambrosius in disbelief. "He means to kill all humans and Nums in one wave of water."

"I believe so," Ambrosius confessed.

"But won't the water flow through the gates and flood the land beyond?"

"Do you recall the armies of Del'Unday we saw north of Woodlen? They were preparing for an attack that they could not win. In hindsight, it is now obvious they had no intention of breaking through the Dovenar Wall. Only to launch an attack against it."

"Why?"

"So the Woodlenders would close their solid doors to defend themselves. If Darkmere has set up a small attack at every gate, then I would assume that every one of them will be closed up tight at the time the wave strikes."

Thorik finished the thought. "Trapping in all the water as well as the people from escaping as the wave blankets the land."

Not a word was spoken for some time as everyone thought about Ambrosius' words and how it would affect their families and friends.

They continued traveling north along the gigantic structure passing several plateaus that extended into the water in half-moon shapes. Hexagon stone tiles with engraved rune symbols covered the constructed beaches, which supported two closed doorways. Each docking plateau looked the same and the group continued to pass them by until Gluic told them to stop once she felt a change in the wall's energy. The group landed the boat along its thick tiles and got out to stretch their legs and backs after the long day.

"I don't think I will ever get onto another boat again." Brimmelle complained as he groaned from his aches. He placed his hands at his hips and stretched as he looked at the various rune symbols below his feet.

Grewen glanced over at him and thought about how Brimmelle was fortunate enough to be able to stand and stretch while in the boat. "It's a long swim home, little man."

Draq had already landed and rested, roosting on a long stone slab which spanned over both entrances into Weirfortus.

Thorik started removing gear from the boat as Gluic and Avanda wandered off to explore the docking platform. He looked up at the constructed stone cliff as it reached high into the sky and then back down and over toward the two closed stone doors. "Which one?" he asked himself out loud.

"I thought you were the one with all the answers," Draq sarcastically stabbed from above.

"Well, just because –," Thorik began to defend himself while watching Ambrosius walk past him and approach the left doorway. Puffing up his chest, Thorik replied to the dragon's comment with a grin. "This one," he ordered, pointing toward the left door. Internally he was hoping Ambrosius wouldn't change his mind.

Grewen looked over at Draq. "He's our leader." He held a straight face before cracking a smirk at Draq.

Draq was not impressed. Frustrated, he yelled at Brimmelle to get his mother before she fell into the lake as she reached out into the water to pet a passing fish.

Thorik and Grewen had followed Ambrosius to the large smooth stone door. The doorway was covered with a row of hexagon tiles, each with a separate rune. The tile placement arched along the inside of the frame and several of them were missing.

Thorik looked confused as he watched Ambrosius search for a way to open the stone door. "I thought you had been here before."

With a frustrated look, Ambrosius replied, "Yes. It was a different reservoir, and the door was open at the time I arrived."

"If Gluic is accurate in saying this is the correct platform, then either Darkmere hasn't arrived yet, or he figured out how to get in and then closed the entrance afterward," Grewen commented as he walked over to investigate the second door.

"It's about time we get the upper hand on him," Thorik gladly commented.

Ambrosius was not ready to join Thorik in his enthusiasm. "We don't have *anything* on him yet. He managed to send a spy into the secret and hidden council meeting. He successfully baited me into attacking Pyrth to strike fear into the populace against me. And he knows my son is out of hiding. I can only hope this is not another trap. No, my friend, we do not have the upper hand yet."

Ambrosius continued searching. "It would appear that these tiles are about the same size as the ones you carry. Hand me one from your collection."

Thorik pulled out his sack of Runestones and looked inside it.

Ambrosius answered Thorik's question before he could utter it. "*Any* of them will do fine."

Thorik reached in and grabbed one. He pulled it out and looked at it briefly as he handed it to him. It was the Unity Runestone. Finding it appropriate for the situation Thorik smiled at the irony. *Who would have ever thought they would see Del'Unday, Ov'Unday, Nums and an E'rudite all working together?*

Ambrosius began to place the stone in one of the missing tile locations. It looked like it was going to fit. He retracted his hand. "Yes, I think these will work. Now, we need to determine the correct order to place them in."

"We have a problem," Grewen announced. "This door already has all of its Runestones in place. So, if our theory is correct, they have entered here and closed the door behind them."

Ambrosius realized that they may already be too late and the water could be entering the spillway any time now. "Thorik, see if the Runestones are in the same sequence on that door frame," he ordered with urgency in his voice.

Thorik ran over and quickly had his answer. "They are completely different." On his way back to Ambrosius, he looked into his full sack of flat Runestones. "We could just start trying them until it opens, although it may take some time."

Scratching his beard, his eyes darted back and forth while contemplating the situation. "No, the wrong combination could cause this door to open with a wave of water behind it, or this entire platform may drop into the lake. I know not what traps lie within this. The same could be true if I force it open. I tread lightly on Notarian artifacts." He ran his fingers harshly through his hair as he tried to contain his emotions.

Grewen returned to the first door and they all continued to gaze at the symbols hoping to see patterns of some type. Every second that passed could be the one that they needed to stop Darkmere's plan. "Death is among us on this day," the giant said to Ambrosius.

"It is not like you to give up so easy, my friend," the E'rudite commented before looked back to see Grewen gazing out onto the water. Following his line of sight, the rest of the group saw Grewen's concern.

Floating on the surface of the water, a lady stood motionless. She was covered in cloths made of shadows and mist, which evaporated as they strayed away from her. Dark smoky ashes gave depth to her body and face as she smiled at the group from behind her pulsing hair.

"Irluk," Ambrosius told them. "To see the Death Witch before a battle is a bad omen." Looking at Thorik with concern, he added, "I saw her in the fog before the battle of Maegoth and again before the destruction of the council. There will be a battle here today, and death is certain."

Thorik watched the ghostly shadow of a woman fade away in the breeze, but her absence didn't calm his nerves. A shiver ran down his spine and the hairs on his body stood on end. *Who will die today?*

Ambrosius struggled with her image as well. Few have seen Irluk and lived to tell about it. He knew she was closing in on him, for he had seen her too often. However, he needed to evade her just one more time.

"Thorik, back to the doorway and the runes. This is your area of expertise. Tell us what to do!" Ambrosius snapped, as he ran his fingers through his hair again, nearly pulling handfuls out by the roots.

Thorik racked his brain over the puzzle with no clear answer. He had looked at the runes in the tiles on the platform they stood on with no common series. "I don't know!"

"Quickly, Thorik. We have no time for this!"

Thorik looked up at him. "I'm sorry." Guilt set in as he tried to determine the answer that Ambrosius demanded.

Brimmelle walked up to them after settling his mothers needs and glanced at the missing tiles. "Looks like you're missing the Justice, Courage, Compassion and Harmony Runestones," he said very matter of fact.

The group turned in disbelief and looked at the hefty Num for an awkward moment.

Abruptly, Ambrosius questioned his comment. "And what makes you say this?"

Like always, Brimmelle didn't appreciate being questioned, especially on Runestones. "The rest of them are in the same sequence as the ones outside the city of Kingsfoot." Periodically, his natural ability to memorize everything he saw did come in handy. He had never been wrong with such things and did not like being questioned.

For the first time, Ambrosius looked at the Fir with respect. "Thank you. I'm glad you came on this journey. Quickly, put them in place."

Reached into his bag and began pulling out the needed stones. It wasn't long before he had all but one of them. And then it hit him. He had given the merchant in the Pyrth market one of his Runestones, but which one? She had selected one from his hand and the rest were quickly set back into the bag.

Frantically he dug in his bag to find it. *Could I have traded the key to unlocking this door and saving the valley for a mere bag of fruit? What have I done?*

"Thorik, please hurry," Ambrosius ordered.

Thorik dumped the bag on the ground, got down on all fours and began to separate them. "Please, Mountain King," he prayed out loud. "I'll never give out another of your sacred Runestones again. I'll cherish them and protect them." As the last word crossed his lips, he recovered the Runestone he needed. With a sigh of relief he solemnly thanked the King.

Thorik placed the stones where Brimmelle pointed.

A low rumbling could be heard and felt in their feet. The group backed away from the doorway, cautious to the unknowns on the other side. Grinding rock moaned as the door slab slowly slid to the side. Ambrosius leaned forward to see the darkness from behind it. He held Thorik back from doing the same.

A long granite corridor was exposed. It's once polished floors and walls were now covered with dust and cobwebs. Carved symbols and unknown writing decorated the walls, which stood a few shoulder lengths apart.

The E'rudite stepped forward and looked deeper into the passage. Stepping one foot inside, he waited for any potential trap or reaction. None emerged. He stepped fully through the archway.

A loud ground-shaking thud followed his entrance. Brimmelle jumped for cover. Thorik leaped in after Ambrosius to save him, startling the man from behind.

Grewen stood calm. "It was the door completing its motion."

Ambrosius removed a common rock from his pocket and focused on it. Intense pressure was placed on it from the E'rudite, causing it to glow. "If Darkmere is already here, time is against us. We must move with haste as well with caution." Levitating the now luminous liquid rock in front of him as a light source, he began to head down the corridor.

Thorik placed the other Runestones back in his bag and followed him. "Mixing fire and water would be easier."

Hunched over, Grewen was next to enter the doorway. Brimmelle waited for Grewen to slowly move forward as the giant's body fit tightly into the available space.

Thorik stopped and turned around as he lit a torch. "Grewen, do you need help?"

"No, but don't let me slow you. Scout ahead and I'll be there as soon as I can," he answered.

Ambrosius looked back at the giant Mognin scraping his shoulder blades across the ceiling. "If there is no time to wait for you, I will not. I would expect the same from you, my old friend."

Grewen nodded. "True enough. Get going."

With that, Thorik and Ambrosius raced up the long corridor.

Chapter 33
Del'Unday Ambush

Draq watched as Grewen attempted to wedge his bulky body into the doorway. Sniffing the air, the dragon lifted his long muzzle upward. Something wasn't right. His instincts were warning him of danger. Searching the platform, all was calm as Avanda and Gluic walked toward the water. "Brimmelle, get Grewen back out here."

Brimmelle didn't like the tone of the dragon's voice, let alone Draq himself. "He's almost through the doorway. What do you need?"

"Now, Fesh!" Draq yelled. "Get him out here, right now!"

"Fine." Tossing his hands in the air, the Fir worked his way under the giant to relay Draq's message.

Draq scrutinized the landscape, looking for anything out of place. Again, all he could see were the two female Nums near the lake.

Avanda could see in Gluic's face that something was wrong. "Gluic, are you ill?"

She did not reply. Lowering herself to one knee, Gluic softly touched the ends of her fingers to the tile platform.

"What is it?" Avanda asked.

Gluic waited a few seconds as she tuned into the vibrations she felt from her fingertips. "Here it comes." She pushed the youth toward Grewen and the doorways. "Run child! Run!"

Avanda was confused and turned after only a few steps. In doing so, she watched in horror as an enormous snake-like tail reached out of the lake, grabbed Gluic, and pulled her underwater.

"Gluic!" Avanda yelled as she stepped forward a few paces with arms stretched out in a wasted effort to help her.

Draq had seen the assault and was in the air and past Avanda before she realized what had happened. After a sudden rotation of his body to fly upside down, he arched his head back to dive aggressively into the water after the elder Num.

Avanda took another step and stopped before looking back at Brimmelle who was running toward the water to save his mother. Behind him, Grewen had finally backed out of the doorway.

Missing the event, Grewen searched for Gluic and Draq as he followed Brimmelle. "Avanda, get to the doorway," Grewen yelled across the platform.

"But Gluic was pulled into the water. We have to do something," she replied.

"Get away from the water, right now!" he demanded.

It was very uncharacteristic of Grewen to order her in such a manner. Knowing she had to follow his words, she struggled with the idea of just running away when Gluic was in trouble. She quickly met him halfway and looked up at him to protest. In doing so, she could see that his eyes were fixated on something behind her. She turned to investigate.

Along the shore was a soft outline of an object coming into view. It quickly materialized into a ship that had been docked on the opposite side of the platform from their rowboat. The illusion of invisibility had been removed and several Del'Unday stood on its top deck watching the new arrivals.

"Delvorian, you're with me," ordered a large white wolf-like creature with two long muscular tentacles extending from its upper shoulder blades. "The rest of you prepare the boat for sailing. Darkmere should return soon."

Controlled movement of the thick tentacles was frequently interrupted by a loose snap, much like a bullwhip. But instead of just the sound of a crack, it gave off a strong electrical discharge that could be heard, seen, and smelled.

The mutated wolf-like creature jumped off the ship and onto the tiled platform. With strong shoulders that were taller than a Num, its tentacles raised up higher than Grewen's head. This was a Wolvian. Intelligent, calculating, and very dangerous.

A second Del'Unday leaped from the ship and landed next to the Wolvian. It was a Brandercat. Landing with a slight favor to one side, Grewen could see a deep scar on his right shoulder.

"So we meet again," the chameleon cat said. "Where is your other short friend? I have a score to settle with him." He limped forward. "Ka'Ru, you can have the Mog. I've got the taste for Num today."

Growls, barks, and cheers from the boat were quickly extinguished as Ka'Ru turned his head toward them. This was not entertainment for him. This was a necessary removal of an obstacle.

The Del'Unday on the ship quickly returned to their duties, under the watchful eye of the Wolvian.

Grewen pushed Avanda behind him. "Run to Thorik. Tell him that it's a trap."

She refused to run, leaving her friends in such peril. She looked to the water and wondered what was happening under the surface.

Draq dove through the clear water behind the fast moving sea snake. Gluic was caught in its forked tail and held her breath as she was whipped back and forth. The snake could easily out swim Draq if it was not for its cargo of Gluic.

Using this to his advantage, Draq simply stayed behind him instead of trying to out maneuver the sea serpent. Trailing in its wake, he caught up to Gluic and reached out to grab the snake. First with his claws on the front of his wings and then with his strong back legs.

His sharp nails pierced the snake's scales causing a trail of blood to spill out, but it wasn't enough to cause it to let go of Gluic who was starting to go limp.

He knew her air was about out and time was of the essence. Raising his sharp red tipped tail, he thrusted it deep into the snake. The snake went straight with pain, releasing Gluic who now began to swim to the surface.

Draq started to follow her until he realized that his tail was still lodged into the snake's body. He was unable to pull it out.

Brimmelle turned to Grewen. "Kill these deformed beasts, I'm going after my mother." He then prepared to dive into the water.

Ka'Ru took offense to the comment. His tentacles snapped in Brimmelle's direction causing an electrical spark to shoot out from them, striking him in the head. Brimmelle stiffened for a moment before collapsing to the ground.

Avanda turned and ran for the doorway. She finally realized the need for Thorik and Ambrosius' help. As she approached the doorway, Delvorian suddenly appeared out of thin air. His Brandercat abilities had allowed him to run around Grewen without being seen in his effort to block her entrance into the doorway.

The Brandercat purred "You're too late to go for help, but not too late to be my next meal."

Chapter 34
Sibling Rivalry

Thorik and Ambrosius reached a side entrance into a huge underground tubular waterway. Empty of water now; this new room looked like it could easily carry the flow of several King's Rivers.

Peering out from behind the entrance wall to the room, Ambrosius and Thorik surveyed the situation before attacking. They did not wish to fall into another trap of Darkmere's making.

Two massive metal doors rested to Thorik's left. They were taller than the Dovenar Wall and as wide as they were high. A long continuous hinge ran along the doorway's stone sides as the closed double doors touched each other tightly. Torch light reflected back off the shiny metal doors into the room doubling the light output. No rust or degradation was evident on the wet metal hinges or decorative door faces.

Wide stone locking pins extended several feet out of the floor and ceiling to cover the seam where the doors met. One locking pin slowly crept into the ceiling and the other into the floor. The pins continued to unlock the doors, which struggled to hold back the massive amount of water from the reservoir on the other side. Shifting slightly as the pins freed the majority of the center from restrictions, gaps between the doors began to release the water's pressure.

Water shot out of from around the doors in every direction causing the water to wash over the door level landing, down into the main part of the room and then out through a long tunnel that ran to the lake.

Following the flow of water into the center of the room on the lower level, Thorik caught sight of several people rotating two of the four enormous valves, as they walked around in circles pushing the valve handles. Each valve apparently controlled one of the locking pins.

Looking at the group, Thorik gasped as he noticed Emilen and Wess working one of the valves along with several others. They all wore red cloaks similar to those of the Red Guards in Pyrth.

"It's Emilen and Wess! We need to save them." Thorik weighed his options to reach them undetected. "I think we can reach them if we go back and use that last branch in the tunnel." Thorik raced off to see if his assumption was correct. Upon turning down the side hall, he placed his backpack down as a signal to notify Grewen where to turn.

Ambrosius was not interested in the workers that rotated the large levers. He was glaring at Darkmere, who stood on the far side of the giant tube-shaped room designed as a spillway for millions of gallons of rushing water. He stood at the top of a far staircase; much like the one Ambrosius was standing on, and watched the door's locking pins continue to open. Ambrosius finally had his opportunity to confront his brother and, with a bit of luck, end his plans of destruction and domination.

With a flick of Ambrosius' finger the stone steps fell out from under Darkmere's feet causing him, and some rubble, to fall onto the ledge in front of the giant metal doors. He rolled and tumbled until he landed face down covered with small pebbles.

Darkmere raised his eyes to see Ambrosius resolutely advancing down the steps, along the wall, and then toward him. Returning to his feet, Darkmere stared contemptuously at his approaching brother.

Startled, the workers had stopped turning the cranks that were unlocking the doors to observe the conflict.

With a disrespectful glance to his side, Darkmere scowled at his crew. "Back to work!" Slowly and methodically, he returned his attention to Ambrosius. "Welcome, my brother. I was beginning to think you had missed the clues needed to get here in time. Bringing Gluic back to life paid off." Smiling, he added, "Surely you didn't think her return was pure luck?"

With only a slight hesitation the workers returned to their tasks, pushing the rods attached to the valve in the center.

The water continued to pour out of the door seams, shooting in every direction. Stray waterspouts hit the workers, knocking some off their feet. A few struggled to get back up.

The room started to flood as water ran its course down past them. Ambrosius and Darkmere stood at odds as they were occasionally slapped with jets of high-pressured water.

Ambrosius spoke first. "Before I destroy you, I want to know why. Why have you spent your entire life torturing me? Killing my wife, hunting my son, destroying everything I've created. Why?"

Arrogant, Darkmere looked shocked at the question. "How can you ask that after destroying everything that was rightfully ours? By our birthright, the entire Dovenar Kingdom was ours to rule. It was *you* who betrayed the kingdom by siding with the Ov'Unday, causing the Civil War. It was *you* who turned Ru'Mere away, and it was with his anger at *you* that he released these waters and flooded our great cities." Darkmere pointed his thin finger at Ambrosius. "You destroyed my Kingdom, now I have destroyed yours, so a fresh start can be made."

Ambrosius looked down at Darkmere's outstretched arm. "Your perception of the truth has been poisoned beyond your comprehension, and outside my ability to rectify." Reaching out with his mind he crushed every bone in Darkmere's hand. "I banish you from this land, once and for all!"

Darkmere's hand imploded as fluids splattered in all directions. It was quickly followed by snapping of bones in various locations of his arm, working from his wrist all the way up to his shoulder. Darkmere screamed out in pain.

Meanwhile, Thorik exited the lower tunnel. Looking to his left he saw Ambrosius and Darkmere standing on the upper tier in front of the huge doors that groaned from the pressure on the far side. In front of him, Emilen and Wess and the others continued to rotate the valve that lifted the top locking pin. There were also eight more servants which rotated the other valve for the bottom pin.

Both groups were wet and tired as they walked in circles, wading in two feet of water. Even with the water running down the spillway, there was enough new water showering in from around the double doors to keep the levels high.

Thorik ran to Emilen. "Emilen, stop what you're doing. You'll flood the whole valley. We need to turn the valves the other way before it's too late."

"Thorik!" She rejoiced. "You've come. I'm so glad you decided to join us."

"No, not join. I'm here to save you and Australis." Thorik walked backwards, in front of her, as she continued to push forward.

"What are you talking about?" She continued pushing. "We need to cleanse the one to regain our Kingdom."

"I don't understand." He grabbed the lever arm of the valve and started to push back. However, the eight others pushing against him continued its clockwise rotation.

"You remember, from the Portent Scrolls. You've known it ever since you were a child. We all have," she said prior to reciting the lyrics of the children's game.

> *"When all the jewels are in his crown,*
> *The mighty king will drop it down.*
> *All but one of the gems will break*
> *As it plummets into a nearby lake*
>
> *The treasure will again appear*
> *Striking disbelievers with great fear.*
> *But if the one is cleansed, you see*
> *Rebirth to the kingdom is foreseen"*

She continued, "It's Ambrosius. He is the one jewel that dropped from the Mountain King's crown and landed in the lake. Returning to Woodlen he caused great fear. Now all we have to do is cleanse him for the prophecy to come true and our Mountain King faith will be reborn to new levels."

Thorik couldn't believe his ears. "No, you've got the wrong Kingdom. It's Darkmere's Kingdom that will be reborn. The Terra King is actually Darkmere in disguise."

Water poured out in greater levels as the water rose another half a foot.

Emilen grabbed Thorik's hands and locked them onto the handle with her own hands. "You're wrong Thorik. This is our chance to make the ultimate sacrifice for our belief."

Thorik looked upon her. Her red hood covered most of her beautiful curly hair and her eyes were shallow and distant. It was Emilen, and yet it wasn't. Her personality no longer was glowing, but the gem in the center of her new brass disk was, as it hung from its leather necklace.

"Em," Thorik asked, "How did you know what happened in Woodlen? And how did you know Ambrosius was coming here?"

"The Terra King already knew he was coming to Pyrth. He then gave Gluic's crystal the information needed to lead Ambrosius here."

Thorik was shocked. "How? Em, how could he have known we were coming to Pyrth? How did he know of Gluic's use of crystals?"

Draq was pulled deeper into the water as he fought to free his tail.

The Giant Sea Snake dragged the Red-Tipped Silver Dragon along the Weirfortus wall in an attempt to kill him. Slapping Draq against the wall only embedded his pointed tail farther into the snake.

Draq's claws scratched at the stone in hopes of finding something to grasp on the smooth wall. His air was limited and he would need to escape soon if he had any chance of surviving.

The wall disappeared from his view, in what appeared to be a large opening into the Weirfortus structure. Draq prepared himself for the other side of the opening. When it came, he flung his body against the inside wall of the entrance and grabbed on with everything he had.

Slapping his body onto the inside wall of the tunnel caused serious pain, but the quick jar released the dragon. Shaking it off as fast as possible, Draq quickly swam through the tunnels entrance. The chase was back on, but this time Draq was the prey and the snake was not encumbered with Gluic.

Draq realized that he had made a critical mistake. He had no idea if this tunnel would lead to air, something he desperately needed. *No time to second-guess myself,* he thought. Faster and faster he pierced through the water as the snake continued to gain on him.

It was getting dark and difficult to see, even for his exceptional eyesight. Nothing was in view and he was hoping he would not run into a wall at this speed. The only benefit to the darkness was, with any luck, the snake also was blinded.

Starting to doubt himself, he considered making a sharp turn in the dark and head back out of the tunnel. But before he began the maneuver, he spied a slight light ahead. Racing with everything he had he breached the water's surface. "Air," he rejoiced with a large gasp.

A faint light could be seen down the tunnel. It was the last thing he saw as the snake attacked him from behind and swallowed him whole.

The large cat, Delvorian, who once chased Thorik north of Woodlen, now blocked Avanda's access to the Weirfortus doorway. Instead of trying to get around him, she turned and ran to the Mognin rowboat.

The cat slowly stalked her. He knew she couldn't get away. The idea of her running only excited him and increased his hunger.

Avanda grabbed her sack of magical items that she had taken from Sharcodi, north of Pyrth. Turning with the sack in hand she reached in and pulled out a vile of liquid. "Stay back or I'll turn you into a pig," she claimed, hoping he would accept her bluff.

He stopped for a moment and looked at the symbols on the sack. He knew it was Sharcodi's enchanted items and came to a stop. "You don't know how to use them. Now put those down before you dissolve yourself, preventing me from my fresh meal." He proceeded toward her.

"I'm warning you. I'll use this."

"Then use it, and get it over with. I'm hungry," Delvorian purred out at her while increasing his speed.

She threw the vile at him, popping him in the nose before it bounced off and shattered on the tile floor. A purple liquid spilled out causing a greasy stain on the ground.

The cat growled as he pawed his bleeding nose. Her attack had only angered him.

Ka'Ru barked as he showered Grewen with sparks from each whip of his tentacles. The tips of these flexible appendages fired small blue lightning bolts in every direction.

Trying to protect his head, electrical burns covered Grewen's forearms and hands. The giant tried several times to grab the powerful whips but only received cuts and scorched skin to show for it.

"Why are you helping Darkmere flood the lands?" Grewen asked him as he defended himself.

"It is our time to take Australis back from the humans," he replied.

"But Darkmere is human. You would lower yourself to follow him?" Grewen pushed to cause friction from within.

"We will allow him to help us until we don't need him anymore," answered the Wolvian.

"So your alliance is not strong with him?" he prodded.

The muscular wolf-like creature was not about to tip his hand to the Mognin. "They are strong enough." He lashed out and struck Grewen's chest with both tentacles at the same time.

Grewen's body straightened up and shook violently for several seconds before falling to the hard stone landing with a loud thud.

Ambrosius and his brother continued their battle. Darkmere's crippled body hunched over as he reached out and touched the ground in front of him. The stone at his finger tips changed into lava and a river was instantly created of the liquid rock heading toward Ambrosius. Steam rose as the water sprayed onto it.

Ambrosius jumped to his left, but his nemesis' power of alteration was strong as the trench of molten rock followed his moves. He ran back up the stairs as the alteration caught up to him and melted the steps below his feet.

Launching himself away from the steps and through the air, Ambrosius landed near the seam of the doors. The powerful jets of water shot inches from his face as he gained his footing. Using nature's own water pressure, he angled the stream toward his brother.

The burst of water shot at Darkmere who raised his arms the best he could. Not to defend himself, but to alter the air in front of him into an inferno.

The air between them changed to a furnace of flame and heat, evaporating the water instantly.

Ambrosius could feel the heat begin to burn his skin as well as his lungs. Unable to breathe, he covered his face. His clothes and staff ignited in flames as he pushed more water toward Darkmere with no effect, except for the additional steam.

Resorting to his non-E'rudite powers, Ambrosius raised up his flaming staff and launched it through the air like a spear. Darkmere had no time to react as the weapon emerged from the cloud of vapors. Striking him in the forehead, it knocked him onto his back, breaking his concentration and ending the firestorm.

Regardless, steam continued to bellow from the magma on the floor, along with the cracking and popping of the water trying to cool it.

Before Darkmere could recover, Ambrosius tossed his brother in the air before reaching down to pick up his scorched wooden staff. Slamming into a far wall, Darkmere fell forward onto the floor. His body now crippled and mangled by Ambrosius. Arms and legs were shattered at every joint. The only thing functional was his head and a few internal organs as he struggled on the upper terrace floor. Heavy waters splashed at him, washing him over the ledge and onto the main floor where his followers stood.

Emilen let go of Thorik's hands and ran over to Darkmere to pull his head above water while Ambrosius walked to the edge and looked down at his dying brother. She cradled his head in her arms as his limp body swayed in the water's flow.

Ambrosius looked down at Emilen for a moment in her hooded robe with the brass disk and gem hanging from her neck. "It's you." It suddenly hit him. "You were Beltrow's assistant. You brought the gem to the Council, but Volnic pushed you and broke the necklace that held it around your neck. Even so, you knew your father would eventually say the word to activate the illusion." His memories erupted as he looked at her. "I remember you pulling me into the boat and saving me. For what purpose? Just to lead me back into Darkmere's trap? Have you worked for Darkmere all along?" Ambrosius' mind raced as all the points finally connected. Beltrow had told him that he sent his daughter for the annual summer trade and yet Dare said they never arrived in Shoreview. "Thorik, how long have you known Emilen?"

Fighting the current of the water, Thorik replied, "She arrived at Farbank about the same time I found you in the forest. But it can't be her; the spirits in the Kingsfoot Statues said that you killed them."

"The statues did not say that I killed them. They asked why the killer had returned. Emilen *had* returned to Kingsfoot and was in the city while we were talking to the spirits."

Thorik also started piecing it together, her comments to the Num merchant in Pyrth, her arguments with Brimmelle, her insistence on helping Ambrosius travel to Woodlen, her knowledge of the Runestones and the sequence needed to enter Weirfortus, everything.

"Why?" Thorik asked her.

"The Terra King speaks the words of the Mountain King. Listen to him. Realize what he could do for us. As a spiritual leader, I was sent on an important assignment for our faith, to destroy the Council and bring Ambrosius to Woodlen." Emilen touched Thorik's face softly to get him to understand. "We must help fulfill the Portent Scrolls and release the waters to cleanse him." She then looked up at the one she was referring to, Ambrosius.

Just then, Darkmere leaped out of the water as a shot of highly pressured water hit Ambrosius in the back. Darkmere's E'rudite abilities had mended his bones and tissues. Reaching up, he grabbed Ambrosius' left ankle and his right calf.

The skin mutated in form as well as the clothes that covered Ambrosius' lower body. Flesh and blood turned to soft rotten wood with frequent cracks and holes. The transformation raged down into the stone floor as well as up his legs.

Ambrosius' right hand reached for the pain racing up his leg. Upon touching it, his hand and wrist became victims of the mutation as well. His now wooden hand was stuck to his wooden trunk that rooted deep into the floor.

"You are not as bright as I thought, brother. I would have expected you to have already figured this out. By following my trail, you have made these people's prophecy complete and rebirth of *my* Kingdom can begin."

Grabbing Darkmere's waist with his mind, Ambrosius began to squeeze tight, preventing any chance of escape for his brother.

Realizing he was captured with few options, Darkmere used his powers of alteration to change his form into Ambrosius' wife Asha in a matter of seconds. She now stood where he once did, still being compressed with her arms tight at her sides. Her long dark hair flailed about as she struggled to get free.

Asha screamed in pain from Ambrosius' grip. "Please dear, no!" she called out to him. Her rich brown eyes and lovely full lips begged Ambrosius to stop his attack.

Hesitation cut Ambrosius' focus as he saw his wife being crushed by his own powers. Understanding it was an illusion did not shield his heart from breaking at the sight of her in pain. Unfortunately, it drove deep into his emotions just long enough to allow Darkmere to break free.

Asha's face changed from a soft tan skin to a coarse white sand. The skin texture quickly expanded to the rest of her body and clothes. Afterward, her face changed back to Darkmere's bony appearance, still of sand.

Regaining control of his thoughts, Ambrosius squeezed with all his might.

The center of Darkmere's body rushed up and down from the point of the crushing grip. His body, now fully comprised of granular pieces had easily been displaced. Each piece of sand fell back into its normal position once Ambrosius let go.

Ambrosius tried several more times to break or crush his brother's body, only to see the scattering of sand that moved back afterward. He unleashed a full wall of force, knocking Darkmere against the far wall. The body parts that had been displaced from the blast quickly reunited with his main trunk.

Darkmere laughed as he waved his minions to leave and he began to follow. "It's too late. I have already won. Even if you were able to kill me, no one trusts you now. You have no friends, no army supporting you, no voice of power. You are already dead."

The words stung more than the pain in his lower body. His mind replayed his brother's comments as he helplessly watched Darkmere begin to leave the room.

Ambrosius had to destroy his brother before freedom was lost forever. The only part of his brother's white granular body that he hadn't seen completely dissolve was his head. As he directed his resources to crush Darkmere's skull, a crack of unimaginable intensity was heard.

Breaking off the remaining stone locking pins, water burst out of the doorway slamming the metal doors to each side. A gigantic wave of water rushed out, the likes of which they had never seen before. Ambrosius rotated his upper body around to face the oncoming threat. Instinctively he raised his staff with his left hand to hold the water back as hundreds of thousands of tons of pressure crashed against his invisible shield.

Quickly slipping out a side tunnel with his minions, Darkmere escaped.

Chapter 35
Flood Waters

Grewen slowly regained his footing after being shocked by Ka'Ru's tentacles. Large scorched flash-points remained red and tender on his chest from the most recent assault.

Brimmelle helped Gluic out of the water as Avanda situated herself between them and the prowling cat, Delvorian.

Beads, powders, strings, and seeds were scattered across the platform. The jar of eyeballs, box of thorns, a mirror, and vile of blood were still intact despite Avanda's attempt to break them against the cat's face. So far, nothing that she had used from her sack of magic had done anything but slow the creature down. All that remained was a stick and a few dozen orange berries. The rest of the odd objects were scattered all over the platform, showing no magical ability. She simply didn't know how to activate them.

It was at this time that a crack rumbled the platform and rock moaned from great pressures. The docking platform's right doorway rumbled open and several Nums rushed out, followed by Darkmere. Emilen was among them, and stopped long enough to remove the Runestones she had added to open the stone door for Darkmere. Wess exited the door and looked at his old friends on the far side of the platform as he was herded toward the ship by one of the Del'Unday.

Ka'Ru looked over his shoulder at Darkmere. "We will be there momentarily, my lord." He gave a slight bow of his head.

The Nums climbed aboard and were followed by the dark lord.

"Set sail," Darkmere ordered. "I want to be away from the wall when the water is released." Looking over at his servants Ka'Ru and Delvorian, he added, "Kill them and board, at once."

With that, the ship started pulling away from the dock. They would have little time to finish their killing before they needed to make the leap onto the ship.

Wess could not stand by and watch Avanda be ripped apart. "No!" he screamed as he jumped off the ship and onto the platform at the final second while the ship launched.

Avanda pulled the handful of berries out of the sack and tossed them at the cat's open mouth. Half of them landed on the ground, rolling in various directions.

The cat chewed the ones that entered his mouth, swallowed, and smiled. Again, no results.

Avanda pulled out the stick, which was the last item in the sack, just as the Brandercat jumped on her and knocked her to the ground. Pinning her down, his mouth opened up to snap her neck off. His head lurched forward to grab her throat.

Wess slammed his entire body against the cat, knocking it off of Avanda. She was free, but now Wess and Delvorian were locked together in a heated battle.

Wess used his strength to squeeze the cat's neck, cutting off its air. The Brandercat changed colors and shades as it bucked and tried to shake Wess off its back. The creature was weakening, but then again so was Wess as he lost his balance. Falling to the platform with a thud, flat on his back, the wind was knocked out of Wess.

Avanda ran to his aid, but Delvorian reached him first. With a quick bite to his neck and a twist of his head, the cat had snapped Wess' neck. The Num's body went limp, his head hanging from the cat's mouth like a sack of rice, and his arms falling to the platform like dead snakes. Delvorian dropped the lifeless Num from his blood stained teeth and smiled at Avanda.

Avanda stood no more than an arm's length away. Shocked at the scene she didn't know how to react. However, the Brandercat did. It took advantage of her fear and stepped up to her.

Opening his mouth and turning his head sideways, Delvorian placed his teeth around the frozen girl's throat. His hot cat breath coated her neck as she stood in shock. It was over, there was nowhere else to run. Avanda winced as she felt a few his teeth graze her skin, but instead of chomping down on her, he stopped and froze in his position.

Rumbling from deep inside Delvorian could be heard, causing his face to tighten and his side to flinch. It began to grow louder as the cat recoiled in pain and arched his shoulders forward. Short deep breaths became loud and inconsistent. Losing his sense of balance, the cat spread his legs to keep from falling over. The orange berries had been activated by his very own actions.

Avanda snapped out of her trance and backed away from Delvorian, for it appeared the cat was going to be sick. Gluic grabbed Avanda's hand and made a dash toward the doorway. They would run for safety within Weirfortus, out of sight of the Del'Unday. However, Avanda attempted to pull away from Gluic to pick up her scattered unused magical items.

"Not now, Avanda. You can collect them later," Gluic instructed.

"But I can use them to save Uncle Wess," the youth responded as she looked at all the magical items scattered across the platform. Each had powers. She just needed to figure out how to activate them to save him. Tears ran down her face as she looked at her uncle's limp body lying among useless magical objects.

Beyond his body, a ghostly dark shadow floated on the lake. Irluk moved toward Wess, preparing to take what was rightfully hers.

Gluic reached around Avanda and gave her a warm hug as she gazed at the Death Witch. "I'm sorry dear, but there isn't any way that we can bring him back now. It was his time," Gluic confessed. "Be proud that he was there for you." She continued to escort the youth to the Weirfortus entrance.

Turning back toward the platform as they reached the doorway, Avanda saw dozens of giant larvae bursting forth from the Brandercat's midsection, consuming the cat from the inside out. Gluic covered her eyes and guided her into Weirfortus and up the long hallway.

Stunned at the scene, Ka'Ru lost concentration just long enough for Grewen to grab the Wolvian's long thick tentacles, one in each hand.

Grewen stepped backwards, pulling Ka'Ru off his feet, before he twisted Ka'Ru's body and began to swing the creature around him. Leaning back, Grewen shuffled his feet and whirled around in a circle with the wolf-like Del'Unday swinging out above the ground.

Around and around, Grewen swung Ka'Ru, each time gaining more and more momentum.

As the initial shock wore off, Ka'Ru energizing his tentacles. Sparks of electricity showered Grewen's face and burned the giant's wrists.

"Arrrrg!" Grewen screamed as the overwhelming pain shot down his body. But he refused to let go as he continued to spin the creature around while making his way to the water near the ship that had already launched.

Every part of Grewen's body screamed in pain as Ka'Ru relentlessly drove electrical pulses into him. The burning flesh on his hands and feet began to smoke as sparks and discharges fired from inside his grip on the creature. "No More!" Grewen yelled. He was in agony as he turned one last time with a massive toss of the Wolvian toward the ship.

Ka'Ru was now a missile heading straight for the side of the ship off shore. He impacted the port side of the ship with a splintering of wooden boards and the sound of breaking lumber. The Wolvian penetrated the hull before coming to rest at the far side of the ship.

The ship rocked violently from the attack, knocking a few of the crew overboard. Upon righting itself, the ship then began taking on water from the gaping hole in its side.

Grewen turned to enter the Weirfortus hallway as the ship's crew struggled to keep it afloat as they continued sailing off into the lake.

After being swallowed whole by the sea snake, Draq had started his attack from within the creature's body. The snake's internal muscles tried to crush him to death, while its stomach acid began burning his eyes.

Using his spear-like tail, Draq punctured the snake from within. His strong back claws ripped his way out of the serpent's side. The snake thrashed about in pain as the dragon fought with everything he had to escape and obtain air to breathe.

But it was too late. Draq blacked out.

The Red-Tipped Silver Dragon woke up on the stone shore of the spillway, at the far end from Ambrosius. Half of his body was still stuck in the ribs of the dead serpent that had washed up. The sea creature's internal organs had spilled onto the stone floor as well as coating the dragon's body.

Weak from his battle, Draq needed time to recover. There wasn't enough strength left to free himself from his awkward position. So, he rested.

Draq looked upstream toward the torchlight. Clearing his eyes, he could see Ambrosius as the lights danced on a wall of water behind him. "Ambrosius!" he screamed. But the raging waters that were starting to flood the spillway soaked up his words long before they reached him.

Struggling again with the snake's large rib bones, he couldn't free himself. He was forced to remain captive while watching his friend struggle.

Ambrosius could not move his legs nor remove his right hand, as he continued the nearly impossible task of keeping the water at bay. The water pounded against his invisible shield as it raced around him on both sides and across the top. He leaned his torso forward and pressed his E'rudite ability to its limits. The shielded area grew slightly.

"Thorik!" Ambrosius yelled over the sound of the rushing water.

Thorik climbed onto the upper level tier and worked his way to Ambrosius.

"Cut me loose," Ambrosius ordered.

"What do you mean?"

"Take your battle-axe and cut me free of my legs and hand."

Thorik was horrified at the thought. "I can't cut off parts of your body."

"They no longer are my body. Now cut me free of these wooden confines before it's too late."

He reached for the axe, strapped to his back. It was the same weapon he had used to bust the lock on the wagon while freeing Brimmelle and Gluic. Raising it over his head, he realized that this would be the only way to free Ambrosius and save the E'rudite's life. He took a moment to steady himself, mentally and emotionally, for what he was about to do.

Standing motionless, he looked at the legs he was about to sever.

"Hurry! Cut me free," Ambrosius demanded.

The wet double bladed battle-axe swung through the air at an angle, slicing off the lower part of Ambrosius' wooden hand, his upper right leg, and his lower left leg.

The wood splintered and sent Ambrosius falling to the ground. His shield faulted for a moment, crashing large waves into the room. Quickly recovering, he pushed back with his one remaining hand.

Ambrosius coiled his body from the pain. "Now close those doors and reset the locks."

Looking at the doors, Thorik was bewildered at how a Num could do such a task. "They are too large. Too thick. Too massive."

"Notarians designed them to move easily." Ambrosius' words were starting to break up from his strain. "Hard at first, but you can do it."

"But the water extends past the doorway."

"I'm going to push the waters back into the bottom of the reservoir. You will have to close the doors behind me before I can't hold it any longer," Ambrosius instructed.

Thorik looked at him. "No, you'll be crushed. You'll be killed."

"I'm already dead!"

"No! We can work together and rebuild Australis, don't give up now," Thorik shouted over the water.

"You don't understand. If I let go, we *all* die, you, your friends, and the hundred thousand that live within the Dovenar Walls."

Thorik pleaded with him. "There has to be a way."

"There is. Close the door behind me. Make my life worth something again." Ambrosius pushed with all his strength and slowly began driving the water back into the giant reservoir.

Tears ran down Thorik's face, mixing in with the water dripping from his hair. The thought of imprisoning his friend in a tomb of water was overwhelming. Thorik's questions of Ambrosius' true character were now clear, too late to act on, too late to acknowledge.

It was now Thorik's own character that he questioned. *I should have prevented this. Somehow this could have been stopped. If only I had been more supportive to him, and not slowed his journey with my doubt.*

His mind raced as he chose a path to take. *Now is not the time to dwell on what I should have said or done. Now is the time to act on what I know is right, regardless of how much I hate it.*

Thorik turned around and looked at the Nums entering the spillway. They looked around the room trying to understand what had happened.

Thorik ran to the ledge to help them up. "Get up here right away to help close these doors." He helped Avanda, Brimmelle, and Gluic to the upper level before giving them additional orders. "Brimmelle, take Gluic and Avanda to the far door and start pushing it shut." Seeing their expressions, he realized what he was asking seemed impossible. "Trust me, they will move if you push." At least he hoped that it would be that easy.

Brimmelle was upset and not in the mood for Thorik's disobedience. "Thorik, you don't know what we've been through out there. Where were you when we needed you?"

Thorik wasn't backing down. "You can tell me about it later. Right now, you need run over and push that door closed," he demanded.

"Are you insane?" Brimmelle asked. "We need to get out of here before it's too late," he added as he grabbed Thorik by the back of his arm to escort him to the side tunnel.

Thorik had been overruled. His mentor had given him a direct order, and rightfully so. The chamber was quickly filling up with water and the chances of them being able to close the enormous metal doors were slim to none. What had Thorik been thinking? Their only options were to run for safety or die trying to close these doors.

"No!" Thorik shouted. "Stop trying to run my life!"

"I'm not trying to run it, you fool. I'm trying to save it." He then added, "Once again."

"I don't want you to save me. I don't want to feel in debt to you for saving my life when I was younger. Quit telling me how to run my life. That's not what I want from you."

Brimmelle stepped forward as he held back his anger at his ungrateful student. "And what is it that you do want from me?"

Thorik stood firm and strong, looking Brimmelle square in the eyes. It was so simple of a statement, and yet so hard to say. "I want you to trust me. Believe in my judgment. Allow me to fail or succeed on my terms."

Brimmelle looked up at the dome of water being held back from Ambrosius' powers. Water gushed out of the sides, splashing at the Num's feet. "You sure picked a bad time to start asking me to trust you."

Thorik replied, "You won't regret it."

"That's because I won't be alive to do anything." He was obvious upset with his decision to support Thorik. "You better be right," Brimmelle continued as he began to run to the far door.

Grewen had finally crawled his way out of the tunnel. He stood up to see a giant wave of water aching over Ambrosius as he laid on the ground holding it back with an invisible force. In front of the impending wave, Thorik looked over at him as he ran to one of the open metal doors.

"Grewen, stand between those large valve levers and get ready to start turning them," Thorik ordered. "You need to lock these doors the moment we get them shut."

Grewen looked over at Ambrosius and then back to Thorik. "We can't trap him in there."

"Grewen, I don't have time to debate this. Get between those levers right now." Thorik's voice had a strong sense of authority.

Ambrosius continued to drag his body deeper into the reservoir using the splintered stub at the end of his right arm, pushing forward as the water randomly sprayed out around the sides. He utilized the wooden appendages remaining on his legs the best he could for gripping the wet floor.

The crippled E'rudite had succeeded in moving one more foot into the reservoir and yelled back to Thorik, "Close the doors." His body was trembling from the intensity of the water around and above him. With his staff overhead in his left hand, the vitality in his face was starting to weaken as he looked up into the darkness. *There is no turning back for me this time. I can only hope that others will carry on in my place.*

Thorik gave the signal. The little Num had already begun to close the huge left door as Brimmelle, Gluic and Avanda started to do the same on their side. Barely inching forward at first, Thorik fought with everything that he had to get the door moving. Perfectly balanced doors and hinges allowed for friction free movement, it was the sheer weight of the door that was causing all the issues. Once in motion, the doors moved slowly and smoothly around to their closed positions.

As the doors started to come together, Thorik positioned himself in the center with one hand on each door looking in at

Ambrosius who has laying on his back under the tremendous pressure of the water above. The staff that Thorik had made for him was still in Ambrosius' grasp but no longer was it over his head. Instead it was at his chest, still pressing up against the inevitable winner of this final contest.

Ambrosius looked over his shoulder at Thorik. His pale expression showed exhaustion and submission to his demise. "Find my son. Keep him safe." he struggled to get out each word from his collapsing lungs. "Tell him I love him." He finished as the doors closed in front of Thorik.

Thorik closed his eyes, holding firmly to his last memory of Ambrosius. A sight he knew would haunt him to the end of his days. The once so powerful man, who had lost his wife, fatherhood, and his Kingdom, was now being crushed to death trying to save those who would wish to see him die. They would never know his sacrifice for them as they continued to live another day and enjoy another meal in their illusion of safety.

He turned and yelled at Grewen, "Lower the locking pins."

Grewen's hands were already on both valves as he sat in his rowing position between them. He began turning both at the same time as one pin shot down from the top and the other up from the floor, locking the doors shut.

Gluic had lowered herself onto her hands and knees. "Stones are rich with life." Her fingers fanned out over the granite floor. She closed her eyes.

Brimmelle fell next to her, out of exhaustion. "Not now, mother."

A crash of water hit the doors and began spilling through the seams. The added pressure of the sudden implosion around Ambrosius caused damage to the doors preventing them from holding the water back. Moaning of the metal quaked in the long tube-shaped room, while new leaks began to spring forth.

Thorik moved everyone from the metal doors and ordered them to evacuate through the side caves before the doors gave way. But it was too late; the water's current was already grabbing the Nums and pushing them toward the lake. Gluic was washed away first, over the edge into the main level near Grewen who reached out and grabbed her as she passed.

Brimmelle followed quickly after her and was whisked past Grewen on his other side, only to grab onto one of the turning rods on the second set of valves.

Thorik held onto the metal door by way of a few decorative insets. Clinging onto the door's artwork, Avanda worked her way over to Thorik. Grasped onto him with both legs and both arms, she held on for dear life.

"Grewen," Thorik yelled over the noise of raging water. "Grab Brimmelle and move them over to the side cave. I'll hang on until you come back for us."

The water was not affecting Grewen. His weight was too much for it at this stage, but even he would quickly be swept away if the doors were to break. Hanging onto Gluic, he waded through the knee-high water away from the reservoirs to the second set of valves to collect the other Num.

"No," shouted Gluic as she pushed away from the giant. "Grewen, drop me and allow us to be washed away."

"Not on your life," he replied as he made his way over.

"It's your only chance to save the kingdom from destruction. Those doors won't hold much longer," Gluic said as Brimmelle's fingers began to lose grip.

"Hang on. I'm almost there." Grewen rounded the large valve and extending rods.

"Turn those back two valves like the ones you did before and it will drop a stone wall in front of the doors to seal it tight," Gluic added.

"How would you know this?" Grewen asked.

"The stones tell us what we need to know," she said. "One must only listen."

Brimmelle looked over at his mother. "I trust her. Do as she says."

It was the last words Grewen's little ears heard from Brimmelle as the Mognin watched the Num let go and get washed away. It was too late; Grewen could never run as fast as Brimmelle was floating away, even on flat ground. He looked back at Thorik who was still hanging onto the door with both hands as jets of water from underneath it kept knocking him off his feet.

Grewen held tightly onto Gluic as he changed course to head toward Thorik.

Gluic looked up at him. "No, you heard me. Turn the other valves, close the door."

Grewen looked up to see the bottom of the stone wall extending slightly from the ceiling, perhaps a foot past the metal doors. There were slots along the sides for the massive wall to be lowered into for a snug fit. The floor had a shallow dip in it where the wall would rest in, once dropped. Attempting to stand in the shallow area was Thorik as he struggled to hang on with his eyes closed to protect them from the spouting water.

The Mognin reached down with one of his gigantic hands to crank one of the levers only to find it stuck in place. He reached over to the other one with the same results, however they did move when he turned them both in tandem. To do this he would have to drop Gluic. He looked around for another alternative.

"It's okay son, you need to do this."

"I cannot let you go and send you to your death," he insisted as the water continued to rise around him.

"I know dear, that's why I will have to help." She used both of her hands to stab his hand with the sharp end of a crystal, driving it in far enough to draw blood.

Crying out in pain and surprise he instinctively released her, only to attempt to grab her back once he realized what she had done. Again, it was too late as she washed away.

The only ones left with Grewen were Thorik and Avanda. His only plan at this point was to drop the wall onto their location. He yelled out, "Thorik, let go, I'm dropping the wall. Get out of the way."

Extreme noise was pounding Thorik's head while he continued to be splashed from the various spouts. Eyes closed tight and rushing water covering his ears, Thorik heard nothing of the new plan and would continue holding onto the metal door until he felt Grewen come back to save them.

Water raged at Grewen's hips as he bent over and reached under the water to turn the large levers. In concert, they spun much easier than when trying to only turn one at a time. Looking up, he could see the wall slowly start to lower.

Grewen would have to sit down in a rowing position to speed up the process. In doing this, the waves now lapped at his face while he pulled rod after rod on both sides, spinning them around in circles.

Between splashes in his face he could still see Thorik hanging onto the giant doors as the stone wall quickly moved downward.

The metal doors continued to bulge to their limits. Flooding from every direction increased as hinges began to snap apart. Grewen knew he only had seconds left and grabbed his last breath as he leaned under the water to pull with all his might. Faster and faster he pulled until he heard the slam of the stone slab door hitting so hard that it vibrated the floor where he sat.

The valves were tight and would not move anymore. He raised his head out of the water, looking at the wall that was now completely lowered. The water was no longer pouring into the room. It was over.

Looking about he also noticed that Thorik and Avanda were gone, swept downstream or trapped between the rock wall and the metal doors. He looked behind him, down the long spillway outlet toward the lake for signs of them. As the waters receded, he spotted Gluic and Brimmelle. Both survived the flood on a raised ledge many lengths down the tube. The others were nowhere to be seen.

Grewen lowered his head. He had lost three great friends on this day.

Looking back at the lowered wall he heard coughing, or perhaps choking. Off to the side, Thorik was wedged into a part of the wall from where they had originally arrived. A spout had kicked him from the metal doors and sent him flying over to the side. Clinging to him was Avanda, with her eyes shut.

Grewen stood up and ran over to them, plucking the Nums from their cramped positions and holding them in his arms.

Thorik was not choking on water, nor crying in pain, but instead was bursting with the agony of losing his friend Ambrosius. He was devastated with a hurt worse than all of his other physical pains before. A piece of him had just died, as though it was cut out with a knife.

Avanda burst into tears, partly because Thorik was crying and partly for the events that recently occurred.

Thorik looked up at Grewen who exhibited the same pain, but only in his eyes.

"I've killed Ambrosius," Thorik told him, tears running down his face.

"You've saved Terra Australis," Grewen replied.

Chapter 36
Return to Farbank

It had been a long quiet journey back across Lake Luthralum as Grewen paddled the boat up King's River, past Longfield and to Farbank. As they approached the village, they could see several children playing along the shore while others fished from the docks, wrapped in warm blankets. Men and women were busy working as they finalized their preparations for winter.

All of the trees had lost their leaves and the few remaining had already turned brown from the freezing night temperatures. The fallen leaves had been cleaned off the roofs and raked out of the streets. Everything was neat and tidy.

The children cheered with excitement as they saw the giant Mognin moving the boat toward the dock carrying Avanda, Thorik, Gluic, and Brimmelle. The adults were more apprehensive about the sight of the giant but came down to the dock all the same to welcome the traveler's home.

Reaching the dock, Grewen held the boat steady as the Nums exited. It took several adults to keep the vessel balanced while Grewen vacated the rowboat without tipping it over. When he did, he stood up to full height to stretch his back.

The short Nums backed up at the sight of Grewen's enormous body. Fearing the giant, many of the villagers sunk deeper into their winter coats as they witnessed the odd sight.

One of the men shouted out, "Brimmelle, what is this creature your have returned with?"

Brimmelle raised his hands to calm everyone down. "This is a Mognin, one of the Ov'Unday of the southern valleys." He looked up at the Altered Creature who he once feared. "You will address him as Grewen, he is our trusted friend."

These were strong words for Brimmelle. He rarely used the words "trusted friend" even among Nums in his village. In fact, no one in the village considered him as a friend, only as a Fir. A friend would put him at an equal level, which he would have never before accepted.

Avanda's parents ran down the slight slope to the river, arms stretched out as they saw her. Avanda met them halfway, jumping up into their arms and disappeared into their thick wooly coats. The three hugged tight.

Wess' brothers walked over to Brimmelle. The eldest, Hyphry, asked the Fir, "Where's Wess?"

Brimmelle's face and eyes lowered as his hands locked together behind his back. A moment later he straightened his body up and looked at the three brothers. "I'm sorry to say that he didn't make it. Wess passed away during our journey."

Those in hearing distance quieted down to listen to Hyphry. "How did he die? Why didn't you save him?"

Brimmelle's eyes shifted back and forth searching for a way out of this uncomfortable public scene. "Perhaps we should refer to the Rune Scrolls for guidance during these difficult times."

"No," Hyphry said. "You asked him to go with you. It was your responsibility. How could you let him die?"

Thorik stepped in, "Brimmelle didn't let him die. Wess was a hero."

"A hero? Our brother?" Hyphry asked in surprise.

Thorik replied, "Yes, without a doubt. He fought off thrashers and living stone statues as well as protected me from unfriendly guards. He saved us from freezing to death in the mountains and helped us save all human and Num life from a tidal wave of death."

Thorik watched as everyone listened in awe to the tale. "Along our journey we discovered that a plot was unfolding to destroy all our lands. We traveled far to the south to stop it from happening. When we arrived, we were attacked and Avanda would have been killed if it weren't for Wess. He sacrificed his life to save hers. Your brother should be remembered as a hero."

Wess' brothers smiled at Thorik's words. "I knew he had it in him," one said as they gave each other hugs and patted each other on the back. Grief would continue, but at least now it was with respect and honor of the tasks Wess had accomplished.

Thorik nodded with a sense of comfort at the sight of the brother's reaction.

Several women, meanwhile, asked Gluic how she was holding up after such a long trek. She dismissed the questions and instead opened a sack to show them. "They have some wonderful stones in Pelonthal." Politely they looked, but were not impressed as she continued to show them off.

Thorik was greeted by many and he returned the sentiment back. "It's good to be home." A sense of peace came over him, which he had not felt in a long time. He inhaled the comfort and easiness of the surroundings that he grew up with.

"We will throw a grand party for your return," Sorla shouted to the crowd who cheered at the idea of it.

Thorik hadn't seen Sorla since the Harvest Festival, when she congratulated her husband Trumette for winning the foot race. She was always trying to make everyone happy and always willing to throw a party for any occasion.

"That is very nice but we will not be staying," Thorik answered back. "We still have more to do to ensure your safety. The threat is still out there."

Sorla looked confused. "But you said you saved us already."

"We did, from one specific danger, but there will be more unless we are there to stop them from happening."

"You've done your part." Sorla nodded to Thorik. "Come home and relax. Others will take over where you have left off."

Trumette pulled her back. "The battle is over, but the war remains to be won, my dear."

Grewen looked down at the frail old Num. "Well spoken."

Trumette looked over at Brimmelle. "Where do I sign up for our next mission?"

Everyone chuckled at the idea before Brimmelle could respond. "I am not going on any more missions. I will be staying here to teach what I have recently learned," he continued to address the shocked faces, knowing that they had never heard him speak of himself learning anything outside the words of the scrolls. "Thorik is the leader of this group. He knows what he's doing and carries my full support."

Silence followed as the Nums tried to rationalize this new Brimmelle attitude. It was still authoritative but showed feelings and depth to his words that were never there before. It was a welcome change.

"But we must have a party before you leave again," Sorla again begged.

"There is no time for that," Thorik replied.

Grewen reached down and patted Thorik on the back. "Enjoy the blessings before you. It is these memories that we are fighting to keep alive."

Thorik looked up at his enormous friend. "All right, one night of festivities and then we're off."

Everyone rejoiced and left to set up the tents and tables.

The party had run late into the night and Thorik finally made his way upstream of Farbank, up the path that had not been kept tidy for a long while. Branches lay across the way as well as leaves, which needed to be raked. He would have to get up all the earlier in the morning to clean it up before they left.

He saw his cottage, small and simple. It was not grand like those he had seen on his travels, nor was it protected by any great walls. Yet it felt like the safest place in Australis. He couldn't wait to make a cup of tea in his own kitchen again and to sleep in his own bed. No Del'Unday, Fesh'Unday, Woodlen Guards, swimming corpses, or carved statues coming to life. It will be a welcomed treat even if it was only for one night.

Stale air hit his face as he opened the door. It wasn't overpowering, just unpleasant. He opened the flume on the fireplace and started a nice little fire. He rotated an angled metal rod over the top of the flame, carrying a pot of water for his tea.

Reaching a boil, he poured his tea into a cup, grabbed his jar of sugar, and scooped out a large spoonful before stirring it in. Wrapping his hands around the large cup helped warm up his chilled body from the night's wintry temperatures. Blowing softly across the surface a few times he took a sip to warm his insides.

His face pursed up as he realized that the scoop of sugar was actually salt. His tea was awful. Checking the labels on the jars, he had grabbed the correct one. Someone had switched the contents. His guess would be Wess, just before they headed upstream on their journey.

He had a soft chuckle and made himself a fresh cup of tea, this time with sugar. He sat back and listened to the approaching storm as the winds picked up and lightning could be seen in the distance. It was uncommon, but not unusual to have thunderstorms this late in the year. All he could think about was how nice it was to be able to ride it out in the safety of the house he had grown up in.

He washed up and prepared for sleep as the winds continued to howl through the trees.

Stretching out on his bed, he closed his eyes and thought back at the adventure he had recently survived. The challenges he had risen to. The challenges he had lost. Most important were the friends that he had met and lost along the way.

He still had deep feelings for Emilen and he believed she did for him. On one hand he hated what she had done. The loss of life that she had taken and the feeling that she had deceived him burned in his mind. On the other hand he wondered if she was a victim of Darkmere's control, carrying out his acts without the power to fight it. His heart still tightened when he thought of her lying with him in the tail of the dolphin statue while the warm mineral water of Kingsfoot Lake splashed up onto their bodies.

It was almost like being back there. He could feel droplets of water hit his body.

"Thorik, are you awake?" Grewen's deep voice broke his peaceful memory as he opened his eyes to see the roof of his cottage lifted off its walls by Grewen, who was looking down at him. Rain was starting to pour into his home and was saturating his bed sheets.

"What are you doing? Close the roof you fool," he announced as he sat up in bed looking up at Grewen, who was leaning over the front wall. The fireplace shed enough light onto Grewen's upper body to see that he was under attack. His shirt was half ripped off and large bleeding scratches marked up his body.

A howl could be heard just as several thrashers jumped onto Grewen's chest and arms. An entire tribe had attacked as Grewen fought to keep them off, falling backward out of sight, taking the roof with him.

A thrasher jumped from Grewen's falling body and landed on the front wall as he spied Thorik still in bed, shivering with fear and confusion. Thorik could see the scar of the three scratches over his eye. It was the Silverhead. Sniffing the air, he remembered the attack on his tribe and Thorik's killing of his family. He jumped off and landed in front of Thorik at the same moment a second creature grabbed Thorik from behind.

Thorik screamed with all his might as he stood up and lunged at the creature attacking from behind. Holding the beast down with one hand, he began taking out his own aggression.

"Thorik! Stop it," Avanda yelled. "You're going to knock us off the boat."

Thorik jolted his eyes open to find himself on top of Brimmelle, in the Mognin rowboat. The rain was coming down hard and lightning lit the sky frequently to give him a clear view of Brimmelle's facial reaction from the unprovoked attack.

Avanda sat next to Gluic as they held a blanket over their heads to hold off the rain. The youth wondered if one of her magical items could stop the rain. She had collected most of them before leaving Weirfortus. However, sitting in a rowboat in the middle of the lake was not the best time for her to test the items for magical properties.

Grewen was still paddling the boat in the middle of the Lake Luthralum with no land in sight as Thorik helped Brimmelle back up and regained his own bearings. Swiping his face with his hand to clear the rain from it, Thorik looked about to see where they were. The disorientation from his dream of returning home was starting to fade.

"Where are we?" Thorik asked.

Grewen spoke up first. "We just passed several rocky islands. We still haven't seen Draq, so we're sailing blind. If I don't see him soon, we'll have to attempt to land on one of these islands until this storm blows past." Grewen continued to row. "And where exactly were you?" he said with a grin.

Thorik looked out at the waves on the lake as he gathered his thoughts, finally realizing he had dreamt the return to Farbank. Turning, he looked at Grewen. "I was home."

The Mognin nodded. "Things okay back there?"

A slight smile crossed the Num's face. "Yes, and I mean to keep it that way."

Grewen grinned. "Understood, little man."

Chapter 37
Assassin
(Prelude to Book 2, Sacrifice of Ericc)

The heart of the mountain churned with heat deep inside its cold exterior, only to be exposed by the occasional steam rising out of the center crater. Above all other mountains this one stood amongst a range of non-volcanic peaks. Unlike the rest, it had fought its way up to its great height on its own instead of being carried up by the shifting of land.

So grand was its size that passing clouds were caught against it like fish in a net, unable to free themselves. Nearly a god of nature, it caused climate changes and shook the earth when it was angry. This happened more often now than it had in the past. In its youth it had fought for great strength and had settled with age, but lately it was no longer at peace. No longer idle or content. Respect had been lost for the great power it had provided the creatures that lived upon it. Damage was done to the mountain by those who it was protecting.

The heartbeat of the magma inside pounded away rising and lowering with each passing emotion. It would explode; there was no doubt about it. It was just a matter of time. Just a matter of pressure, frustration, and anger. It would explode.

Steam escaped out of its various vent holes with gray smoke that contrasted with the glacier of white around the funnel's peak. Halfway down its slope, steam bellowed out from caves under the deep snow. And below that, in a half-circle valley, smoke rose from the neck of a headless statue standing with its back against a sliced out section of the mountain.

The statue only stood a thousand feet high, now that its head was crushed against its feet in the heated mineral lake below. Dried streams of lava ran down the Mountain King's body, originating from the steaming vent at his neck. The cupped hands in front of the Mountain King Statue had been destroyed in the attempt to catch its own head. The once proud King now stood in snow covered grief.

Excluding the warm steaming lake, the valley was blanketed with several feet of snow. It had been for quite a while. Paths of deer and wild cats had been erased by the current blizzard that lashed out at the valley. Perhaps brought on by the mountain itself.

Snow fell at an angle and drifts built up like the dunes of the Kiri Desert. Only the lake fought to stay free of ice. The wind churned in the valley, down the mountainside, past the city of Kingsfoot, across the lake and back up the southern mountain range before coming back for another pass. Like a wagon-wheel, the storm rotated in the valley for days.

Through the windblown snow a figure moved down the southern mountain into the valley, against the flow of the storm to the north. Leaning forward on two powerful legs, the stranger fought for every step he took over the harsh landscape. Tall thick boots of skins rose to his knees, but still didn't protect his feet from all the cold. A bulky coat of firs covered the rest of his body, bundled up as best he could. The hood of the coat was pulled down as tight as he could without impairing his vision.

Once he reached the valley floor, he worked his way from one white dune to another. Snow clumped onto his body, weighing him down all the more. It was as though the storm was fighting him, preventing him from entering the valley, keeping him from his destination.

Nearing the lake, the winds picked up water and sprayed the traveler again and again. The water instantly froze into layers of ice, making it nearly impossible to move his joints anymore. Trying to keep his distance from the water, the wind continued to splash as much his way as possible.

Now, nearly frozen, the traveler reached the bridge, in the center of the valley, which arched over the water outlet into the King's River. The bridge was coated with layers of ice and required him to pull himself across using the slippery arm rail. After passing the apex of the bridge his feet began to slide down the other side. Using his right gloved hand for balance on the arm rail he allowed the slide to continue until his hand hit a broken section and got knocked against the sharp edges of the stone railing afterward. He fell, but landed on one knee, a foot, and his left hand, protecting the bruised right one.

His hood had been flung off from his fall and the wind, exposing his long snout of a face. Dark red in color, the skin sunk in around his bony features. His eyebrows lowered in disgust with fighting the storm. Exhausted from the constant attack he rested a moment, looking at the last leg of his trip, the city of Kingsfoot. Growling a bit at the frigid wind pounding his face, he raised his frozen hood over his hairless Blothrud head.

Picking himself up, he moved forward around the lake to the city. Plowing through snowdrift after snowdrift, his momentum increased as his body tired. He had to reach the city before his body gave out on him. Pushing with all his might, he was at a full run, busting his way across the last section of open land. Blasting through the last wave of snow, he reached the perimeter wall of half exposed statues.

He stopped and leaned against one of the stone scroll statues to catch his breath and shield him from the ever-ferocious wind. Reaching under his robes he pulled out a small dagger covered with runes along the handle. It was a glorious design of twisted blades as it shined with virginity. Not a scratch on it, never used, never damaged. It was as fresh and sharp as it was the day it was made.

Holding the dagger in his fist tightly, he looked at his reflection within the blades. Still breathing heavily, he nodded to himself. *Are you ready for this? This could be your undoing.*

Glancing around the statue, he saw a courtyard of half-submerged statues before the three vaguely distinguishable terrace levels up to the city's wall. Wind blasted him in the face as he looked about.

Placing the dagger back under his coat of ice and snow covered firs, he made his way up to the city in a slow gallop. The stairs in the center were useless under all the snow but his large wolf-like legs on his eight-foot body conquered them with ease.

He pushed one of the two doors open quietly and peered in to see a large room with many vats of oil fires lighting the room with yellow light. Several doors and halls exited the room in every direction as he looked for signs of life.

Closing the main door behind him, a wave of warmth covered his body. He quickly removed his gloves and coat that weighed more of snow and ice than of firs. He removed his shirt that was soaking from the sweat of his trek. To freeze in some body parts while sweating to death in others was no way for this Blothrud to travel. He hated the cold.

As he patted himself dry, a large scar could be seen on his back from his upper left shoulder blade down below his belt. It had been a deep gouge that never fully healed. It scarred much wider than the rest of the whip marks on his back. Several wide blades extended from his spine a few inches, many had been chipped and damaged but dangerous all the same. Spikes could also be seen on shoulder blades, knuckles, and elbows. They also were rough from battles of the past. He was a seasoned veteran with many a battle to his name.

He put on a dry leather vest that gave him freedom to move before leaving the front doors. He checked the blade one last time. Sharp, clean, and ready. He rotated the dagger in his fist a few times to make sure he had a good hold on it.

Looking about for a direction to follow, he spied a green light coming from a room at the end of one of the many hallways. The door was shut and the light trimmed the bottom with shadows moving in front of the sickly light.

He looked at the blade one last time and rotated it in his grip again until he felt he was ready. He was.

Standing up tall with his chest out firm he proceeded down toward the closed door, dagger to his side. He walked with confidence and composure as he reached the door and opened it.

The room inside was half that of the first room. Two vats, one in each corner on the far side, gave off a smoky green light that danced on the walls, covered in stone carvings of wilderness. The flickering light made the tree leaves above appear to sway in the breeze as well as the ferns below. Several small stone and crystal statues stood in the room with a throne on the far side between the two vats. The throne was solid crystal and carved out to look like it was the base of a tree with roots reaching out for the seat and arms.

Sitting in the throne was a cloaked figure. It looked to be short and standing on the seat, seeing that no legs came forward and then down in front. The other possibility was that the figure was sitting with its legs crossed. The Blothrud didn't care either way.

As he advanced into the room, blade in hand, he noticed the animal statues moving and walking about. He slowed his pace as the animals looked up at him and began to surround him. Keeping his eyes on the cloaked figure, they followed close behind.

A large black marble panther stood in his way just prior to reaching the throne. It growled and prepared to pounce on the Blothrud who stood defiantly. A wave of a hand from the cloaked figure caused the panther to back down and sit next the throne.

The Blothrud lifted his precious dagger and pointed it at the other. "This is Varacon, the blade of your request. Countless lives have been lost to bring this to you."

The cloaked figure sat up slightly from its previously hunched over position. In doing so, the cloak moved and exposed his upper legs that mutated into cracked and fragmented wood, splintering and decaying. His left hand reached out to grab the dagger from him as the Blothrud turned the handle for him to grab.

Lifting it from the red creature's hand, he inspected the blade. Polishing it on the right arm of his cloak, he exposed his deformed right hand. It also had been turned to shards of rotten wood. "You have done well." His voice sounded raspy and tired.

The Blothrud could see excessive burn damage along the cloaked man's neck. "What shall you have me do with it?"

The cloaked man looked up from his hood. "You shall kill my son, Ericc."

Continue the adventures of Thorik Dain and his friends in...
Sacrifice of Ericc
Essence of Gluic
Rise of Rummon
Prey of Ambrosius
and
Plea of Avanda

Further adventures in the same realm include...
Nums of Shoreview Series (Pre-Teen Adventures)

Future series in the same realm include...
Ambrosius' Exploits
Santorray's Journeys
Darkmere's Path

Pronunciation Guide

CHARACTERS
Ambrosius: aeM-brO-zee-ahs
Asentar: as-en-Tar
Avanda: ah-Van-Dah
Bakalor: Bah-Kah-Lor
Beltrow: beL-trO
Bredgin: Brehd-gehn
Brimmelle: Brim-'ell
Darkmere: Dark-Meer
Deleth: deL-'eth
Draq: draK
Emilen: ehM-il-eN
Ergrauth: erR-gRahTH
Ericc: ehR-iK
Feshlan: FehSH-Lahn
Gluic: Glu-iK
Grewen: Gru-'en
Irluk: uhR-luhK
Ovlan: ahV-lahN
Sharcodi: shAR-kO-dEE
Thorik: Thor-iK
Trumette: truhm-et
Wyrlyn: Wer-Len

LOCATIONS
Corrock: koR-RahK
Cuev'Laru Mountains: Koo-ehV Lah-Roo
Cucurrian River: Koo-kuR-ee-uhn
Doven: dO-ven
Govi: Gah-Vee
Kiri: kE-rE
Lu'Tythis: Loo-Tith-is
Pelonthal: peL-ahn-THahl
Pyrth: perTH
Wierfortus: wEer-fort-us
Woodlen: Wood-lehn

Pronunciation Guide

SPECIES

Blothrud (AKA Ruds): BlahTH-Ruhd

> *7' to 9' tall; Bony hairless Dragon/Wolf-like head; Red muscular human torso and arms; Sharp spikes extend out across shoulder blades, back of arms, and back of hands; Red hair covered waist and over two thick strong wolf legs. Blothruds are typically the highest class of the Del'Undays.*

Del'Unday: DeL-OOn-Day

> *The Del'Unday are a collection of Altered Creatures who live in structured communities with rules and strong leadership.*

Fesh'Unday: FehSH-OOn-Day

> *The Fesh'Unday are all of the Altered Creatures that roam freely without societies.*

Gathler: GahTH-ler

> *6' to 8' tall; Hunched over giant sloth-like face and body; Gathlers are the spiritual leaders of the Ov'Undays.*

Human: Hyoo-muhn

> *5' to 6' tall; pale to dark complexion; weight varies from anorexic to obese. Most live within the Dovenar Kingdom.*

Krupes: KrooP

> *6' to 8' tall; Covered from head to toe in black armor, these thick and heavy bipedal creatures move slow but are difficult to defeat. Few have seen what they look like under their armor. Krupes are the soldiers of the Del'Unday.*

Mognin (AKA Mogs): MahG-Nen

> *10' to 12' tall; Mognins are the tallest of the Ov'Unday.*

Myth'Unday: Meeth-OOn-Day

> *The Myth'Unday are a collection of Creatures brought to life by altering nature's plants and insects.*

Ov'Unday: ahv-OOn-Day

> *The Ov'Unday are a collection of Altered Creatures who believe in living as equals in peaceful communities.*

Polenum (AKA Nums): Pol-uhn-um

> *4' to 5' tall; Human-like features; Very pale skin; Soul-markings cover their bodies in thin or thick lines as they mature. Exceptional Eyesight.*

Made in the USA
Charleston, SC
28 January 2015